THE FORTUNE TELLER OF KATHMANDU

ANN BENNETT

✿ Created with Vellum

For Maggie

PROLOGUE

KATHMANDU, NEPAL

THERE WAS little natural light in the cell-like room, tucked away in the back of an ancient building in the maze of narrow, cobbled streets in the heart of old Kathmandu. Despite that, Devisha had the sense that daylight was fading quickly outside, and that darkness would soon envelop the neighbourhood.

It had been quiet that day. But the usual mix of people had made their way through the backstreets and alleyways to her door, crossed the outer chamber lit only by flickering candles, and drawn back the velvet curtain that divided Devisha's alcove from the chamber. As they did every day, they had sat down opposite her with their timid, hopeful faces, extended their palms across the table, raised their eyes tentatively to hers before she dropped her gaze to read the future mapped out in their lines. The Line of Life, the Line of Fate, the Line of Heart, the Line of Fortune. The mounts of Jupiter, Saturn, Apollo, Mercury and Venus. Devisha knew every permutation of every line intimately, as well as what they signified.

Today had been much like every other day. There had been the young daughter of a rice farmer from Nagarkot who had arrived with her mother. They'd walked the length of the Kathmandu valley to Devisha's rooms. They wanted to be sure that the girl's chosen betrothed was auspicious, and to get Devisha's advice on the best date to set the wedding. There had been the old, stooping carpenter from Bodinath, his brow furrowed with worry. His business was failing as well as his health. He'd asked if things would pick up in the future. Then, there had been the middle-aged woman from Thamel who'd already lost three babies in childbirth. With a pleading look in her eyes, she'd wanted to know if the one she was now carrying would survive.

All Devisha could tell them was what she saw in their palms. She could usually see, as soon as she turned a hand over in her own, peered at the palm and traced the lines with her own fingers. Their futures played out in her mind. She would try to tell them exactly what she saw, what they craved to know.

It wasn't always easy living with the gift that had been passed to her down the generations. She'd learned it at her mother's knee and her mother from her grandmother before her. To witness the pain in people's faces when she told them what she could see was sometimes hard to bear. Their heartache would often become her own. She knew she would be thinking about the woman from Thamel long into the night. But in amongst the pain was joy too, joy and light and hope for the future. She'd foreseen that the rice-farmer's daughter's marriage would be happy and prosperous, and that she would have a long, rich life, filled with love and laughter.

With a sigh, Devisha got up from her chair. It was time to get ready to go home. But as she held back her veil and stooped to blow out the first candle, she heard the click and creak of the outer door. Then came footsteps. Someone was walking slowly across the chamber towards her. The footsteps stopped and, as often happened, the newcomer hesitated for a couple of seconds before pulling back the curtain and peeping through.

The face of a stranger appeared in the flickering candlelight. A young woman, with soft dark hair and pale skin. She looked different to most of Devisha's customers. She wasn't local, and in this hidden quarter, it was rare to see a foreigner. Although the newcomer had Indian features, she was wearing western clothes. Devisha noticed the scepticism in the woman's narrowed eyes, but there was a hint of curiosity, and a sort of yearning there too.

Devisha quickly sat down and beckoned the young woman forward. 'Don't be afraid,' she said. 'Please, come in. Sit down. Give me your hand.'

The girl's eyes flickered hesitantly, darting around the room, taking in the smoking candles, the incense and the wall hangings. Then she took a couple of steps forward, sat down in the chair opposite and extended her right hand across the red tablecloth.

Devisha took the soft, manicured hand in her own, studied it for a few seconds. Her eyes widened and she stifled a gasp.

This was unusual indeed. There was a lot to see in this palm. There was everything there she'd expected from such a subject, but there was more. Much, much more.

Devisha narrowed her eyes and peered closer concentrating deeply. Whatever it was, was elusive. She traced the Line of Luna with her long, painted fingernail, letting it rest briefly on the Mount of Mercury.

This young woman would be tested, that was clear. But she was strong too. Stronger than she looked. There was something more there though... something dark, something troubling. Something that even Devisha couldn't fathom, not straightaway. She bent forward, her many necklaces clanking against the table, and looked closer.

1

HAMPSHIRE, 2015

A BITING wind whipped around her legs as Chloe followed the coffin out of the church with the other mourners. As they left the chilly shelter of the stone porch, stepping out into the slate-grey afternoon, it started to drizzle, compounding the bleak sadness of the day, ice-cold rain mingling on her cheeks with hot tears.

Grief pressed down on her chest like a lead weight. It was hard to believe that her grandmother's tiny frame lay inside that simple, wooden box, borne aloft on the shoulders of six strangers, black-suited men from the funeral parlour. Hard to believe, too, that Gran wouldn't be there, back at the house, sitting in her favourite armchair beside the fire in the snug, ready to while away the evening with a cup of tea and comfortable but entertaining chatter.

Through a blur of tears, Chloe followed the coffin as it was carried sedately between the graves to the plot near the edge of the cemetery next to Grandpa's grave, beside a mound of red earth where there was a sinister-looking rectangular-shaped hole in the ground.

'Monty's buried over there,' her cousin, Daniel, said, bending down to speak to her, nodding towards the opposite corner of the windswept graveyard.

'Monty?' Chloe frowned.

He raised an eyebrow, exasperated with her, as he often seemed to be. 'Field Marshall Montgomery? Desert Rats? Ring any bells?'

'Oh, of course,' she muttered, remembering being brought here from the village school to be shown the rather understated grave in the corner of this obscure Hampshire cemetery where a great war hero lay.

'It's part of the reason Grandpa wanted to live round here, I expect, when they came back from India.'

'Perhaps...' Chloe said, not wanting to speak, and wondering why Daniel was trying to distract her with these seemingly irrelevant facts at this precise moment.

She moved discreetly away from him, making her way between the mourners towards the graveside, where the vicar was now intoning the burial service.

'Man that is born of a woman hath but a short time to live, and is full of misery. He cometh up, and is cut down, like a flower; he fleeth as it were a shadow, and never continueth in one stay.'

Chloe wiped away a tear as the vicar continued reciting the prayer, and the men started to lower the coffin on its black ropes into the grave. Her throat ached with emotion. It was hard to imagine life without Gran's twinkling smile, her irreverent laugh, her original take on life. Looking around at the rest of the congregation, old ladies from the village dabbing their eyes, friends Gran had made over the years through her numerous interests, distant relatives who'd driven miles to be here, Chloe realised that she wasn't alone.

When the bearers stepped away from the grave, the vicar nodded in Chloe's direction.

She moved forward and threw the single white rose into the pit. 'Goodbye, Gran. Thank you for everything.'

She was followed by Uncle Andrew, Daniel's father, himself a military man, who now, at the age of sixty-nine, walked with a stick, his Falklands injury finally coming home to roost, but he still carried himself with soldierly bearing. He threw a red rose down into the grave, then Daniel followed with a stem of lilies. As they turned towards her, the pain on both their faces was plain to see. Uncle Andrew, normally so composed, dabbed his cheek with a white handkerchief. Chloe watched them with a heavy heart. This all felt so final.

≈

BACK AT THE HOUSE, Chloe milled around in the high-ceilinged drawing room, sipping tea and nibbling from the buffet she'd hastily organised via some outside caterers.

'What would Lena have made of these sandwiches, love?' one of Gran's friends asked her with a twinkle in his eye.

'Not much, I suspect,' Chloe said, laughing. It hurt to laugh.

'If she'd have known she was going, she'd have made the snacks herself. Popped them in the freezer.'

'You're quite right,' Chloe agreed, thinking that only someone very old, who knew her grandmother very well, could have made that comment. But it had cheered her up all the same.

'She had a long life, dear,' one of the old village ladies reminded her, gripping Chloe's hand when she said goodbye. 'A long, full, and colourful life. To be celebrated, not mourned.'

Of course, she was right. Gran had lived to the ripe old age of ninety-five and had died peacefully in her sleep. But, even so, the loss was hard to bear.

One by one, the guests trickled away. Guests, not mourners, Chloe reminded herself as she said goodbye to each and every one of them, thanking them for coming. Then, there was just herself, Daniel and Uncle Andrew left, and a room full of dirty teacups, half-eaten sandwiches and cold sausage rolls.

'I expect you need to get home, don't you, Dan? It's a long drive to Orpington,' she hinted.

'Yes, perhaps we should get going, Dan,' Uncle Andrew said, tapping his stick on the floor. He lived near his son, having moved there to be closer when his wife had died a couple of years before.

'Not yet, Dad. The M25 will be murder at this time, building up to rush hour. We can help you clear up if you like, Chloe?'

Her heart sank, she just wanted to be alone. 'There's not much to do. I just need to stack the cups and plates up. The caterers are coming for them in the morning.'

Uncle Andrew shuffled out of the room, evidently not impressed with the offer to help.

'I'll help you.' Daniel began to stack saucers. After a while, he said, 'I suppose you'll be thinking about putting the old place on the market soon?'

He spoke with studied casualness, but it stopped Chloe in her tracks. Daniel had been acting awkwardly all day. She'd thought it was just the pain of losing Gran, but realised now that this was what was behind it all.

'I haven't decided yet,' she said, trying to keep her voice even, trying not to sound prickly. She knew he'd been put out when he'd discovered that their grandmother had left the house to Chloe alone. But he and Uncle Andrew had been amply compensated in her grandmother's will in terms of shares and savings.

'I suppose it must help, you being an estate agent and all that. You'll know how to play the market.'

'Correction, Daniel. I *was* an estate agent. I left my job a couple of months ago.'

He stared at her, eyes popping. She couldn't help smiling. Of course, being without a job would be anathema to someone like Daniel.

'I had to move back here,' she said, at the same time

wondering why she felt the need to justify herself to him. 'Gran needed someone to be around for her.'

'But you only worked in Guildford. It's hardly a million miles away.'

Chloe sighed and sat down on the nearest chair. 'Gran couldn't be left during the day. And besides, I'd had enough of it. I'd done it for ten years, don't forget. I needed a change.'

'Oh yes, I'd forgotten that you'd dropped out of university.'

Irritation and anger rose in her chest. How was this any business of Daniel's, him with his well-mapped-out city career, his path to success and financial security smoothed over by his army connections? His doting wife Charlotte and their two perfect children – a girl and a boy – perfectly spaced two years apart, notable by their absence that day.

'What has that got to do with anything, Daniel?'

'Nothing, I suppose,' he said, sitting down heavily beside her. 'But I could never understand why you and Gran were as thick as thieves like you were. Especially after poor old Grandpa died.'

Chloe stared at him, shocked, realising that jealousy must be behind his comments. 'She looked after me, Daniel. After poor Mum died and Dad took off to Australia with that woman, Gran was all I had. And she was kind to me, like a second mother, really.'

The pain of those years came back to her afresh. Losing her mother to breast cancer at seventeen, and effectively her father too, shortly afterwards, had dealt Chloe a devastating blow. He had buried his grief by plunging straight into another relationship that took him half way across the world. No wonder she'd been blown off course for the next few years and hadn't been able to complete her education.

'I suppose she must have been good to you,' Daniel said, his tone conciliatory. 'I'm sorry. I know things weren't easy for you at the time.'

Chloe recalled how Daniel had hardly ever come to see Gran.

She had a sneaking suspicion that he rather looked down on the old lady, with her part-Indian blood, and her eccentric, unpredictable ways. He preferred to align himself with Grandpa, with his stiff upper lip and military background. But, despite their differences, Gran and Grandpa had fitted together like hand and glove. They'd appreciated each other for who they were. In fact, their differences had brought them closer.

Then Chloe recalled how she and Gran would discuss Daniel after one of his rare visits and suppressed a smile.

'I wish that boy would lighten up,' Gran would say. 'And as for her! Talk about po-faced. Like a Stepford wife. I thought women were meant to be liberated nowadays,' and as she spoke, she would be rocking with laughter.

'Would you mind if I took one or two of Grandpa's things? Military memorabilia really. To remember him by?' Daniel asked now, breaking into Chloe's thoughts.

She shrugged, thinking that it was strange he didn't ask for a memento to remember Gran by.

'Take what you like. Gran didn't touch Grandpa's study, as you know.'

Daniel jumped up. 'Thank you. I'll take a look now. And I'll see if I can find Dad while I'm at it.'

And he was off, hurrying out of the room, following his father along the echoing flagstone passage towards the study.

Chloe began stacking plates again, clearing the screwed-up serviettes and scraps of food into a binbag. Lena's drawing room was huge and square, at the front of the comfortable old rectory with a big bay window. It took her a while to make any progress into the mess.

Daniel soon came back, Uncle Andrew trailing behind. Daniel was carrying a framed photograph that must have hung on Grandpa's wall since he and Gran had moved into the house in 1947 after Indian independence.

'11th Gurkha Rifles,' he pronounced proudly. 'Look, Grandpa's here in the middle. His wartime regiment.'

'Oh yes,' she said, remembering how Gran had told her how she'd accompanied Grandpa on recruiting campaigns for the Gurkhas in Kathmandu in the early forties.

'I've taken a couple of Papa's medals,' Uncle Andrew chimed in. 'I hope you don't mind. Sentimental value.'

'Of course not, Uncle. He was your *father,* after all.'

It was funny how they wanted to take these things now. It was over ten years since Grandpa had died and they'd never asked before. Perhaps they didn't really believe that Chloe wouldn't be putting the house on the market straight away. Maybe they thought that she was heartless enough to get rid of all the old memorabilia too now that Gran had gone.

They left soon after that. Daniel pecked her cheek briefly on the doorstep.

'If you need anything, just give me a call,' he said.

Uncle Andrew had taken both her hands in his.

'Well done today, my dear. Thank you for organising everything. Do take care of yourself.'

'Thank you, Uncle,' she said, forcing back the tears. She could see the suffering in his face and suddenly felt sorry for him. It must have been a tough day for him too, saying goodbye to his mother.

Chloe shut the front door with a sigh after watching them get into Daniel's BMW and speed off down the drive, spraying gravel in their wake. She went through to the kitchen and opened the door. Kip, Lena's black Labrador, bounded towards her, wagging his tail. He'd been pining for Lena and each time Chloe had popped through to the kitchen to check on him, he'd jumped up eagerly, hoping no doubt that it would be Lena coming through the door, not her. She stroked him to calm him down and topped up his water. Then, she wandered back towards the drawing room, feeling an overwhelming emptiness descend suddenly upon her.

She picked up the binbag and carried on tidying, but before she'd had time to reflect properly on her relatives' strange behaviour, the doorbell gave a shrill ring, making her jump. Had Daniel and Uncle Andrew forgotten something?

But when she opened it, a tiny, white-haired old lady stood on the step. Chloe vaguely recognised her as having been at the funeral service, although she didn't recall seeing her at the wake.

'Miss Winter?' the old lady asked, looking up at her through thick glasses.

'Yes. It's Chloe actually.'

'I'm Mildred Lightfoot. An old friend of your grandmother's from the war. I wanted to speak to you in private.'

Chloe drew back the door, puzzled, her interest piqued. 'Do come in, please.'

The old lady looked around Gran's age, perhaps a little younger. But she was clearly in good health. She walked without difficulty, in fact, she was rather sprightly.

'I waited until everyone had gone,' the old lady said, mysteriously.

'Oh, there was no need to do that. Where did you wait?'

'In my car, a little way up the road. I kept the engine going and the heater on.'

'Well, I hope you didn't get too cold. Come through, please.'

Chloe took her through to the large, square kitchen, where the Aga kept the room warm. There were two armchairs beside it and Chloe took Mildred's coat and invited her to sit down. Kip came up to the old lady, wagging his tail.

'Hello boy. You must be missing your mistress,' Mildred Lightfoot said, patting his head.

Chloe wondered how the old lady knew the dog belonged to Lena, but supposed she would have guessed.

'Would you like something to drink? Tea, coffee – something stronger perhaps?'

'Oh no, dear. I'm driving, but I wouldn't say no to a cup of tea, if it isn't too much trouble.'

Chloe put the kettle on the Aga and sat down opposite Mildred. 'Now, what was it you wanted to tell me, Miss Lightfoot?'

'*Mrs* Lightfoot, actually... but it doesn't matter. I thought you might be interested in Lena's diary from the war years. I kept it for her because she didn't want your grandfather finding it. And after he died, she must have forgotten to ask for it back. She had a very interesting war.'

Chloe stood up to take the boiling kettle off the hob. She poured the water into the teapot. 'Yes, she told me that she worked for Grandpa in the Regimental HQ. She was his secretary, I understand.'

'She was, dear. But there was much, much more to it than that.'

Mildred was looking straight up at her, beaming, her false teeth gleaming under the bright kitchen lights.

Chloe stirred the teapot and left it to brew. 'Whatever do you mean, more to it?'

Gran had always been very circumspect about the war, playing it down whenever the subject came up. 'It's all in the past now. No use looking back,' she would say with an air of finality.

'Well, dear Lena played her own part in the Burma campaign. We served together actually in the Wasbies. That's the Women's Royal Auxiliary Service (Burma) to be precise.'

'The Wasbies?' Chloe repeated bemused, this was a real surprise.

'I know she didn't tell any of her family. There were certain... well, let us say certain *sensitivities* around her time at the front that she didn't want resurfacing.'

Chloe shook her head, still mystified. She was coming to the conclusion that perhaps Mildred Lightfoot was getting a bit confused in her old age. What she was saying made no sense, but it would be fascinating to read her grandmother's diary all the same.

She poured the tea and handed the old lady a cup.

'I'd love to read her diary,' she said. 'Then perhaps I'll understand a bit more about what you're talking about.'

'I'm sure you will. I have brought it especially for you.'

'Well, thank you. Thank you for bringing it, and thank you for coming here today. It means a lot that such a longstanding friend was here for Gran at the end. Presumably you hadn't seen Gran for a long time?'

'Oh no. We saw each other regularly until her recent illness. I live in Wiltshire, you see. So not too far away.'

Chloe's mouth dropped open. 'But... she never mentioned you.'

'No. As I said, she wanted to keep her wartime past a secret from the family, and because I was part of that, she was unlikely to have mentioned me. I don't mind. I was happy to keep her secrets for her.'

Mildred finished speaking and sipped her tea noisily.

Chloe thought about Gran's gallivanting, while she could still drive. 'I think I'll pop up to London today... I think I'll drive down to Portsmouth. See the sea...' Chloe could never keep up. She could easily have driven down to visit a friend in Wiltshire and not mentioned it. But what did Mildred mean about her grandmother's secrets? Chloe was about to ask her to explain when Mildred put her cup down abruptly and said, 'The diary will explain it all. You'll understand once you've read that, my dear.'

She began to rummage in her large, brown handbag, muttering to herself, then produced a battered paper bag and handed it to Chloe.

'Once you've read it, if you want to talk about it, please do come and see me and I might be able to explain things.' She drained her cup, put it down on the Aga and stood up. 'Now, I really must get going. I don't really like driving in the dark and I need to get home and feed the cat. Poor old Tibs. He doesn't like being alone.'

Chloe showed Mildred back down the corridor and opened the door for her. The paper bag in her hand felt like an unexploded bomb.

'As I said, don't hesitate to get in touch,' Mildred said, stepping out into the windy evening. 'Lena will have a note of my number in her address book.'

'Thank you, Miss... Mrs Lightfoot.'

'I'm so sorry for your loss, my dear girl. I know Lena loved you a great deal and that you two were very close.' Mrs Lightfoot closed her hands around Chloe's for a brief second, looking deep into her eyes with a piercing, sincere look.

'Thank you,' Chloe muttered again, biting back tears. She stood there watching as the old lady crossed the drive, got into her tiny car and drove off, hooting the horn as she went.

She turned back inside the house, a whirlwind of emotions coursing through her. The strange conversation with Mildred Lightfoot had unsettled her deeply, stirred up a hornet's nest of questions in her mind. She walked slowly down the corridor , Kip at her heels, and paused outside Gran's snug. She'd avoided going in there since Lena's death. She opened the door, clicked on the light and stood there in the doorway, her heart aching with her loss.

Gran's presence was palpable here. There was the comfortable armchair beside the fireplace where she used to sit to read or to watch TV, with its brightly coloured patchwork quilt thrown over the threadbare upholstery. On the walls were her favourite photographs. Pictures of Darjeeling in the 1930s, photographs of her wedding in the church there, other family weddings, Uncle Andrew and Chloe's mother, Selina as children. Then there were Chloe and Daniel's school photographs, pictures of Grandpa in military uniform and hiking in Wales, holding a staff in one hand. There was only one portrait of Gran when she was young, and she'd been proud of it. It had been taken when she'd first joined the Regiment as Grandpa's assistant. She was photographed with mountains as a backdrop and was wearing a neat black skirt and simple white shirt, her black hair pulled off her face. She was staring out at the camera, her beautiful dark eyes brimming with pride, her full mouth turned up in a warm smile.

Chloe went up to the photograph and peered at it closely, until the features and lines blurred before her eyes. 'Oh Gran, what were the secrets that you couldn't share with us?'

How she wished her grandmother was still here, so she could ask her directly, speak to her once more.

She left the room, closing the door firmly, and went back to the kitchen to sit in the warm. And there, in front of the Aga, she opened the paper bag and took out a little black notebook, crammed full of Gran's dense handwriting. She opened the first page and saw that the entry was dated 5th September 1943. Chloe read the first line and was instantly drawn in.

I've decided to start a diary. Today felt like a turning point in my life and I want to chart what happens next!

2

DARJEELING, 1943

LENA HAD COME to loathe Monday mornings, when it was her job to take the senior girls' English class. Whatever she did to try to interest them in the syllabus she'd been instructed to teach, their eyes would quickly glaze over, and they would begin to chatter amongst themselves, giggle, pass notes, and sometimes even throw things across the classroom. For the rest of the week, Lena oversaw the junior girls. She had far less trouble with them. They were more malleable, more compliant, better behaved all round than the older girls. But despite her own love of English literature, she could never seem to ignite any spark of enthusiasm in these girls.

That day, they were studying *Jane Eyre* and were going round the class, reading a passage at a time out loud. The girls' English was patchy, some were better than others, but all of them had the tendency to slip into that sing-song accent that marked them out as Eurasians that the school was so desperate to stamp out of them.

These girls were the illegitimate daughters of British officers and officials of the Raj. The result of illicit liaisons with native Indian women, they had been packed off to the establishment at a very early age. The hope was that here in Darjeeling, this sleepy, remote hill station, far away from the seat of Empire, they could be discreetly forgotten, while their Indian heritage was gradually educated away. Each and every one of them was well aware of the shame of their existence and that they were here at St Catherine's to try to remove the Indianness from them, although their antecedents would always be obvious from the colour of their skin.

Lena herself had been one of those girls. She'd been brought here by her reluctant mother, Sita, at the age of three, and had entered the 'orphanage'. She'd been here ever since. When she'd been old enough, she'd started lessons with the other little ones in the schoolroom. They were taught English, rudimentary arithmetic, geography, history and a smattering of science. The teaching was seldom very good, because they were mainly taught by ex-pupils like Lena herself, who had never left the place and had certainly never been trained to teach. It didn't seem to trouble the school authorities or the parents that the education was far from first-class. Far more important than the main subjects were the lessons on deportment and English habits and culture that formed a large part of the curriculum. More usefully, they were also taught shorthand and typing to equip them for the outside world.

Lena's attention wandered, and she stared out of the window, while a girl on the front row stumbled ineptly through a passage about Jane Eyre's arrival at Thornfield Hall. Whenever Lena was bored or frustrated, all she needed to do was feast her eyes on the distant vista of Kanchenjunga. It towered over the neat lines of the tea gardens around Darjeeling, the coloured roofs of the buildings scattered around the nearby hills, the blue-tinged Himalayan foothills, those mystical mountains, whose jagged series of snow-covered peaks seemed to change minute by minute with the angle of the sun, like a living kaleidoscope. The sight of those far-off mountains both chilled and thrilled her.

They represented mystery and adventure, wonder and beauty, and the fact that the world and life in general contained infinite possibilities. But they also represented the harshest environment on earth and all the dangers that went along with that.

The view of those incredible peaks had been ever-present in her life for as long as Lena could remember. Wherever you went in Darjeeling, apart from when the monsoon shrouded it in mist, it was there. Glimpsed from between tall buildings at the end of an alleyway, from the narrow streets of the Indian town, from the botanical gardens, the railway station. And just the sight of it lifted Lena's spirits.

The girl carried on reading and Lena's mind drifted to the conversation she'd had with her mother the day before. Her mother had not been content to leave her only child in the care of strangers and take the train back to Calcutta all those years ago. Instead, she'd found cheap lodgings in Darjeeling and had lived there ever since, scraping a living together, working in menial jobs or taking in sewing, living in tiny, damp rooms in a back alley near the bazaar. That must have been hard for someone who'd been brought up in the prosperous Main Sewer Road area of Calcutta.

'You really need to get away from that place, daughter,' Sita had said when Lena had dropped round for tea. 'It's not healthy, staying in the same place you've always been, forever. And you're not happy either. I can tell,' she'd noted, pinching Lena's pale cheek between her chubby fingers.

'But what else could I do, Ma?' Lena had asked, aware that the thought of leaving St Catherine's filled her with panic, even though she knew her mother was right, and she loathed the cloistered boredom of her life there.

'I don't know, my little one, but life is full of possibilities, never forget that.'

That was rich, coming from her mother, Lena thought, who had done nothing with her own life, other than enter into an unwise liaison with a British officer at the age of twenty and spend the rest of it suffering the consequences.

'I know you despise me, Lena,' Sita had said quietly, looking deep into her eyes. Lena had dropped her gaze. Were her thoughts that transparent? 'But I've only ever had your best interests at heart, you know.'

'I know, Ma,' she'd replied, her heart growing heavy at the memory of her mother bringing Indian sweetmeats to pass through the school fence to her when she was small, before being shooed away like a pi-dog by the school porters.

She was pulled back into the present by a commotion in the classroom. Someone had flicked ink at another girl. Jane Eyre and Mr Rochester completely forgotten, a group of girls at the front were standing up, pushing each other, talking in raised voices.

Lena rushed over to where the trouble was bubbling. 'Hey, what's going on...'

At that moment, the classroom door opened and the headmistress, Miss Woodcock, entered, and strutted to the front like a tall, haughty bird.

'Quiet!' she boomed and there was instant silence.

The troublemakers slunk back to their desks, looking sheepish.

'There is no excuse for this behaviour, girls. No excuse at all. You are taking advantage of a young and inexperienced teacher and you should all be ashamed of yourselves!'

All the girls stared down at their desks. Shame coursed through Lena at the older woman's words. How unfair of her to draw attention to her own lack of experience. It only served to humiliate her further. She felt her cheeks grow hot with anger and embarrassment.

'And as for you, Miss Chatterjee,' Miss Woodcock turned her focus onto Lena, 'this isn't the first time I've had to intervene in one of your classes.' She spoke in an imperious voice, looking down her long nose at Lena, her mean, blue eyes narrowed.

Lena looked up and met her gaze defiantly. She knew the woman felt she could treat her as she liked because she was an ex-pupil. Miss Woodcock had once been her headmistress. As such Lena had no status to answer back. She didn't have much choice but to take it on the chin.

The headmistress's eyes flashed angrily when she saw that Lena was determined not to be cowed by her words, and her cheeks grew pink. 'I don't expect this to happen again, Miss Chatterjee,' she said, drawing herself up. 'You need to up your game, or there will be serious consequences.'

With that, she left the room, slamming the door behind her, and the class erupted in excited chatter.

Lena banged a book on her desk, feeling hot and uncomfortable, her blouse sticking to her body. 'Quiet! You heard what the headmistress said. Now let's get straight on with the next passage. Jennifer. Over to you.'

After school that day, Lena ran over to the newsagents on the main shopping square, Chowrasta, and bought herself a copy of the *Darjeeling Mail*, taking her mother's advice for once. She took herself up to the top of Observatory Hill, where she watched the rainbow colours of the sun as it set on the mountains, while scanning the classified ads. There were numerous ones for ladies' companions, nannies, governesses to English families, but none of those appealed to Lena. She wanted to get right away from teaching. She had a suspicion that she had absolutely no talent for it, and she knew it was sapping her confidence.

The sky was darkening, and she was about to close the paper and give up for the evening, when something caught her eye on the next page. *Organised and efficient young woman required for the role of secretary to the senior officer at the Military Base, Jalapahar, 11th Gurkha Rifles. Must be proficient in typing and filing, smart and intelligent with impeccable references.*

Lena's eyes widened at the words 'impeccable references', but she hoped Miss Woodcock wouldn't be mean enough to sabotage her chances of getting away from a job that they both knew she wasn't suited to. This job sounded perfect. All the girls had been taught shorthand and typing at school, to prepare them for the world of work, and she was grateful for that.

She got up and hurried down the hill and back through the darkening streets to St Catherine's. There, in the dormitory she shared with three other girls, she started writing her application.

'What are you *doing*, Lena?' Mary, the girl on the opposite bed, asked and when Lena told her that she was applying for a job, all the girls looked at her with astonishment and sneaking admiration.

'You mean you'd really do it? Break away from this place?' asked Mary.

'Of course,' Lena answered, nibbling her pencil. 'Today was the final straw. Old Woodcock tore me off a strip right in front of the class for not keeping discipline. It wasn't the first time. It's so humiliating.'

'I envy you,' said Vicky, lying on her front on the bed, kicking her legs back in the air. 'I wish I had the courage to make a break.'

'You should do it too. You should *all* do it. They take us for granted here, treat us like slaves. They think they can do so because we've been here all our lives and that nobody cares about what happens to us,' she said vehemently and she meant it. She hated to see her friends treated that way.

'You're right,' Joan, the fourth girl said. 'I think I'll start looking for another position right now.'

~

I STOPPED TALKING THEN and buried myself in the application. I certainly didn't want all of them to apply for the same job. One of them might get it instead of me! Perhaps I'd gone too far, trying to encourage them all to break free!

Chloe smiled at her grandmother's reflections. How typical of her, with her naturally generous nature, to have encouraged the other young teachers to break away from the stifling regime at St Catherine's, even if it might be at her own expense. She thought how her grandmother had sacrificed so much, giving up her homeland to return to England for her husband's career, putting her own life on hold to care for her children, taking in Chloe herself when her mother had died, without a second thought. Chloe's eyes misted over with tears. Her grandmother had been a truly unselfish human being.

She wiped the tears away, anxious to continue with the diary.

I sat up long into the night perfecting my application, writing it out in my neatest handwriting by the light of my tiny torch. I had to screw up several early attempts and keep starting afresh...

Lena skipped lunch in the staff dining room the next day and took a rickshaw to the army base at Jalapahar cantonment.

She'd underestimated how long it would take to reach the base along the rough roads that wound around the hill. Like all rickshaws in Darjeeling, this one was pulled by two men, with three others running behind to push it up the hills. Despite all this manpower, it took a good half-hour to get there. Even before she got to the army base, Lena was worrying about being late back for the afternoon's lessons. She didn't want another reprimand from Miss Woodcock, especially as if all went to plan, she might need a reference from her one day soon.

When she reached the gate to the cantonment, the guard there wouldn't let her through.

'You have no identification on you, miss,' he said, waggling his head from side to side, almost as if it amused him to deny her entry.

Lena didn't have time to argue, so she gave him her letter. 'Please could you hand that into the office?' she asked with pleading eyes. It would be so unfortunate if, after all this effort, her application didn't even get to the right person.

She hurried back to the school, worrying incessantly about the application and whether she was going to be late for the afternoon lessons.

A few days later, an official-looking letter arrived at St Catherine's for Lena. Miss Woodcock handed it to her after breakfast with her trademark raised eyebrow and pursed lips. Perhaps she'd guessed what it was about...

Lena took the letter and hurried to the lavatories, the only place in the building where she was guaranteed privacy. Sitting on the big wooden thunderbox, she ripped the envelope open. The letter thanked her for her application and asked her to attend an interview the following afternoon at the cantonment. That sent her nerves into a flutter. She was filled with pleasure and pride that she'd actually got an interview, but she was supposed to be teaching that afternoon and teachers were not allowed time off during term time. Lena sat there thinking about it for a while and soon realised that the only thing for it was to fake an illness.

The next morning, while the other girls were getting dressed, Lena lay in bed clutching her belly, saying that she had stomachache and diarrhoea. Her friends informed Miss Woodcock she was unwell and that was it, the stage was set.

Lena lay there feeling guilty for a while, but she knew she would need to get up and dressed if she was going to make it to the interview. She listened to the sound of the children in the passageway going to prayers, the strains of 'The Lord is my Shepherd' floating up the stairs from the hall, the chanting of the Lord's Prayer, then the door opening and the chatter of the children and the clatter of their shoes in the passage as they trooped to their classrooms.

Her next difficulty was leaving the building without being noticed. And even if she did manage to get out, there was another potential problem. It was not unknown for Miss Woodcock to check up on sick teachers in their dormitories in case they were 'swinging the lead', as she termed it, and if that happened while Lena was out at the interview her cover would be blown.

Listening out for steps on the stairs, Lena slid out of bed, showered quickly in the communal bathroom, wound her long black hair into a bun on the back of her head and got dressed in her best clothes – a narrow black skirt and white blouse and black leather slingback shoes with little bows on the front. They weren't particularly good clothes – on her wages, she could only afford to go to the bazaar tailor, who used inferior material and was a little slapdash, but they were the best she had. Looking at herself in the blemished dormitory mirror, Lena patted her shiny, immaculate hair and smiled at her reflection. She realised she looked the part, that she could hold her head up.

Letting herself out of the fire escape door, she crept down the metal staircase and slid round the outside of the building, ducking under the windows. Then, she went out through the side gate and was standing in the street, her heart soaring. All she had to do now was get to the cantonment and convince whoever interviewed her that she was right for the job. Excitement and nerves fizzed through her in equal measure.

She hired a rickshaw from Cart Road and hardly noticed the precipitous journey along the rough roads that circled through the tea gardens around the mountain and on up to the cantonment at Jalapahar. She would normally have gazed out at the landscape, the misty mountains, layer upon layer of them, fading into the distance, but she was too preoccupied to notice them today, thinking about the upcoming interview and worrying about Miss Woodcock strutting around in the dormitory and finding her missing. When they arrived at the cantonment gate, she had her identity card at the ready for the guard. He studied it carefully, clearly trying to find an excuse to turn her away, but in the end handed it back with a snort and waved her through officiously.

Lena had never been on an army base before and as the rickshaw trundled down the bumpy concrete road between row upon row of long, neat, green-painted Nissen huts, she looked about her in awe, taking it all in. It was another world here, and so orderly in comparison with the centre of Darjeeling which she was used to, all chaos and noise. But despite the appearance of calm, there was a lot of activity. A platoon of Gurkhas was on exercise on the parade ground when she reached the central square. A sergeant stood ramrod straight in front of the soldiers, barking out orders, and the soldiers were marching up and down, performing turns and salutes at his behest.

She got down from the rickshaw and had to ask around for the lieutenant's office. A young officer, who drew up in a jeep, blushing furiously, guided her to one of the corrugated iron Nissen huts on the other side of the parade ground. There was a sign on the door saying 'Lieutenant George Harper'.

She knocked tentatively and it was immediately opened by a grey-haired Englishwoman, the same generation as Miss Woodcock who looked almost as frightening. She looked Lena up and down with barely concealed contempt. Lena was used to this treatment from the British, so it didn't faze her.

'Miss Chatterjee?' the woman barked. 'Lieutenant Harper is expecting you, but I need to ask you some preliminary questions first. I'm his current secretary, Mrs Spooner. Sit down behind that table please. In front of the typewriter.'

Lena obeyed, looking round at the neat but austere office with its metal filing cabinets, antique typewriters and wooden furniture. The woman sat down opposite her and put a pair of pince-nez on and studied Lena's application, frowning deeply and letting out sighs of dissatisfaction.

After what seemed like an age, she looked up at Lena and said, 'I see from your application that you are claiming to be proficient in shorthand and typing and yet you have no actual experience of having worked in an office.' Lena detected a note of triumph in her voice. 'Can you explain that to me?'

'Everyone at St Catherine's is taught shorthand and typing, to help them get a job,' Lena replied in her sweetest voice. 'I also type my lesson plans out on the staffroom typewriter. All the staff there do that.'

The woman regarded her sceptically from over the top her of her pince-nez. 'Yes, I would imagine that girls at St Catherine's need all the help they can get. I know all about that school.'

Lena felt a flush of humiliation heat her cheeks, but she didn't respond, realising a reply wasn't expected. She knew that if she did say out loud what she was thinking, it might seriously damage her prospects of getting the job.

'Well, let's not dwell too much on that,' the woman said finally. 'In view of your lack of experience, I'm going to give you a shorthand and typing test.'

She pushed a pen and shorthand pad over the desk to Lena, then sat back and started to read something out of a military report about a boundary dispute between Nepal and India. She read quickly in a loud voice. There were some long, fearsomely difficult words in it, as well as map co-ordinates and technical terms, but Lena had studied her shorthand lessons well and the words didn't throw her.

When she'd finished reading, Mrs Spooner looked at her. 'Got that all down, did we?'

Lena nodded.

'Well, in that case, I don't suppose you'll have any difficulty in typing it up. What's your typing speed, as a matter of interest? I note you don't state that on your application.'

'Eighty words per minute,' Lena said, and the other woman raised her eyebrows.

'Well, we'll see about that,' she said, looking at her watch. 'I will time you. Off you go.'

Lena rolled a piece of paper into the machine and began typing the document. The typewriter was old and jumpy with missing keys. It rattled and pinged alarmingly, but she pressed on.

She looked up when she'd finished. Mrs Spooner didn't say a word, she just held out her hand for the paper and scrutinised it quickly. Then, with another deep sigh, she crossed the room and knocked on an inner door and put her head round it. There followed a brief conversation between Mrs Spooner and the occupant of the room, which Lena couldn't hear properly.

Mrs Spooner turned round. 'The lieutenant is ready for you now, Miss Chatterjee. Come on through, please.'

Lena had been a little nervous on the way to the base in the rickshaw, and during the shorthand and typing test, but now her nerves really came to the fore. Her palms began to sweat, her throat went dry and her heart was beating ten to the dozen. It felt as if everything she had ever learned had vanished from her brain. She imagined the lieutenant to be an ancient, be-whiskered gentleman with a florid face, puffing on a pipe. He would surely be even more frightening than his secretary.

As Lena went towards his office door, she realised how much getting this job meant to her and made a valiant attempt to get her nerves under control.

Lieutenant Harper was sitting behind an elaborate wooden desk that looked incongruous in this temporary, makeshift building. When Lena entered, he sprang to his feet, held out his hand and shook hers vigorously. Her mouth dropped open in surprise. He was not the old retainer she'd imagined, and he was actually smiling.

'Miss Chatterjee. Very nice to meet you. Please do sit down.'

Lena did so and surveyed Lieutenant Harper discreetly. He didn't seem half as fierce as Mrs Spooner and was clearly a good deal younger. He was probably in his mid-thirties, and had a clear-featured, handsome face with a square jaw and gentle grey eyes. This surprised Lena as from the novels she'd read, she'd imagined all soldiers to be tough and decisive.

'First, may I congratulate you on getting through the short-hand and typing test. You did extremely well. I know Mrs Spooner makes it very difficult and not many pass the test.'

'Thank you,' she breathed, relieved. Her heart was beginning to slow down at last.

'Now, let me explain a bit about the job,' he said. 'Mrs Spooner is retiring very soon, and I need a replacement. There is quite a lot of admin work and the usual secretarial work, letters to type, records to file, and so on. Some of it might be regarded as quite tedious. Could you cope with that?'

'Oh yes,' she assured him. 'I'm quite used to boredom.'

He smiled. 'Well, that's good to know. The job has another side to it too. Mrs Spooner is marvellous in every way, but she doesn't like to travel. Whoever I take on will need to be prepared to come with me on trips into Nepal. I need to go to Kathmandu and sometimes to more far-flung places to recruit more soldiers into the regiment. I need someone with me to take notes and keep a record.'

'Oh!' Lena's eyes lit up. She'd always wanted to travel, to see the world beyond the confines of Bengal Province, that, to date, had been the only place she knew. She'd always been fascinated by Nepal, whose border was only a few miles away from Darjeeling but, as a closed kingdom, was completely out of bounds. The market in Darjeeling though, was frequented by Nepalese traders, in their colourful, traditional clothes, come to ply their crafts and wares from across the Himalayas. She was entranced by them, and by that magical, mystical mountain kingdom they came from.

'So, what do you think?' Lieutenant Harper smiled. 'We've had a couple of girls pass the shorthand and typing test, but sadly they were daunted by the prospect of travelling, so pulled out.'

'I'd absolutely love to go to Nepal,' Lena replied, unable to keep the excitement from her voice. 'Nothing would give me more pleasure.'

'Then the job is yours, Miss Chatterjee,' he said with a warm smile that lit up his whole face. 'When can you start?

∼

I could barely speak to say thank you, and my hand is trembling now I as write these words. I can't believe that I'm actually going to leave St Catherine's!

Chloe closed the diary, a smile spreading over her face. Reading about the first time her grandparents had met was almost like being there, experiencing that momentous event first-hand. She wanted to read on, but she was tired now. Her eyes would barely stay open. It had been an exhausting day. The strain of the funeral had taken its toll, and she found herself longing for bed.

Yawning, she said goodnight to Kip, ensuring his water bowl was filled and his door closed. She went through to Lena's snug to switch the lights off.

'Goodnight, Gran,' she said. Then, wiping away a tear, she picked up the diary and went upstairs to bed.

3

HAMPSHIRE, 2015

THE NEXT MORNING, Chloe woke early, the sad events of the previous day coming back to her as soon as she opened her eyes. She could hear the rain on the window and she had half a mind to stay in bed and nurse her sorrow, but then she remembered her grandmother's journal. She couldn't wait to read more, even though there were plenty of other things she knew she should have been doing; sorting out the house, dealing with her grandmother's paperwork, even looking for a new job.

She reflected on what she'd read so far. How awful it must have been for her grandmother to have been sent away to an institution at such an early age, to be torn away from her mother, to be taught to despise everything Indian and then feel the pain of guilt at having rejected her mother and her mother's gifts. Her mind ran over Lena's words again:

Guilt still burns through me because as a tiny child, I was embarrassed that that woman dressed in a saree and shawl had come specifically to see me, and because I'd actually hated the sweet, cloying taste of the sweetmeats she brought and had thrown them away at the first opportunity...

What a burden for a child to bear. No wonder it had played

on her mind. Chloe sighed, thinking how sad it was that Lena had never felt able to share these things about her past with her, despite how close they'd become after Chloe's own mother, Selina, had died.

Soon, the compulsion to read more of Lena's diary drove Chloe out of bed. She showered quickly, dressed in comfortable old jeans and a sweater, took the diary out of her bedside cabinet and went straight downstairs to the kitchen, where she let Kip out into the garden, put food into his bowl and made herself toast and tea. Even before the tea was brewed, she was sitting down at the table and opening the next page of her grandmother's diary, keen to find out more about her past in India.

Miss Woodcock's eyebrows shot up in surprise when I told her that I was giving my notice to St Catherine's, but she didn't try to persuade me against it. She was quite rude, though, in her own inimitable way...

~

'QUITE FRANKLY, I didn't think you'd have it in you,' Miss Woodcock said drily when Lena told her she would be taking a secretarial job on the army cantonment.

'You don't need to stay on until the end of the term,' she added in a withering tone, and Lena felt a little wounded, even though she was desperate to move on. She'd fully expected the headmistress to try to get her to stay, to insist she worked until the end of the term.

'Beware the outside world, Lena,' Miss Woodcock said then. 'St Catherine's is all you've ever known. Girls here lead a very sheltered life and you might find yourself ill-equipped to deal with some of the hardships out there in the real world.'

'I will be careful,' Lena said dutifully. She'd wanted to tell Miss Woodcock that she had no need to worry, that she was perfectly capable of existing away from St Catherine's, but now she was on the brink of this dramatic change, her confidence seemed to be deserting her.

'You can leave at the end of the week,' Miss Woodcock stated, standing up and glancing at her watch, indicating an end to the meeting. 'Mary and Joan can take over your English lessons. Neither of them have enough to keep them busy at the moment. They'll be glad of the extra work.'

While Miss Woodcock's reaction had been less than impressed, her mother's was quite the opposite. 'Thank the gods!' she said. 'I must go to the temple and make puja. I will give thanks to the goddess of education, Maa Saraswati, for this great honour she has been bestowed upon my child.'

'It's nothing to do with the gods, Ma,' Lena said, laughing. 'They didn't go to the interview. They can't type at eighty words per minute!'

'Lena!' Her mother looked shocked. 'You mustn't say such things. But, of course, you've been brought up a Christian by those wretched Britishers. What can I expect.'

Lena laughed. This was a common refrain from Sita, even though she knew she'd had no choice but to bring her daughter to St Catherine's.

'Perhaps you're right.'

'And where are you going to live when you leave the school?' her mother asked then.

Lena put her cup down. 'Well, I was hoping – just at first, of course – that I might stay with *you*, Ma.'

Her mother gasped and her eyes filled with tears of joy. 'This is only a humble hovel, my Lena, and very small too. But nothing would give me greater joy than having my only daughter back to live with me again, after almost twenty years of separation. There is room for a sleeping mat on the other side of the living room. It will be cramped, but we will manage.'

'Thank you, Ma. And when I have saved up, we might be able

to find somewhere a bit bigger. It's one of the reasons I wanted to get another job.'

~

CHLOE PUT the diary down and got up to let the dog in and to make some more toast. Kip hurried straight to his food bowl and started gobbling his breakfast. Chloe hadn't eaten much the previous day, but this morning she'd regained her appetite.

She read the paragraphs about her great-grandmother over twice, fascinated to have some insight into the woman she'd never known, but from whom she'd inherited her dark eyes and glossy black hair. Chloe had known her great-grandmother's name was Sita, but that was about all she'd been told. It was clear, from reading the diary though, that Sita had given up any life she'd had in Calcutta to be near Lena, and that she had a huge, generous heart. How sad, and how strange it was then that Lena had spoken so little about her own mother, when she'd clearly had such a warm relationship with her in her youth.

Chloe buttered the toast and spread some of her grandmother's gooseberry jam on it before sitting down with the diary again. She turned the page and began reading the entry dated 12th September 1943.

It felt strange this morning, to pack my clothes and the rest of my meagre belongings in the holdall I bought at the bazaar, say a tearful goodbye to my roommates, who all promised to keep in touch, and to walk out of the front gate of St Catherine's for the last time...

~

'GOODBYE, MISS LENA,' Abdul, the guard, said, and gave her a neat salute, clicking his heels together. 'Do come back and see us sometime.'

Then the gate clanged shut behind her, and on all those years she'd spent in that big, rambling building as part of that large community of Eurasian girls just like her. For a moment, Lena felt cast adrift, unsure where to turn. But then a shrill cry from across the road reminded her.

'Lena!' It was her mother, running towards her, her bright pink saree flailing in the wind.

A lump rose in Lena's throat at the sight of her, and at the thought that all those years ago, Sita, just a young woman then, had been forced to bring her little girl here against her better judgment, leave her behind those tall gates and walk away. She had suffered the pain of being parted from her daughter. But she'd not given up, despite hardship and poverty. This must feel as though all those years of waiting had been worth it.

Lena crossed the road, put her holdall down on the pavement and they embraced.

'I'm so happy to have you back,' her mother said, holding Lena at arm's length and smiling into her eyes. 'Let me carry your bag, Lena dear.'

Lena shook her head, suddenly overwhelmed herself at the reunion. 'I can carry it myself. You mustn't pamper me, Ma.'

They walked through the town together, rubbing shoulders with the crowds of thronging shoppers, Tibetans, Nepalese, Gurkhalis and Bengalis, where the chatter of many different languages mingled in a cacophony of voices. They strolled past market stalls plying every type of produce – colourful and ripe fruit and vegetables, bright fabrics and woollens for the mountains, brightly coloured spices that filled the air with their exotic aromas, sweet-smelling flowers, and glittering jewellery. The vendors called out to them, enticing them to buy their wares as they passed. There was so much clamour and colour here, and Lena realised that now she was part of it all. She was part of the fabric of this vibrant, busy community, not separated from it by the school gates and the strict regimes and prejudices of St Catherine's.

She turned to her mother smiling. 'Thanks for coming to meet me, Ma. I'm glad to be free of that place.'

They took a side street and walked down several narrow flights of uneven steps to get to the lower part of the town. The bazaar here was even noisier and more chaotic than the market they'd just passed through. The pungent smell of cooking spices hung on the air and here, too, vendors were shouting about their wares. Lena and her mother passed stalls where chicken carcasses hung by the neck from racks and where butchers jointed animals with meat cleavers on bloody blocks in the open air. The smell of drains, ever present in the town, was even more rank down here. What a contrast this was with St Catherine's. It was a different world.

Lena's mother's home was tucked away in an alleyway just behind the bazaar, an open drain running down the hill in front of the building. When they got inside, surveying the place as her new home for the first time, Lena realised how tiny it really was. But it was clean and colourful, and her mother had done her best to make it homely. Sita slept on a truckle bed behind a tapestry curtain at one end of the room. At the other end were some low cushions for relaxing and a small altar for her daily puja. The tiny kitchen opened out beyond that, and the lavatory and wash-house were in a courtyard just behind it.

Her mother cleared a space for Lena to sleep and unrolled her sleeping mat. Then they unpacked her holdall, hanging her clothes up beside Sita's on the single rail.

THERE WASN'T time for me to worry too much about my new living arrangements because I'm starting my new job tomorrow! I busied myself with preparations, making sure my clothes were clean and neat, my smart leather shoes with the little bows on the front polished, and that I have everything I need in my handbag, including enough change

for the rickshaw-wallahs. And now I must sleep, because tomorrow is going to be a big day for me, the first day of a new phase of my life.

Chloe paused and put the diary down. She cleared up the breakfast things and made herself another cup of tea. As she was doing so, the doorbell rang. She went to answer it wondering who it could be. A young man in white overalls stood on the doorstep.

'I'm from the caterers. Come to collect the crockery?'

'Oh! Oh of course. I'm so sorry,' Chloe said, flustered. She'd been so absorbed in her grandmother's story that she'd completely forgotten about them.

She helped the young man load the boxes into the back of his van, then went back into the house as he drove away, pulling her cardigan tightly around her. It was even colder than it had been the day before at the funeral, and that day had felt bitterly raw.

Chloe had promised herself that she would start sorting out the house today, but now she told herself that it could wait for a while, that there was no hurry. She wanted to read a little more of the diary, to immerse herself in Lena's world.

She went back into the kitchen and picked it up again. Kip slumped at her feet with a deep sigh.

I barely slept last night, finding it impossible to get comfortable on the thin sleeping mat in Ma's sitting room. I was also disturbed by her loud snores coming from behind the curtain and the sounds of the street outside. There were stray dogs howling, neighbours talking and laughing into the night, cockerels crowing even before dawn. And on top of that, my whole body was racked with nerves at the thought of what the morning might bring.

AS THE FIRST light crept into the sky, Lena heard her mother stir and tiptoe cross the room, then move about in the kitchen. Soon the smell of cooking spices wafted through the room.

A few minutes later, her mother crept to her bedside with a cup of chai. 'I've cooked you some breakfast, child. You'll need some fuel for your important day.'

Lena's heart sank a little. If she ate spicy food for breakfast, her breath would smell of it all day. This was a taboo that had been drummed into them at St Catherine's as the staff had tried to instil into all the girls a fear and loathing of spicy food. But as Lena had grown older and had tasted illicit food from the market, or had eaten what her mother had prepared for her, she'd begun to love it, and she resented being taught to despise it.

She didn't have the heart to tell her mother that she couldn't eat spicy food for breakfast, and in any case, when she bit into the succulent, fresh puris stuffed with peas and spices, they tasted so delicious that she devoured three of them, washed down with the sickly-sweet cardamom chai that Sita had brewed just for her.

Just before eight o'clock she kissed her mother goodbye and made her way up to Cart Road, where she found a waiting rickshaw and negotiated a price to Jalapahar cantonment. This time, the rickshaw-wallahs dropped her at the gate. She asked them to return at five fifteen.

She made her way on foot down through the cantonment, where Gurkhas were already exercising in stiff lines out on the parade ground, to Lieutenant Harper's office. There, she was dismayed to see that Mrs Spooner was still installed behind her desk. Lena had anticipated that the former secretary would have left by now and that she would have free rein over the work.

'Miss Chatterjee,' Mrs Spooner greeted her with a sour smile. 'The lieutenant asked me to stay on for another week to show you the ropes. I hope that will be useful for you.'

'Of course,' Lena replied politely, now dreading the coming hours and days ahead.

But she need not have worried. Mrs Spooner had changed her tune towards Lena, now that she'd actually been appointed, and although she wasn't exactly friendly as she showed Lena the filing system and explained the routines, she was at least civil. Lena did notice her wafting the air rudely with her hand and putting her handkerchief over her nose when she came close to Lena, clearly not happy with the spicy smell of her breath, but she wasn't rude enough to say anything about it. Mischievously, Lena vowed to ask her mother to cook her a spicy breakfast every day that week.

Lieutenant Harper greeted her warmly. 'Come on in, Miss Chatterjee,' he said, waving her into his office. 'Mrs Spooner has probably told you that she's kindly agreed to stay on to help you settle in, which is good news, because I haven't the faintest idea how the office is run,' he said with a hearty chuckle. 'Now, let me explain a bit about what we do here. Our job is to train new Gurkha soldiers for the front line in Burma. Do you know anything about the campaign?'

Lena shook her head. 'Not really. I've read a bit about it in the papers,' she said. It was true, but just as when she read anything about the war or the news in general, it always seemed remote and far away, and to have nothing to do with her own life.

'Well, please sit down and I'll tell you a bit about it. Look at this map, here on my desk.'

She leaned forward and stared at a large map of the Indian-Burmese border.

'Now, this border here is crucial to the defence of the British Empire in India,' Lieutenant Harper said, tracing a line on the map with his finger. 'The terrain there is terrible, though – jungle-covered mountains populated by hill tribes, no proper roads. Despite that, the Japanese are bound to try to take India by this route. Their aim is to make the whole of Asia under Japanese rule. They call it the Co-Prosperity Sphere, but really they just want to dominate the region.'

Lena stared at the contours on the map. From her school geography classes, she understood what they meant, and from looking at them, she could visualise the remote, soaring mountains he described, covered in jungle, with fast-flowing rivers and no roads, seemingly impassable by an army.

'Now, last year,' Lieutenant Harper went on, 'the Japs took the British by surprise in Burma and overran the whole country. We Brits didn't have the manpower at that time; we were concentrating on Europe and the Japs caught us napping. The Japs took Rangoon in March '42 and drove out our troops. British forces were forced back as far as the Irrawaddy River – here,' he pointed to a long blue line on the map, snaking the length of the country.

Again, Lena tried to picture a wide river, meandering across an arid plane, and the fierce battles between two modern armies playing out on its banks.

Lieutenant Harper pointed to another landmark on the map. 'This is Mandalay – Burma's second city. It fell to the Japs in May last year. In trying to hold off the Japanese though, the British sustained around thirty thousand casualties. Many of them were brought over these mountains to India, to hospitals here. British and Indian troops later tried to recover some ground in the Arakan – which is further south, here,' his finger moved to an area in Southern Burma beside the coast.

Lena peered at the spot he was pointing to. From the contours on the map, she could see that the whole of the coastal plain was cut off by another mountain range.

'In February this year, the 77th Indian Brigade, better known as the Chindits, set out from Imphal in India – here.' His finger jabbed at a spot deep in the mountains. 'Their job was to penetrate behind Japanese lines through these hills. They are fighting in the jungle in very dangerous conditions. They have had some success – pushing on down to Mandalay and cutting off some railway lines. Other brigades have been continuing the fight further south in the Arakan. But the Japs are now advancing through these mountains towards India. General Slim has just been appointed to command the 14th Army to defend those hills. And that's where we come in...'

Lena imagined the Chindit soldiers in camouflaged combat gear, creeping through the jungle with their weapons, silently and unseen, only coming out at night to cut railway lines, before heading back to the shelter of the trees. It sounded like something she might have read about in an adventure story, rather than something really happening.

'As I mentioned before, our job is to recruit and train Gurkhas from Nepal, ready to defend the front line as part of the 14th Army. Gurkhas are the toughest soldiers in the world. So we'll be planning a trip to Kathmandu in a couple of weeks. I'll need you to help me with that, Miss Chatterjee.'

'Of course,' she said, excitement bubbling inside her.

'But, in the meantime, there's something else I'd like you to do. As I explained, many soldiers have been wounded in Burma and brought to India for medical treatment. I don't know if you are aware, but there are several of them here in Darjeeling, in the various hospitals and convalescent homes. There are some Indians, some Nepalese, but many are British. They are all a long way from home, and it might help their recovery if they were to have some visitors. I was wondering if you could go along to the Eden hospital tomorrow afternoon, take them some fruit and try to cheer them up.'

This wasn't quite what she was expecting, but she couldn't refuse, so she agreed.

'Mrs Spooner will give you some change from the petty cash. Go to town at lunchtime tomorrow, buy some fruit from the market and take it to them. I'm sure they'll be delighted to see you and the quicker they are on the mend, the quicker they'll be able to go back to the front and help the war effort.'

'All right.'

'Good,' Lieutenant Harper said with a smile. 'I'm sure it will make a big difference.'

It flashed through Lena's mind that her visits would be part of a cynical strategy to put those men back in the battle zone, rather than any genuine concern for their health and well-being. But this was the army, after all, and its business was trying to win the war.

THE FOLLOWING DAY, after a tedious morning spent filing soldiers' records with Mrs Spooner, Lena set off to town, stopping off at the market on Chowrasta to buy some fruit, which she put into a large basket, before making her way to the Eden hospital on Mount Pleasant Road. It was an imposing, whitewashed building and as she entered through the wrought-iron gate, showing her identity card to the guards, she felt a little nervous. She'd never been there before and had to suffer the disparaging looks she received from the British nurses on duty in the reception area.

'I've come from the Military Base at Jalapahar to visit some of the British soldiers,' she explained.

'Really?' The young nurse looked at her with suspicion.

'Yes, Lieutenant Harper sent me. I am his secretary.'

'Oh! Lieutenant Harper. Of course,' the nurse said, her demeanour changing at the mention of his name 'Now, let me see... some of them are too sick to receive visitors, but there are others who are on the mend. I'll take you upstairs. Please, come this way.'

Lena followed the white-clad nurse up the wide, marble stair-case, along an echoing corridor and into a ward at the end. The room was huge, with high ceilings and tall windows. Ceiling fans turned above their heads, cooling the air. There were about ten beds in the room, evenly spaced on either side. From where she stood in the doorway, Lena couldn't get much sense of how sick the patients were.

'All of these chaps are British,' the nurse said. 'They've been serving with either Indian or British Army regiments and were all wounded in Burma. They might look shocking to you, but I'm not showing you the really serious cases. Those patients can't receive visitors yet.'

'Oh dear,' Lena muttered, her heart going out to those poor men.

'All right,' the nurse said briskly, 'I'll leave you to it then. Just introduce yourself. I'm sure they'll be delighted to have a visitor. I'll be downstairs in reception if you need me.' She turned on her heel and left Lena standing there alone.

Lena approached the first bed tentatively. The man in it was either asleep or unconscious, his head lolling on the pillow, heavily bandaged. She decided not to wake him up, so continued to the next bed. The man in that bed was in an even worse state. His whole face was bandaged, but for one eye, which was also closed. Lena carried on, becoming increasingly shocked by what she saw. All the men were in varying states of consciousness, with either amputated limbs or wounds to their head or face. One or two opened one eye and smiled weakly at her. She handed fruit to those she thought would be able to eat it, and she sat down beside a couple of the beds where the men were conscious and held their hand for a few minutes.

As she sat there, she thought about these young men, probably about her own age. They had left their homes in a cold country to travel halfway across the world to fight a fanatical enemy in thick jungle in a tropical climate. The lines and contours on the map of Burma that Lieutenant Harper had traced out with his finger for her the day before were becoming clearer to her now. It struck her forcefully that this wasn't just far-off war written about in newspapers and talked about in army HQ, it was a real conflict that had sucked these young men in and spat them out and would probably affect them for the rest of their lives. And these were just the ones who had made it out alive...

Lena said a quiet prayer for these young men and for all the others caught up in the conflict.

She moved on to the last bed, the one in the corner of the

ward. As she approached, she was surprised and gratified to see that the soldier in this bed was awake and in full possession of all his limbs. He even smiled at her as she got closer, and she saw that he had a mop of dark hair and hazel eyes with long dark lashes.

'Private Billy Thomas,' he said, holding out his hand to shake hers. 'I thought you'd never get to me, miss.'

Lena shook his hand in return and sat down beside his bed with a silent sigh of relief.

'A few weeks ago, I was in a really bad way like some of the other lads, but I'm on the mend now,' the young man said. 'It's so good to see a living, breathing person for once,' he added, smiling up into her eyes.

I SMILED BACK at him and I saw genuine joy and pleasure in his eyes. It lifted my heart, and I realised that this was just the beginning of a whole new world opening up to me.

CHLOE STOPPED READING, trying to envisage her grandmother on that ward, visiting those badly injured men alone, dealing with the shock of seeing their horrific injuries.

She'd smiled when reading how her grandfather had described the Burma campaign with the aid of maps. She could recall many times that he'd described battles and other historical events to her, poring over maps on his desk. Seeing the maps with their contours, rivers and mountains had helped her visualise the scenery. It interested and amused her that he'd done the same with her grandmother when they'd first met. Those little details about him made the whole thing feel so real.

4

KATHMANDU, 1943

I AM NOW in Kathmandu with Lieutenant Harper! We've come here for his next Gurkha recruiting campaign. We flew by light aircraft from a remote airstrip near the Jalapahar cantonment. Lieutenant Harper drove me to the airstrip himself in an open-topped jeep along the unmade roads.

Lieutenant Harper's driving was fast and reckless, and by the time they arrived at the tiny airstrip, Lena was already feeling a little light-headed. She had to suppress a gasp of dismay when she saw the flimsy aircraft, settled on the airstrip like an insect ready for flight. It was a tiny, four-seater propeller plane with camouflage fuselage, and looked battered and battle-worn, as though it had already seen a lot of action. This was to be her first ever flight and she knew that the route through the mountains to Kathmandu was likely to be hazardous.

Her mother's attitude hadn't helped.

'Kathmandu! Oh, my dear daughter,' Sita had said, clutching her chest. 'I must pray to Ganesh, the god of travel, for your safe delivery,' and she had hurried off to the temple.

Until the morning Lena departed, her mother had been offering sweetmeats and lighting candles, prostrating herself before a statue of Ganesh, the elephant god, that she'd put on her little altar in the living room. She'd even decorated the statue with a garland of marigolds.

Lena was careful to keep her views to herself, but she couldn't help being a little sceptical about Ma's offerings. Even though she didn't want to offend her, she couldn't resist saying at one point, 'Ma, it's really kind of you to pray for me, but I can't see how any of this is going to stop the plane from plunging into the mountains.'

Yet, as the time approached for Lena to board the aircraft, she found that she was praying under her breath for a safe flight to her own god too.

Now, mounting the aircraft steps behind Lieutenant Harper, she was so nervous that her heart was hammering and she felt her legs shaking beneath her. She narrowly missed bumping her head as she entered the plane through the low doorway.

'Duck!' Lieutenant Harper yelled, and she did, automatically.

Once inside, she was dismayed to see how tiny the interior of the plane was, how flimsy the bucket seats, and how shabby everything appeared.

'You mustn't worry about the state of the aircraft,' Lieutenant Harper explained with a reassuring smile. 'The RAF uses it to fly supplies into the troops in Burma. It's certainly seen some service in recent months. It's a hardy little bus and the crew are second to none.'

Lena attempted a smile but was too afraid to answer. She told herself to calm down. If she felt sick while they were still on the ground, what on earth would she be like on the flight itself?

She didn't have long to wait to find out. The pilot and navigator, both wearing RAF jumpsuits, flying helmets and goggles, climbed on board, greeting Lena and the lieutenant with a cheery wave. Lena didn't feel reassured by their relaxed manner or by their appearance. The two men looked impossibly young. They couldn't have been much older than Lena herself. They quickly buckled their seat belts, fired up the engines, and the aircraft started to taxi towards the flat grassy strip that served as a runway.

'Put your seat belt on, Miss Chatterjee!' Lieutenant Harper shouted over the noise of the engines, and she hastily buckled the inadequate-looking webbing belt across her lap. It was difficult though, with trembling, clumsy hands.

The roar of the engines reached a deafening pitch, then the plane started picking up speed along the airstrip. It went faster and faster until the trees along the edge of the airfield became a green blur, and with a slight bump they were airborne and climbing steeply. Then, without any warning, the plane was banking and turning left to fly over the cantonment.

An involuntary gasp escaped Lena when she looked out of the window. There was the whole of the cantonment, its neat rows of Nissen huts, parade ground and buildings, all laid out beneath her. She was astonished; it looked just like a toy town. But it quickly disappeared from view as the plane straightened up and flew above the ridge of the Darjeeling hills.

Lena pressed her forehead to the window and stared down at the ground, forgetting her nerves for a moment, marvelling at what she could see. There was the pale line of the unmade cart track that she came to work on by rickshaw each morning, the dark forest that the track wound its way through, and beyond that the tea gardens. Even from that great height, she could make out the brightly coloured sarees of the tea pickers amongst the emerald strips of tea bushes.

Soon, they were flying over the town, partially hidden by wispy clouds, the aircraft still climbing. Lena picked out St Mary's Church, the Indian bazaar, teeming with people, and there were the grey roofs of St Catherine's. Children in the playground were staring up and waving madly. Lena waved back, remembering looking up from that same playground in wonder at passing aircraft. Back then, she'd never dreamed that one day she might actually be flying in one herself.

They quickly left Darjeeling behind and were soon soaring high over the little town of Ghoom, where the Darjeeling Himalayan railway went through a series of loops to cope with the gradients. Lena could make out the silver outline of the rails, and her heart leapt to see the plume of steam rising from the little train itself as it puffed its way around the loop towards Darjeeling. But the railway and the communities around the town were soon left behind and the plane struck out over the wooded mountains separating Bengal Province from Nepal. She could see the tree-lined contours of the mountains beneath, looking like a relief model or an aerial photograph from a geography lesson.

All the time, they continued to climb higher and higher. Lena watched the propellers nervously. They were turning so fast, they were just a blur, but what would happen if they decided to simply stop? Sometimes the plane flew through pockets of cloud which made it rock and buck in the currents. When that happened, Lena's stomach did a somersault, but the pilot and the navigator appeared unperturbed, so she tried not to worry, though she did glance across at Lieutenant Harper.

He smiled reassuringly again. 'It's just a bit of turbulence. It will pass,' he said, and she felt a bit better then.

The flight took about an hour and a half, most of it over rocky, mountainous terrain. In the distance, Lena caught glimpses of the higher peaks of the Himalayas, including the familiar jagged summits of Kanchenjunga. They were covered in snow, with fluffy white clouds clinging to the peaks, the morning sun lighting them up in pinks and golds.

Lena reflected that these mountains had been a constant presence every day of her life, but she'd never seen them that close up before. The sight was awe-inspiring.

As the plane cruised between the mountains, she started to

relax and think of other things. Her mind went back to her visit to the hospital earlier in the week. She still couldn't get over the shock of seeing all those young men with such devastating injuries.

Seeing them close-up like that had really brought home to Lena that the war was actually real, not just something to read about in the newspapers. It was being fought by innocent young men who had no real interest or understanding of the underlying politics. They were just caught up in events beyond their control, in the wrong place at the wrong time.

The conversation with the young private, Billy Thomas, had stayed in her mind.

He had seemed such a disarmingly open and friendly Englishman. Lena had never met one like him ever before. Most of the British in Darjeeling thought they were above the locals and especially superior to a Eurasian like Lena, and they mainly either treated her with contempt or simply ignored her. In contrast, Billy had treated Lena as an equal and seemed genuinely pleased that she was there to visit them.

Lena had asked Billy whereabouts in England he came from.

'The East End of London, for my sins. You ever been there?'

When she shook her head, he'd said, 'You wouldn't want to, either. It's not a nice place.'

She had been puzzled. It was the first time anyone British had ever described their home country in anything other than glowing terms.

'I'm sure that can't be right,' she'd murmured.

Billy Thomas had given a short laugh. 'Have you ever been to England, miss?'

Lena had felt her cheeks colouring. 'I'm afraid I haven't,' she'd replied quietly. 'I was born in Calcutta and I've lived most of my life in Darjeeling. In fact, I've never been outside Bengal Province.

'You're joking! How come you talk like a proper English lady, then?'

That had made Lena laugh. 'I didn't know I sounded like that. But if I do, I suppose it's because I went to a school where we were taught to speak the King's English. We were also taught all about British values and customs, and what a wonderful place England is. All the girls I know at St Catherine's yearn to go there one day.'

When he looked back at her, his eyes were serious.

'You know, there are some good things about Britain, but there's a lot wrong with it too,' he'd said. 'There are far too many people who are poor and struggling. Like my parents. My dad was a docker in the Port of London. Worked his whole life all hours, a heavy, dirty job, but he earned next to nothing. We lived in a tiny, damp terraced house, eight of us in two bedrooms. And we're not the only ones. The country's good for those born into money, but the rest of us have a struggle. There's a huge class divide. There are things about Britain that would make your hair curl if you heard them.'

Lena suppressed a smile at this odd expression. But it unnerved her to hear this about the country that had been built up in her mind as somewhere to look up to, certainly not somewhere that suffered some of the same problems with poverty that India did.

'It's nice having someone to talk to,' Billy had said, breaking into her thoughts. 'These poor lads on the ward aren't any company, and the nurses all turn their noses up at a lad from the East End. Do you think you could come again soon, miss? Oh, and the fruit isn't too bad either.'

Lena had promised to visit again, although she had no idea when that might be. When she'd left, Billy's face, with its open, warm expression, his earnest eyes, had stayed in her mind.

Looking out of the aircraft window, Lena saw that the rugged tops of some mountains looked very close. The plane had begun its descent. She realised she was more interested than afraid. By the time it had crossed the mountains south of Kathmandu and was coming down into the Kathmandu valley, Lena had completely forgotten her initial fears. The landing on a grass airstrip north of Kathmandu was bumpy, but the plane soon came to a juddering halt and the door was quickly thrown open.

A Land Rover driven by a Gurkha soldier, dressed in khaki uniform, was there to collect Lena and Lieutenant Harper. He drove them to an army base on the outskirts of the city, not far from the airstrip.

As they drove onto the base, Lena realised that it looked very much like the cantonment at Jalapahar, with its neat rows of Nissen huts, functional, square buildings and flat, featureless parade grounds.

The driver stopped outside an accommodation block and Lena was shown to her room, which was sparse and functional. She sat down on the narrow bed, disappointed that she wasn't able to see any local colour, but within minutes there was a tap on the door. It was Lieutenant Harper.

'Would you like to join me in the canteen for lunch once you've had a chance to freshen up?'

'I'd love to,' Lena answered, relieved that she wasn't expected to stay here alone, trapped in this soulless room.

'Sorry about the drab room....' the lieutenant said, glancing around. 'Standard army issue, I'm afraid. By the way, I have to meet the colonel in command here after lunch. There's no need for you to come along. You won't be needed until tomorrow morning. If you'd like to take a look round the city this afternoon, I'll have a word with the driver.'

'Oh. I'd love that!'

Her spirits rose instantly. How kind and thoughtful her new boss was.

After a basic lunch of fried rice and vegetable curry, Lena met the driver outside the accommodation block. She got into the front of the Land Rover beside him, and they set off.

They passed through the straggly outskirts of Kathmandu,

which to Lena looked very much like the shabbier suburbs of Darjeeling, but before long she sensed that they were approaching the historic heart of the city. The buildings narrowed and closed in around them, shutting out the sky, and as they crawled along the crowded streets, she found herself looking out at carved wooden houses, whose upper floors jutted out above them. The whole place had a medieval feel to it, like something from a fairy tale. Street stalls were laid out on the pavement – fruit, nuts and spices were displayed in bowls, or set out on blankets, and shoppers were standing at the roadside bargaining with stallholders.

Occasionally, there was a break in the buildings, and a colourful shrine or stupa would be wedged in between, letting in a chink of sky. People were kneeling and making puja on the steps, laying flowers and offerings, incense and candles filling the air with their heavily scented smoke. Most of the buildings had open-fronted shops on the lower floors where shoppers thronged. Wares and produce hung from the shopfronts – brightly coloured fabrics, shoes, baskets, leather bags, cooking equipment. There was no other motor traffic there, most people were on foot, on bicycle or travelling by rickshaw. In amongst the shoppers were tradesmen hauling their wares in boxes, or pushing sack-barrows, bringing produce to the markets.

As people surged past the Land Rover, they stared in at Lena through the windows. Lena realised that she must look something of an oddity in her western clothes. They were such a contrast to the traditional dress that everyone else was wearing – brightly coloured tapestry sarongs, silk sarees and woollen shawls. People didn't seem to be shy of staring, and it felt strange and oddly exciting to be there in this closed, secret kingdom, where normally foreigners weren't allowed to venture.

They carried on crawling through the old city centre, and the crowds closed in behind the vehicle, increasing the claustrophobic feeling of being imprisoned in a forbidden city.

Lena looked out at the street signs – they were written in Devanagari script which she could understand because she could speak and read Hindi. Eventually, when it felt as though the streets couldn't get any narrower or congested, the driver stopped the Land Rover and turned off the engine.

'I cannot go any further, miss,' he said. 'You need to walk now. Up ahead is Durbar Square. It is very historic, very beautiful. I wait here for you for one hour.'

Lena thanked the man and got out of the vehicle. She was a little apprehensive, especially as once out of the Land Rover, she got even more odd looks from the locals who stopped to stare at her neat skirt and white blouse. She found herself wishing she'd brought one of Ma's sarees, but she plunged forward into the crowd anyway, curious to see the medieval heart of this unique city that was steeped in history and mythology.

Rounding the first corner, she found herself in a wide, open space, a square surrounded by temples with tiered red roofs, mounted above flights of stone steps. People sat on the steps taking in the afternoon sun, smoking and chatting. A couple of rickshaws stood empty beside a group of men.

A boy approached Lena carrying a box of brushes. 'Shoeshine, miss?'

The boy couldn't have been more than eight or nine and had the most beautiful, gappy-toothed smile, but Lena shook her head and carried on walking across the square. In front of her was an imposing three-storey red-brick building, with shuttered windows and elaborate roofs. The steps to the entrance were guarded by two huge, mythical creatures. They looked like enormous painted dogs, extravagantly decorated in reds and golds. Lena stood staring at the building, wondering what it might be, when the shoeshine boy plucked at her sleeve.

'This is Kumari Bahal, madam,' he announced. 'Home of the Kumari Devi.'

'Who is the Kumari Devi?'

'She is a child, miss.'

'A child?' Lena was intrigued.

'Yes. A living goddess. She lives in that building. People say it is very lucky if you happen to see her. Sometimes she comes to the window and looks out. I have seen her many, many times,' he added with another huge smile.

'Thank you for telling me. I had no idea.'

Lena realised then how little she really knew about Kathmandu; she should have bought a book about the city from the bookstore on Chowrasta. But she'd been kept so busy by Lieutenant Harper making preparations for the trip and by Mrs Spooner, with general office duties, that she'd had no time for shopping. She realised it was probably impossible to buy a tourist guide in Kathmandu itself. There were no other tourists and no concessions to foreign travellers. She would just have to learn about the city first-hand. Everyone seemed friendly enough, even if they did stare at her strange, modern clothes.

Shading her eyes, Lena looked up at the palace. One of the shutters in an upstairs window was thrown back. A child appeared in the window and stared down at the crowded square. Lena couldn't take her eyes off the little girl. She was like no child she'd ever seen before. She wore an elaborate gold headdress, and her forehead was painted bright red, with the image of a white and blue eye in the centre. Round her neck, she wore many garlands of flowers, marigolds and chrysanthemums.

'Kumari Devi!' said the shoeshine boy with subdued excitement, pointing up at the window. 'You are very lucky, madam. She brings luck to everyone who sees her.'

Lena tore her eyes away from the little goddess and smiled down at the boy, but when she lifted her eyes to the window again, the girl had vanished, and the shutters were already swinging shut.

'She is gone, madam, but the fortune teller will be able to tell you how lucky you are.'

'Fortune teller?'

Lena's scalp tingled at the thought. There was a fortune teller in the bazaar in Darjeeling, but everyone said she was a charlatan who preyed on people's fears and superstitions and that she had no special powers at all. Perhaps it was being in these ancient, mystical surroundings, so far from home, completely alone, but the idea of going to a fortune teller here in Kathmandu appealed to Lena then in a way that it wouldn't normally have done.

'Would you like me to take you to her?' the boy asked.

'All right...' Lena said slowly, and the boy laughed, flashing her another wide smile.

HE WAS OFF THEN, tugging her arm to follow him. She hurried along behind him, across the wide Durbar Square and into a side alley filled with jewellers' shops. The boy was moving quickly, darting between the shoppers.

Lena struggled to keep up with him in her slingback shoes. But at the end of the alley, he waited for her, then ducked into an even narrower passage, where there were no shops at all. It was dark there, and looking up, Lena saw that the eaves of the buildings were almost touching, shutting out the light, and the air was heavy with the smell of drains mingled with the spicy, smoky perfume of incense. A chill went through her then and she suddenly felt vulnerable and alone. How far she was from home here, how far from the base even.

The boy stopped at an entrance halfway along the passage. 'It is here,' he said, pointing at some carved wooden doors. 'You just go inside, and she will see you.'

Lena hesitated.

'I will wait for you here,' the boy said, 'so you don't get lost.'

Putting aside her qualms, Lena thanked him, pushed the heavy door open and entered a darkened room. There were no windows, and for a couple of seconds, she stood behind the door wondering whether to turn round and go straight back out again, but her eyes soon acclimatised, and she could see that the room was lit by candles, flickering from every surface, giving off a smoky, waxy smell. Ahead was a red, velvet curtain covering an entrance. Lena walked across the dark room towards the curtain, pulled it aside and peeped round it.

A woman sat in a tiny room behind the curtain, on a high-backed chair. In front of her was a small round table, spread with a red velvet tablecloth and a white crystal ball that glinted in the candlelight. Lena was surprised to see a little girl sitting beside her, dressed in a red tunic. Her eyes were rimmed with heavy kohl and looked huge in her tiny, pale face. She reminded Lena eerily of the Kumari Devi. The room itself was lined with silk wall-hangings depicting scenes from the Ramayana, and the air was filled with the smell of incense.

The woman was reading from a book to the child, but when she looked up and saw Lena, she put the book aside hastily and stood up to greet her. She was dressed in colourful robes, her hair covered with a shawl fringed in gold braid. Around her neck she wore many gold chains. She was heavily made up with thick black kohl around her eyes, just like the child's, and deep red lipstick on her full lips. In her nose and ears were rings and studs and when she put her hands together in a gesture of greeting, numerous gold bangles jangled together.

'Good afternoon, madam,' she said in Nepali, which Lena could understand, given her knowledge of Hindi.

'Good afternoon, to you,' Lena replied, and the woman motioned for her to sit down on a stool in front of the table.

Lena perched on the stool, feeling a little nervous and a little foolish too. Why had she come here? She hadn't even had to be persuaded, she'd just gone along voluntarily at the very first suggestion. It would be very difficult for her to leave now, though.

She glanced at the little girl, and was startled that her intense dark eyes were fixed on her face. She quickly looked away again.

'Don't be shy,' the woman said with a welcoming smile. 'Give me your hand, please.'

Lena held her hand out over the table and the woman took it and turned it over to look at the palm. She bent her head forward to study it carefully and stayed like that, motionless for a long moment. Then she began tracing the lines on Lena's hand with her forefinger and muttering to herself, as if in a trance. The fortune-teller's nails were long and sharp and painted the same deep shade of red as her lipstick.

When she was beginning to wonder whether this was a normal palm reading, the woman lifted her head and looked into her eyes. She was still holding Lena's hand, palm up, in one of hers. 'You will have a long life. Long and happy for the most part, but I do see tragedy there too.'

'Oh?' A prickle of unease stirred in Lena's chest. She felt herself frowning.

'You have a new friend,' the woman announced, peering intensely into Lena's eyes.

Lena frowned. A new friend? 'I don't think so...' she murmured.

'That is what I see. A new friend. Someone who has suffered badly and who still suffers. Your friend may be in danger,' the woman said, still looking into her eyes.

'In danger?' she asked in alarm. Was the woman actually genuine?

The woman dropped her hand and put her hands over her eyes and rocked back and forth. 'I can't see what it is at present,' she murmured. 'It is shrouded in mist and clouds, but danger lurks in the future for him. You must warn him, try to stop him.'

'But... what do you mean? Stop him?' Lena asked weakly.

'Yes. You must try to stop him, save him from the danger that threatens. It will not be easy, he will be resistant, but you must try.'

Lena withdrew her hand, deciding that the visit had been a waste of time. She stood up and felt in her bag for her purse.

'Twenty rupees,' the woman said. 'And don't forget my words.'

Lena put twenty rupees down on the table and hurried out of the place.

5

THE SHOESHINE BOY guided me back to Durbar Square and I handed him a few rupees for his trouble. He rewarded me with another big smile, before I bade him goodbye and found my way back to the Land Rover. The driver turned the vehicle around and drove me back through the busy streets to the base. But this time I wasn't really looking at my surroundings, I was thinking about the woman's words. Although I'd tried to dismiss them in my mind as nonsense, a waste of time, in reality they had chilled me to the core.

Chloe put down her grandmother's diary and slowly came back to the present. It felt incredible to be reading the words that Lena had written over seventy years ago. She could barely equate the young woman who had penned those lines with the older woman she'd known so well. As with the entries she'd read the day before, the parts she'd read that day were so vivid, so colourful, conjuring a world that Chloe had never imagined, a world that her grandmother had certainly never spoken of.

Chloe was fascinated to read her grandmother's first impression of Kathmandu. It sounded such a magical place. She read it again, to experience Lena's words to the full. She wondered if it remained the same, or if the modern world had obliterated its charm. How she would have loved to have been there by her grandmother's side to experience it in all its magic in the 1940s.

But the thought kept returning, why had Lena been so circumspect about her childhood and life as a young woman in Darjeeling?

Chloe recalled trying to get her to speak of India on more than one occasion.

'Oh, you don't want to hear about that. It is not at all important,' her grandmother had said dismissively. 'My life is here now. When I came to England with your grandfather after the war, I put all that behind me and started afresh. I don't want to start talking about it now. Besides, it is so long ago, I can barely remember it at all now. It's almost like another life.'

'But, Gran,' Chloe had coaxed, 'it's important to *me*. It would be so interesting to hear about India. It's part of my heritage, after all.'

But Lena wouldn't be drawn. Instead, she'd said, with a touch of impatience, 'If you really want to find out about India, Chloe, why don't you go there yourself, some day? Then you will see that it isn't all exotic palaces and fabulous landscapes. You will see that there is cruelty and poverty and ugliness there too. Some people have wealth beyond their wildest dreams and others have to scavenge on rubbish tips for a living. It is a land of contrasts, Chloe, of unimaginable beauty and of unimaginable suffering too.'

Lena's descriptions of her life in Darjeeling, and of her visit to Kathmandu, had certainly ignited in Chloe a real desire to go there, to see those places for herself, to see how much had changed since her grandmother had written about them in the early 1940s. How fabulous it would be to travel there and see it all for herself. Perhaps now was the time to do that?

She sighed, thinking back to her recent, painful split from Fergal, the latest in a series of unsatisfactory relationships. It had left her reeling, her ego in tatters. Fergal worked hard as a financial analyst in the city – he was a go-getter. She'd met him when she'd shown him round some new-build flats which he was looking at as an investment opportunity. Foolishly, Chloe had mistaken his Irish lilt and swarthy good looks for something interesting and out of the ordinary. Here was someone different from the men at the office, and all the other men she'd dated.

But, after a short time, she'd realised her error. Fergal didn't want to be out of the ordinary. Far from it. He wanted to settle down with Chloe, buy a three-bedroomed house in Guildford within easy reach of the train station, work hard in the city for a few more years and save up to have children.

But Chloe hadn't wanted that. She hadn't wanted to settle down yet. There was something inside her that yearned for something more, something different from life. She had no idea where that restless spirit inside her had come from, but she couldn't keep it down.

But some of the unkind things Fergal had said to her at the end had cut her to the quick and now she was wondering if she wanted to get involved with anyone ever again. It would certainly take a while for her wounds to heal and, for now, she knew that she desperately needed a change of scene.

But, she wondered, was a trip like that possible right now? With everything she had to organise in the house, with her grandmother's affairs to sort out. She'd been truthful when she'd assured Daniel that she didn't want to sell the house, but at the very least, she needed to clear it up, to sort through her grandmother's things, get rid of the stairlift and the low bed Lena had had installed in the snug when she got too ill to go upstairs. It pained Chloe to see those things about the place. She wanted to remember Lena as the vibrant, quick-witted woman she had been for most of her life, full of laughter and joy, not the invalid she'd become in her last few, painful weeks.

With a sigh, she got up from the armchair beside the Aga and began to wander around the house. Kip got up from his rug under the window and trotted at her heels. Chloe was trying to look at the home her grandmother had made with fresh eyes, to understand Lena a little better. But there was very little evidence of her grandmother's connection with India, apart from the couple of anonymous black and white scenes from Darjeeling in the 1930s, and the photograph of her wedding in the church there – Lena and George - George in uniform, Lena in a simple white dress - their arms tucked into one another's, beaming into the camera.

In her grandfather's study, there were little statues of Hindu gods on the mantlepiece, a watercolour of the Taj Mahal on one wall, silk wall hangings depicting colourful Indian scenes above the fireplace, and a painting of the Himalayas. But there was nothing in the rest of the house to suggest that its occupant had ever spent any time outside the British Isles. In fact, looking closely, Chloe realised that the whole place was studiedly English. From the chintzy curtains and loose covers in the living room, the English hunting scenes on the walls, to the Aga in the kitchen, the comfy armchairs, willow-pattern china and gingham tablecloths, everything about this house proclaimed it to be that of a stolid, old-fashioned Englishwoman.

Chloe was puzzled as to why that was. She wondered if her grandmother had kept any mementoes from her former life at all. What about in her most private place, her bedroom? Would there be anything there to give any insight into the early years before her marriage?

Feeling a little like a snooper, Chloe told the dog to stay in the hallway. Then she crept upstairs, approached the bedroom door and put her hand on the handle. She'd rarely been inside the room before. It wasn't that she'd been forbidden, she'd just not been encouraged to enter. Mrs Bull, the housekeeper, came in weekly and cleaned and swept, stripped the bed and polished the furniture, but Chloe hadn't been in there for a while. The door was a little stiff, so she had to put her knee against it to push it open. She switched on the light and stepped inside.

A blast of cold air hit her as she entered – someone had switched off the heating, so she went over to the old-fashioned, bulbous radiator under the window and turned the knob until she heard hot water gurgling through its valves. Then she turned to her grandmother's large mahogany wardrobe and opened the door. Inside hung Lena's favourite clothes. Here were her colourful dresses, tunics, blouses and brightly patterned scarves. Chloe pulled a handful of them towards her and buried her face in them. She caught the smell of her grandmother's favourite perfume – Diorissimo. She felt a lump rise in her throat; the scent brought back so many powerful memories and in all of them her grandmother was smiling or laughing. She'd been a happy, contented woman, Chloe realised, so why had she been so reluctant to talk about her past?

At the bottom of the wardrobe were some deep drawers. Chloe pulled them open one by one and investigated the contents. Inside were hats and shoes, some of them positively antique-looking. There were a few boxes of Grandpa's shoes too, and a collection of his ties. But there was nothing more personal than that.

She moved on to the chest of drawers, a large elaborately carved Victorian mahogany monstrosity that matched the wardrobe. She opened the top drawer tentatively and took a deep breath before diving in. It pained her to riffle through her grandmother's sturdy, white cotton pants and vests, the T-shirts she used to wear for gardening, her thick jumpers, and her old woolly socks which she'd darned rather than thrown away. But again, there was nothing to reflect her connection with India at all.

Her dressing table revealed nothing either. Various bottles of perfume and cosmetics were arranged beside her grandmother's hairbrushes and jewellery box in front of the mirror.

In the bedside cabinet, Chloe found her grandmother's stash

of medications, the tablets she'd taken to alleviate the headaches that had plagued her in her latter years, her heart pills, cough medicine, and numerous food supplements and vitamins. There were also the books she loved to keep close. She'd loved literature to the end. There were hardback copies of *Jane Eyre*, *Wuthering Heights*, and several different Jane Austen novels, but nothing more. There was no insight into her former existence here at all.

Feeling thwarted, Chloe left the bedroom, went back downstairs and along the corridor to the snug. Kip hovered in the doorway. Ever since Lena's death he hadn't wanted to go inside. This was the room in which her grandmother had spent most of her time, that she'd made her own. Surely, if she hadn't kept anything in her bedroom, if there was anything at all to find, it would be in here.

Trying not to look too hard at the daybed, which still sent shivers down her spine, Chloe went straight to the bureau. It was where her grandmother used to sit to do her paperwork – the household bills, the bank accounts, her tax returns. Chloe had been putting off tackling the paperwork; her grandmother had not been very organised in recent years and Chloe was dreading the muddle that she suspected had been left behind.

She started to go through the drawers at the side of the bureau. In the top three drawers, there was nothing remarkable, just the usual array of random stationery items, paper clips, treasury tags, old biros and pencils, even an ink bottle. But when she tried the bottom drawer, it refused to open. Thinking it was just a little stiff, she tried once again to pull it open, but quickly realised that it was actually locked. She felt a little thrill of anticipation while she searched for the key. It wasn't hard to find, it was in one of the tiny drawers inside the top of the bureau itself.

Her hands were shaking with excitement as she unlocked the drawer and eased it open. Chloe peered inside, holding her breath. There was a slim book in there with a gold padded front with one word embossed in elaborate script. *Photographs*. This was what she'd been looking for. She opened it carefully and already she could tell that there weren't many photographs in there. That made the ones that were there all the more preciously tantalising.

She turned the first page and there was a black and white photograph of a young Lena, in her early twenties, Chloe guessed, dressed in uniform, a smart jacket and a peaked cap. She was smiling, but her eyes held a slightly anxious look. Underneath the photograph, she had written in her familiar scrawl, 'First day with the Wasbies!' So, she *did* have evidence of her time with the Wasbies here in the house, Chloe thought. What was it then about the diary that meant it had to be entrusted to a friend for safekeeping?

She turned the next page of the photograph album and there was a picture of Lena with three other girls. This was a slightly younger Lena, dressed in a simple black skirt and white blouse. Her face, devoid of make-up, was full of innocence. All the other girls looked to be Eurasian like Lena, and roughly the same age. The photograph had been taken in a dormitory by the look of the background. The girls stood together in a line slightly formally, their arms linked, and they were all smiling. Underneath the picture, Lena had scrawled, 'Graduation day – from pupils to teachers – with dormitory pals Mary, Joan, and Vicky'.

Chloe looked hard at the photograph of the four girls. She already knew about these girls from the journal, but the sight of these young women standing together brought home to her how big a part her education at St Catherine's and the relationships she'd forged at the place must have played in her grandmother's life. They all looked so close, so comfortable in each other's company, almost like sisters. How strange that these friendships hadn't lasted, or at least that Lena had never mentioned any of these names to Chloe.

She turned another page and there was Lena again, this time a little older, her arms around an amply proportioned Indian lady, dressed in a saree and shawl, with a prominent tikka mark in the middle of her forehead. They were standing in front of some railings and behind them was an astonishing mountain landscape, soaring peaks covered in snow. It was so dramatic that Chloe assumed that it must be a studio background. Both had huge smiles and, under the photograph, Lena had written, 'Me and Ma and Kanchenjunga'. The backdrop was real!

Chloe looked at the photograph for a long time. So, this was her great-grandmother, Sita. It was the first time Chloe had ever seen a picture of her, and looking at her now, she could see a likeness between the two women, even though Lena was slim and young, Sita older and running to fat. In a rare moment of openness, Lena had told Chloe her mother's name, that she came from Calcutta, that she'd died well before her time, but that was all. Here, the two of them looked close, as if they got on well and enjoyed each other's company. In which case, why had her grandmother been so circumspect about her mother?

Turning the page, Chloe took a sharp intake of breath. There was one more photograph in the album. It was of someone Chloe had never seen before – a young soldier, in soldier's uniform, with a forage cap perched on his dark hair. He had no officer's stripes, so was clearly a private. He was looking out at the camera with an open, friendly expression in his dark eyes, although he wasn't smiling. Unlike on the other pages, her grandmother had not written anything underneath the photograph, so there was no clue as to the identity of the young man. Nevertheless, there was something vaguely familiar about him and, looking closely, Chloe had an uncanny feeling that she'd seen him somewhere before.

There were no further photos in the album, so Chloe peered into the drawer again, felt around its edges, but there was nothing else in there. She was glad to have found the album, though. At least she now had a little more insight into her grandmother's past. Perhaps Mildred Lightfoot would be able to shed some light on the identity of the mystery soldier, or perhaps the diary would? Could it possibly be Billy Thomas? Chloe wondered. The young man Lena had met in the Eden hospital? Did their friendship blossom enough for him to have given Lena his photograph? Chloe supposed she would have to read on to find out.

After reading so much of Lena's diary that morning, she decided that she needed to at least make a start on clearing her grandmother's room out. She was dreading it, and all the emotions it would inevitably bring up. She went back up to the bedroom and started sorting through her grandmother's clothes. There were one or two pieces that she wanted to keep for sentimental reasons or because she might wear them, but generally she folded items and slipped them into a bin bag to take to the charity shop. It pained her to be doing this. It felt so final, but the thought of her grandmother's journal was keeping her going. As she worked, Chloe's mind was filled with the sights and sounds of the bazaar, the view of the snow-capped Himalayas close-up from a light aircraft, the hubbub of the medieval centre of Kathmandu, the Kumari Devi, peering down from a high window with her kohl-rimmed eyes and finally the fortune teller, with her necklaces and bangles and her mysterious prophesies.

6

I FOUND it very hard to drop off to sleep last night. I've got used to the hubbub at Ma's place over the past couple of weeks, and the room here at the barracks in Kathmandu seems very quiet in comparison.

As Lena lay awake, the fortune-teller's words went round and round in her mind. What exactly did they mean? And that look in the woman's eyes as she spoke! Filled with mystery, but also so all-seeing. Who could she possibly have meant when she said that a friend of Lena's was in danger and that she needed to warn him? It was a puzzle.

Leading such a sheltered life in St Catherine's, Lena had never had an opportunity to make any male friends. The only men she knew were those who served the school in some way – the guards, porters, gardeners, cooks and sweepers, and those she happened to chance upon in the market or in cafes and shops in the town. So, it was difficult to work out who the fortune teller might have been referring to when she mentioned a new friend, when it was obvious from what she said that she was referring to a man.

Could the fortune teller have been referring to Billy Thomas, Lena wondered. She hardly knew him. She'd only had one conversation with him and, in any case, what danger could he be facing? She supposed that if he was sent back to the front, he would be facing danger every day, so perhaps that was it. But how could she stop him? How could she tell a soldier that he couldn't go back to the front because he would be in danger? That was self-evident.

But the more she thought it over, the more her thoughts inevitably led back to Billy. There was something about him that had resonated with her immediately. Some connection that seemed to go very deep. Perhaps it was because he'd confided that his family was poor and that he grew up struggling and in poverty. She was still surprised to have heard that from an Englishman, but could relate to it completely. Her own mother had been poverty-stricken for as long as she could remember. Lena's school fees and expenses were paid by her father, but she had no idea who he was, or even if he was in India anymore. All she knew about him was that he was a British officer. She didn't even know what rank. He'd never been in touch with Lena, nor with her mother since she went to live in Darjeeling, as far as she knew. And Ma flatly refused to talk about him.

Lena's heart twisted when she thought of her mother, always having to scrimp and save and live in tiny, dark quarters. Obviously, the stain of having a child out of wedlock with a British officer had meant that she was never able to find an Indian husband. Lena was aware that the family in Calcutta never got in touch, having cut Sita off without an anna when they found out about Lena's impending birth.

So, she understood precisely what it was like to be poor and to live as an outcast on the fringes of society. She was keenly aware that Eurasians like herself were not properly accepted either by the Indian community or by the British. They were truly outsiders. Perhaps that was what connected her so powerfully to Billy, she thought, and what the fortune teller had seen in her palm.

But it suddenly occurred to her, that there was one other Englishman she'd recently met, who was also kind and considerate and who also didn't appear to judge people on their background – Lieutenant George Harper. She'd never expected to be working for such a genuinely decent human being and she counted herself lucky to be doing so.

She would hardly describe him as a friend, though, so surely the fortune teller couldn't possibly have been speaking about him? No, the more she thought about it, the more she was sure the fortune teller must have been talking about Billy.

She thought back once again to their conversation. She realised that she had never spoken to an Englishman who was so friendly and open, had so little pretension about him and who was prepared to speak to her as an equal, and not look down upon her because of the colour of her skin. Her heart filled with pleasure thinking back over their conversation again, and she vowed to go to the hospital and see Billy again as soon as she got back to Darjeeling.

Later that morning, after breakfast in the canteen, Lieutenant Harper took Lena along to the gymnasium for the first day of recruiting. She carried a notebook and pen, ready to take notes. She was looking forward to seeing how the process of recruiting Gurkhas for the British Indian Army worked.

They entered the gymnasium through a back door. It was an enormous, high-ceilinged building, with a springy wooden floor, its walls lined with climbing bars and ropes. Lena was astonished to see how many young men were waiting. They all stood in line patiently, under the hundreds of whirring ceiling fans. Lena knew about the tradition of sending young Nepalese men to fight for the British, but seeing so many there made her wonder if there would be any left in the villages when they'd all gone to defend the empire abroad.

'These boys are just the ones from the Kathmandu Valley,' Lieutenant Harper told her. 'Tomorrow the driver will take us to

Pokhara, about a hundred and fifty miles west of here, and from there we will go by pony into the mountain villages. That way we will reach those boys who find it difficult to come down to the recruiting centres.'

Lena blinked in surprise. It was the first time Lieutenant Harper had mentioned going into the hills. She hadn't brought any clothes suitable for riding. She couldn't possibly get on a pony in her black skirt and slingback shoes. Perhaps there would be an opportunity to buy some trousers in the market either in Kathmandu or in Pokhara?

But there was no time to worry about outfits. Lieutenant Harper was already calling the first man forward. Lena sat down at the trestle table beside him and opened her notebook. He spoke to each man in turn while Lena noted down their names, addresses and dates of birth. Watching their young faces as they spoke, she suspected that many of them were exaggerating their age or perhaps didn't know their date of birth, but she transcribed what they said anyway. Many could speak little or no English.

The recruits then moved on to queue up for a medical inspection. There were army doctors waiting to examine each candidate, though the examinations didn't look very thorough to Lena. The doctors measured the boys' height and weight and chest, looked into their eyes and down their throats. Then, if the doctor was happy, he made a huge white tick on the recruit's chest with a piece of chalk.

Lena collected up the forms that the doctors had completed and matched them to the recruits' details. Those who passed the medical assessment were sent out onto the parade ground, where they had to report to a sergeant.

Lena followed Lieutenant Harper outside to watch. He explained that the candidates would have to complete a series of physical exercises. They would have to lift a bar thirteen times, then do twenty-five sit-ups in one minute, after which they would have to run three miles in twenty-five minutes. Lastly, they would be given a traditional Nepalese basket filled with stones and asked to complete an arduous assault course whilst carrying it. If they couldn't complete the course within a certain time, they would be rejected.

Lena watched in awe as the boys hauled the baskets onto their backs and set off at a run across the parade ground. The first obstacle was a brick wall which they had to scale carrying their basket. After that, they disappeared from sight, but Lieutenant Harper told her that the course included some uphill stretches, swimming through a pond and more climbing.

When the test was over, the sergeant stepped forward to dismiss those who hadn't made the grade. Only a handful out of all those hundreds of young men were told to get dressed and to leave the base. The look of utter dejection on their faces as they shuffled away was heartbreaking to see.

'Perhaps it's some consolation to them that they won't have to go to war,' Lena said to the lieutenant.

'Well, there's a lot more to it than that, Miss Chatterjee,' he replied. 'Many of these boys come from very poor villages, where the harvest might have failed, or where the villagers have to pay high rents to unscrupulous landlords. You have to understand that a boy in the army has the chance of a regular wage, medical treatment, education, sick pay. Often, whole families will be counting on that pay packet. Those boys may be responsible for several people's welfare.'

Lena added slowly, 'So, if they are rejected, they might feel that they have failed their family in some way.'

'Precisely,' the lieutenant nodded.

It seemed sad to Lena that these young boys were prepared to risk their lives defending a foreign power in a war that had nothing to do with them, simply because their families were so poor.

AFTER THEY'D FINISHED for the day, Lieutenant Harper asked Lena to go to dinner with him in a nearby restaurant.

They walked off the base and into the surrounding town, which Lieutenant Harper informed her was called Patan. She realised as soon as they began to walk down the cobbled streets that the centre of Patan was very much like the centre of Kathmandu, with many ancient temples and ornately carved houses whose upper floors jutted out above the street. It was complete with its own Durbar Square too, similar to the one she'd seen in Kathmandu but a little smaller and a little less grand.

Lieutenant Harper guided her to a restaurant one of the side streets leading off the square. It was a small, simple place, filled with steam and delicious cooking smells, where locals were eating and talking in noisy groups. There was a free table, though, a small one in the window, and they squeezed into the tiny seats.

Lena had felt a little nervous when the lieutenant had suggested the outing, but quickly realised that she was glad that he had taken her there. Not only was the food bland on the base, but the canteen was a soulless place to spend an evening, especially as Lena was virtually the only woman there.

'May I recommend you order a thali? You won't find a more nutritious, balanced meal anywhere in the world,' Lieutenant Harper said, smiling.

Lena accepted his recommendation and when she started eating, she realised that he was right. A thali was a complete meal served in a round, metal dish divided into different compartments. It consisted of dal baht, a sort of spicy lentil soup, plain rice, greens, a bit like spinach, vegetable curry and chapati breads. The fresh flavours exploded on her tongue. It was delicious – hot and succulent and tasting subtly of spices.

While they ate, Lieutenant Harper explained a bit about the

relationship between Nepal and the British and how there was a tradition of Nepal supplying men to the British army. 'The Maharajah of Nepal has authorised the recruitment of 12,000 men this year. They are keen to keep good relations with the British in order to maintain their independence. Those men are certainly needed,' he went on between mouthfuls of curry, 'if we are to do anything other than retreat from the Japs in Burma. With more manpower, we might have a chance of driving them back from the border. But, at the moment, India itself is at real risk of invasion, I'm afraid.'

Lena stared at him, a prickle of nerves running down her spine. It was hard to believe. She'd been brought up with the notion that the British empire was inviolable, but hadn't she read for herself in recent years about the fall of Malaya, Hong Kong, Singapore and Burma? Perhaps India would be next.

'Have *you* been on the front line in Burma, Lieutenant Harper?'

It was a question she'd wanted to ask before. Lieutenant Harper was still a young man, yet he wasn't out there fighting with others of his age.

He drew a deep breath and put his fork down. 'Yes. I fought in the Arakan campaign in southern Burma last year. I'm afraid the regiment suffered heavy losses – so many good men were cut down.' He paused and shook his head. 'Such a tragic loss of life... But I was one of the lucky ones. I was shot in the chest and wounded. Afterwards, I'm afraid to say, I became very ill. I was taken back to hospital in India, where the doctors eventually discovered that I had a heart defect.'

'How terrible for you,' Lena said.

'Yes. That was the end of my fighting days.'

She could see in his eyes that not being at the front rankled with him still, that he was putting a brave face on it. He quickly moved the subject on.

'Enough about me. As I said, I've been lucky in lots of ways.

But what about you, Miss Chatterjee. What about your life. Have you always lived in Darjeeling for example?'

As ever, Lena was worried about revealing too much about her background, but for some reason she felt safe with Lieutenant Harper. She took a deep breath and told him about her time at St Catherine's and a little about her mother too. He listened to her story with a genuinely interested expression on his face, occasionally shaking his head or making sympathetic noises. As she spoke, Lena realised that she didn't feel awkward talking about it with him at all. She decided that it was because Lieutenant Harper was a thoroughly decent human being. She knew he wouldn't treat her any differently because he knew the truth about her background.

When they'd finished eating, they walked slowly back to the base, through the dimly lit streets of Patan, past the shadows of the ancient temples. The moon was high in the sky and the whole place seemed infused with mystery and mythology. Lena was pleased that she'd had the chance to come here to experience this beautiful country for herself. She was looking forward to the next day when they would travel to Pokhara and she would get to see more of it first-hand.

7

TODAY WE ARRIVED in the little town of Pokhara, in western Nepal, after a very long and uncomfortable journey in the Land Rover from Kathmandu. We were on the road for about twelve hours in all.

The road from Kathmandu was very rough and bumpy, full of ruts and potholes, and for most of the way was an unmade track. It traversed mountain ranges, skirted along the side of precipitous drops, and ran for miles alongside river rapids. In several places, there had been rockfalls or landslips and the road had been covered in rocks and earth. When that happened, the driver stopped the Land Rover and he and Lieutenant Harper got out and went to help the villagers who were clearing the rocks from the road in wicker baskets. Lena got out too and went to help.

'No need for you to get out of the Land Rover, Miss Chatterjee,' the lieutenant said as Lena followed him. 'The driver and I can deal with this.'

'But I want to help,' Lena insisted. 'I wouldn't be the only woman, after all.'

It was true, there were many village women, dressed in their colourful costumes, black skirts with tapestry borders, hoisting baskets of rock on their backs, trying their best to clear the road.

The road must be important for their livelihoods, Lena realised, the only means by which they were able to get produce to local markets and receive supplies.

'I suppose you're right,' the lieutenant agreed, and Lena took her place beside him and the locals, clearing away the rocks that had obliterated the highway.

It was back-breaking work. All she could do was to pick up the smaller stones and carry them by hand to a pile at the side of the road. Her heart went out to all those poor local people for whom this was a regular occurrence, not just a minor inconvenience, a short hold-up on a long journey. While they were working, a queue of vehicles built up on the road in either direction. The drivers and passengers got out and helped to clear the highway.

Soon it was done, and they were on the road again. But the same thing happened in two more places and they repeated the same routine, helping the locals to clear the road and to get the traffic moving again before carrying on their way.

It was growing dark by the time they finally rolled into the narrow streets of Pokhara so Lena had little chance to see the place, but she did notice as they approached that the town was in a great, wide valley, surrounded by hills with the snowy peaks of the Annapurna range as a fabulous backdrop.

The town, little more than a village, was built along the shores of a beautiful lake, whose still surface reflected the mountains, lit up with the reds and golds of the sunset. They drove through the centre, which was lined with terraces of beautiful old houses, built with decorative red bricks with intricately carved wooden windows and balconies. People sat out on their porches watching the Land Rover pass, their open faces curious but friendly.

In amongst the houses was the occasional temple, like in Kathmandu often elevated on a pedestal of stone steps. People were kneeling on the temple steps, lighting incense or candles or making offerings. There was no electric light here, only gas lamps and candles, the smoke from which mingled with incense and woodsmoke and added to the sense of mystery and magic of the place.

The driver took them to a small guest house on the edge of the old town. Lena was glad to get out of the rattling, vibrating Land Rover, to stretch her legs, to go upstairs and lie down on the narrow bed. The room was high-ceilinged with bare white walls, with just one picture on display, a portrait of the King of Nepal, decorated with a chain of marigolds. There was a washstand with a chipped bowl and jug and a small chest of drawers.

Lena went to the window and pushed the shutters aside and leaned out into the street. She drank in the atmosphere – the smoke from woodfires mingling with the mist coming down from the mountains, the voices and footsteps of people going to and fro in the street below, on ponies or in rickshaws, and everywhere lit by candlelight or gas lamps which cast their flickering light on their surroundings. It felt magical to be here, when to think, only a month or so before, her life had been so dull and confined.

Later, as she and the lieutenant ate dal baht, downstairs in the guest house in front of a smoky fire, he told her more about the recruitment of Gurkhas.

'It's a never-ending process,' he said. 'Until this war is over, we will need a constant flow of men for the front line.'

Lena went silent then, thinking about the implications. If the front line needed constant replenishment that meant that men were dying every day. Young men like the ones who'd been recruited in Kathmandu. They were barely more than boys and had everything to live for and the hopes of their whole families on their shoulders.

But then Lieutenant Harper said, looking straight into her eyes, 'It's not like you think, you know. We need more men for the front line because new theatres of war are opening up all the time, not simply because of casualties. We will need many, many men to defend Imphal and Kohima and the border between Burma and India, to stop the Japs breaking through into India.'

Lena was amazed that he had discerned, just from the expression on her face and her silence, exactly what she was thinking.

Lieutenant Harper went on to reassure her that he wouldn't actually be recruiting on this trip into the hills, just gathering the names of boys who wanted to try, and to give them details of lorries that would take them to Pokhara for the next recruitment day, in a couple of weeks' time.

As she lay down in her little bed later, Lena reflected on the conversation. Lieutenant Harper was full of surprises and a far more sensitive person than she'd expected from someone in his position.

THE NEXT MORNING, after a breakfast of porridge and jasmine tea, Lena rushed out to a little market near the guest house and bought some baggy cotton trousers with a drawstring waist, and some soft boots for riding. She also bought a small knapsack, as Lieutenant Harper had said that they could only take minimal luggage – the rest was to be left at the guest house. When she got back to her room, she quickly changed into her new purchases, relieved that at least she wouldn't have to travel into the hills in her work clothes.

The driver collected them in the Land Rover and took them through the mountains as far as a tiny settlement at the end of the road. As soon as they left Pokhara behind, the dusty, white road began to rise, through areas of farmland but also through patches of wild, rough vegetation. The road rose steeply, often doubling back on itself, all the time climbing steadily. Sometimes they passed little settlements – thatched, stone houses built along the road where people and animals scattered at their approach. The villagers stood staring as they passed through. Once, they had to stop while a herd of goats crossed the road, driven by children. They carried on through scrubby forest, steep-sided banks on one side, a steep drop to the bottom of the valley on the other. Up ahead reared the snow-covered peaks of a group of huge mountains.

'That's the Annapurna range,' Lieutenant Harper told her.

Lena stared up at the incredible mountains. They were getting close to them then and the closer they got, the bigger and more majestic they appeared.

Eventually, they reached a larger village and the road petered out into a stone-built path which wound its way up through the long valley ahead. The driver stopped the Land Rover and turned off the engine. A farmer, swathed in blankets against the brisk mountain air, approached, leading two ponies, who also wore blankets under their saddles. The animals looked shaggy and rough, but also hardy and strong – one was a dirty white and the other dark brown.

Lieutenant Harper spoke to the owner and gave him some money. The man handed the reins over to him.

'You *can* ride, can't you, Lena?' Lieutenant Harper asked, turning to her, and she burst out laughing. It amused her that he'd waited until she was about to mount a pony and ride into the hills before he asked that question. He laughed too and the man stared at them, bemused.

'Of course I can,' Lena replied when the laughter had died down. Everyone who grew up in the hills as she had done learned to ride at an early age. It was often the only way to get out of town, there were so few proper roads around Darjeeling.

'I'm sorry,' Lieutenant Harper said with a rueful smile. 'I've had a lot on my mind these past few days.'

Lena got up onto the smaller pony and adjusted the stirrups. The man told them, in Nepalese that Lena's pony was called Snowy and that he was very strong and willing, but a little stubborn on occasion.

They bid the pony man and the driver goodbye, arranging to meet the driver back there in four days' time, and set off along the path into the hills, riding side by side where the path was wide enough.

'This is the start of the ancient highway that goes up into the hills and leads through several villages.' Lieutenant Harper explained. 'It is only on this path that farmers and villagers get their supplies, including building materials, food, medicines, household goods, clothes. They are brought in either by pony or by sherpas.'

Sure enough, before they had been riding for twenty minutes, they passed a group of sherpas carrying huge wicker baskets on their backs, secured by bands around their foreheads. Lena couldn't see what was in the baskets, but they looked very heavy. The men appeared incredibly strong though, their calves bulged with muscles as they climbed the steep hill.

'These men are born to this life,' Lieutenant Harper explained. 'They start helping in the fields and carrying loads from village to village from a very early age.'

Sometimes they saw groups of women on the path too, some lugging heavy loads too, others carrying baskets of hay or vegetation for their animals or logs for their fires.

The path wound up through a long valley. A fast-flowing river rushed through rocks deep in the valley bottom and the banks ran steeply down to it. They rode through forests and passed terraces where villagers had planted rice, maize and other crops. After about an hour, they came to the first village of simple stone-built, thatched houses, painted white and terracotta red. In the village square, under a banyan tree, the village elders sat around playing dice and chatting.

The village headman came up to greet Lieutenant Harper warmly, his face wreathed in smiles. 'We are pleased to see you. We have many young men interested in joining up this time, Lieutenant,' he said.

The lieutenant thanked the headman respectfully. This time he was speaking yet another language, the language of the hills, which Lena didn't understand. They got down from the ponies and the village women brought them tea and vegetable pakoras, which they ate sitting on a bench under the banyan tree.

The headman set up a trestle table and brought two chairs. Lieutenant Harper and Lena sat down side by side at the table. Then the headman disappeared off into the passages between the houses and returned with a group of about ten young men.

The boys lined up in front of the table and came forward one by one. Just as in Kathmandu, Lena took down their details, while Lieutenant Harper spoke to each of them in their own language.

The lieutenant told Lena that to be accepted into the regiment, they should really be between eighteen and twenty-one.

'But many of these boys have no concrete proof of age. We have to take a lenient view in this time of war. As I told you, the army is desperate for new recruits.'

Lena noticed that these village boys seemed less self-assured than the boys they'd seen at the recruiting centre. Many were dressed in dirty, ragged clothes and their hands and faces were grubby and often smudged with earth.

Lieutenant Harper explained that they were farm boys and had probably been out tending the crops or animals that morning. 'They may look rough,' he said, 'but they are strong and hardy, and if they're willing to serve, and pass the physical tests, they will make excellent soldiers.

He told each of them to report to village at the end of the road in two weeks' time at nine o'clock in the morning, when a truck would come and collect them to take them down to Pokhara. Recruitment tests would be held at an army camp just outside the town.

When Lieutenant Harper had spoken to all the boys in turn and had made sure they understood his instructions, Lena and he said goodbye to the villagers and carried on their way on the ponies. This time, the road left the valley and began to rise up into the hills, with many flights of stone steps to break the climb. The ponies took it in their stride, though, and were sure-footed on the steps, obviously completely at home in the terrain.

They passed through more tiny villages and farms, all old stone-built houses thatched with reeds and straw and often painted white and terracotta. The road went on for a long way along another steep-sided river valley and at one point they had to cross the river on a narrow bridge. It looked very flimsy to Lena, strung high above the rocky torrent, made of string and bamboo. She started to dismount from the pony, thinking that it would lighten the load.

'There's no need to do that,' Lieutenant Harper said, kicking his own pony past Lena and onto the bridge. She watched him cross the swaying structure and step off safely on the other side.

With her heart in her mouth, she kicked Snowy on, and he stepped onto the bridge and began walking across it slowly and deliberately, as if he knew it was important to keep the pace steady. Halfway across, though, he stopped, lifted his head and whinnied, and for a few tense moments, Lena thought he was going to take some persuading to carry on. But with a gentle nudge of the heels, he continued on to join Lieutenant Harper on the other side.

'Well done!' the Lieutenant said to Lena, and they carried on along the stone path, the short distance to the next village, her heartbeat gradually slowing down.

There, they repeated the ritual established at the first village, this time enrolling eight young men for the tests. Then they were shown by the headman to the house where they were to stay that night. The family greeted them warmly with smiles and a small boy led the ponies off to a nearby stable for the night.

They ate supper on the front porch, watching the sun go down over the mountaintops.

'Have you been up here many times?' Lena asked the lieutenant. He appeared very comfortable in the surroundings and seemed well known and well-liked by the locals.

'I've been so many times that I've lost count, Miss Chatterjee,' he said.

'Do you think the villages might run out of young men at some point?' she asked.

'The village elders are very careful who they allow to join up. Young men are reaching the recruitment age all the time, but the elders don't allow all of them to join the army. They need some to stay and farm the land, take care of the villages.'

'You seem to have a real rapport with the villagers, Lieutenant Harper,' Lena remarked.

'I hope so. You won't find more loyal, generous people anywhere in the world.'

But then Lena noticed his face take on an awkward look, as if he wanted to tell her something but was holding himself back, or didn't think it was the right moment.

'Was there something you were going to say?' she asked, but he shook his head and got up to ask for another helping of dal baht.

When they had finished eating, the lady of the house, a stout, middle-aged woman dressed in long black robes with a colourful, embroidered waistcoat, showed Lena and Lieutenant Harper upstairs via a ladder to the sleeping quarters. So, there was no chance to ask the lieutenant what had caused him to reflect while they had been speaking about his rapport with the villagers.

Lena lay down on the lumpy bed, listening to the bleating of goats and the lowing of cattle in the stable beneath her. There were gaps between the floorboards, so if she looked down, she could see goats, cattle and chickens beneath. The family was staying at one end of the house, Lieutenant Harper somewhere in the middle and Lena at the other end, behind a thick curtain and with only a candle for light.

I am tired now and must get some sleep, although I'm not sure how easy that will be with the animals shifting about underneath me and the ever-present smell of woodsmoke curling up through the floorboards from the cottage fire. I am intrigued by Lieutenant Harper's reaction when we were talking about the villagers and hope that tomorrow I will be able to get him to speak about it.

THE NEXT DAY, when they arrived in Ghorepani, which was bigger than most of the other villages they'd passed through, Lieutenant Harper took Lena aside. He looked very awkward and apologetic as he broached the subject.

'Lena, I have to tell you something,' he said. 'It's a bit tricky, actually, but when we get to the centre of the village, you will be offered a bed in a local villager's house like last night, but I will be staying elsewhere.'

She stared at him for a moment, unsure quite what he meant.

'The fact is, I have a… an… er… understanding with a young woman in the village. I always stay with her and her parents when I come up into the hills.'

She felt a blush creep into her cheeks then. What he was telling her was so out of character for this seemingly stiff-upper-lipped Englishman that it was hard to take on board. She just stood there, staring at him, her mouth open, her cheeks pink with embarrassment.

'I'm so sorry for putting you in an awkward position, Miss Chatterjee,' he said at last. He cleared his throat. 'It's a difficult situation, but I do have the most honourable intentions towards the young woman. I just need to find a way of squaring it with my superiors in the Regiment. I'm afraid that they will regard it as a very unconventional arrangement.'

What an understatement, Lena thought, still reeling with surprise herself.

But when she saw the girl in question, she began to understand his sentiments. She was exquisitely beautiful with long
silky black hair, delicate features, high cheekbones and tip-tilted
black eyes. Her face was full of smiles and her eyes lit up when
she saw Lieutenant Harper. Lena could instantly tell that they
were deeply in love. She watched them embrace and sit down
together under the village banyan tree to exchange news, their
expressions full of love, immersed in each other's company.

Lena turned away, not embarrassed any longer, but glad for
Lieutenant Harper that he had found such happiness in the most
unexpected of places, although she was fearful for him too. She
couldn't think that the intractable old colonels in Darjeeling
would ever stand for an arrangement like that. If the news ever
reached them, Lieutenant Harper would surely be hounded out
of the army, no matter how good a recruiting officer he was.

She left the two of them to their conversation and went into
the village house where she was lodging that night. The owner, a
very old lady, with blackened stumps for teeth and a face creased
with smile lines, showed her upstairs. This time, she had a room
of her own, albeit with a bare wooden partition and a curtain for
a doorway, but it did have a little window, and from there she
could look out over the snow-capped Annapurnas. They were a
stunning sight, bright white against a clear cobalt sky, and the
spectacle made up for the impending discomfort of the wooden
bed and its wafer-thin mattress.

Lena set out her things on the little chest. She was glad that
they would be staying for at least two nights. After so much travelling, it was good to be able to pause and soak in the rhythm of
the life in the village. According to Lieutenant Harper, potential
recruits would come from neighbouring villages to see him in
Ghorepani, so there was no need to go further into the hills.

When Lena went downstairs again, the old woman was
tending the cooking fire and her family sat around the table
peeling vegetables and preparing the food for supper. She went

outside and stood admiring the fabulous views of the valley and the surrounding mountains.

Lieutenant Harper spotted Lena and came over, arm in arm with the beautiful Nepalese woman.

'This is Alisha,' he introduced. 'Alisha, this is Lena, my new assistant.'

The young woman smiled and put her hands together in the traditional greeting. 'Namaste,' she said, smiling into Lena's eyes.

Lena returned her greeting.

'George says you are very good at your job,' Alisha said in English. 'He says you are a great help to him, and that this trip has been a success because of you.'

Lena couldn't help but smile at the generous words. She thanked Alisha and asked if she would be joining them for supper.

'It will be an honour,' she replied.

'You speak perfect English,' Lena said, surprised.

'Well, I teach English,' Alisha explained. 'At the local school. But, of course, George teaches me a lot,' she added, turning to gaze into his eyes with a teasing smile. 'He often corrects my grammar.'

Lieutenant Harper laughed, gazing into Alisha's eyes and the love between them was plain to see. Then he picked up his bags and took Alisha's arm. 'We're going to drop my bags at Alisha's house. We'll be back here for supper.'

As they turned to go, Lena caught sight of Alisha in profile and almost gasped in surprise. Because, as she turned, she saw that Alisha had a gently protruding belly, in stark contrast to her slim frame.

≈

I GLANCED AGAIN at her discreetly to make sure, but I realised immediately that Alisha is pregnant and that in all likelihood Lieutenant Harper is to be a father in the next few months!

Chloe stared at her grandmother's writing, hardly able to believe her eyes. She read the paragraphs about Alisha several times over, wondering at the words each time she did. Knowing her grandfather as she had done, it was difficult to believe that as a young man he'd had an unconventional relationship with a Nepalese beauty in a remote Himalayan village and that she'd borne him a child. If it had really happened, he must have been very different as a young man to the man she'd known. The years must have changed him significantly.

What had happened to Alisha, Chloe wondered, and to her child? Were they still alive? Did she have some distant part-Nepalese relatives somewhere in the hills beyond Pokhara? Yet another reason to make the journey to Nepal, she thought, and a compelling one at that. Then she smiled, wondering what Daniel and Uncle Andrew would make of this momentous news. Uncle Andrew in particular had worshipped his father, but would surely have been surprised and, knowing Uncle Andrew's conventional nature, a little shocked too at this revelation. Chloe tried to imagine the expressions on their faces as they processed the information. Perhaps it would be better to keep it to herself until she was quite sure of her plans.

8

HAMPSHIRE, 2015

CHLOE LOADED up the back of her car with bin bags full of her grandmother's old clothes, shoes and assorted belongings. Lena had been a hoarder – Chloe had realised that as she'd gone through the bedroom cupboards that morning. Some of the things she had kept were so old-fashioned that Chloe assumed she must have bought them when she first came to England shortly after the war. It seemed a shame to be getting rid of them, but perhaps some of them would find their way to people who really cared about old clothes, and who might give them a new lease of life and actually wear them. There wouldn't be much point in keeping them for sentimental reasons, just for them to hang in the wardrobe for yet more decades.

When she'd loaded up the bags, Chloe brought Kip out to the car too. While she was out, she planned to take him for a run on one of the commons near Farnham, where she'd arranged to take the clothes to one of the charity shops on the high street. Kip leapt up into the back of the car, tail wagging furiously. He'd been pining for Lena ever since her death, looking up with expectant eyes every time anyone entered the kitchen, only to put his head down on his paws again, disappointment clearly

visible in his liquid brown eyes. He'd missed out on walks over
the past few days too. He had hated being shut in the kitchen
while the wake was going on. Chloe had heard him whimpering
every time she'd gone down the passage. She wondered how
much he understood. Perhaps he would forget Lena eventually
and accept Chloe as his mistress? She hoped so, hating to see
him unhappy.

She locked up the house, drove out of the drive and down
through the narrow lanes to the main road, then the fifteen
minutes or so it took to get into town. She found a space in a car
park near the high street. Leaving Kip in the car, she took the first
two bags to the British Heart Foundation charity shop, where the
woman in charge received them gratefully. It took Chloe three
journeys to deliver all the bags she'd brought, and she'd felt
strangely bereft as she'd handed over her grandmother's effects to
a stranger.

On her final journey back to the car, she bumped into her
friend and former colleague, Sophie, who worked at one of the
estate agents in the town. Sophie was dressed smartly in a black
suit with high heels, her blonde hair tied back in a ponytail.
Chloe felt instantly scruffy in her old jeans, trainers and worn
waxed jacket.

'How are you?' Sophie asked, her voice full of sympathy. 'It
must be such a difficult time for you.'

'I'm OK, thanks. Bearing up.'

'I'm sorry I couldn't stay long after the funeral.'

'It doesn't matter at all. I know how busy you are. Thank you
for coming.'

'Look, I'm on my lunch break now.' Sophie glanced at her
watch. 'Why don't we go for a quick drink at the Queen's Head?
I've got forty minutes. We can grab a sandwich in there too.'

Chloe hesitated. 'I'd love to, but the dog's in the car. I was
going to take him up to Caesar's Camp for a run.'

'Well, why don't you go and get him? I'm sure dogs are

allowed in the pub. You look as if you could do with a drink and some company.'

It was such a long time since she'd been for a drink and a chat with a friend. Throughout the long months of caring for her grandmother, the traumatic final days, the lead-up to the funeral, she'd cut herself off from all social contact and focused on what she had to do.

'All right,' she said, brightening. 'I'll go and fetch him.'

'Good! I'll go along to the pub and get a table. I'll see you in there,' Sophie said with a warm smile.

Chloe went back to the car, let Kip out and put him on the lead. When she arrived at the pub, she was surprised to see Sophie standing in the doorway, scanning the pavement for her.

'I've changed my mind,' Sophie said as soon as she saw Chloe. 'Let's go somewhere else.'

'OK,' replied Chloe. 'But I thought you hadn't got much time. We'll have to walk to another pub.'

Sophie hastily tucked her arm through Chloe's. 'Come on, then. The Hop Blossom's always nice at lunchtime. It's far too busy in the Queen's Head at the moment.'

Chloe shrugged and allowed herself to be ushered away, but as they walked past the pub window, she glanced through and instantly saw the reason why Sophie hadn't wanted her to go inside. There was Fergal, seated at a corner table opposite a woman with long blonde hair, with her back to the window. Their hands were entwined on top of the table.

The shock went through Chloe like a lightning bolt. She'd thought she was over Fergal, but seeing him there with someone else sent her emotions into turmoil.

'I know why you didn't want me to go in there,' she said to Sophie, pulling her arm. They both stopped walking. 'I just saw him through the window.'

'I'm so sorry, Chlo,' Sophie said and put her arms around Chloe. Chloe felt tears of hurt and shame prickle her eyes. 'I didn't know what to do when I saw him there, so I just turned around and came back out again.'

'Why is he here anyway? He works in London.'

They began to walk again, both of them realising at the same time that the two of them standing still with a large dog were causing an obstruction on the narrow pavement.

'I don't know. Perhaps he's taken the day off. She lives in Farnham...'

Another wave of shock passed through Chloe, this one less strong than the first, but there all the same. 'You knew! You knew before and you didn't tell me?'

'I'm sorry,' Sophie said. 'I haven't known about it for long. I found out on the grapevine. I just didn't know what to say to you. I knew you were having a tough time, what with your gran and everything. I was going to tell you; I just hadn't found the right moment.'

They walked on in silence for a few minutes, back through the busy cobbled streets and across the car park, towards the other pub.

'I don't know what to think about it. I'm surprised it's bothered me so much, to be honest,' Chloe admitted.

'It's probably because you're feeling fragile anyway. At times like this, everything gets on top of you more than it would normally.'

'I suppose so,' Chloe said.

They reached the pub and went inside, shouldering their way through the lunchtime crowd to get to the bar.

'Gin and tonic?' Sophie asked.

'I'm driving, I shouldn't really.'

'A single won't hurt. You need it!'

'All right.'

Chloe found a table in the back of the pub next to the roaring open fire, and settled Kip down under the table. She stroked his head, and he looked up at her with mournful eyes. Perhaps he understood her sadness too. It often amazed her how in tune with human emotions dogs were.

Sophie came over with the drinks and a lunch menu. 'I'll treat you,' she said.

Chloe took a sip of her drink and scanned the menu. There were some delicious-looking options, but she didn't feel like eating. The gin coursed through her, relaxing her limbs instantly.

'I'm really sorry about Ferg,' Sophie said. 'That was the last thing you needed right now.'

Chloe took another sip. 'It's just reminded me what a total bastard he was to me at the end. I've tried to put it behind me, Sophie, but seeing him again has brought it all back.'

'Do you want to talk about it?' Sophie asked. 'I knew things got heated when you split up but you never really told me the details.'

Chloe put the menu down and took another sip of her drink. She hadn't told anyone what had passed between her and Fergal at the end. It was too shaming somehow, too demeaning. She'd shut it up inside and tried to forget about it. But perhaps it might help, she reasoned, to talk about it now. She looked at her friend, who was looking at her expectantly.

'Well,' she began, 'he said that he'd never felt completely comfortable and at ease with me, that I didn't know how to love, that I was too buttoned up. He said he was glad it was ending and he would be free to go and find someone normal. He said...' She swallowed. 'He said he'd never really enjoyed making love to me.'

Sophie gaped. 'Chloe, that's terrible! No wonder you're angry at him.'

Chloe hung her head. 'I suspect he only said those things because he was upset that I took the decision to leave, but they hurt me all the same.'

She felt Sophie's hand taking hers and squeezing it. 'Look, you mustn't take it to heart. Like you say, it was him hurting. I'm sure he didn't really mean any of it. You need to put it behind you and get on with your life.'

'I know... In fact, I was thinking of taking a trip...' Chloe said on an impulse. The idea had started to consume her thoughts over the past couple of days, but it was the first time she'd voiced her plan aloud.

'A trip? What, some winter sunshine? There are some great deals to the Canaries and Southern Spain at the moment. I saw them in the travel agent's...'

'No. No, not winter sun at all. I was thinking of going further afield... Nepal and India.'

'Wow! What's brought that on?' Sophie asked, surprised.

So, Chloe explained about how Lena's friend, Mildred Light-foot, had paid her a visit after the funeral and had handed her Lena's wartime journal. She told Sophie how what she'd read of it so far had made her want to travel to the places her grandmother had written about and see them for herself.

'There are some incredible revelations in the journal,' she added. 'Apparently, my grandfather had an affair with a Nepalese woman, and she became pregnant.'

'Your grandfather!' Sophie stared at her, her eyes incredulous. 'I can't imagine it!'

Chloe laughed. 'Yes, that's exactly how I reacted when I first read about it. But why would Gran lie about that? So, you see, I want to go there and find out more. I need to see if I have any relatives still living in that little village in the Annapurna foothills.'

'That's incredibly brave, Chloe. Especially as you haven't done very much travelling before.'

'Only because of Fergal! I was always trying to get him to go somewhere more adventurous than Mallorca. Not that Mallorca isn't lovely, of course, but there are so many other places in the world to explore. I've only recently realised how confined the relationship made me feel.'

'I'm envious,' Sophie said, taking a sip of her drink. 'I would offer to come with you, but we're so short-staffed at the moment, I'd never be able to get more than a week's holiday.'

'That's a kind thought, but the more I think about it, the more I'm convinced that I need to do this by myself.'

It would be an opportunity, Chloe thought, to reconnect with her grandparents and to reflect on her own life and the choices she'd made.

One of the barmen was hovering over them. 'Did you want to order any food, ladies?' he asked. 'Only the kitchen will be closing soon.'

Chloe ordered soup and a roll, not feeling hungry, but when it came, she found it slipped down easily. She realised that she hadn't been eating properly since her grandmother's death. It was the first food that she'd tasted properly and that she'd actually enjoyed for several weeks.

When they'd finished, she walked back through the centre of town to Sophie's office on Castle Street. They stopped outside and kissed goodbye.

'Let me know when you decide to go,' Sophie said. 'I really think you should do it, Chloe. You owe it to yourself and it would do you so much good. And if you ever want lunch again, or to meet for a drink after work, let me know. I'm always here for you.'

'Thanks, Sophie.'

Chloe led Kip to the car through the backstreets. She didn't want to walk past the Queen's Head and risk bumping into Fergal and his new love interest.

Once in the car, she drove up to Caesar's Camp, parked on some waste ground, and took Kip onto the huge, rambling common. He bounded off gratefully as soon as he was off the lead, sniffing round the bushes and trees, and banks of winter heather and bracken. She walked after him, zipping up her coat and tightening her scarf. The February breeze was really brisk, especially up here in this exposed place, but the sky was bright blue and there wasn't a cloud in sight. Chloe loved this sort of winter weather, it made her glad to be alive.

She walked further on into the common, passing a lake where ducks were swimming. Kip paused to bark at them, which set off a lot of noisy quacking and flapping of wings. 'Come on, Kip!' Chloe called him away and they headed on towards Caesar's Camp itself. It was really just a group of pine trees on a plateau, high above a vast plane.

Chloe sat on a bench to watch the planes taking off and landing at Farnborough Airport a couple of miles away, while Kip ran about sniffing rabbit trails. These were private jets, ferrying businessmen between high-powered meetings, but all the same, just watching them heading into the blue, stimulated her sense of adventure and desire to travel to pastures new.

When she was too cold to sit there any longer, she called Kip and they headed back to the car. She couldn't wait to get back to the house. She wanted to read more of her grandmother's diary and to carry on sorting through her things. But there was no longer any doubt in her mind about her medium-term plans. She couldn't wait to start looking up flights to India and Nepal. She was buzzing with a sense of anticipation of the adventures to come, suddenly feeling free of the restrictions that had so stilted her in recent years.

9

DARJEELING, 1943

WE ARE NOW HOME in Darjeeling, having flown back from Kathmandu this morning.

It was the same tatty aeroplane as before and the same young flight crew. But this time Lena had no fear of flying whatsoever. She was just overjoyed to be up in the air and in the privileged position of seeing those stunning mountains up close from that incredible vantage point. They flew so close to some of the peaks that she could actually see the contours of the granite and the way the snow clung to the crevasses in the rocks. It was truly beautiful.

The flight gave Lena the chance to reflect on the past few days. She realised that she'd learned a lot on the short trip. Firstly, she'd discovered a great deal about human nature from meeting so many warm, welcoming people. The hill villagers were very poor but still extended their hospitality generously and graciously. She'd also got to know a lot about Lieutenant Harper by spending so much time with him, and by seeing him and Alisha together. The experience had taught her not to judge people hastily. Someone whom she'd originally assumed to be a regular, conventional British officer, she now knew to be more a more complex and interesting personality.

The two days and nights up in Ghorepani had proved uneventful. Lieutenant Harper had completed several rounds of recruitment and Lena had almost filled her notepad with the names of all the keen volunteers. As for the romance between Lieutenant Harper and Alisha, the more she saw them together, the more she was sure that they were truly in love and made for each other, but also the more fearful she grew for their future. Lieutenant Harper hadn't mentioned Alisha to her again, nor her condition, and Lena hadn't seen fit to raise the subject with him. But he had told her that they were due to go on another recruiting trip in a couple of months' time. Perhaps it would be discussed then, when the pregnancy would have become more obvious. Lena couldn't wait to go back to Nepal again. It had certainly worked its magic on her in those few short days.

Despite that, she was also looking forward to getting back to Darjeeling and visiting Billy in the hospital again. The fortune-teller's words had been going round and round in her head as the time she was due to go home drew closer. She was trying to think of a way of introducing the subject to Billy without alarming him unduly. How do you tell someone that they are in danger, but that you have no idea what from? There was a chance, though, he would understand better than she did what the fortune-teller's prophesy might mean.

The fortune teller describing Billy as a friend had made Lena reflect on whether that was true or not, and she'd realised that it certainly was. Even after one short meeting, she felt certain that Billy could be described as a friend and one that Lena was keen to see again and find out more about as soon as she could. It struck her that she'd been thinking about Billy a lot and looking forward to talking to him again. She realised that he was one of the very few people – outside of the St Catherine's girls obviously – with whom she seemed to have a great deal in common, who hadn't judged her for her background or race, and who seemed to understand her instinctively.

SITA WAS OVERJOYED to have Lena back. She was sitting cross-legged on some cushions, sewing some clothing when Lena arrived, but she threw her work aside, jumped up and hugged her daughter, crushing the air out of her lungs.

'I'm so happy to have you home, my daughter. I've been praying for your safe return since the moment you left home and I've been making puja several times a day. Now that you are home safely, I can relax, my Lena. The fact that you came back has proved that it was all worth it!'

'Oh, Ma. It's so lovely to see you. And thank you for praying for me.'

'Sit down, and I will make some tea.'

Lena was tired from the journey, so she was glad to sit down and let her mother fuss around her.

As she poured the tea, Sita said, 'Now, tell me all about Nepal. What was it like over there?'

As they sat together and sipped their drinks, Lena told her mother everything she could about the trip, but Sita didn't seem impressed.

'It must have been very cold indeed up in those mountain villages,' she remarked with a shudder.

'It was cold, it's true. But it gets chilly in Darjeeling too, Ma.'

'Hmm. And you say you went up by pony? I don't think I would like that. It sounds dangerous.'

'It wasn't dangerous at all really. The horses are very sure-footed.'

'And what was the food like, daughter?'

'We ate a lot of dal baht. It was delicious, actually.'

Sita eyed her sceptically. 'Tonight I will cook you a Bengal mutton curry, with aloo bhaja, fried potatoes. You look as though you could do with building up.'

'That would be lovely, Ma. Thank you,' she said, sensing with surprise how comforting it was to be home after her travels.

Sita drained her tea and got up, pulled her shawl around her shoulders. 'I'll get along to the market now and get some mutton before it's all sold out.'

Lena waited until her mother was at the front door, then said, as casually as she could, 'I was going to pop out this afternoon, Ma. I will probably still be gone when you get back.'

Sita gave her a sharp look, 'Surely the lieutenant doesn't want you back at work straightaway?'

Lena was reluctant to tell her mother that she was going to the hospital to see Billy. Something told her she wouldn't approve, so dropping her gaze, she said, 'Not quite. I have to go along to Raj Bhavan, Government House, on an errand.' The Eden Hospital was quite near Government House, so she reasoned that it was only a little white lie.

In truth, Lena was itching to see Billy again. For some reason, she felt drawn back to him as if by an invisible thread.

After Sita had finally closed the front door behind her, Lena got ready quickly. She brushed her hair and tied it back in a ponytail, then she put some powder compact on her face, a touch of rouge and a lick of lipstick. She hoped that Sita wouldn't come back while she was doing it because she knew her mother disapproved of make-up. When she'd seen Lena wearing lipstick once, she'd said, 'You look I like a loose woman, daughter!' so, since then, Lena had been very careful about it.

Lena put on one of her best blouses, a pale pink one of fine cotton that set off the colour of her skin, a clean skirt and some pretty sandals. Then, picking up her shopping basket, she set off, taking care to go in the opposite direction to the Indian bazaar where her mother had gone. In her handbag, Lena carried some cotton wool so that she could pop into the ladies' room at the hospital and wipe off the make-up after the visit.

She went straight up to the stalls on Chowrasta, bought a selection of fruits and put them into her shopping basket. She didn't want to go to the hospital empty-handed, nor did she want to the nurses to think she was visiting without a reason.

When she arrived at the hospital, the nurse on reception recognised her. 'Good morning. You are Lieutenant Harper's assistant, aren't you? I'm sorry, could you remind me of your name?'

'I don't think I told you before, actually. I'm Lena Chatterjee.'

The nurse gave Lena one of those withering looks she'd come to expect from British people on hearing her Indian name, then scribbled the name down in the visitor's book.

'I'm afraid, since you were last here, two of the men on the ward have sadly died,' the nurse informed her.

Lena's heart gave an unpleasant lurch.

'The others haven't improved very much, I'm afraid... But Private Billy Thomas is getting better every day.'

Lena's heart beat a little faster at those words, but it suddenly occurred to her that if Billy was improving so quickly, he might be sent back to the front before long. She was glad that she'd come straight to the hospital. She might have missed him if she'd delayed the visit.

Once up in the ward, as she'd done before, Lena dutifully stopped beside the beds of all the men who appeared conscious. She said a few words to each of them, held their hands and left them a piece of fruit if she thought they would be able to eat it. She tried her best not to hurry through this part of the visit, but she was anxious to see Billy.

Finally, she reached the end of the ward. Billy was sitting up in the last bed, staring out of the window at Kanchenjunga. His face was peaceful, his eyes faraway. Lena recognised that look and knew that he was lost in imaginings, just as she herself had been many, many times. There was something about that view that just transported you, whatever the situation you were facing in your daily life.

'Hello,' she said tentatively. She was a little reluctant to disturb him, but when he turned towards her and she saw his eyes light up and his wide, unreserved smile, her heart swelled with pleasure.

'Miss Chatterjee! How nice to see you. I've been hoping you would come back. I wasn't sure that you would, though. It's been quite a long time...'

'I've been in Nepal...' she said on an impulse, then wondered if she should really have kept the details of her visit secret.

'Nepal? I've fought alongside many Gurkhas from Nepal. Strong, and courageous they are. Loyal mates too.'

'I can well imagine that they are,' Lena remarked, sitting down beside him and offering him some fruit. 'I have mangoes, papaya, bananas, apples.'

'I'd love an apple, Miss Chatterjee,' Billy said, his eyes brightening again. 'It'll remind me of home. Mother used to bring beautiful Cox's apples home in the autumn, when she came back from visiting her folks in the country. They lived on a farm.'

Lena tried to imagine a sun-kissed orchard deep in the English countryside, its lines of apple trees loaded with luscious autumn fruit.

Billy continued to reminisce. 'She used to take me and my brothers down there on the train when we were nippers. We had a lot of fun playing in the barns, climbing the haystacks, helping the farm boys out with the animals.' Then his eyes took on a wistful look. 'That all ended when we left school. Then me and Harry had to go and work in the docks with our father.'

'How old were you then?' Lena asked.

'Twelve. Harry was only eleven. I'll always remember my first day. We were set to work loading metal bars onto a ship. Lifting them up and slipping the ropes from the crane around them.

They were so heavy, we could barely pick 'em up. Once they were loaded on the crane and it was swinging them onto the ship, we had to get inside the hold and unload them there and stack them safely so they wouldn't move. It was backbreaking work and it never ended, neither. When we went home on that first day, our hands were bleeding. The next day, we went back in the morning and there were more heavy things for us to load. Sometimes it was sacks of coal or sugar, sometimes iron bars, sometimes crates. It didn't matter that we were nippers. We were expected to work as hard as the men.'

'Oh, Billy,' Lena said, realising that it was the first time she'd spoken his name out loud. 'It sounds terrible.'

She was shocked at hearing about Billy's childhood. She knew that children were exploited mercilessly in India, in the cotton mills, working on farms and in factories, but she'd had no idea that the same thing happened in England. Her image of English children was shaped by having seen the spoiled young offspring of the planters and officials who lived in Darjeeling. Pushed about in perambulators by their doting Indian ayahs, dressed in silks and ribbons, they were shipped off to be educated in England when they were very young, not even returning for holidays.

'What about your father?' she asked. 'Was he there when you were working?

Billy snorted. 'My dad was a drunk. He spent all his money in the pub, so we were always poor. Mother depended on the money that we lads could earn on the docks. I even had a job on my days off, helping out in the local street market selling flowers. It was good to be out of the house, to be honest. When Dad came back from the pub, he would knock Mum about, as well as any of us children who happened to get in his way.'

Looking at Billy, it was hard to imagine that he'd had that sort of childhood. His face was sweet, even innocent-looking, with a friendly, open expression. The only bitterness he displayed was when he spoke of the hardships he'd suffered at his father's hands, and the shame he felt at being unable to defend his mother against his father's violent outbursts. He told Lena that when he and his brothers were small, they would try to hide when his father was angry, but sometimes he would pull them out of their hiding places and beat them too – just for the hell of it. When they grew older, they would step in and defend their mother, but they were no match for their father, who was strong and tough from a lifetime heaving cargo on the docks.

'Are your parents still alive?' Lena asked, not really knowing what to say.

'Not Dad. He died just before the war. Liver failure.'

'What about your mother?'

'After the old man had died, Mum went back to her family in Kent. She's happy now, but all those years of living with him and in a house riddled with damp and vermin has sapped her health. She suffers from pleurisy and asthma. Rheumatism too.'

Lena shook her head in sympathy. 'I'm so sorry, Billy. You must miss her. What made you join the army?'

'Well, I lost my job on the docks during the depression in the early thirties. Harry and me would go down to the docks and wait in line for work. Sometimes we would get a few hours, sometimes not. I tried to get another job, but there was nothing about. I wasn't qualified for anything else and labourers were two a penny. In the end, Harry and I decided to sign up for the army. After a few weeks' training, we were sent out to India to fight on the North-West Frontier.'

'The North-West Frontier? It's tough there I've heard,' Lena said.

'Incredibly tough. I'd never seen anything like it before. It was freezing cold, the mountains were covered in snowdrifts. The Afghans are the fiercest fighters in the world. But, even so, it felt like a bit of an adventure, and it was far better than being at home.'

'How long did you serve there?'

'Around five years, I suppose. Then the chance came up to volunteer to fight in Burma. Me and Harry jumped at it. We were sent on a troop ship to Rangoon and ended up fighting in the Arakan campaign. The Arakan is an inhospitable place to fight. As inhospitable in its own way as the North-West Frontier. There's a line of mountains, ninety miles long and twenty miles wide, with rocky peaks no one can climb. They're covered in jungle. Between the mountains and the sea is mudflats. The idea was to take an island off the coast from the Japs, so that the RAF could launch bombing raids on Rangoon from there. But we weren't equipped to fight in those conditions. That's where I got my injuries. And that's why I'm here.'

'And what about Harry?' Lena asked and immediately regretted doing so. The light went out of Billy's eyes instantly.

'Harry was killed,' he said quietly. 'One of the first skirmishes. A mate had been shot and Harry ran out into this clearing in the jungle, to bring his body back. It was against orders. Typical of Harry. He was so brave. Never a thought or a care for his own safety. He'd almost got back behind the lines, carrying his mate's body, when he was mown down by Jap machine-gun fire. I'll never forget the expression on his face when he was hit – for a split second he looked shocked, then he dropped like a stone. He died instantly.'

THERE WERE tears in poor Billy's eyes when he'd finished telling me about his brother's death and my heart went out to him. Without thinking, I took his hand in mine and squeezed it in sympathy. I felt like crying myself, I was so sad for him.

Chloe put down the journal and thought for a moment about her grandmother's growing friendship with Billy. It was touching to read, and fascinating to learn about Billy's background and wartime experience. He sounded very far removed from Chloe's grandfather, but she could see why Lena, with her stigmatised birth and tough upbringing, had felt an instant kinship with this boy from the poverty-stricken East End. From her grandmother's description of Billy, she was almost certain that he was the young man in the unnamed photograph in Lena's album. She was curious to learn more...

Billy said that it was hardly surprising that the Brits were no match for the Japs in the Arakan. He was still holding my hand when he said this. I wondered if he'd forgotten about it, but didn't say anything. I was happy just sitting there with him, hand in hand, listening.

'WE BRITS WEREN'T REALLY TRAINED for jungle warfare,' Billy acknowledged. 'Those of us who'd been in India were used to mountainous conditions and snowstorms, the rest of the lads were trained to fight in the desert.'

Lena found the terror of battle hard to imagine, although listening to Billy gave her some idea of how it might feel. He told her about an ambush, when his platoon was surrounded by Japanese soldiers and all but him and one other man were mown down.

'It was hell on earth. Bodies everywhere... Joe and I looked at each other. We could hear the Japs crashing through the jungle towards us and knew we had to take cover or we were done for. I spotted a hollow tree-trunk. We managed to squeeze inside. We crouched in there, holding our breath while the Japs strutted round the clearing, kicking the bodies, poking them with their bayonets. They cleared off eventually. When we climbed down, we had to step over our mates to get out of there.'

'Is that when you got injured?' Lena asked quietly.

Billy shook his head. 'That happened a few days after the

ambush. I was assigned to another unit and sent out again into the jungle. We were outnumbered once more by the Japs. Outsmarted by them too. We were ordered to advance and I was shot in the leg and shoulder.'

Lena gasped.

'I thought I'd bleed to death right there in that godforsaken jungle, or that one of the Japs would put another bullet through my head. The pain was unreal. Two mates picked me up and carried me back behind the lines. The doctors patched me up in a field hospital and before long I was on a train back to India. And here I am,' he said, looking into Lena's eyes.

She met his gaze, then asked what she'd been wondering, 'Are they going to send you back to the front soon?'

'I'm raring to get back there, to tell you the truth,' he said, 'but the Brits have been in retreat for months in Burma now. When there's a new offensive, they'll need all the men they can get.'

This must be why they needed all those extra Gurkhas, but thinking of Kathmandu gave Lena a prickle of anxiety as she remembered the fortune-teller's words. She knew she had to tell Billy – to warn him, but now she was with him, she felt awkward raising it especially after hearing about his ordeal. But in the end, she took a deep breath and blurted it out.

'When I was in Kathmandu, I went to see a fortune teller.' She tried to sound matter-of-fact but realised how strange it must sound. 'She told me that someone I knew was in danger...'

To her dismay, Billy laughed out loud. 'And what does that have to do with me?' he asked, a teasing look in his eyes. 'She could have meant anyone.'

Lena felt the colour rise to her cheeks. 'Well,' she went on, 'she said that I have a new friend and that that new friend could be in grave danger.'

She couldn't look into his eyes. It made her self-conscious to admit that he meant something to her.

'Well,' Billy said, more gently now. 'When I go back to the

front, I *will* be in danger. We are all in danger out there. It would be strange if we weren't.'

'But I think the fortune teller might have been referring to something different. Not the front line, perhaps. Something else...' she couldn't keep the fear out of her voice.

Billy laughed gently again and looked into her eyes. 'I promise to be careful,' he said, but it sounded a little as if he was mocking her.

Lena got up to leave soon after that.

'Will you come again?' Billy asked, and she caught the longing in his eyes.

'Of course. I'll come next week.'

She walked away from the ward feeling unhappy, as if she hadn't achieved what she'd set out to do. She was disappointed that Billy hadn't taken her seriously. As she'd suspected he might, he clearly thought anything to do with fortune-telling and mystics was pure bunkum. Lena concluded that she would normally have agreed with him, but she was equally sure that the fortune teller was telling the truth. By not being able to convince Billy that the danger was a reality, she felt as if she'd failed him somehow.

But despite her distress, Lena remembered to slip into the ladies' room to wipe off her make-up.

10

KOLKATA, 2015

CHLOE STOOD on the pavement in Bunder Street in Kolkata outside the hotel with her bags. She stared in shocked amazement at the street scene before her as the yellow and green taxi drew away, disappearing into the traffic. She'd never been in such an incredible, colourful, vibrant place before. Cars, taxis and motor rickshaws were crawling along the narrow road tooting their horns, and in amongst them were pedestrians ambling along chatting, unperturbed at holding up the traffic, rickshaws pulled by men who ran between the shafts in their bare feet dressed only in dirty vests and ragged sarongs, old-fashioned bicycles, and men wheeling handcarts and sack barrows loaded with goods. They were heading towards a market that Chloe could just about see, spilling out onto the road further up the street.

On the opposite side of the street was a food stall set up under a corrugated-iron roof for shelter, where a man in a sarong was cooking up something in an oil drum that smelled deliciously spicy. Customers sat around cross-legged on the pavement, waiting for their meals. Beside that was a drinks stall with a tatty awning from which hung bags of fresh lemons and limes. Behind the counter, a man was squeezing the fruit by hand into a large, metal jug. A fruit and vegetable stall sat alongside it, on which an array of ripe marrows, mangoes and papaya were laid out. Washing was hanging out to dry on some wrought-iron railings which ran the length of a tall building. A dirty tarpaulin was stretched from the railings to a point halfway across the pavement. A pair of bare feet protruded from under the tarpaulin, which was clearly home to street dwellers.

Feeling a little overwhelmed, Chloe turned towards the hotel, The Tea Planter's Club, and walked to the front gate. She would be in the city for three days, so she would have plenty of time to explore.

There was a little sentry box outside the hotel gate, and a few men sat around it on plastic chairs, chewing betel nut and whiling the time away. The sentry himself emerged from the box when he saw Chloe approaching. He saluted her rather officiously and made an elaborate fuss of opening the gate. She went inside the grounds and in front of her was an elegant-looking two-storey, white-painted building, complete with balconies and grand pillars. It was set in beautiful, flower-filled gardens around a spreading banyan tree.

At that moment, a porter in a white uniform with a red turban hurried out of the hotel. He took Chloe's bag from her and gestured for her to follow him into the reception area, where she checked in at the desk.

She was shown to a room at the back of the hotel, overlooking a quiet, tree-lined side street. The room was large and square, with a big, old-fashioned bathroom, a large, comfortable-looking bed and a couple of antique armchairs and a ceiling fan.

When the porter had left, Chloe pulled the shutters and windows closed, turned on the air conditioning and fan, took a quick shower, then, wrapped in white fluffy towels, sank down on the bed. She was exhausted from the journey, which had lasted around sixteen hours, crammed into an economy-class seat. Now, she stretched her legs out gratefully and closed her eyes. As she did so, the bed seemed to lurch and tip alarmingly. She realised that she was still experiencing the motion of the aeroplane, the gentle swaying and dipping from the turbulence. It was her first long-haul flight and it had been far more tiring than she'd expected.

She drifted off to sleep eventually and when she awoke and checked her watch, she was amazed to see that it was six o'clock in the morning. She'd managed to sleep right through the evening and for the whole night. Her stomach clenched with hunger, so she got dressed and made her way down to the restaurant on the ground floor.

Walking through the gracious public areas of the hotel, she noticed that they were furnished in the old colonial style, with planters' chairs, mahogany furniture, potted palms and paintings on the walls. Amongst them hung sepia photographs of old Calcutta, where rickshaws and horse-drawn vehicles stood outside grand buildings, and photographs of groups of colonial Brits, the ladies in evening gowns, the men in dinner jackets standing under palm trees, in amongst photos of famous guests and former owners of the hotel.

Her eyes were drawn to one photo a formidable-looking woman standing in front of the hotel. She had dark hair, styled in 1940s curls, and she was smiling into the camera. Underneath it, the inscription said, *Edith Mayhew, owner, 1940–1980*. In Mrs Mayhew's determined look, Chloe caught something of the old colonial spirit that Brits from that era must have possessed to survive and even thrive so far from home. Chloe's grandfather had had that same look, which he hadn't lost, even in old age.

Over a traditional English breakfast which she ate seated at a table with a linen tablecloth and silver cutlery, Chloe studied her map of Kolkata. Chatterjee was a common name, she knew that, but her grandmother's journal had also yielded a street name. Sita's family had lived in the vicinity of Main Sewer Road, in southern Kolkata. Chloe had scoured the maps in her guide-books but couldn't find any road with that name.

If the street did still exist, she could go there and ask around. It would be fascinating to know if she had distant relatives living in the city and to see if anyone remembered her great-grand-mother, although she acknowledged that that was highly unlikely.

In the end, she went to the front desk, where the concierge spoke good English. He smiled when she said the name of the road.

'The road is not called that name anymore,' he explained. 'It has changed its name twice over the years, once to Ballygunge Avenue, and then in the early 1930s it became Rashbehari Avenue. It is named after a philanthropist.'

Chloe thanked him profusely. 'I would never have found it if you hadn't told me that,' and he smiled and bowed his head in appreciation.

She went back to her guidebook, which didn't yield much information, but she also had her tablet with her in her handbag. She connected to the very slow hotel internet and did a search for Rashbehari Avenue. There wasn't much information about it and what there was was sporadic, but she managed to find out that the area had been settled in the early part of the twentieth century by Indian middle classes who'd wanted to move away from the cramped streets in northern Calcutta, which had been designated to them and consigned the name Black Town, whereas the British occupied the airier parts of central Calcutta known as White Town.

Chloe was sure that even by going down to Rashbehari Avenue she wouldn't find much out. After all, Sita must have left home in disgrace around 1920, but even so, she was keen to walk around the area and try to get a feel for what it must have once been like.

The concierge called her a taxi and when she asked the driver to take her to Rashbehari Avenue, he frowned disapprovingly.

'That is not a tourist area, madam,' he said, shaking his head.

'No, I know. I'd like to go there just to see it. I have some family connections there.'

The taxi driver shrugged and pulled out into the traffic of Bunder Street. They crawled to the end of the street behind a rickshaw, then turned left onto Chowringhee Road, a four-lane carriageway that ran south past the huge expanse of green known as the Maidan. The traffic on this wide road was as crazy as in the narrower streets, rickshaws vying for space with overloaded lorries, with the occasional horse-drawn cart or bullock cart plodding patiently through the traffic. Chloe noticed that even though this was one of the major thoroughfares of the city, the pavements were still lined with ramshackle food stalls and the makeshift homes of street dwellers.

She gazed across at the Maidan. It was reminiscent of a London park behind its green-painted railings with its shady spinneys and large lily ponds. People were out strolling in family groups, dressed in their finest suits and sarees. Chloe realised that it was Saturday. With the long journey from England and travelling through different time-zones, she'd lost track of the days.

On the other side of the road to the Maidan were large, solid buildings, built by the British, she guessed, to impress and intimidate its colonial subjects, but halfway down was a huge, white church. She remembered that it was called St Paul's Cathedral, and, but for the beggars sitting on the front wall and the overgrown grounds, was identical to many churches she'd seen in English towns.

A little further south, the enormous, white edifice of the Victoria Memorial rose up in front of a huge lake. Chloe stared at it as they drove past, impressed by its size and grandeur, its huge white dome and pillared façades reflected in the still waters of the lake.

'*That* is tourist place,' the driver said approvingly, nodding towards the memorial, his face still sullen. Chloe guessed it was because she was going somewhere where he would have no chance of getting any commission.

'Perhaps I'll go there another day,' Chloe replied, and he instantly brightened.

'I take you there tomorrow,' he said, putting his foot down and driving on a little faster.

They headed into the built-up streets south of the Maidan, crawling between office blocks and apartment buildings amid a constant flow of buses, taxis and motorbikes. After fifteen minutes or so battling the heavy traffic, the driver turned off onto an equally busy dual carriageway. He slowed down.

'This Rashbehari Avenue,' he said.

Chloe stared about her in disbelief as traffic roared past the crawling taxi, horns blaring. Some of the buildings flanking the carriageway looked as if they could have been built in the early part of the last century, but she was shocked that her great-grandmother had grown up on this busy thoroughfare. It couldn't have been like this in the nineteen twenties, surely. But this was definitely the name of the road the concierge had given her, and there were old buildings here, so she was keen to investigate further. She asked the taxi driver to drop her wherever he could.

He pulled off the busy road onto a side street and drew up in front of a grand old house.

'You can walk around here,' he said. 'I will wait for you.'

'There's no need to wait,' she said. 'I don't know how long I will be.'

'No matter,' the taxi driver replied, pulling out a newspaper from the glove compartment and turning his attention to the headlines. 'I wait anyway.'

Chloe got out of the taxi into the clammy heat of the morning.

She made for the shade of the trees that lined the side street and consulted her map. It appeared that there was a network of residential streets on either side of Rashbehari Avenue that made up the neighbourhood. She wandered for a little way, looking at the crumbling old houses that must once have been beautiful. They were the sprawling homes of wealthy and professional Indians who wanted to make a statement by building a prestigious home for their families. Many of them were neglected now, their gardens overgrown, their plaster peeling, and many had been divided into apartments. In between the old houses, newer apartment blocks had sprouted, several storeys high, filling their plots completely, where there once would have been trees and gardens.

Chloe carried on wandering through the shady streets, taking care not to lose her way. The neighbouring roads all looked much the same. It was very quiet, apart from the rumble of traffic on the main road and the occasional tooting horn. There was hardly anyone about. A few children playing in the garden of one derelict mansion stopped and stared at Chloe as she passed, and a few stray dogs trotted about. Just when she was about to go back to the taxi, she wandered past an old woman sitting in the shade of her porch of a smaller house. Chloe stopped, smiled at the old lady and made the namaste gesture in greeting.

'I wonder if you can help me?' she asked. 'My great-grandmother grew up here many, many years ago. I've come from England and I'm trying to find out where she might have lived.'

'Come and sit,' the old lady said, motioning Chloe to sit in the other chair on her veranda.

'Thank you.' Chloe went up the short garden path and sat down beside the old lady on the creaking veranda.

'I have lived here many years,' the woman said. 'I will try to help you if I can. But there have been many changes around here. Many people have left and new people have come to live in the area. I don't know many of them anymore.'

'I don't have much information about my great-grandmother.

All I know is that she grew up in this area. She left around 1920, so it was a very, very long time ago.'

'Oh, that is a long time ago! Before I was born, I'm afraid. What was her name?'

'Her name was Sita. Sita Chatterjee.'

'Chatterjee! Oh then, I *will* be able to help you. There is a very large house, the Chatterjee house, on Rashbehari Avenue itself. Nobody lives there now. It is closed up. It has many, many rooms. Over fifty, it is rumoured. It was built in the early nineteen hundreds and many branches of the Chatterjee family lived there all together for decades. It has many separate courtyards inside. The family is all gone now. Moved abroad or to other parts of India. The house is neglected, like so many other beautiful houses around here.'

'That's amazing. Thank you so much for telling me,' Chloe said, incredulous and delighted in equal measure. 'I will go and look at the house. Where is it?'

'Number seventy,' the old lady said. 'There is much traffic on the road, so do be careful, please.'

Chloe thanked the woman and made her way back through the streets towards the main road. When she reached it, she looked at the numbers on the buildings; here they were all apartment blocks, some of them close to the road, some with shops on the ground floor. To her relief there was at least a shady pavement running along the road, albeit cracked and uneven. She worked her way along, checking the numbering of the buildings until she reached number seventy.

There were metal barriers all along the lower floors to stop squatters from entering, and on the upper floors the bay windows were boarded up. It was clearly a huge house that had once been beautiful but was now sadly crumbling and neglected. The ochre-yellow paint was peeling from the upper walls, along with clumps of plaster from the pillars of the porch. There were tiles missing from the roof too, which must once have been terracotta-coloured but was now blackened with lichen and pollution.

Chloe felt sadness wash through her as she looked at this forlorn relic of her ancestral past. She tried to imagine the house in its prime, with family members going in and out of the grand entrance, the upper windows open to catch the breeze from a much quieter neighbourhood. She thought about her great-grandmother, Sita, the stout, capable-looking woman in Lena's photograph album. Had she been born here in this house, spent her childhood here? Was this where the rift took place that had forced her to leave home? Where had she gone to give birth to and care for her baby? Chloe knew those questions would probably remain unanswered, but standing there looking at the gracious old house, she felt a connection to it that she hadn't expected. Growing up, she'd never explored her Indian ancestry, but now she felt a strange feeling of belonging, a notion that part of her root system had been established here, in this huge, chaotic city.

11

DARJEELING, 1943

THERE IS a famine ripping through Bengal Province, decimating the poor in the countryside. The newspapers are full of it. We haven't really been touched by it up here in the hills, although rice has been more difficult to get than before. Local people mainly earn their living in Darjeeling from the tea plantations, but down in the plains, the shortage of rice has been devastating.

Everyone Lena had spoken to who'd travelled through the countryside and to the cities beneath the hills was shocked by what was happening.

One day in early October 1943, Lieutenant Harper had to go down to Calcutta by train to meet his superiors. 'There's no need to come with me, Miss Chatterjee,' he said. 'I can manage perfectly well by myself.'

Lena was sure he went alone in order to spare her the experience of seeing so many people dying on the pavements, even children and babies, and the horror of it all.

When he came back, he was visibly shocked. 'It was terrible... unbelievable,' he told her, ashen-faced. 'Government lorries go round collecting up the dead and taking them down to the ghats to be cremated. The whole place is filled with the stench of rotting bodies. Everywhere, there are poor, emaciated people too weak to move. It is a dreadful situation and very distressing indeed.'

Everyone Lena knew was deeply concerned about the famine. Sita had started helping out at a charity in the town that put on afternoon teas in aid of the famine fund. It had given her a new lease of life, mixing with the burra memsahibs, as she called them, and all the important citizens of Darjeeling.

When Lena went to see Billy in the Eden Hospital, he had a lot to say on the subject. To his mind, the famine had been caused by the actions of the British government.

'It's them who should take the blame for the death and suffering,' he told Lena, his eyes deadly serious. 'The Jap invasion of Burma is part of the problem. Rice can't be imported from Burma anymore. But British policies are to blame too. Did you know that they've prioritised supplies of rice to the military and civil servants rather than to the locals?'

Lena nodded. 'I've read something about that...'

'It's made prices go up. Ordinary farmers can't even afford to feed themselves.'

'Yes, it's a terrible situation, Billy.'

'And there's something else too. Even worse, it's called the Denial policy.'

Lena frowned. She hadn't heard about that.

'I read about it today. The Government in its wisdom has gone out and confiscated all the rice supplies near the coast in case the Japanese invade. It's so they wouldn't be able to feed their troops. They've also confiscated all the local boats. Fishermen can't operate anymore. The poor are unable to feed themselves now, just because of this... it makes my blood boil... I grew up hungry myself,' he told Lena. 'I can't bear to see poor people suffering, especially when it could have been avoided.'

Lena had never seen him so passionate about anything before. He even told her in confidence that he was against the

British Raj and that India should have its independence as soon
as the war was over. She looked around the ward nervously– it
wasn't the sort of thing one said where there might be officials of
the Raj about and some of the doctors in the Eden Hospital were
stalwarts of British rule.

'Why are you fighting to preserve the empire, then?' she asked
him in a low voice.

'Because it's my job,' he said with a trace of bitterness. 'I told
you it was the only one I could get when I joined up. But when I
stop to think about it, I realise that I'm against the very thing
we're fighting for...' But then he reflected, rubbing his chin, 'On
the other hand, I wouldn't want the Japs to take over here either.
They would be even worse rulers than the Brits.'

*ALTHOUGH THE FAMINE IS IMPORTANT, I tried to change the subject. I
wanted to remind him about the fortune-teller's words again. Each time
I do that though, he smiles and pats my hand. 'Thank you for worrying
about me, Lena,' he says, 'but I know how to take care of myself.'*

Chloe thought about Billy and Lena. It was the first chance
she'd had to read the journal since she'd arrived in Kolkata. She'd
got back to the Tea Planter's Club from Rashbehari Avenue
exhausted from walking around in the heat, and jet lag was
catching up with her. She'd collapsed on the bed and slept for a
couple of hours. Now it was mid-afternoon. She knew she needed
to make the most of the city for the few short days she was here,
but the pull of Lena's journal was strong. She'd picked it up and
told herself she would just read a few pages before she went out.

Now she was musing on Billy's views on the Raj. They were
probably radical from a soldier who, as Lena had pointed out,
was fighting to support the empire. Chloe recognised that anti-
establishment streak in her grandmother too. Chloe had often
heard her gently mocking her husband for his conservative,

imperialist stance, and now she was discovering where the first seed of those ideas might have been sown.

I've been to see Billy nearly every day for the past fortnight. I've slipped in quietly during the evenings after work, when most of the nurses have gone home, and the nightwatchman is sitting outside the door of the hospital. If I hand the old man a few rupees, he is happy to let me in.

DURING THOSE VISITS, Lena and Billy got to know each other very well. She told him all about her sad beginnings, how her mother had to leave home when she became pregnant, and how she had to leave Calcutta altogether to take Lena to Darjeeling to school. He listened quietly, his gentle eyes on her face, sometimes shaking his head and exclaiming at the things she told him. She knew he understood.

Every time she went to see him, they grew a little bit closer, and although neither of them said so, Lena could feel in her heart and her bones that they were falling in love. She knew she cared deeply for him, although it was a strange feeling, one she'd never experienced before, and from the way he looked at her and the way he kissed her hand so tenderly before she left, she could tell that the feeling was reciprocated. Whether there was any future for them, with the Burma front looming for Billy, Lena no idea, but if there were, it would make her happier than she'd ever been in her life before.

But, on 11th October, Lena's world was turned upside down.

She was coming home from work a little later than usual. They had been very busy in the office that week, filling out the records for all the soldiers that Lieutenant Harper had recruited on their trip to Nepal. Mrs Spooner was no longer working in the office. Although Lena was relieved about that, it meant more work for her. It occurred to her, that as she was late anyway, it would be good to go straight to see Billy now, instead of waiting until later. She asked the rickshaw-wallahs to take her along to the Eden Hospital.

As they made their way through the town, she began to notice that things looked strangely different. The sky was brooding and dark, the colours sharper and brighter. Then, on the way along Mount Pleasant Road, that led to the hospital, something unimaginable happened. The ground began to shake violently all around the rickshaw and cracks started to appear in the road. All this was accompanied by the most terrible thundering, vibrating sound from deep within the earth. The trees were shuddering too and even the buildings on either side of the road were shaking. At first, Lena couldn't believe her eyes.

'Earthquake!' the rickshaw-wallahs dumped the rickshaw, with Lena still sitting in it, and hurtled off down the road, not even stopping to help her. Not that she wanted to be helped. Her mind was on one thing. Getting to Billy. She suddenly knew. This was surely what the fortune teller had been trying to warn her about. Billy was in danger from the earthquake, now she needed to help him.

She tore down the road, dodging the gaps that were opening up in the surface and the branches that were crashing down from the trees. She rushed into the hospital grounds and up to the front door. There was no one on the front desk. All the nurses must have been helping patients, so she made for the staircase. Running up the juddering stairs two at a time, she met wave after wave of hospital staff coming down, carrying or supporting patients between them. Lena searched desperately amongst the strained and terrified faces, but could see no sign of Billy.

A doctor who was on his way down, helping an old lady connected to a drip, tried to bar her way. 'You must go back down. The building is going to collapse.'

Lena ignored him and tried to push past, even more determined to get to Billy now..

'Didn't you hear me? It's not safe upstairs.'

'I've got to go up there. My friend is up there.'

She barged past the doctor, reached the top of the stairs and struggled along the corridor. The floor was heaving and buckling under her feet and her heart was in her mouth. She was terrified to go on, and every instinct was telling her to get out of the building, but she put her terror aside. She needed to find Billy at all costs and help him to get out of there.

She moved as fast as she could along the corridor to the ward. The door stood open and the beds were empty – the sheets cast aside in piles, trays of medicine upturned in the chaos. The hospital staff must have taken the sickest patients to safety already. She ran straight to the end of the ward and her heart leapt with relief. There was Billy. He was out of bed, staggering around precariously in his blue striped pyjamas, holding his head in his hands.

'Lena!' he shouted when he caught sight of her. She ran to him and threw her arms around him. They held each other for a few seconds.

'We need to get out of here,' Lena urged. 'Put your arm around my shoulder.'

Unsteadily and slowly, they began to walk across the ward towards the corridor. Billy was limping badly and leaning heavily on her shoulder, wincing with pain. Lena was desperate to run, knowing they had to get out of there quickly, but it was impossible. He couldn't move that fast.

As they reached the doorway, the floor of the ward seemed to rise and buckle under their feet. Then, with a great rumble and booming sound, the wall in front of them collapsed, spraying bricks and dust everywhere, quickly followed by the wooden ceiling, which crashed straight down on top of them. They fell to the ground face down under the weight of it and lay there panting, Lena not knowing what to do next. The lights had gone out and it was dark under the collapsed ceiling, thick white dust swirling everywhere, getting into Lena's mouth and eyes. They were both coughing and spluttering.

Lena felt around above her head and realised that that part of the ceiling at least had fallen down in one huge piece, so it might be possible to crawl along in the space underneath it.

'Come on, Billy,' she said, urging him onto his knees and starting to crawl ahead of him.

At the end of the room, where the door to the ward should have been, a fallen beam blocked their way. When she felt it there, she lay back sobbing. *We'll never get out*, she thought, but then she felt Billy squeeze her hand.

'Don't give up now,' he said. She knew he was having great difficulty; every movement of his leg appeared to cause him pain, but he still had the strength to encourage her and that galvanised her.

'You stay here, Billy. I'll crawl ahead and find a way out.'

She set off towards the left side, then to the right, but after a few paces in each direction, her way was blocked by piles of bricks and rubble. All the time, the building was groaning and straining. She could hear falling masonry and cracking beams and she was terrified that the roof of the hospital itself would cave in. They would surely be crushed under its weight.

Lena was beginning to despair when she saw a gap up ahead. She raced towards it on her hands and knees and managed to haul herself through. When she stood up, she saw that she was standing on the upper side of the ceiling. Looking up, she could see the rafters of the floor above, and above that the roof beams of the hospital itself.

Terrified that the roof might collapse at any moment, she got back through the hole and crawled over to Billy. He was lying where she'd left him, groaning and holding his injured leg.

'Come on. I've found a way out.'

Lena managed to lead him to the edge and help him squeeze out through the gap. From where they stood, they could see the top of the staircase ahead. Above them, planks from the fallen floor were hanging off the rafters. As they looked up, one splintered off and crashed down, narrowly missing them.

'We need to get out of here,' she urged and they carried on. Slipping and stumbling on the uneven surfaces, clambering over piles of stones and debris, they managed to fight their way along the half-collapsed corridor. Finally they reached the stairs. There they stopped and looked down in dismay. Several stairs at the top of the staircase had collapsed. It was impossible to go down it.

There was chaos and confusion at the bottom of the stairs too. Hospital staff and patients were rushing about in the light of a few hurricane lamps. No one seemed to know what to do.

'Help!' Lena shouted but no one heard, so she shouted again, this time louder. She gripped Billy's hand and glanced at him nervously. Drops of sweat stood out on his pale face. He was clearly in a lot of pain. Waiting was unbearable.

Finally, one of the doctors looked up and saw them. His face fell. 'Stay right where you are,' he shouted. 'I'm going to get help.'

He left the building and came back a few minutes later with a couple of orderlies carrying a ladder. The two men got to work quickly, cleared a path in the debris in the hallway and propped the ladder up against the top of the stairs.

'The patient must come down first,' the doctor shouted. 'I'll come up to you.'

He climbed up the ladder towards them. As he got close to Lena, she saw the perspiration running through the grime on his face, his pebble glasses coated in dust.

'You'll need to turn round,' he said to Billy. 'Put your feet on top of the ladder.'

Billy did his best, all the time wincing in pain. Lena helped him to get into position and the doctor put his arms around Billy's waist and eased him down the ladder. Lena watched nervously, holding her breath.

Then it was Lena's turn. She hadn't realised how much she

was shaking until she put her foot on the ladder, but it was quivering so much, she wondered if it would dislodge the ladder and she would fall. Her heart was beating fit to burst too, but she knew that Billy was safe and that was all that mattered. But as she began to ease herself down, there was that hideous rumbling sound again and the building started to shudder and shake. The ladder was shaking too. Lena screamed in terror.

'Hang on!' the doctor yelled. 'I'll come up and get you!'

He put his foot on the bottom rung and before he'd managed to reach Lena, the shaking miraculously stopped and she was able to climb down, even though her legs felt like jelly.

As soon as she was on the ground, she burst into tears.

Billy was sitting on the ground outside the building, being checked over by one of the nurses. Lena longed to put her arms around him, but instead looked into his eyes and smiled – and he smiled back. At last, they were safe, when five minutes earlier they'd thought they were going to die. She was still shaking all over, but her heartbeat was gradually slowing down.

The fortune-teller's prediction had come true, she realised. Billy had been in danger, and she had managed to help him out of it.

The doctor turned to her. 'We're going to move him to another wing. Not all of the building has been damaged. Only this part, which is the oldest.'

'Can I come too?' Lena asked, but the doctor shook his head.

'I'm sorry, but it is already overcrowded in there. Why don't you come back tomorrow?'

The orderlies brought a stretcher and lifted Billy onto it. Lena held his hand for a brief moment and looked down at him. He looked pale, almost grey in the light of the hurricane lamps. He looked up into her eyes and smiled, and then he was gone, carried off into the night.

Someone lent Lena a torch and she walked back along the rutted surface of Mount Pleasant Road towards home. The ground still gave the occasional tremor. On either side were damaged buildings, although most of those had managed to stay upright, but when she entered the narrow passages and alleys of the Indian bazaar area, she sensed that all was not well. There was that by now familiar smell of brick dust in the air and people were rushing about and shouting.

She emerged from the alleys into the marketplace and saw by the light of the torch and the hurricane lamps that all around the market were piles of stones and rubble where buildings had collapsed.

Her heart started to thump again. She could hear wailing and crying as bodies were pulled from the rubble. She held her breath and hoped. She needed to get to her mother and check that she was all right. She cursed herself. In all the trouble and panic over Billy, she hadn't stopped to think that her mother might be in danger. Sita's home was flimsy and badly built, a mixture of wood and bricks with a corrugated iron roof.

When she turned the corner into their alleyway, Lena's heart lurched with shock. There was Ma's little house, now reduced to a pile of rubble, completely blocking the alley. Men from the market were digging in the pile with sticks and spades. Her first panicked thought was that Ma might not have been at home. Perhaps she was still helping with the teas up on Chowrasta, although in her heart of hearts she knew it was too late in the evening for that. Sita would have been preparing their supper, as she always did at that time, when the earthquake struck.

Lena flew to the heap of rubble, her eyes blinded with tears. Falling on it, she started to dig with her bare hands.

A neighbour, Sunil Gupta, a stallholder from the market, came and lifted her gently off the pile. 'There is no need for you to dig, Miss Chatterjee, the men will do that. Come and wait in my house.'

Sunil's humble home was in the next street. As Sunil headed back out to help the searchers, his wife, Lakshmi, sat Lena down on her cushions and gave her some sweet chai. Lena could only sip at it. She could barely swallow, her nerves were in such turmoil. Lakshmi clearly didn't know what to say to her. She just sat there, wringing her hands, her eyes full of dread.

Lena didn't know how long it was before Sunil came back for her. When she saw the tears in his eyes, she knew. She could barely stand up. Sunil had to support her as they walked back to the alley and the heap of rubble that had once been Ma's home.

They had found her. Her body had been crushed under the roof beams, purple bruises blooming on her face which was covered in white dust. They had laid her out beside the rubble. Her eyes were closed and she looked so peaceful. Lena fell down and hugged her stiff, lifeless form, her tears splashing onto the dust on her face.

'I'm so sorry, Ma. I wasn't there when you needed me. I'm so sorry...'

She was riddled with guilt. She'd had no thought of her mother when the earthquake struck – the woman who had given her life to care for Lena. Her sole thought had been for someone else. Someone she barely knew.

Eventually, when her tears were spent, the men helped Lena to her feet.

Sunil said that we will have her funeral tomorrow and insisted that I should stay with them tonight. So here I am, in a tiny spare room on the top floor of Sunil and Lakshmi's house. One of the men brought a pile of dusty belongings from the ruin of Ma's house. There were some of my western clothes amongst them and this journal. I dusted it off, amazed that it had survived. It looks battered, but most of the pages are intact.

I'm grateful for Sunil and Lakshmi's kindness in offering me a bed. The room is bigger than the space I had at Ma's but how my heart aches to be back there, to be folded in her ample arms once again, to feel nurtured and loved as only she knew how. The trauma of helping Billy out of the hospital is still in the back of my mind, but it has been eclipsed by a far greater pain, one that I know will never leave me as long as I live.

Chloe closed the journal, a lump in her throat. She looked at the battered cover and imagined it covered in the dust and rubble of Sita's home after the earthquake. A chill went through her. Through this little book, she had a real connection to the past and that terrible day when her great-grandmother had perished. Sadness washed through Chloe at the thought of Lena losing her beloved mother like that. What a terrible, tragic loss, inflicted in such a cruel and sudden way. It was true what Lena had said about her; Sita had been taken before her time. Clearly Lena had never come to terms with the guilt she must have felt at not being there for her mother, and that was why she'd never ever spoken of that day to Chloe, to Chloe's mother or to the rest of the family.

12

WEST BENGAL, INDIA, 2015

CHLOE LAY on the top bunk in a first-class compartment on the night train that was trundling north from Sealdah Station in Kolkata towards New Jalpaiguri station in a town called Siliguri, south of the Himalayas. There, she would change trains and get the Himalaya Railway up to Darjeeling. She stared up at the moving images and lights on the ceiling, unable to sleep. The constant jolting and frequent stopping of the train at remote country stations, and in other places for no explicable reason, kept her awake, as did the recurring thoughts that went round and round in her mind.

Her senses were still reeling from three days in the most chaotic, most colourful and most surprising place she'd ever set foot in in her life. The city of Kolkata had offered up fabulous temples and majestic buildings, wide-open green spaces, as well as the most shocking poverty, squalor and cruelty she'd ever witnessed. One moment she would be strolling through the cool, palatial halls of the Victoria Memorial, gazing upon extraordinary landscape paintings, sculptures, armoury and other fabulous relics of empire, and the next moment would see her walking past pitifully thin street dwellers, who lived under tarpaulins on the pavement and who used their malnourished or disabled children to help them beg for a living. She always stopped and gave them money, feeling sorry and a little guilty for her own comfortable existence when there was so much poverty in the world.

She was still reeling too from the discovery of Sita's family house on Rashbehari Avenue. She'd taken many photographs of the crumbling ruin and had thought about sending them to Daniel and Uncle Andrew. Would they even be interested, though? She'd messaged Daniel with a few photographs of Kolkata when she'd first arrived in the city, but his response had been lukewarm. Wasn't he even interested in his Indian roots? She supposed she shouldn't be surprised – he'd never shown any great interest in Lena or in anything to do with India, and nor had Uncle Andrew. He seemed far more interested in Chloe's grandfather and the success of his military career.

She thought back to how they'd responded when she'd told them about her trip. Daniel had said, 'I'm all for broadening horizons, Chloe, but what about your next step career-wise? You've had rather a lot of time off now haven't you?'

Uncle Andrew, when she'd called him, to say goodbye had said. 'Interesting, of course, to see the former seat of empire, Chloe dear, but do take good care of yourself, won't you? India isn't what it once was, you know.'

By contrast, Sophie had responded instantly and warmly when Chloe had sent her photographs of the house in Rashbehari Avenue. 'That's incredible, Chloe. What a find,' Sophie had written in return. 'You must be so thrilled to have found it. It looks as though it must have been fabulous in the old days.'

Chloe sighed now, remembering, and remembering too what she had read in the journal about her great-grandmother's final day.

Thinking of Sophie, Chloe's mind wandered back to the day they had met for lunch and she had happened to see Fergal through the pub window. Recalling that image of him and the blonde woman sitting so intimately in the corner of the pub made her spirits plummet anew. She stopped herself. She'd vowed that she wouldn't torture herself any longer by thinking about it. She knew that she needed to move on. This trip was part of that. She turned over to face the wall and, closing her eyes, succumbed to the gentle motion of the train, and before long had drifted off into a fitful sleep.

At New Jalpaiguri station, rickshaws and taxis converged on the forecourt to meet the passengers from Kolkata with much clamour, tooting and beeping of horns. Shouldering her backpack, Chloe ignored the frantic haranguing of the taxi drivers and made her way through the crowd across the station yard to a separate platform, where a train from the Darjeeling Himalayan Railway was waiting to depart. She was a little disappointed to see that the engine was a diesel and not a steam one.

She bought a ticket and found a seat in one of the blue painted carriages. There weren't many people boarding the train that morning. A couple of middle-aged Englishmen – trainspotters from Yorkshire, she later found out – got into her carriage. A few straggling tourists turned up just before departure and got onto other carriages. Then, with a lot of tooting and jolting, the train jerked into life and set off on its long journey into the hills.

'Most people don't do the whole trip nowadays,' one of the Yorkshiremen told Chloe. 'They go up by road. It's far quicker. But we wouldn't miss the magic of the train. This is our fifth time here.'

For most of the way, the railway ran beside a road, which wound its way up the steep mountains through thick evergreen forests with hairpin bends, precipitous drops, tunnels and tight loops. Cars, lorries and jeeps overtook the little train as it laboured up the hill. The railway too went through many bends and loops, at one particular point completing a 360-degree turn before doubling back on itself. It took several hours and stopped at many tiny stations on the way up into the hills. Chloe was content to sit and watch the scenery and was glad she hadn't gone by bus or car. Sometimes, through a gap in the trees, there were stunning views of the plains below, flat and green from the monsoon rains, shimmering in the heat of the morning.

At last, the gradient levelled out, and they were travelling through hillside towns and villages, and, in between them, the vast tea plantations that Lena had written about in her journal. Chloe stared out at them, fascinated. She recognised the straight rows of emerald-green bushes, planted on stepped terraces. The bright sarees of the tea pickers as they moved between the lines, huge baskets on their backs, were visible even from a long way away. As well as plantations, complete with their factories, municipal buildings, and living quarters, they passed temples and churches, monasteries and hotels. The hillside was so steep that it looked as though the buildings were spilling down its side.

Beyond the hillside, in the far distance, was a magnificent vista of the Himalayas, including the many snow-covered peaks of Kanchenjunga. Chloe caught her breath, looking at it. It was incredible. No photograph she'd ever seen had done it justice. Now she understood why Lena had never tired of watching the sunlight move over its ever-changing face.

Before long, they were trundling through the outskirts of Darjeeling town itself, rattling past small dwellings, shops and stalls where people sat out on the steps to watch the train go by. As they got nearer to the centre of the town, the buildings closed in on the track and then they were arriving at a station. With a triumphant blast of its horn, the train shuddered to a halt.

Chloe got down from the carriage and pulled on a cardigan. The temperature up here was much colder than down on the plains. She was instantly surrounded by a crowd of taxi drivers and rickshaw-wallahs touting for trade. They were all trying to grab her attention at once. She chose one that looked vaguely trustworthy and asked him to take her to the Elgin Hotel, which she'd already booked online. She got into the back of the battered old Toyota and was driven through the narrow streets. She looked out at the multitude of colourful shops and stalls lining the roads, selling a vast array of goods – fresh fruit and vegetables, clothes, materials, spices. She wondered whether this was where Sita used to shop. She would have to explore on foot with a map.

Despite the busy shops, as they drove slowly through the town, she got the sense that Darjeeling was more laid-back, far less frenetic than Kolkata. Looking at the people, she noticed people of many different races here – Ghorkalis from Nepal, Tibetans with their wide, open faces and colourful robes, and amongst them, taller Indians. As Lena had written in her diary, Chloe was now seeing for herself that Darjeeling was still a melting pot for different ethnic groups.

The Elgin Hotel was a gracious colonial building, perched on the edge of the hillside, overlooking the town and, beyond that, the tea plantations that fell away steeply below it. In the distance, snow-covered peaks of Kanchenjunga sparkled in the afternoon sun. Chloe's room at the front of the hotel had a picture window with a marvellous view of the Himalayas. She was glad to sit down in the window to rest after her long journey and watch the spectacular sunset.

Later, after a short nap and a shower, she noticed that it was already dark outside. Her stomach was rumbling with hunger, so she went downstairs to eat in the hotel dining room, the walls of which were lined with black and white photographs of old Darjeeling. She went round and peered at each in turn, intrigued. There were photographs of an old market, with stallholders selling crafts and produce, laid out in baskets on the ground; another picture of a rickshaw with four rickshaw-wallahs pushing and pulling a fat Englishman in a pith helmet up a hill; another of soldiers from a Ghurkha regiment standing to attention in Chowrasta, the central square; as well as pictures of the Darjeeling railway, in particular one of a steam train labouring around the Batasia Loop. There were photographs of vintage vehicles, and people strolling about in groups in old-fashioned clothes. She half-expected to catch a glimpse of Lena and George wandering down one of the streets of the town in these photos but, of course, was disappointed. All the faces were of strangers.

AFTER BREAKFAST THE NEXT MORNING, Chloe strolled out of the hotel gate with her map of the town. There were several places she was keen to visit, but first on her list and closest to the hotel – along the same road in fact – was St Catherine's School. Chloe had already discovered from her research on the internet that the school itself had closed down shortly after Indian independence. The building had survived, though. It was no longer a school, but a hotel, 'The Himalaya View'.

She walked along the road and there it was, a few doors along towards the edge of town. She stood outside the wrought-iron gate looking in at the large grey building with its steep roofs, its row upon row of gothic-style arched windows and its central clock tower. Despite the new owners' attempts to brighten it up with beautifully stocked gardens, the place retained a slightly austere air. If she half closed her eyes, she could just imagine groups of uniformed girls playing in the yard, the school bell ringing from the front steps and them rushing inside for their next lesson.

A watchman sat in a little booth beside the gate. She sensed he had noticed her peering at the building, so she went over to speak to him.

'Can I help you, madam?' he asked, hastily putting out a bidi cigarette with his heel. 'Do you have a reservation at the hotel?'

'No, I'm afraid not. I'm just interested in the building. My grandmother was a pupil here before the war when it was still a school.'

The man's face brightened. 'Ah, St Catherine's? It was closed when I was small. I remember all the smart young ladies in their uniforms walking in the town two by two.'

'Well, she would have been one of them, although perhaps even before that time,' Chloe said.

'Those were good days,' he remarked, his eyes growing misty with memories.

Chloe smiled. 'Do you really mean that?'

'Yes. Of course!' He suddenly became animated. 'My father worked for the British at Government House. He was a driver for the Governor. It was a good job, but when the British left India in 1947, he couldn't get another job. We lived in poverty until my older brother was able to go out to work. Under the British, things worked well. Things aren't so good now.' He trailed off shaking his head.

Chloe's mouth dropped open in surprise. She didn't know what to say. She hadn't expected to find an Indian man singing the praises of British rule.

'There are photographs,' he announced, brightening. 'Inside the hotel. Photographs from that time. They are in the reception hall. Many pictures of the pupils. You should go and ask the receptionist. She will be glad to show you.'

'Thank you for telling me,' Chloe said, her heart quickening. 'That's very kind of you.'

He opened the side gate and let her through.

The austere building soared up in front of her. She imagined how intimidating a place it must have been for a three-year-old girl, separated from her mother, and everything she'd known before, to arrive in that spot for the first time and look up at the building. From the journal, she'd discovered that it was still intimidating for Lena right into her twenties. Chloe recalled how she'd had to creep down the fire escape and let herself out of a side gate simply to go to her interview at the military base. Being here, Chloe could see exactly why the establishment had had that effect upon her grandmother. Just the building itself was frightening enough, even without female dragons like Miss Woodcock to contend with.

Chloe went up the front steps and into the reception area. There was a smell of wood polish and lavender. The floor was herringbone parquet and the walls panelled in dark wood. A wide wooden staircase rose up out of the hallway with wrought-iron bannisters. But for the fans on the ceiling, it could have been an English country house.

'Can I help you?' The elegant receptionist was full of smiles.

Chloe explained that her grandmother had been a pupil at St Catherine's and that she'd come to find out more about her life in India before the war. 'The watchman said that there are some photographs of the school in here. I hope you don't mind me having a look.'

'Of course not.' The receptionist came out from behind the desk and showed Chloe over to an alcove beneath a window where there were a few armchairs and a coffee table spread with newspapers. 'They are on that wall,' the woman said, pointing to a large, white wall almost covered with framed photographs.

'Wow!' said Chloe, approaching it, wondering where to begin.

'They are vaguely in date order, but slightly random,' the receptionist told her. 'So, feel free to browse. Would you like a cold drink while you do? On the house, of course.'

'I'd love that, thank you,' Chloe said.

'We do a very nice lemongrass cordial to welcome guests. I will bring you one of those.'

The receptionist disappeared, and Chloe started peering at the photographs. They were all black and white, rather faded, mainly of groups of pupils, all girls, from tiny children to young women. All stood stiffly, looking nervously at the camera, there were very few smiles amongst any of them. The dates on the photos ranged from 1920 to 1948. There were some gaps, and some years had been missed out altogether.

Chloe calculated that Lena must have been admitted to St Catherine's nursery around 1923, and she knew from the journal that she'd left in 1943. She began with the earliest photos and worked her way through. She quickly realised that not every year group had been photographed annually. There was one photograph of very young girls in 1923, dressed in pinafore dresses with starched white blouses underneath. The photo was very grainy, though, and the quality poor, so it was virtually impossible to make out the details of the children. She looked at it for a long time but couldn't discern Lena's features in the group.

She moved on, examining each one carefully. There was one taken in 1933, when Lena would have been around thirteen. Chloe's eyes were drawn to one girl in the centre of the group who had something of the look of Lena about her. She stared boldly out of the photograph. She was one of the very few pupils smiling and had a mischievous look on her face. Chloe's heart beat a little more quickly as she scrutinised the girl. It was surely Lena. Who else could have smiled like that? And as she looked, Chloe felt a deep connection to the girl in the photograph, clearly bored with her lot and yearning for so much more from life.

She carried on systematically, scanning the photos taken during the early 1930s without seeing another one that contained any girls that resembled her grandmother, but then she came upon a photograph of a small group of older girls, which was inscribed '*Graduation, 1938*'. That was about the right date. Her eyes were drawn to the middle of the group and, again, there was that girl with that same knowing smile she'd had as a thirteen-year-old. There was no doubt about this one. It was definitely Lena.

With a prickle of déjà vu, Chloe realised that she recognised some of the other girls in this group. Then she remembered that she'd seen them in the informal snap taken in their dormitory that Lena had stuck into her photograph album and kept for seven decades. They were wearing the same clothes in both photographs. Perhaps the two photos were even taken on the same day? Chloe wished she had brought Lena's album with her so she could compare the two, but it was back in the hotel, stashed safely away in her backpack.

The receptionist came over with a glass on a small tray. It clinked with ice as she put it down on the coffee table near Chloe.

'Is it all right if I take pictures of a couple of these on my phone?' Chloe asked.

'I don't see why not. Have you found your grandmother in any of the photos?'

'I think so,' Chloe said and pointed to the two photographs of Lena.

'She looks such fun,' the receptionist smiled.

'Oh, she was!' Chloe agreed with feeling, realising with a jolt how much she missed Lena's optimistic but irreverent presence every day.

The receptionist returned to her desk and Chloe got out her phone and took the photos she wanted. Then she looked at the rest of the pictures – there were some of the building itself, some of the grounds, one of the old watchman, his face creased with smile lines. This must have been the one whom Lena had described as having saluted her when she left for the final time. Then there were a couple of group photographs of the staff – the cooks and kitchen porters, cleaning staff and the teachers who stood in the middle. It was dated 1939. Most of the teachers looked British, their faces unsmiling, their hair pulled back into tight buns, their clothes neat and understated. The one in the centre on the front row was clearly the headmistress. With dark hair and severe eyes, she looked like the sort of woman you wouldn't want to cross. Chloe peered a little closer and saw a pair of pince-nez dangling on a chain round her neck.

'Miss Woodcock!' she breathed and yet another of Lena's descriptions came properly to life for her.

Chloe took a photograph of that one too, then sat down to drink the lemongrass drink. It was delicious and aromatic.

The receptionist came to take her glass when she'd finished. 'Where are you staying?' she asked.

'Just up the road at the Elgin.'

'Lovely hotel, but you could come here. We have an incredible spa,' she smiled conspiratorially.

'I did look at the website, but it's a bit beyond my price range, I'm afraid,' Chloe said. What she didn't say was that she wouldn't want to stay in the hotel, knowing what a traumatic childhood Lena had experienced here. Despite the changes that had been made and the all-pervading sense of luxury, the atmosphere of those days seemed to prevail. The building was too unwelcoming and institutional, it hadn't shrugged off the feeling of a boarding school yet. Chloe shuddered inwardly, then got up to leave, handing the receptionist the glass and thanking her.

'Well, do come back anytime if you need to look at the photos again,' the woman said with a smile.

Lena left the building with a definite sense that she was getting closer to her grandmother's past. She was glad she'd come to Darjeeling and that she'd visited St Catherine's. She thanked the watchman on her way out, then set off towards the area that her guidebook told her was the old bazaar quarter. She wanted to find where Sita had lived, and where she had sadly perished. Although she didn't have an address, she had a picture in her mind of what it would be like.

She wound her way down through the narrow streets and alleys and flights of steps that led to that part of town where there was now a vegetable market, the Chowk Bazaar, a little way west of the railway station. Chloe soon found herself wandering through the aisles of the market, breathing in the scent of spices and fresh vegetables, walking past stalls selling ground spices out of open sacks, vegetables so fresh that clods of soil still clung to them, sacks of lentils and rice of many different varieties.

Around the edge of the market and immediately behind it, the streets were narrow and cramped. Some of the buildings looked as though they were temporary, made of wood or corrugated iron. As Chloe had feared, it was impossible to get a sense of where Sita's house might have been. It didn't look as though anyone lived in these dilapidated buildings anymore. But, standing at a crossroads between two of the busy market aisles, she began to understand what it must have been like to live in close proximity to this bustling place and how different it must have been for Lena coming from the stiff, subdued atmosphere of St Catherine's.

Standing there on the corner, Chloe watched an ample, middle-aged woman in a deep pink saree, a basket over her arm, test vegetables at a nearby stall. She pinched them for ripeness, smelled them for freshness and then started bartering energetically with the stallholder. Observing her, Chloe smiled. This could have been Sita, all those years ago, buying her daily provisions. This place and what went on here was so timeless.

Chloe bought a couple of apples from a fruit stall and started to make her way back to the hotel. She was a little disappointed that she hadn't been able to work out where Sita had lived, although she now had a good idea of what it might have been like living around the market, even in the 1940s.

Later that day, Chloe asked the hotel receptionist to find her a taxi to take her to Jalapahar. The taxi took her up through the back of the town and onto a quiet road that wound up the mountain past the occasional isolated house and through deep pine forests. At one point, they passed a seated white Buddha under a red canopy. Sometimes, the trees opened out and from the road, especially on the hairpin bends, there was a magnificent view of the whole town with the Himalayas spread out in the distance.

'Is there an army base up here?' she asked the taxi driver.

'In the days of the Raj, there were barracks here and an army camp.' They passed a high brick wall. 'Army camp was there,' the driver said. 'Look up ahead. There is the soldier's memorial.'

At the side of the road was a statue of a Gurkha soldier holding a gun, and behind it a wall with gold writing entitled 'A soldier's prayer'.

Chloe asked the driver to stop beside the memorial. She got out and read the words to herself. *God make me fast and accurate, may my aim be true, and my hand faster than those who want to destroy me. Grant me victory over my foes and those who want to do harm to me and mine.*

Reading the words several times over, and looking at the life-sized statue of the soldier, it made her think about her grandfather, George Harper, and Billy Thomas and the stories of the Burma campaign that Lena had related in her diary.

She wandered to the other side of the road and stared out at the fabulous view – of layer upon layer of mountains fading into the blue, with fluffy white clouds nestling between them. She felt very close to her grandmother at that moment, standing there, in the place where Lena had once gone to work and where she'd met Chloe's grandfather. But, once again, her mind returned to Billy. What had happened to him? Had he survived the war? What had happened between him and Lena? She hoped that the diary would give her the answers.

13

DARJEELING, 1943

TODAY WE SAID farewell to my dear mother and my heart is aching with the knowledge that she is no longer with me. I pray that her soul is on its way to a good place now.

Sita's body was taken into Sunil's house and laid out on a bamboo stretcher that the local men had put together hastily. Lena hardly slept. The grief and guilt were overwhelming. How had she not been there for Ma when she'd needed her most? She kept torturing herself with thoughts of how Sita had given up her life to be near to Lena while she was at school, and she'd welcomed her into her humble home when she needed somewhere to stay.

She'd cared so much for Lena, and yet Lena had hardly given her a thought when disaster struck. Lena supposed it was because her mother had always seemed so capable, such a force of nature, such a survivor. In the back of her mind, Lena must have thought that Sita was indestructible. And yet there she was, lying cold and stiff downstairs in Sunil and Lakshmi's living room. Her big, generous heart and her huge presence gone for ever.

Now, Lakshmi and Lena washed her body with water from a

stream that ran through the valley at the bottom of the market. There was no running water in the taps in the town after the earthquake, and they had to clamber over the piles of stones and rubble and several times they had to make their way down a muddy path to the stream with their buckets.

It felt surreal removing Ma's clothes and bathing her big, soft body. At first, Lena was a little embarrassed. She'd rarely seen her mother naked, she was always very modest. But then Lena reminded herself that Sita was no longer occupying her body and also that she would have approved of what they were doing. She was so devout, and they were following traditional Hindu rituals just as she would have wanted. It felt terrible touching her face that was now blue and purple with the bruising she'd suffered. Looking at her injuries, Lena realised that she must have suffocated to death under that pile of rubble. Lena hoped and prayed fervently that she hadn't been conscious, and that the end had come quickly.

Once they'd washed and dried her body, they dressed Sita in one of Lakshmi's best sarees. All of Sita's own clothes had been buried in the earthquake, but they chose a beautiful white cotton one with gold embroidery. Lena felt a little guilty about that, but Lakshmi was insistent.

It was difficult to ease the cloth under Ma's stiff, heavy frame, but Lakshmi was strong and was able to lift while Lena pushed the saree under Ma's body. They smeared turmeric on her brow as was the tradition. In all that time, they didn't speak. This was partly out of respect for Sita and partly because the whole process was so profound it would have seemed like sacrilege to breathe a word.

When she was dressed, they laid Sita out on the stretcher in the room again, and a procession of neighbours came to view her body. They trooped through the room slowly and respectfully, their heads bowed, some in tears. Some brought rice balls and flowers as offerings to place near Sita's body. All looked sad, shocked and subdued, and Lena realised how much her mother and her big personality had been taken to the heart of this poor but lively community.

She knew that others in the neighbourhood had died in the earthquake too. Sunil had told her that they would all share a funeral and be cremated by the edge of a stream down in the valley. Lena was dreading the rest of the day. How would she get through it without breaking down?

Around noon, a pony cart arrived and the men from the neighbourhood loaded the stretcher carrying Sita's body onto the back of the cart. The driver shook the reins and the pony started off through the group of onlookers. Lena and the others followed on foot and when she glanced behind, she saw that there was a huge crowd surging through the streets behind them. At the edge of town, two other carts joined the procession. They proceeded at a stately pace along the mountainside, and after a while turned off the road onto a track which wound down through the plantations and terraced farmland to a fast-flowing stream in the bottom of the valley.

On a pebbly beach beside the stream, three funeral pyres had been built with logs and kindling. Lena's heart caught with emotion to see them there. It brought home the finality of what had happened. She watched through a veil of tears as the bodies on their bamboo stretchers were carried gently to the pyres and eased onto them. She recognised the families of Sita's neighbour, an old blacksmith, and one of the stallholders from the market. People stood around chanting and praying, their heads bowed. Her heart went out to all those families who were grieving their loved ones, just as she was.

Her eyes scanned the crowd. She didn't know many faces, but her heart did a little jolt of surprise to see an Englishman amongst the mourners. It was Lieutenant Harper, dressed in uniform. He must have heard what had happened and come to pay his respects. He looked up and caught Lena's eye and gave her a nod and a sympathetic smile. What a generous act of compassion it was for him to come to the funeral, Lena thought. He didn't know her mother, so he must have come to show support to Lena herself. She was touched and surprised once again by the man's kindness.

When the prayers were over, the funeral pyres were lit. People stood around watching the flames and smoke rise. Lena could hardly bear to look as the flames licked around Sita's body, quickly engulfing her. She knew it was a Hindu ritual, but it made everything seem so final. Lena would have preferred to bury her body in a churchyard where she could go and visit her, bring her flowers, kneel by the graveside and tell her about her life. But that wasn't to be. Ma was a devout Hindu and that was what she wanted. When the flames died down and her body had been reduced to ash, the men who were to stay there to watch the pyre all day would push the ashes into the fast-flowing river, so they would begin their journey down to the holy river Ganges and Sita's soul would find its next home.

The crowd began to wander back up the hill towards the town. Lena felt Lakshmi's arm through her own, helping her to take each difficult step away from her mother's burning corpse. Somebody spoke to her on her other side.

'My condolences, Miss Chatterjee.'

Lena turned to Lieutenant Harper. 'Thank you for coming. It means a lot to me,' she said.

'It was the least I could do. When I heard your mother had been killed, I came straight away.'

Lena wondered how he had found out, but assumed that everyone had heard that the earthquake had struck the market area and he knew that she lived there. Plus, the fact that Lena hadn't turned up for work that morning. She hadn't given it a single thought.

Lieutenant Harper fell into step beside her and the three of them walked together in silence. There was something comforting in the knowledge that the lieutenant was there by her side at this most difficult time. There was no need for words, it was enough that he'd come and that he was there to walk her back to Darjeeling after one of the saddest hours of her life.

She'd hardly noticed her surroundings on the walk down the hill, but going back up, she realised that it was a beautiful crisp, clear day, the view of the snow-covered peaks against the bright blue sky. *Ma would have loved this view*, Lena thought. Sita had always appreciated the beauty of the hill town that she'd made her home.

After a while, Lieutenant Harper asked, 'Do you have anywhere to stay?'

'My neighbours, Lakshmi here and her husband Sunil, are kindly putting me up.' They spoke in English, which Lakshmi didn't understand. Lena glanced at Lakshmi, not wanting to offend her. 'I have no idea how long I'll be able to stay there, though.'

'I understand. If you want to come and live up at Jalapahar, there will always be a room up at the base for you.'

Lena was touched. 'Thank you. You are very kind. I'll think about it.'

She quickly decided though that she really wouldn't want to live up there. The thought sent chills right through her. She would be isolated and miles from anywhere, with only soldiers to keep her company. She would far prefer to stay in this bustling town that she knew so well, with its markets and shops, and to be amongst familiar people.

When they got back to the centre of town, Lieutenant Harper's driver and jeep were waiting for him.

'Take as much time off work as you need,' he told Lena as he got into the back seat. She thanked him and watched him drive away.

When they arrived back at Lakshmi's house, Lena was astonished to see Joan, Mary and Vicky waiting for her. They were sitting outside the house on a pile of stones that before the earth-quake had been the front wall. Her eyes welled up and she couldn't help bursting into tears when she saw them.

'We're so sad to hear about your mother,' Joan said. 'We heard about it from the watchman at St Catherine's.'

'We wanted to come to the funeral,' Mary put in. 'But Miss Woodcock wouldn't let us miss lessons.'

'But lessons have finished for the day now and we came as soon as we could get away,' Vicky explained.

Lena embraced them all and Lakshmi and Sunil invited them inside, where they drank tea and shared their memories of Sita.

Lena was so pleased to see her friends. She realised that she'd been missing them since she left the school, even though it had only been a few weeks. It was such a comfort to her that they'd come to be with her. They stayed until it got dark, then left to go to supper at the school. They all embraced and vowed to keep in touch and meet again soon.

THIS TERRIBLE DAY is over now and I'm dropping with exhaustion, but wanted to write all this down before I sleep. Before we went upstairs to bed, Sunil found an old photograph of Ma which he put on the little altar in the living room and surrounded it with marigolds. In the photograph, she is smiling her big, generous smile. Just looking at it made fresh tears come to my eyes. We will keep it there for the next ten days or so, which is the Hindu period of mourning. On the thirteenth day, Lakshmi told me that another ceremony will be performed, the 'preta-karma', to release Ma's soul for reincarnation.

The next morning, when she went downstairs, Lakshmi brought her tea and porridge.

'I've made it specially for you, Lena,' she said. 'I know you've been brought up in British ways.'

Lena was touched by her thoughtfulness and sat down to eat

at the low table, although she had little appetite. As she sipped at the porridge, Lakshmi told her that she and Sunil had decided to ask Lena to stay on with them as long as she needed to.

'We have never been blessed with children, sadly. It is good to be able to care for someone, especially Sita's daughter. We both loved her dearly as you know.'

'That's very kind of you, Lakshmi. I would love to stay, but you must allow me to make a contribution to the household.'

At first, Lakshmi shook her head but Lena insisted, knowing that Lakshmi and Sunil didn't have much money.

Lena was touched again and grateful that they had offered. They were kind and generous and it was good to be able to stay in the town after all, especially with people who knew Sita and were mourning her loss just as Lena was.

After breakfast, she headed to the Eden Hospital to find Billy. She'd thought about him on and off all day the previous day, wondering how he was, worrying whether he was safe.

As she made her way to the hospital, she could hear the sound of hammering and sawing. Workmen were already repairing the earthquake damage, which seemed to be confined to the area around the bazaar and the hospital. Only a few buildings had collapsed completely, like Sita's house, but many had some sort of damage – mostly to the roofs, windows or porches.

The road leading up to the hospital was full of cracks and potholes still, so Lena had to tread carefully. Walking that way reminded her of how frightened she'd been when she was trying to get to the hospital and the ground was literally shaking under her feet. How terrified her mother must have been too, alone in her little house as it had tumbled down around her. Once again, Lena was filled with guilt and remorse that she hadn't been there for her. She realised that she would have to live with that feeling for the rest of her days.

When she reached the hospital, the place was a hive of noise and activity, with maintenance workers hard at work repairing the damaged building. She wondered how long it would take them, the damage inside was extensive. She'd assumed that they might need to pull the whole wing down, but it looked as though they were patching it up instead. They would have to replace the staircase and the ceilings upstairs as well as several roof beams, so it was bound to take a long time.

There were no medical staff around, so Lena went to another entrance in the side wing. There was no one on reception either, so she made her way into a ground floor ward. The place was chaos, with doctors and nurses rushing around looking harassed and seemingly double the number of patients on the ward. Some were lying on stretchers or camp beds in between the normal beds. Lena wandered around the ward trying to find Billy. She caught a glimpse of a couple of his former roommates, heavily bandaged and unconscious, still unable to speak, but there was no sign of him at all.

Lena's mind started to run wild, imagining that he'd somehow got injured after she'd left, or that his condition had deteriorated badly since he'd been moved. She stopped one of the nurses and asked her if she knew a Billy Thomas. She shook her head, but asked a doctor who came over to speak to Lena.

'Billy and a couple of the other soldiers were actually moved yesterday to a convalescent home. Their condition was less serious than many of the men here and their beds were needed for gravely ill patients.'

'Oh, I see,' Lena said, relieved.

'The intention is for Billy and the others to rejoin their regiments as soon as they are able.'

'Could you tell me where it is please? I'd like to visit,' her relief now turning to panic.

He scribbled an address on his notepad, tore it out and handed it to Lena.

She didn't recognise the address in Gurungni Road, Connaught Lodge, but she knew it would be too far for her to walk, so she went back towards the centre of town and Chowrasta, where the rickshaw-wallahs squatted on the ground waiting for trade, playing cards and dice. She negotiated a price for them to take her there and back and to wait for half an hour. Half an hour didn't seem very long to spend with Billy, when she'd been aching to see him, but the rickshaw-wallahs wanted double the price to stay any longer.

It took a while to get there. They had to avoid certain streets that the earthquake had made impassable. There was a fair amount of grumbling from the rickshaw-wallahs about the extra distance, but Lena stood firm and refused to pay more.

Connaught Lodge was a big, rambling, mock-Tudor house perched on the edge of the hills, overlooking the Happy Valley tea plantation. It looked as though it had once belonged to a wealthy British family, but now it appeared a bit run-down with peeling paint and overgrown gardens.

A severe-looking matron came to the door and looked Lena up and down. Lena knew instantly what was going through her mind. She was wondering what a Eurasian girl was doing visiting a British soldier.

Lena took no notice and asked in a firm voice if she could see Private Billy Thomas. The matron reluctantly showed her through the corridors, and up the stairs, and there was Billy in a sunny room all of his own with views of the tea terraces.

'It's not visiting time, I'm afraid. Fifteen minutes only, please,' said the woman. Then, with another disapproving look, she closed the door behind Lena.

Billy had been sitting up in an armchair and he got up to greet Lena. She ran over to him and they held each other tight. With the rush of relief at finding him safe, and all the pent-up emotion about her mother, Lena couldn't hold back the tears. Billy just stroked her hair and kissed her forehead and waited until the crying had died down. Then he asked her to sit in his chair and he pulled a stool over and sat down too.

'Tell me what's wrong,' he said.

'My mother is dead. She was killed in the earthquake.'

Billy's face fell. 'I'm so sorry,' he said. 'What a terrible, terrible thing.' He took Lena's hand. 'You must have been with me when it happened. I'm sorry.'

'It was my decision. It didn't cross my mind that Ma might be in danger.'

They sat together and looked out over the plantation with its rows of neat tea bushes and the pickers in their brightly coloured sarees moving between them, and Lena talked about Sita. She told Billy how Sita had given up everything to be near her at school and how guilty she felt because, when Lena was small, she was a little ashamed of her when she came to the school gates to give her Indian sweetmeats. He held Lena's hand and she sobbed with guilt and grief.

'As long as I live, I'll never get over how I treated Ma and how I might have been able to prevent her death if I'd been at home.'

'You mustn't think like that. Nobody could have predicted the earthquake. You mustn't blame yourself.'

'It was because of the fortune teller that I came to help you that night. I knew she was trying to warn me about the earthquake.'

Billy looked at her with those earnest, brown eyes and shook his head. 'You need to stop believing in that fortune teller. If the fortune teller had been trying to warn you about the earthquake,' he said, 'she would have told you to protect your mother too.'

Lena stared at him. It was true. Why hadn't the fortune-teller predicted that Ma would be in danger? And why hadn't Lena thought of that herself? She supposed her mind had been at sixes and sevens and she hadn't been thinking straight.

The precious time with Billy seemed to fly by, and it felt as if she'd only just arrived when the matron was knocking on the door saying that time was up. It seemed so unfair, but Lena wasn't in any mood to protest, she was just glad to have been able to talk to Billy, glad that he was alive and looking better and stronger than she'd ever seen him before.

Billy walked her over to the door. She was sure he would have kissed her had the matron not been there holding the door open impatiently. Lena could see the longing in his eyes – the same longing that she knew was reflected in her own.

'I will come again tomorrow,' she promised.

14

AND NOW I am back at my new home, overlooking the market where there is much activity as the stallholders work to get everything back to normal. From where I sit in the window, I can see people clearing piles of rubble, raking earth over cracks in the ground, hammering nails into stalls and buildings, climbing up roofs on ladders to mend holes in them. With this much activity, all the damage will soon be repaired and the earthquake will fade into memory. But not for me. The pain of losing Ma like that and the guilt I feel at the way she died alone will follow me for the rest of my days.

Chloe put the diary down once again and reflected on the contrast between the deep sadness of Lena's situation and her growing closeness with Billy. It was extraordinary reading this for the first time. She thought she'd known her grandmother very well. She'd always assumed that Lena would have been able to confide in her. It was a bit of a blow that she'd kept all this to herself for the whole of her life.

Although she was keen to read the rest of the diary and find out what had happened, Chloe didn't want to rush through it. She wanted to make sure that she took in and understood every detail, everything her grandmother had gone through during those terrible days after the earthquake and beyond. But for the time being, she wanted to work out the next stage of her own journey. In another day or two, she would have seen most of the things in Darjeeling that she'd come to see, and she was looking forward to moving on to Kathmandu. Her grandmother's descriptions of the mysterious city were fresh in her mind, and she wanted to see if it was still the same. Perhaps there were still fortune tellers near the Kumari Devi's palace. But getting there could be tricky. There was no obvious route and she didn't have access to a light aircraft, as Lena had. She needed to find out how to get there by road.

Chloe headed down to the front desk, where the receptionist greeted her with a smile. She asked him if it was possible to get to Kathmandu by road. He assured her that it was, but that it was quite difficult to travel there overland.

'It is very far,' he said frowning. 'It might be better for you to take a taxi or minibus down to New Jalpaiguri and then fly to Kathmandu. It would be much quicker.'

'I'd far rather go overland. I'd like to see the country while I'm here.'

He raised his eyebrows and looked at her quizzically.

'Have you ever been on an Indian bus, madam?'

Chloe laughed and shook her head.

'Well, I'm afraid it is not an easy experience,' the man acknowledged. 'But if you're quite sure, I will help you.'

He told her that there were no direct buses to Kathmandu and that, as a foreigner, there were only certain places where she would be able to cross the border.

'You will need to get a taxi down to Kakarbhitta on the border. Then from Kakarbhitta you will be able to get a bus to Kathmandu. But it is a long journey even from there. Eight hours at least.'

'It sounds interesting,' Chloe replied, mulling it over in her mind. It might be uncomfortable and a very long journey, but as she'd said, she wanted to be able to see the country she was travelling through, not jet over it at 30,000 feet seeing only clouds and blue sky. 'How will I find a taxi to take me to Kakarbhitta?'

'I can find one for you. We can only recommend certain drivers, though. Some in Darjeeling may not be the safest and we wouldn't suggest them for our guests. So, you have to be careful. When do you want to go? I will fix it up for you if you tell me which day.'

Chloe pondered this. There were still things she hadn't done in Darjeeling. For example, she hadn't visited the Botanical Gardens or the zoo, or walked up Observatory Hill to see the view. There were monasteries and temples she hadn't visited yet. She supposed she could always come back here again. Her heart was pulling her in the direction of Kathmandu and the mountain villages where her grandfather had gone to recruit Gurkhas. She wanted to find out about the fortune teller and she also wanted to walk up to Ghorepani and see if anyone remembered Alisha and her grandfather seventy years on.

'I'll go tomorrow,' she said suddenly, surprising even herself.

'It might be an idea to stay overnight in Kakarbhitta. Then you can get an early bus the next morning up to Kathmandu. That way, you won't be travelling in the dark. There are a couple of hotels there, if you'd like me to book.'

'Thank you,' she said, wondering how she would fare when she was off the beaten track, not relying on the support of the English-speaking staff in a luxury hotel. A thrill of excitement went through her at the thought. This was so good for her, she knew that. Too long she'd been hanging on Fergal's coat tails, stifling her adventurous spirit, and now she was branching out on her own. It was a little frightening, but exhilarating and life-affirming at the same time.

So, that evening, before sunset, following the map in her guidebook, Chloe walked up to Chowrasta and from there found a little pedestrian walkway that took her around the edge of the mountain, past market stalls selling clothes, artwork and trinkets for tourists. After a few hundred yards, a flight of stone steps branched off the walkway with a sign pointing to Observatory Hill and the Makhani Temple. Following a procession of local people, she began to walk up the steps and after a little way passed under the entrance arch of a temple. Some bells dangled above her, and she noticed that all the locals were ringing them as they went through the arch, so she did the same, feeling a little self-conscious.

An old man next to her paused and gave her a crooked-toothed smile. 'It brings good luck to ring the Makhani Temple Bell,' he said.

She thanked him and carried on along the narrow walkway which climbed steadily upwards, winding round the hillside beside tall pine trees. Sometimes it went very close to houses that seemed to perch on the edge of the rocks, sometimes even through people's gardens. As she got higher, Chloe caught the tinkle of bells on the air coming from a temple on top of the hill. She passed through a covered market, then carried on climbing, under yet more elaborate temple archways. Thousands of multi-coloured prayer flags were wound round the trees, flapping in the breeze.

At the top, Chloe reached the Makhani Temple, and she stopped to admire her surroundings, bowled over by the bright colours all around. There were multiple small prayer halls covering the top of the hill, their walls painted in orange, red and yellow. These buildings were surrounded by a circular wall into which were embedded hundreds of prayer bells. Worshippers were walking around slowly, turning each bell, each one making a different-pitched ring, so there was a cacophony of discordant sound.

Feeling a little shy, but very curious, Chloe stepped inside the temple. There was a strong smell of incense on the air. People were kneeling and making offerings to the statues of gods, which

were garlanded with flowers; others were bowing and kissing
images of gods on the walls. Chloe wandered around, awestruck
by the mystical atmosphere. At one point, she watched a sturdily
built Indian lady in a beautifully embroidered red saree, kneel
and offer a garland of marigolds to a statue of Ganesh, the
elephant god. Chloe caught her breath. Here, in this vibrant
temple, just as she had in the bazaar the day before, she caught
something of the immortal spirit of Sita, her great-grandmother.
Colourful and loud and bursting with joy. Perhaps Sita had
walked up here to make offerings and pray to the gods too?

Chloe headed along another walkway, away from the temple,
and found a viewing point where people were gathered to see the
sunset. She stood amongst the crowd and watched the display of
reds, pinks and golds light up the sky and illuminate the far-off
peaks, as the sun descended swiftly behind the Himalayas.
Watching it made her think of her grandmother and how she
must have witnessed thousands of sunsets just like that, how they
must have shaped her young mind, but how she kept all the
beauty inside, never sharing it with anyone once she left her
home country.

15

DARJEELING, 2015

When Chloe got back to the hotel, she ordered a snack to be brought to the room, then she settled down in the armchair and, nibbling samosas and pakoras and sipping Indian beer, she picked up Lena's diary again. The next entry was dated 16th October, 1943.

I've been to see Billy every day since that first visit to the convalescent home. The matron always gives me that same appraising, disapproving look when she opens the door, but she lets me in anyway. She has no choice really as I am always careful to go at visiting time.

Lena loved the fact that Billy's eyes lit up when he saw her. He would get up from his chair and come over to greet her with a kiss. It worried her a little how agile on his feet he was getting, it surely meant he might soon have to leave Darjeeling as the doctor had implied.

They would sit down opposite each other in the window overlooking the mountains and hold hands, asking each other about how their days had been going and discussing everything under the sun. Conversation always flowed so easily and there was never any awkwardness between them. Sometimes Billy talked about his family, sometimes about England, sometimes about his time in India. He spoke about the war less often. Lena wondered if he thought that hearing about the battles he'd fought in would worry her and sour the atmosphere, or perhaps it troubled him to speak about it. Either way, since he'd described how he got injured, he hadn't mentioned the Burma campaign.

Sometimes, they talked about the famine in Bengal Province, although it had been eclipsed slightly by the earthquake. Lena had read that things were gradually improving in Calcutta and that not so many people were dying each day, although the fact that anyone at all was dying of hunger in a country with such rich natural resources, Billy maintained, was an outrage. He still blamed the British government for the famine and his face clouded over with anger whenever the subject came up.

The more Lena got to know Billy, the more they seemed to have in common. Their views on almost every subject were aligned and even where they didn't agree completely on something, they were both happy to accept the other's point of view. She had never met anyone with quite such an equable and sunny nature as Billy.

The first time she felt any sort of awkwardness with him was the time that he took her hand, leaned towards her, looked into her eyes and said, 'You know I'm in love with you, don't you? Do you... well, is there any chance that you might feel the same?'

At first, Lena couldn't look him in the eye because her cheeks were flaming. She felt so self-conscious about revealing how she felt. But then she remembered that Billy could be sent back to the front at any time. If that happened, she knew she would be devastated if she'd not told him how she felt. She forced herself to lift her head and look into his eyes. 'I'm falling in love with you too, Billy.'

He kissed her on the lips then. A long, lingering kiss that sent shivers right through her.

They only stopped because there was a knock on the door. They broke apart and Lena jumped up from the chair just as the matron opened the door. Her eyebrows shot up and she gave Lena a scandalised look. She must have seen how bright Lena's eyes and cheeks were and put two and two together.

Later as she walked home, Lena went over and over what had happened between them, the words they had spoken, the magical kiss they had shared. A feeling of well-being filled her heart.

But when she got home, there was a note waiting for her from Lieutenant Harper.

My dear Miss Chatterjee,

I hope you are as well as can be expected given your recent sad loss. You are welcome to take as much time off work as you need, but I thought I would let you know that I will be setting off on another recruiting trip to Nepal tomorrow. If you would like to accompany me, I would really value your presence. As well as spending time in Kathmandu, I will be travelling to Pokhara and up into the hills again.

Please think it over. I will send my driver along to your house at ten o'clock tomorrow morning. If you don't feel able to come, do send a messenger along to the base to let me know.

Lieutenant George Harper

The note sent Lena into a flutter of confusion. She would love to go to Nepal again – in fact, if she went to Kathmandu, she would certainly go and speak to the fortune teller to let her know what happened and to ask her why she didn't warn her of the danger her mother was in.

She knew it would do her good to get out of the house after all those days of mourning and to go to Nepal again would be marvellous. However, she was also conscious that Billy had limited time left before he was returned to his regiment and she wanted to spend as much time with him as she could. She felt very torn, but she made a decision. She would up early and go and knock on the door and plead with the matron. Perhaps she wouldn't be on duty if Lena went early enough, but Lena didn't think she could bear to leave without seeing Billy one more time.

So, very early the next morning, she was knocking on the

door of the convalescent home. The kind old night porter let her in for a few rupees, and she spent a wonderful but tearful few minutes with Billy. Breathlessly, she told him that she was going away for a few days, but that she'd be back soon.

'I love you, Billy. I'll think about you all the time.'

'I love you too. Make sure you come and see me as soon as you get back.'

They kissed passionately again but were conscious that the matron would be on duty within minutes and that they didn't have long. Indeed, when she left the building, Lena saw the matron getting out of a rickshaw. As luck would have it, the woman didn't see Lena as she was busy haggling with her rickshaw-wallahs and Lena managed to slip past when her head was turned.

LENA ARRIVED in Kathmandu on 17th October and found herself in the same cheerless room in the barracks. Her heart felt full of love for Billy and she was already missing him.

On the flight over, Lieutenant Harper had explained that the British needed to recruit more Gurkhas. They were completely loyal and trustworthy soldiers, where some soldiers in the British Indian Army had been defecting to the Indian National Army and fighting with the Japanese against British troops.

'This is the worst type of betrayal,' Lieutenant Harper had said, worry furrowing his brow. 'It's all the more dangerous because when they go over to the Japs, they go with inside knowledge about Allied plans. The Japs have been able to use that to their advantage.'

When they arrived on the base at Kathmandu, as before, Lieutenant Harper told Lena that he needed to see the local colonel again and that her afternoon was free to spend as she wished. Leaving behind the austere barracks, the driver drove her into the city in the Land Rover and dropped her near Durbar Square. This time, she had no hesitation about where she was going.

She hurried past the splendid façade of Kumari Devi's palace and looked around for the shoeshine boy. There he was hard at work on the steps of a temple, polishing a man's shoes. Lena didn't want to disturb him, and she remembered the route through the alleys and backstreets behind the square to the fortune teller's place.

When she reached the house, Lena hesitated outside. Now that she was there, she was besieged by nerves. But she took a deep breath and walked inside the darkened room. There was the fortune teller and her child sitting in the same position and dressed exactly the same as before. It was almost as if they hadn't moved since she'd left.

The woman beckoned Lena forward and, looking at her with those intense, kohl-rimmed eyes, she said, 'I remember you.'

Lena sat down in front of her, took a deep breath and started to speak. But as soon as she did, her voice wobbled and she couldn't hold back the tears. She told the fortune teller all about the earthquake and about how she'd rushed to help Billy, thinking of nothing else, and how her mother had perished.

'Why didn't you warn me about the danger my mother was in?' she asked, sobbing. 'I could have helped her. I could have saved her.'

The woman looked confused. 'Let me look at your hand again,' she said. She held Lena's hand close to the candle and examined it for a long time. Then she shook her head and looked into Lena's eyes again in her direct, searching way. 'The connection with your friend is very strong. So strong that it has displaced everything else around it. Because of that I didn't see the danger your mother faced. But looking at your palm now, I can see that it wasn't the earthquake that I was warning you about.'

Lena stared at her, open mouthed. 'Not the earthquake?' she murmured.

'No, child. It was something else completely. Some other form of danger. Danger that is still present, I'm afraid. I can see it there still.'

'But what is it?' Lena asked, incredulous.

'It is something that hasn't yet come to pass, my child.' She peered at Lena's hand for a long time. 'All I can say is that it has something to do with your friend… and someone else. Someone trusted by your friend.'

Lena stared at her, barely understanding. It was hard to comprehend that the woman hadn't been warning her about the earthquake but about something else. Lena asked her again and again what she meant, but the fortune teller shook her head.

'I cannot tell you exactly what it is because I cannot see it fully. All I know is that that it hovers like a dark cloud around you.'

Lena left the fortune-teller's house puzzled and distraught, her mind full of fresh fears. She ran back through Durbar Square and, in her distress, tripped on a paving stone. She must have scraped her shoe because the little leather bow on the left shoe was missing when she got back to the base. She asked in the canteen kitchen for some scissors and cut the one on the right shoe off to match it. For some reason, this felt like a bad omen, on top of everything else.

16

WHAT IS the danger that Billy will be facing in the not-too-distant future? It must be related to his return to the front line. I need to get back and warn him. If I write to him, it is unlikely that the post would get there before me. So, I must sit tight and accompany Lieutenant Harper on this trip and hope and pray that I'm not too late to save Billy from this fresh threat to his wellbeing, or perhaps even his life.

Chloe closed the diary. She wanted to read on, but it was getting late and she had an early start in the morning. The fresh revelations of the fortune teller had been a surprise to her. Like Lena, she had assumed that the fortune teller's prophesy had related to the earthquake. If it hadn't, what was it really about?

With a sigh, she slipped the diary into her backpack, which was packed and ready for the morning. Then, with images of the fortune teller in a smoky, incense-filled booth and her mysterious prophesy in her mind, she laid down and waited for sleep to overcome her.

∽

A TAXI DRIVER came to collect Chloe from the hotel in a four-wheel drive the next morning. She paid her bill and said goodbye to the staff, thanking them for having looked after her so well. Then she climbed into the front next to the driver. He nodded and smiled amicably but indicated that he spoke little English.

They set off through the narrow, bustling streets of Darjeeling and as the taxi edged its way between shoppers and pedestrians, Chloe felt a wave of nostalgia that she was leaving this pretty, vibrant town behind and striking out into the unknown. She'd learned so much about Lena and her painful early years, about Sita and her life of poverty and devotion which had ended so tragically. She was glad to have seen the place where her grandmother had grown up. She'd been stunned by the majestic setting of the town too. It oozed charm and history and its inhabitants had shown her nothing but kindness and hospitality. She'd felt an incredible connection with Lena and Sita here, far greater than she'd felt in Kolkata. She would definitely return, she promised herself, but she needed to get to Nepal and continue her quest.

When they drove past Darjeeling station, a real steam train sat puffing out smoke and steam while tourists clambered aboard its blue, wooden carriages. As they headed out of the town, Chloe peered up at a Buddhist temple with white and golden stupas rising above the road, where a huge, seated Buddha gazed out over the hills, then marvelled at a Tibetan temple elaborately decorated and painted every colour of the rainbow. Layer upon layer of houses rose steeply up from the road which ran on beside the railway.

Soon, they were passing through the little town of Kurseong, its narrow main street lined with tall, brightly painted shophouses with shoppers spilling out over the road. Then onto Ghoom, built in tiered layers that ran up and down the mountainside. At one point, Chloe cried out in surprise when she saw a monkey swinging on an electric cable above the road. The driver shook his head and laughed.

Having left the towns behind them, they drove on through forests, and neat, green tea plantations. The road was descending steeply now through a series of tight hairpin bends. Mist was shrouding the valley, obscuring the distant mountains. The driver put on the windscreen wipers and they carried on their descent through jungles and wild countryside. The road was so narrow in places that they had to squeeze right over to pass lorries and buses coming in the other direction. Each time they pulled over, Chloe had to hold her breath and closed her eyes to avoid looking down the precipitous drop right beside her.

After an hour and a half or so they had left the mountains behind, the road straightened out and they were travelling across the plain towards Siliguri. Still, the railway ran beside the road and Chloe remembered looking out at this road and its traffic jams on the way up to Darjeeling only a few days before. The rest of the journey, on a flat, busy dual carriageway, to Kakarbhitta was less fascinating than the first part. They passed towns, factories and warehouses and the heavy traffic moved quickly. Eventually, they crossed a wide river over a long bridge and passed under an elaborate gateway to reach the town of Kakarbhitta.

'This is the border town,' the driver said, joining a line of heavy lorries, buses and motor rickshaws queuing for the border. 'I take you through to your hotel.'

They queued for a long time to reach the border post, where stony-faced guards checked their papers, then they turned off the main road and went through a maze of narrow backstreets to reach the Jasmine Hotel where Chloe was booked in for the night. She got out, paid the driver and felt a wave of anxiety as she watched him drive away. She was on her own now, in a remote, inhospitable place where there seemed to be no tourists and next to no tourist facilities either.

The reception area of the hotel was as unpromising as Chloe

had feared from the exterior, but the man on the desk was friendly enough and spoke reasonable English. A porter carried her luggage up to her room on the second floor. He hovered around for a tip, so she handed him a few rupees. Then she asked him if there was any room service at the hotel. It was a silly question in a place like this and his lips twitched in amusement.

'No, madam. No food in this hotel. There are restaurants in the town, though. We can give you a map on reception. Motor rickshaw will take you there.'

When he'd gone, Chloe examined the room, which was a little gloomy, with pine-clad walls, brown polyester curtains and a purple bedspread. In the bathroom, with its brown tiles and old-fashioned bathroom suite, the shower dripped erratically. She sat down on the bed feeling dispirited. This place, although relatively clean and well-run, lacked the luxury and charm of the Elgin Hotel in Darjeeling. Still, it was only for one night. Tomorrow she would be in Kathmandu.

She had a couple of hours to kill before dinner, so she took Lena's diary out of her backpack, turned to the entry dated October 21st 943 and started reading.

I haven't been able to write in this journal for a few days. Lieutenant Harper and I were very busy in Kathmandu with the same recruitment activities that we went through a few weeks ago. There weren't quite as many recruits this time, and I wondered if the Kathmandu valley is finally running out of young men after so much recruitment for the Gurkha regiments fighting on the Burma front in recent months.

IN THE EVENINGS, the two of them ate in the same little restaurant that the Lieutenant had taken Lena to before, then returned to the base exhausted after their busy days.

Lena felt she knew Lieutenant Harper quite well now and

found it easy to relax in his company. One evening, during the meal, he asked her about her mother, so she told him something of Sita's story and a little about her own schooldays. He looked very perturbed to hear about her experiences at St Catherine's.

'Such a shocking story,' he said, frowning deeply. 'Although British rule has a lot to commend it, it has its dark side too.' After a pause, he asked, 'And what about your father? Does he keep in touch?'

Lena shook her head. 'I have never had a letter or word from my father in my entire life. Ma never even told me his name! All I know is that he was an army officer and that he paid my school fees. But since I left school, there is no longer even that connection. Frankly, I've never had any interest in finding him or finding out any more about him and that hasn't changed even though Ma has passed away.'

'It all sounds very sad,' the lieutenant remarked.

'Not all of it,' Lena replied, not wanting the lieutenant to feel sorry for her. 'Perhaps I've given you the wrong impression. Despite the harsh regime at St Catherine's, I made very good friends there, and Ma was always around.'

She thought again wistfully about when she was young and foolish and had rejected Sita's love for a time, but she didn't want to mention that to Lieutenant Harper. Then, having talked so much about herself, she asked him to tell her about his home.

'Oh, there's really not much to tell,' he said.

It turned out that Lieutenant Harper's father had been in the Indian Army too, so his early years had been spent in India on a British cantonment, near Bombay.

'But I was packed off to boarding school in England at a very early age. It was a tough time. I didn't see my parents for several years. I missed them and I missed India too.'

'Did you not come back for the holidays?' Lena asked, surprised.

'No. I spent all my holidays with an elderly aunt. When I'd

finished school, I joined the army myself and went to Sandhurst to train as an officer. After that I came back out to India to join the regiment. I hadn't been in the army long before the war came along.'

Lena was struck by the parallels in their stories. They'd both been sent away to school at an early age; both had suffered homesickness and trauma. Lieutenant Harper's was probably worse than her own, she reflected, because he'd had to leave his family behind and travel halfway across the world, whereas her own mother had lived in the same town and was a regular presence at the school gate, even though she hadn't always welcomed that presence in the early days.

Given they were sharing confidences, Lena felt bold enough to ask Lieutenant Harper about Alisha.

'We want to marry,' he said, sadness entering his eyes, 'but I'm worried that the army will never give permission.'

'What will you do?' she asked, with feeling. How terrible it would be for the lieutenant, if this happiness were denied him.

'I've come to the conclusion that I'll have to leave the army. I couldn't bring myself to while the war is on, but I plan to afterwards if there is no other way for us to be together. You know I'm to be a father, don't you?' he asked.

'I had guessed,' Lena said.

'I'm so looking forward to it.' His eyes brimmed with pleasure and pride. Then he turned to Lena. 'And what about you? Do you have anyone special?'

The question took Lena by surprise. She stared down at her tarka dhal, unable to meet his eyes.

'You do, don't you?' he asked, teasing her a little.

Eventually, her embarrassment dissipated. 'Well, there is someone actually. Someone I care deeply for. His name is Billy Thomas. He's a soldier and I've been visiting him in hospital in Darjeeling. I've been to see him many times, sparked off by that first visit that you sent me on.'

'I had no idea it would have had such deep consequences,' Lieutenant Harper said, smiling. 'I'm happy for you. You deserve to find happiness, just as I have with Alisha.'

The rest of the meal passed in companionable ease, before Lena returned to the solitude of the barracks. The next day they would travel by Land Rover to Pokhara and from there on into the mountains by pony. Lena knew Lieutenant Harper couldn't wait to get to Ghorepani to see Alisha, even though he was being very professional about the trip and trying not to let his excitement show too much.

THREE DAYS LATER, Lena was back in the tiny bedroom with its partitioned wooden walls in the village house in Ghorepani, but this time with a heavy heart. The last few days had been very busy. First there had been the trip from Kathmandu to Pokhara by Land Rover with its usual hold-ups and delays, the recruitment at the base there, then the journey up into the hills, again by pony, stopping off in the same villages to recruit more local boys.

When they had reached Ghorepani though, Lena sensed something was wrong as soon as they'd started to ride through the narrow village streets. There was a subdued atmosphere all around. No one was sitting outside on their porches, and the people they did encounter, who before had rushed out to greet them waving and smiling, had hurried into their houses or looked away as they rode through.

At the guest house, the old woman came out of the front door and immediately cast her eyes to the ground. Lieutenant Harper jumped off his pony and walked over to speak to her. Lena couldn't hear what they were saying, but when the woman had spoken a couple of sentences, Lieutenant Harper sat down heavily on a chair in front of her house, his shoulders heaving.

Lena got down from her pony and ran over to him. His face was ashen. He looked haggard, with tragedy etched in every line of his face. Tears were running down his cheeks, and he was sobbing quietly. Lena looked at the old woman in despair, but she shrugged. With the language barrier, she couldn't tell Lena anything. At last, when the lieutenant was finally able to speak, he swallowed hard and told Lena stumblingly that there was some terrible news about Alisha. She had contracted diphtheria a fortnight ago, had gone downhill quickly and had died only days before.

Shock washed through Lena at his words and tears sprang to her own eyes. She couldn't believe that that vibrant, beautiful young woman, so full of love and life, had been struck down so suddenly, that she and her unborn baby were gone from the world. She felt so bad for Lieutenant Harper. He had lost his love and his child. What a heavy blow to bear, one that many would never recover from. Lena had no idea what to do, but instinctively she put her arm around him and held him while he cried his heart out. After a time, he took a deep breath and got to his feet.

'I must go up to Alisha's house. I need to see her parents.'

Lena felt very sad watching him leave and trudge up the hill towards Alisha's family home. He looked so alone and so beaten, his shoulders drooping, his head bowed. Some boys came to take the ponies away to graze and Lena gathered her things together and went upstairs. There, she washed in the bowl of water that the old woman, she now knew was called Hema, had put out for her and got changed out of her riding clothes. She pushed the shutters aside and watched a train of pack ponies with their loads pass along the village street.

Life goes on, she thought. Despite the tragedy of the death of a young woman, the life of that village community felt little changed. Lena thought about Alisha and about Sita too. They must have died within weeks of each other. It was a tragedy for both. But at least Sita had had a longer life and hadn't been cut down in her youth like Alisha when such a bright future lay ahead.

With this fresh sadness to bear, Lena's mind kept returning to Billy and the fortune-teller's words. She knew her place was there with Lieutenant Harper, to help him with the work and support him through those dark days, but she longed to see Billy again, to warn him of the fresh danger that hovered over him like a dark cloud.

Lieutenant Harper came back an hour or so later, his eyes full of pain. Lena went to join him and Hema brought them tea. They sat outside looking at the mountains, not saying much. The lieutenant told Lena that in accordance with Buddhist tradition, Alisha had been carried down the mountain to the stream in the valley and cremated on a funeral pyre the day after she'd died.

'I'm going to go down there and spend some time in that place to think of her.'

'Would you like me to come with you?' Lena asked, but he shook his head.

'I need to do this alone.'

Lena watched him go, feeling helpless.

IT IS GETTING LATE NOW. Hema has prepared our supper and is keeping it warm, but there is no sign of Lieutenant Harper. The sun has started to go down over the mountains, the snow-capped peaks of the Annapurnas are tinged with pink and orange. It won't be long until it's completely dark. How will Lieutenant Harper find his way back alone? He has no torch. If he doesn't come back soon, I will need to try to make the village men understand that he is lost and persuade them to go out with torches to look for him.

Chloe was deeply saddened by Alisha's death. Her poor grandfather! What a terrible loss he'd suffered. His baby had never been born, and he'd never realised his dream of marrying

Alisha. Prior to reading the diary, Chloe had had no idea what he'd gone through in his youth and what was carefully hidden behind that buttoned-up exterior. She'd always thought her grandmother and grandfather were an indivisible unit. She'd never considered that there might have been other loves in their lives before, but she knew now that both Alisha and Billy were fundamental to their stories.

While she wished to continue reading, the light was fading outside the hotel window. It was time to venture out to find some food. She went downstairs. The man on reception gave her a map of the town and marked on it with a cross where there was a good restaurant beside the river.

'It is only ten minutes' walk, madam,' the man said. 'But be sure to get a motor rickshaw back afterwards. Kakarbhitta is a border town, madam,' he added, shaking his head. 'Many strangers here. It may not be safe.'

She thanked the man, left the hotel and followed the map through the backstreets of the little town towards the wide Mechi river. There were few people about, but because there was still light in the sky, Chloe didn't feel intimidated.

The restaurant was set behind a tall red wall, and she entered through an archway. As she wandered around, she saw that the tables were set in booths outdoors, sheltered by bamboo screens, overlooking the lazy waters of the river. Waiters rushed to and from the indoor kitchen, but there was also an outdoor barbeque from which delicious smells were emanating.

Chloe felt a little self-conscious being a single, western woman in this place where most of the tables were filled with groups of noisy locals. The waiter found her a table with a good view over the river and the flooded paddy fields in which the setting sun shimmered reds and golds. She settled herself down. There was only one other lone diner, she noticed, a young Nepalese man fashionably dressed, who looked a little out of place himself, she thought – far too sophisticated for the rustic setting.

She ordered some momos, delicious Tibetan pastries which she'd discovered in Darjeeling, a chicken curry and a local beer. She sipped the beer and ate her food watching the sun go down over the wide river and the flat, waterlogged paddies in the valley below. She wished she'd brought Lena's diary along, because without anyone to talk to, she ate her meal far too quickly. When she'd paid the bill, she asked the waiter if it was possible to call a taxi. He told her that there would be some waiting outside the gate and she could agree a fare back to the hotel.

Sure enough, there were a few motor rickshaws lined up outside the restaurant waiting for customers. The drivers were hanging about under the trees smoking and chatting. One left the crowd and approached her. His clothes were dirty and a cigarette hung from the corner of his mouth.

'Where you going to?' he asked, peering at her.

'Jasmine Hotel,' she said. 'How much?'

'Three hundred rupees,' he replied.

Chloe did a swift mental calculation and worked out that was the equivalent of about two pounds. It seemed very cheap, so she agreed and got into the back of the rickshaw.

The man started the engine and revved the throttle. Chloe was perturbed to see that he then took a bottle of whisky from under the steering wheel and took a long swig. She was about to jump out and find another driver to take her, but before she'd had time to do that, he had set off, screaming down the road, the engine roaring. At the end of the road, he took the turning at breakneck speed, and sped down the next road, going far too close to other vehicles, people and animals. Chloe hung on for dear life, wishing she hadn't got into this particular rickshaw. She cursed under her breath, hoping that he would take her straight back to the hotel.

She heaved a sigh of relief when they turned into the road

where the Jasmine hotel was. The rickshaw accelerated down the street and squealed to a halt outside the front door. Chloe jumped out. The man looked at her with bloodshot eyes and said, 'Three thousand rupees.'

Chloe's mouth dropped open. 'We agreed three hundred.'

The man laughed and banged his hand on his dashboard. 'Three hundred too cheap. You pay three thousand. It is far.'

'It isn't far, and we agreed three hundred.' She felt her voice wobble but tried to look him straight in the eye. She took three hundred rupees out of her wallet and held them out. Instead of taking them, he got out of the vehicle and came up to her. He put his face close to hers and she could smell whisky and cigarette smoke on his breath.

'Pay me three thousand,' he snarled. 'You can afford it. Otherwise, I make big trouble for you.'

She carried on holding out the three hundred, her hand shaking now, but he wouldn't take it.

Just then, another rickshaw pulled up behind and a man got out. She recognised him as the young Nepalese man who'd been eating at the restaurant. He paid his fare, then came up to her.

'Is everything all right?'

Chloe was near to tears now. 'He's saying I owe him three thousand, but we agreed three hundred.'

The young man immediately took charge. He stepped forward and had a swift, angry exchange with the driver who got straight back into the rickshaw and drove away quickly.

'Thank you!' Chloe said as the sound of the high-pitched engine died away. 'He didn't even take the three hundred.'

The young man looked at her and frowned. 'You should be more careful, miss. That man's a known cheat. He gives the other rickshaw drivers round here a bad name.'

Despite the fact that he'd just defused a difficult situation and saved her from trouble, Chloe felt irritated by his words. 'How could I have been more careful?'

'Well, you can tell by looking at him that he's a drunk. You shouldn't have got into the vehicle with him to start with.'

She stared at him. 'I don't see how I could have known that, but thank you for helping. Goodnight.'

Chloe went inside the hotel and started up the stairs. As she turned a bend in the staircase, she saw the front door open and the young man enter the lobby. He must be a guest here too. She hoped she wouldn't see him at breakfast, after their prickly exchange and the upsetting incident with the driver, she just wanted to put the whole thing behind her.

17

GHOREPANI, 1943

THE VILLAGE MEN found Lieutenant Harper asleep next to what remained of Alisha's funeral-pyre, beside the fast-flowing stream in the valley bottom where, a day or two before, her ashes had washed away. I wanted to go with them, but they wouldn't allow me to. They said there weren't enough lamps to go round, that I didn't know the path, and that it would be dangerous for me. I watched them set off at midnight down the street with their sticks, pegs and ropes, in case they had to climb. The light from their oil lamps cast eerie, flickering shadows as they moved between the village buildings.

THE WAIT WAS INTOLERABLE. Lena sat outside Hema's house watching for the men to return, growing colder and colder by the minute. The air from the peaks was sharp and cold and stars studded the velvet sky above. Hema brought her a blanket, then, after a time, came to beckon her indoors. She wanted her to eat the meal of dal baht that she'd prepared. Lena didn't really want to eat without Lieutenant Harper there, her stomach was churning with anxiety for his safety, but out of respect for the old lady, she sat down at the table. Hema brought the food on chipped china plates, smiles creasing her nut-brown face, and once Lena had started to eat, she realised that she was actually ravenous. She hadn't eaten properly since breakfast time, and she devoured everything– delicious potato curry, greens, rice and dhal sauce.

Afterwards, she sat in the smoky living room, by the light of candles, and waited for the men to return. She must have dropped off to sleep in the chair because when she next checked her watch it was past two o'clock in the morning. There were noises outside, which must have woken her, because when she looked out of the window, she could see the lamps bobbing up the road towards the house. Her heart lifted with hope and she rushed outside.

Lieutenant Harper was walking between two of the young village men, a blanket draped around his shoulders. The headman brought him into the house, while the others waited outside. Lieutenant Harper sat down at the table and Lena sat opposite him. His face was deathly pale and pinched with the cold night air. He didn't speak and he hardly looked at her, he was so caught up in his own thoughts.

The old man spoke to Hema rapidly in the language of the hills, giving her instructions. She returned with a large earthenware pot which she put in front of Lieutenant Harper. From the yeasty smell, Lena gathered that it was the local brew.

Absently, Lieutenant Harper lifted the pot and took a couple of sips, then Hema went to the oven and brought his food to the table. He took a few spoonsful of curry, then pushed it away, but seemed content to carry on sipping the beer. When he'd finished the pot, Hema brought him another one.

'Are you all right, Lieutenant Harper?' Lena asked tentatively.

He looked at her vacantly, his eyes swimming, and she could see that the brew must be incredibly potent. 'I'm fine thank you,' his voice was slurred. 'Just very tired.'

Hema made a bed for him in the corner of the kitchen, piled up with blankets and goatskins, and when he slumped forward on the table, Lena and Hema went either side of him and half-carried him over to the mat. He collapsed down on it and they covered him with the skins. Hema stoked up the fire. Then they left him there, snoring gently, and went upstairs to bed.

In the morning, Lena awoke when the sun came up over the mountain and the village cocks started crowing. She pulled on her riding clothes and crept downstairs to check on Lieutenant Harper. To her astonishment, he was already sitting at the table eating porridge and Hema was hovering over him, bringing sugar and plying him with cups of tea.

Lena sat down opposite him. She noticed that he was clean-shaven and his eyes bright and clear as if he hadn't taken alcohol in days. He smiled at her, but through his smile she saw the deep sadness in his heart.

'I'm so sorry for last night,' he said briskly. 'Going off like that. It won't happen again.'

'Please don't apologise, Lieutenant Harper,' she replied. 'I understand what you must be feeling.'

'Thank you. But now, we're going to get straight on with the business of recruiting. Are you ready to help me get started?'

'Of course...' Lena replied frowning. She was concerned about his reaction. It seemed to her that he was trying to suppress his grief and carry on as if everything was normal. She was sure that wasn't the best way to deal with it but didn't feel able to say so to him.

They spent the rest of the day speaking to new recruits and taking down their details. As in Kathmandu and Pokhara and the other villages, there weren't as many as last time. Perhaps the village elders were trying to stop them joining up, afraid that the villages wouldn't survive without the strong, young men, or perhaps people knew that a big push was to be made on the Burma front and they didn't want to send their young men to face such a battle. Either way, the supply of recruits for the Gurkha regiments had definitely tailed off.

At the end of the day, Lieutenant Harper told Lena that they would set off back to Pokhara first thing in the morning and from there drive straight back to Kathmandu. Lena knew that Lieutenant Harper would find it hard to leave the village behind, but she was anxious to get back to Darjeeling, to see Billy again and tell him about what the fortune teller had to say.

A FEW DAYS LATER, they were back in Kathmandu having been driven straight back to the base from the end of the unmade road when they'd arrived there by pony. Lena was exhausted having awoken just after dawn in a tiny guest house in one of the remote hill villages and having travelled a very long way that day. It felt as though the Gurkha base in Kathmandu was a very different world from that simple village in the hills, with its ancient, timeless ways.

That evening, Lieutenant Harper didn't offer to take her to their usual restaurant.

'I'm sorry, Miss Chatterjee, but I really need to turn in and get some sleep. I'm not going to have supper this evening.'

So, Lena went along to the canteen alone for a dismal meal of tasteless stew and boiled potatoes. She was worried about the lieutenant. Despite the brave face he had put on when he was talking to the young recruits in Ghorepani, as soon as it was over and he was able to relax, his face had taken on that same exhausted, haggard look that it had when he'd first heard of Alisha's death. Lena wanted to speak to him, but there had been very little opportunity. On the drive from Pokhara she'd asked him several times if he was all right and had made it clear that if there was anything she could do to help him, to please let him know. That was all she could do. Just be there to offer support. It was what he had done so recently himself when Ma had died. Lena's concern was that Lieutenant Harper was too proud to ask for help of any kind.

Lena and Lieutenant Harper flew back to Darjeeling on 28th October. The weather was bad on the flight back. Mist had descended over the mountains and there were no views at all. It was turbulent too, the little plane being rocked and buffeted by high winds, so Lena was very glad when they landed safely on the small airstrip near the army base.

Lakshmi greeted her warmly when she arrived back at the house. She made pakoras for lunch and took Lena's clothes from her.

'I will take them to the dhobi for you,' she said, gathering them up. 'Oh, your friends called while you were away. One of them left a note.'

She handed an envelope to Lena. She ripped it open and saw that it was written in Vicky's familiar scrawl.

Dearest Lena,

I've finally found a way out of St Catherine's! I came round to say goodbye, but as you're away am leaving this with your kind landlady.

I have some wonderful news. I've signed up for the Women's Auxiliary Service, Burma, known as the Wasbies. I saw an advert in the newspaper and applied on the off chance, and was accepted! I'm about to set off for their headquarters in Shillong for my initial training. I will then be sent to Burma where the Wasbies operate mobile canteens for the front-line troops, serving mainly tea and cake, I think. It is a great morale booster for the men apparently. I can't wait to go!

By the way, they are always looking for new recruits. You should really consider it if you have nothing tying you to Darjeeling.

Do write to me in Shillong, c/o the Wasbie HQ.

All my love,

Vicky

Lena read the letter with mixed feelings. She was pleased and proud of Vicky for having the strength and initiative to break away from St Catherine's, to do something so courageous and selfless for the war effort. But she couldn't help admitting to a little tinge of envy reading her letter. Although the trips to Nepal had been fascinating and she was sure the recruiting she'd helped with had been useful for the war effort, the weeks pushing paper in the office in the base had made her feel restless and as though she should be doing more. Vicky's suggestion was food for thought. But, at that moment, she had something more pressing to think about – a visit to Billy.

When she arrived at the convalescent home, the matron opened the door. She gave Lena her usual scornful, disdainful look.

'Could I see Private Thomas please?' Lena asked.

'I'm afraid he's no longer in residence here.' The matron's eyes gleamed triumphantly.

Lena's mouth dropped open. She couldn't take in what the woman was saying. 'I'm sorry. I don't understand.'

'He left, I'm afraid. Two days ago. To rejoin his regiment at the front. An officer came to collect him and some other soldiers who've been convalescing here in Darjeeling. They went off in an army truck.'

Lena was devastated, but she couldn't possibly let the old battle-axe see her cry. 'Do you know where he's been sent?' she asked.

'I'm afraid I don't.'

Lena suspected that even if she did know the woman wouldn't tell her.

'Did he leave anything for me? A message or anything?' she asked, her voice wobbling a little.

The matron shook her head and narrowed her eyes. 'Of

course not. I expect he came to his senses and wondered why he'd been associating with the likes of you.'

Lena felt the blood rush to her face, but before she could say anything she might regret, she turned on her heel and left. The matron's words stung her to the core. It was just the sort of thing she might have expected from Miss Woodcock and the other old harridans at St Catherine's. It took her right back to how she'd felt as a miserable schoolgirl, whose self-esteem had been destroyed by the very people who should have been nurturing and protecting her.

She walked home from Gurungni Road as quickly as she could, her vision blurred with tears. Lakshmi looked up in alarm when she saw Lena's tear-stained face. She put her gentle arms around her.

'Whatever's happened, my dear?'

Stumblingly, Lena told her what had happened, and she listened patiently. She didn't reveal in words the depth of her feelings for Billy, but she suspected that Lakshmi must have seen it in her eyes.

'I need to see Billy as soon as possible,' Lena finished. 'Not just because I care about him but also to warn him again about the fortune-teller's prophesy.'

18

So now I'm up in my room writing this with a heavy heart. I was so looking forward to being reunited with Billy, to put my arms around him, to hold him tight and kiss his sweet lips. I wonder now when I'll ever get to see him again.

Chloe had been reading her grandmother's diary over breakfast at the Jasmine Hotel, partly because she wanted to find out what happened next in Lena's story, and partly because she still felt self-conscious about sitting down alone to eat. It was still early in the morning – just after six-thirty – but the bus to Kathmandu was due to leave Kakarbhitta at eight o'clock. After her unsettling experience with the rickshaw-wallah the evening before, she wanted to make sure she had plenty of time to walk to the bus stand from the hotel.

She put the diary down, tucked into her scrambled eggs and thought about her grandmother. How devastated she must have been when she rushed back to the convalescent home only to find that Billy had already left for the front. It was wartime, and she must have had a niggling feeling that she might never see him again, which was why she was so rattled by him leaving. Chloe had been shocked, too, at the blatant rudeness shown by the matron towards Lena. Her blood boiled to read that that attitude towards Eurasians was common amongst the British at the time of the Raj. Such injustice against her grandmother was hard to imagine. How had Lena managed to keep her optimistic and sunny nature intact through all of it?

When she looked up from her breakfast, her heart sank to see the young Nepalese man who'd helped her the evening before enter the dining room. He wore a black leather jacket that didn't look cheap, a white T-shirt and designer jeans. He clearly cared about his appearance, which Chloe quickly interpreted as vanity. But she had to admit too, that he did have film-star looks, with his perfect skin and sharp haircut.

He glanced across the room and smiled when he noticed her. She smiled briefly in return but looked away quickly. She still felt embarrassed and a little irritated by their previous exchange and had no desire to have anything more to do with him. So, when she'd finished her eggs, she got up and left the dining room, without looking his way.

When she arrived in the lobby with her rucksack and went to the desk to pay her bill, Chloe asked the man on reception if he could call her a taxi.

'There are many motor rickshaws waiting outside to take you to the bus station,' he said.

She thought about voicing her concern that rickshaws could be unreliable and insist on a taxi, but decided against it. It could take an age for a taxi to come. She went through the swing doors of the hotel and out onto the pavement. Sure enough, several motor rickshaws were lined up in the street outside, the rickshaw-wallahs leaning against their vehicles waiting for customers. Chloe looked along the line. To her relief, there was no sign of the driver from the previous evening. But which one could she trust?

'Going to the bus station?' a voice behind her said.

Chloe spun round to see the young man standing behind her,

a huge rucksack on his shoulders. He held out his hand and she took it out of natural politeness.

'I'm Kiran,' he smiled. 'We got off to an awkward start yesterday evening. I apologise if I was abrupt, but I hate to see tourists taken advantage of and I can't help letting it show sometimes. Would you like to share a rickshaw to the bus park now?'

His handshake was warm and the look in his dark eyes seemed genuine. Still, she hesitated. Was she really so easily won over? But thinking about it quickly, if she did go along with him, she was unlikely to get ripped off.

'I'm Chloe,' she answered. 'And yes. I am going to the bus park, and it would be good to share a rickshaw.'

The man negotiated with the rickshaw-wallah and they both got inside. The rickshaw took off down the street and they passed the five-minute journey in awkward silence. Chloe hoped that Kiran wasn't going to Kathmandu on the same bus as her, but the fact that he was setting off from the hotel at exactly the same time and going to the bus park meant that he probably would be.

When they arrived at the outdoor station where many dilapidated buses were lined up and passengers were milling about, Kiran got out of the rickshaw and paid the driver. Then, he helped Chloe out of the back seat.

'Thank you,' she said as he handed her rucksack out to her.

'The Kathmandu bus is over there,' he said, pointing to a ramshackle multicoloured vehicle at a nearby stand. 'I take it that's where you're going?'

She nodded.

'Me too,' he said. 'It's a long journey. But a beautiful one.'

Her spirits sank. So he was going on the same bus as she'd feard. They walked over to the bus together and, before they boarded, he stopped her.

'Do you have water?' he asked, a solicitous look on his face.

'Yes,' she said.

'That's good. It can get hot on there. They do stop at food

stalls, so you don't need to bring supplies of everything, but it's a long journey. Fourteen hours.'

Once again, Chloe felt slightly irritated that he seemed to be telling her what to do, but she suppressed the thought. He was just being kind, she told herself, helping out someone who was in a foreign country and didn't know the ropes.

They climbed on board the bus. Inside, there was a rank smell of animals and, sure enough, looking down the aisle, Chloe saw several cages of chickens balanced on people's laps, and in the aisle lay two small brown and white goats with horns. Boxes and bags cluttered the aisle and the racks above. People didn't travel light here, she noted.

'Best to sit near the front,' Kiran advised. 'Less sick-making that way. There are several mountain passes on the journey.'

She slid into one of the seats near the front.

Kiran held out his hand for her rucksack, which he swung onto the rack above them. He put his own up next to it, then he hesitated.

'Do you mind if I sit here?'

'Not at all,' she said, not knowing how to refuse. At least if he sat there, she reasoned, she wouldn't have to sit next to someone carrying a basket of chickens. He smiled his thanks and sat down beside her.

'I do this journey often,' he said. 'So, I know the ropes.'

In spite of her original antipathy, Chloe decided that the journey would pass more quickly if she put aside her qualms and talked to him as if nothing had happened. 'Oh? Why is that?' she asked.

'I work as a tour guide in Nepal. I've just brought a tour group down to Kakarbhitta from Kathmandu. They are going on to Delhi from here.'

'Do you live in Kathmandu?' she asked, genuinely curious now.

'My parents live in Pokhara and I sometimes live there, sometimes in Kathmandu, but mostly I'm on the move with my job. What brings you to Nepal?'

Chloe paused, wondering how much to share with him, then threw caution to the wind. 'I'm on a sort of pilgrimage. My grandmother was in Nepal during the war when she was young. She died recently and I've been reading her wartime journal. I'm retracing her steps to find out a bit more about her.'

'Was she Indian?'

Chloe smiled. She could see he was appraising her dark hair and features and wondering about her antecedents.

'She was half-Indian. She grew up in Darjeeling in the thirties, but when she married my grandfather, she came to the UK and never returned to India.'

'I'm not surprised about that,' he said with a hint of sadness. 'The way Eurasians were treated by both Indian and British communities. It can't have been a very comfortable existence.'

At that moment, the driver climbed on board and took his seat. A skinny boy got in too and sat down beside him on the bench seat.

'That's the co-driver,' Kiran explained, with a wry smile. 'His job is to lean out of the window and shout at other drivers, and to make sure we don't go too close to the edge on mountain roads.'

'He looks very young,' Chloe said, eyeing the boy nervously.

'He's probably been doing it for years. I wouldn't worry.'

The door slammed shut and the bus roared into life. The driver manoeuvred it noisily out of its parking space, then set off out of the bus station with several triumphant blasts of the horn. The co-driver leaned out of the window, shouting at approaching rickshaws to stop while they pulled out into the traffic. Then they were heading through the town on a busy main road, past rows of modern buildings, offices, factories and apartment blocks. On the edge of the town, they crossed a wide river, then carried on through flat, green countryside, towards some distant mountains, over more rivers and through remote villages strung out along the road.

The road started to climb, and Chloe stared out at the lush, green valley below, with its shallow, meandering river, either side of which were flooded rice paddies and huge square fields full of bright yellow crops that she couldn't name.

'Those are mustard flowers,' Kiran said, following her gaze. 'The valley is famous for them. Kathmandu too.'

'It's beautiful here,' she remarked.

'Of course. Nepal is a beautiful country. But then, I've never been anywhere else – apart from India, of course.'

She looked at him in amazement. He seemed so sophisticated, so westernised. But she hid her surprise, not wanting to offend him.

Flamboyant, multicoloured lorries thundered in the opposite direction, many of them bearing fairy lights, the driver's name displayed on sun visors across the windscreen.

'I'd never been out of Europe before I flew to Kolkata about ten days ago,' she confided.

'That was quite brave of you, then, to come so far on your own. India isn't the easiest place to travel. Especially for a woman alone.'

'I haven't had any trouble at all. Most people have been really friendly... Apart from...' She stopped, biting her lip, deciding not to mention the rickshaw-wallah who had tried to trick her, not wanting to revisit those prickly moments of their first encounter.

The road began to rise higher into the hills, ascending above the wide valley where the shallow river, strewn with boulders, still meandered from side to side. Out of the corner of her eye, she saw Kiran smiling privately, obviously remembering the sharp exchange of the previous evening too.

'Why did your grandmother visit Kathmandu?' he said after a pause. 'In those days, entry to the Kingdom was tightly restricted. It would have been hard to get a permit.'

'She worked for the British Indian Army, and she came to help her boss recruit Gurkha soldiers for the Burma campaign.'

He looked at her with renewed interest. 'Oh, how fascinating.'

'They spent time in Kathmandu before going on to Pokhara and then up into the hill villages.'

'Kathmandu must have been incredible back then,' he said, his eyes dreamy. 'A forgotten land. Full of myth and mystery.'

'That's exactly what my grandmother thought.'

And, without thinking about it, as the bus continued on its rattling climb to the high mountain pass, its engine straining, diesel smoke belching out from its exhaust, she was telling him all about the fortune teller and her prophesy and how Lena had misinterpreted it as being about the earthquake. She told him about Sita's death too, although she felt a little guilty about mentioning it. It seemed a little personal and tragic to be confiding in a complete stranger.

Kiran said how sorry he was to hear about it, and had looked fascinated while she related Lena's story, and Chloe realised how good it felt to tell someone all about it. So far, she was the only one alive who knew all of this apart perhaps from Mildred Light-fooot. Of course, in her emails to Sophie, she'd told her some of what the diary contained, but not the details. Once she'd started speaking about it, the floodgates had opened, and she didn't want to stop. Before she knew it, she was telling Kiran all about Billy and her grandfather, about Alisha and the tragedy of her death.

'That's quite a story,' Kiran said, gazing out at the rocks on the other side of the ravine they were traversing.

'Yes. It's very sad,' she replied. 'Until I read about Alisha's death, I thought that I might have some relatives living in that village up in the hills beyond Pokhara.'

'That would have been incredible,' he agreed. Then he said, 'Would you like to go up there one day?'

'Yes. That's one of the reasons I'm making this journey. I'd love to go up there.'

He smiled. 'There are no roads up into those hills, you know. Just paths. Supplies are taken in by mule train or on the backs of sherpas. The only way there is to walk, or to ride.'

'Gosh,' she said, surprised. 'Even today?'

'Even today. Most of those villages up there have no roads to them. They are very remote. Visiting them is like stepping back in time.'

Chloe fell silent, thinking about his words, then Kiran spoke again.

'Do you know what happened in the end? To your grandmother, and to Billy?'

She shook her head. 'I haven't finished reading her diary yet. I've sort of rationed myself. I want to make sure I take it in properly, soak up the details, not just race to the end. It helps that I'm here while I read it. It means I can see the places she was writing about.'

They both contemplated the beauty of the wild, mountain terrain they were passing through, watching the mountain goats grazing on rocky outcrops, the birds of prey soaring above. It was all accompanied by the vibrating rattle of the bus and the throaty roar of the engine, the clucking of the chickens and the loud chatter of the other passengers coming from the back of the bus.

When they started to descend on the other side of the pass, Kiran turned to her again. 'There are still fortune-tellers in Kathmandu. There are definitely some based around Durbar Square. Have you any plans to visit one?'

'I hadn't thought about that.' She was surprised at the question. 'Perhaps I will...'

'Where are you going to stay in Kathmandu?'

'I hadn't thought about that either,' she laughed. 'I was going to read my guidebook on the journey and find something I like when I get there.'

He laughed too. 'And I've been distracting you. I'm sorry.'

She shook her head. 'No, it's really good to have someone to talk to,' she said, her words heartfelt.

'Well, because I've taken up your time, let me save you the trouble of looking in your guidebook. You should see if you can get a room at the Kathmandu Guest House in the Thamel area. That's quite near to Durbar Square. It's the old city, the main tourist area too. There are many backpacker hostels around there, but the Kathmandu Guest House is a cut above. It has dormitories, but it also has some private rooms.'

'I wouldn't want to stay in a dormitory,' Chloe remarked with a shudder, imagining teenagers on their gap years coming in drunk or worse in the middle of the night.

'You wouldn't have to. They have some very nice private rooms, as I said. Trust me. It's a great place to stay. I always recommend it to my tourists, no matter what their budget.'

Chloe looked out of the window, straight into the darkness of a forest they were travelling through, suspicious suddenly, wondering if Kiran was on some sort of commission. Perhaps she'd been too hasty, trusting him with Lena's life story. Someone she'd only just met. Perhaps she should be more circumspect, more wary. But it was a bit late for that. He was sitting right beside her, and they'd only been going for a few hours. There were at least ten hours still to go.

'You needn't worry,' he said. 'I don't get anything for recommending the place. It's just that everyone who stays there loves it and thanks me for telling them about it. But the choice is completely yours.'

The bus was travelling on a plateau high in the mountains now. They came to a hilltop village and the driver pulled into a village square, where there were a couple of open-air tea shops and some simple food stalls. There was also a crude, painted sign with an arrow saying 'WC' pointing to a place behind a barn. Chloe shuddered again. She needed a bathroom stop but was apprehensive about what it might be like.

She queued up with all the other female passengers on the bus to use a smelly, squat toilet with a large gap under the ill-fitting door. Afterwards, she washed her hands carefully in a bucket of cold water and went over to one of the tea stalls. There was only chai available and as she sipped the sweet, cloying liquid, she looked around at the squalid pit stop with its collection of unsavoury-looking food stalls. Two more buses had pulled up now and there were a lot of people milling about.

It would have been much easier to fly, she acknowledged to herself, but then she wouldn't have got to see the mountains close up, or to travel like a local.

She was getting hungry, but none of the food being served up looked safe to eat or even remotely appetising. So, ignoring her rumbling stomach, when she'd finished her chai, she got back on the bus.

Kiran got on soon afterwards, carrying some packets of food.

'Where did you get those?' she asked enviously.

'There's a village shop for the locals a little way down the road. Here, I bought some for you too.' He handed her a packet of crisps and some biscuits. She thanked him and opened the crisps without ceremony, realising how ravenous she actually was.

The bus resumed its descent towards the Kathmandu valley. The light began to fade and the passengers gradually quietened down. Chloe realised that, so far, she'd done all the talking. Although Kiran had said what he did for a living, he hadn't told her much about himself at all. She wondered if he would be as forthcoming as she had been.

She turned to him, 'How did you come to be a tourist guide?' she asked.

'Well, I grew up in one of the hill villages not too far from Pokhara. It was a hard life and we worked the fields. When my grandfather died, somehow all his land went to my father's older brothers, so we were left without an income.'

'That's terrible,' Chloe said. 'How old were you then?'

'I was ten. But my father wasn't one to be daunted. He had some contacts in Pokhara. That was when trekking was just getting popular. He got a bank loan and bought a guest house in the town. We moved down there and he and my mother worked all hours looking after the guests. I missed the village but the school was very good in Pokhara. Better than the village school. And I loved meeting the young westerners who stayed in the guest house. I learned so much from them. British, French, Germans – I began to learn their languages and when I was old enough, I got a job with a tour company, guiding trekkers up into the hills. Because I could speak European languages, I was always in demand. Everything was going really well, but then came the revolution...'

He lowered his voice and his eyes darted around the bus. Chloe had read about the Maoist revolution in her guidebook.

'Everything stopped for us. No foreigners wanted to visit Nepal for over ten years,' he muttered. 'We had to scrape a living as best we could, labouring on farms, on building sites. My older brother went abroad, to work in the Gulf as a construction worker. He used to send money home. Without that, we would have starved.'

'It must have been terrible,' said Chloe.

'It was a dreadful time for this country. It was a time of great fear and violence. Neighbours couldn't trust one another, young people were taken from their home and recruited by the insurgents, turning against their parents. Many people were killed, many disappeared.'

Chloe looked around the bus, at the passengers chatting away happily, playing with their children, reading or sleeping. It was hard to believe that just a few years before, this country had been at war with itself.

'But that is behind us now. It has been over for more than nine years,' Kiran went on. 'Tourists are back now and we tour guides have plenty of work. I went back to work for the original company and after a few years, I left the company and went freelance.'

'How interesting,' she said. 'And do you enjoy it?'

'I love it. I love meeting new people and helping them discover our beautiful country, seeing the look on their faces when they see the sunrise over the Annapurna range. It's priceless.'

'You are lucky to have found your vocation,' Chloe acknowledged.

'Have you not?' he asked, his eyes on her face.

She shook her head. 'I worked as an estate agent,' she told him. 'The money was good, but it felt unfulfilling. I'd like to do something worthwhile, but I haven't worked out quite what yet.'

As she spoke, she realised she hadn't thought as much about her future since leaving home as she'd intended. The journey into her grandmother's past had been all-consuming.

'Perhaps this trip will give you some perspective on that,' he said.

'I'm hoping so. It's been really good, finding out about where Gran spent her early years. It's helping me understand myself better in a funny sort of way.'

He smiled. 'Travel often works its magic like that.'

'You're right. I hadn't realised it would have that effect,' she said, suddenly feeling drowsy.

She leaned against the window and closed her eyes, and before long, she'd drifted off into a restless sleep.

When she awoke, they were travelling through the straggly outskirts of a city. An assortment of buildings lined the road, some looked like the badly built homes of the very poor, others were more substantial. It was difficult to see properly because it was dark now and there were few streetlamps.

Chloe glanced at Kiran. He was asleep beside her, his head slumped forward, his fashionable fringe flopping over his eyes. She smiled. How strange, she thought, that she'd come full circle since the previous evening. She'd enjoyed his company on the bus journey and was glad that they'd got over that initial awkwardness.

Twenty minutes or so later, the bus pulled into a large bus depot, with the sign Gongabu Bus Station above the entrance, and came to its final stop. Kiran blinked awake and looked around, rubbing his eyes.

'We've finally arrived,' she told him.

He got up and stretched, then took their rucksacks down.

'I will find you a taxi to take you to Thamel,' he said.

'What about you?' she asked.

'I have a place not too far from here,' he replied. 'I'll just get a motor rickshaw.'

They climbed down from the bus, and Chloe followed Kiran through a milling crowd of passengers, porters, animals and touts, to a place on the other side of the station where some taxis were lined up. He went to the one at the head of the queue and spoke to the driver. Then he turned to Chloe.

'He will take you to Thamel. He will drop you outside the Kathmandu Guest House, but if you decide you don't want to stay there, there are many other hotels and guest houses in the area.'

'Thank you,' she said and opened the taxi door.

'Look,' Kiran began. 'I've been thinking, since you told me about your grandfather and the girl from Ghorepani. I've got some work to do in Kathmandu for the next couple of days, but after that, we could go up to Pokhara on the bus together and I could show you the way to Ghorepani. You probably wouldn't want to go there alone. I often take small groups up there, so I know the route well.'

She stared at him, slightly taken by surprise, not knowing what to say.

'You don't have to make up your mind now,' he said. 'Let me know when you've decided. Here's my card. Send me a text or give me a call at any time. In the meantime, enjoy Kathmandu!'

Chloe thanked him and took his card. As she got into the taxi and it pulled away, she watched Kiran disappear into the crowd, then looked at his card – *Kiran Rai, Tour Guide, fluent in English, French, German and Hindi*. She thought about his suggestion and how much she'd enjoyed his company on the journey. It might not be a bad idea to have someone to show her the way to Ghorepani, especially someone who was as congenial and entertaining as Kiran Rai.

19

DARJEELING, 1944

I HAVEN'T HAD the heart to write in these pages for a long time. It has been over two months in fact, but yesterday was New Year's Day and I made a resolution to do so. Life has been so dull and so dispiriting lately. Ever since poor Ma died, and Lieutenant Harper and I went to Ghorepani and found out about Alisha's death. Then when I returned home to discover that Billy had left for the front, all the joy seemed to have gone out of my world. November and December just crawled by.

There seemed to have been very little, if anything, to say, and each time Lena had picked up her diary to write, she'd put it down again. All she had to write about were her dull days at the office, her rides home in the rickshaw, her occasional visits to the bazaar or the shops on Chowrasta, or her quiet evenings at home eating Lakshmi's homely cooking and listening to updates about the war on the BBC World Service on Sunil's crackly radio.

That was how she had spent almost every day, apart from the occasional weekend when Mary and Joan came to visit and they would stroll out of the town and into the hills, to Tiger Point or Observatory Hill. They would gossip about girls they'd known at St Catherine's and exchange news. Sometimes Mary and Joan would bring a letter from Vicky, which she'd written c/o St

Catherine's to all three of them. Lena wondered what Miss Woodcock made of that. Vicky's letters had mainly been about the training she'd been doing up in Shillong, but in her latest missive, she told them that she'd finally been sent to Burma. She couldn't say where because of the censors. She did say, though, that life in the Wasbies was hard but rewarding, living in tents and makeshift accommodation, driving to different places near the front line and serving the active troops.

Lena had dreaded the thought of Christmas without her mother. Even though Sita was a Hindu, she would go out of her way to make Christmas special for Lena when she was growing up. She had even carried those traditions on when Lena reached her twenties. When she was at St Catherine's, Lena used to go and stay with Sita for a few days. They would walk up into one of the nearby forests and find a small evergreen tree to cut, then put it up in the living room and decorate it with baubles her mother bought from the bazaar.

Sita would even bake little coloured sweetmeats and hang them from the branches. She used to place candles all around the room and light them on Christmas morning before Lena woke up. And, of course, she bought Lena a Christmas present. Something small that she could afford on her limited income, but which she would have chosen with great care. It would often be a book from the bookstore on Chowrasta, something by Jane Austen or one of the Bronte sisters. She couldn't read English very well, so Lena never knew how she managed to choose them so accurately. Once Lena had opened her presents and had breakfast, her mother would walk her along to St Mary's Church and wait outside while she attended the Christmas service and then walk her home again.

So, of course without her, Lena wasn't looking forward to Christmas at all. Up at the base, Lieutenant Harper made sure that there was a small tree in the office and a tall one in the canteen. They had a work Christmas lunch with some of the officers. The cooks managed the roast dinner very well, using capons instead of turkey, but their plum pudding was too moist and fell apart when it was served.

Lena was touched when she came home one day to find that Lakshmi and Sunil had bought a small tree from the market and decorated it just like Sita used to. She went to church on Christmas morning and many people, including the vicar, came and held her hand and said how sorry they were for her loss. That made her sadder than ever, and she walked home feeling very low. But when she got back to the house, Lakshmi had been cooking.

'I couldn't do a roast, I'm afraid, but I have cooked a very special curry for you.'

They sat down straight away to eat it and it was delicious. So, Christmas wasn't quite as bad as she'd thought it would be.

She went back to work after the short break and spent a dismal, rather tedious day in the office at the base, filling out record cards for the latest batch of new recruits. Lieutenant Harper came and went all day. He spent time on the parade ground and time talking to the other officers in the mess, and whenever he walked back over to his office in the Nissen hut, Lena watched him through the window, his shoulders hunched, his head down, his brow furrowed. Although he had been putting a brave face on when others were around, Alisha's death had clearly hit him very hard, and whenever he dropped his guard, the ravages of grief were apparent on his face.

A couple of times since their return from Nepal, Lena had managed to get him to talk. On one occasion he'd spoken about how he and Alisha used to trek into the hills together.

'We would enjoy the pure air and stunning beauty of the mountains. While we walked, we would make plans for the future.' His face always brightened a little at the memories, but when he came back to reality and remembered his loss, the pain entered his eyes again.

Lena had her own sadness too. Moment by moment, she yearned for Billy and worried constantly about what was happening to him at the front. He hadn't written to her, which was another source of sadness, although, she reasoned, he probably didn't know her address. She'd never given it to him because she didn't expect him to leave so suddenly.

The words of the fortune teller went round and round in her mind. If only there was a way of contacting Billy. She even asked Lieutenant Harper to find out what he could about Billy's regiment. He did what digging he could, but even he didn't have any way of knowing where Billy had been sent.

'What I do know is that Private Thomas's regiment has been absorbed into the 14th Army under General Slim,' he told Lena. 'But I'm afraid that army is stationed all over Burma at present, so we have no way of knowing where he might have ended up. I'm so sorry, Miss Chatterjee.'

Lena had also been trying to find out what was happening in the Burma Campaign by listening to the BBC World Service and reading the *Darjeeling Times* assiduously. She was sure that news was suppressed and censored, so it was difficult to get a clear picture of what was happening at the front. She had gleaned, though, that Allied planes were out on raids every day and night attacking Japanese positions and dropping supplies to troops on the ground, and that although the Allies had suffered setbacks, there seemed to be renewed hope for a push to recapture the country, with Lord Mountbatten leading the campaign.

Through it all, Lena often closed her eyes and tried to imagine what Billy was going through on a daily basis. She knew that conditions in the jungle and mountains in Burma were very harsh for British troops. It was hot there and incredibly humid, with constant, heavy rainfall throughout the monsoon. There were leeches and malarial mosquitoes, snakes and other dangerous animals, so sleeping in the open air or in small, flimsy tents must have been frightening and unpleasant. She'd also read that it was often hard to get supplies of food and drink to the troops there, so they were frequently hungry. If only there was a way of getting in touch with Billy, to send him her love and to let him know that she was thinking of him, willing him to return to her, hoping that day would come very soon.

ONE EVENING during the first week in January 1944, Mary came to see Lena on her own. She looked excited and agitated, her eyes were bright and she couldn't stop fidgeting. She told Lena that she'd made a decision; she'd decided to sign up for the Wasbies. Vicky's letters always said that the Wasbies were short-staffed, so Mary was confident that she would be accepted. She showed Lena her letter.

While she was reading it, Lena had an idea. It wasn't exactly a new idea. It had been bubbling around in the back of her mind ever since she'd found out about Vicky joining up. Why didn't she go too? It would take her nearer the front, and although it was a long shot, there was a remote chance that she might be able to find out something about Billy's whereabouts. But it wasn't just that. She felt that she could be doing so much more for the cause. Lieutenant Harper had told her that there wouldn't be another trip into Nepal for several months because the Gurkhas had almost exhausted the supply of young men in the villages. So, her immediate future consisted of counting paper clips and filing record forms in the office on the base. Although that was a lot better than teaching at St Catherine's, it was deadly dull, especially when she had so much more to offer.

'Would you mind if I applied too?' she asked Mary, looking up from the letter.

'Oh Lena! That would be wonderful. What a relief. I tried to persuade Joan to sign up too, but she won't because she doesn't want to leave her younger sister at St Catherine's without her.'

'Oh yes. I'd forgotten about Lillie. She's only fifteen, isn't she?'

'Yes, and she's having a tough time at the moment. Joan wants to be there to keep an eye on her.'

'What does Joan think about you going?'

'She was all for it. She even helped me write the letter. Look, if you're serious, why don't you write now. I'll wait while you do it, if you like.'

'Are you sure?'

'Of course.'

So, Mary sat down on Lena's bed and waited while Lena wrote her own letter. It took several drafts, with Mary making suggestions. When it was finally done, with her fingers crossed, Lena sealed it in an envelope and handed it to Mary.

'I'll take them both to the post office at lunchtime tomorrow,' Mary said.

So, Lena's decision was made. She pictured her letter winging its way to the Wasbies HQ in Shillong. She wondered how long they would take to get back to her. If they needed new recruits, she reasoned, they probably wouldn't take too long. For the first time in months, she was excited and optimistic for the future.

20

MY ONLY QUALMS are about leaving Lieutenant Harper, especially with the way he is feeling at the moment. I am almost certain that I am the only person here in Darjeeling who knows about Alisha and his terrible loss. I just hope that if I am to leave, it won't cause him more pain. I am not looking forward to having that conversation with him, but I know him to be a fair-minded man who has the war effort in the forefront of his mind, so I'm sure he will see the benefit of me signing up.

Chloe had been reading Lena's diary, lying on her bed in her room on the third floor of the Kathmandu Guest House. Glancing at her watch, she realised she had slept far later than she thought and had missed breakfast. She put the diary down and stretched, reflecting on Lena's decision to sign up with the Wasbies. It was a brave one, a leap into the unknown. Far braver, she thought, than her own decision to come here and that had felt daunting enough for someone who'd done so little travelling before and had never been outside of Europe.

She'd arrived at the guesthouse in the dark, late the evening before. As soon as the taxi had stopped outside the building, Chloe had understood why Kiran had recommended it. It was floodlit, a beautiful, calm oasis in the middle of the busy Thamel district which was full of down-at-heel hostels, cheap cafés and tourist shops. To her surprise the Kathmandu Guest House didn't look like a guest house at all. It looked more like a mansion or a palace. The elegant building was painted primrose yellow with dark green shutters and white wrought-iron balconies. It stood behind huge gates, and once she was inside, she saw that it was surrounded by large lawns that were lit by fairy lights. She'd checked in and had been shown up to her room. She was so exhausted from the journey that as soon as she lay down on the bed, she'd fallen asleep.

Now, she got up, showered and pulled on some clothes. Then, she went downstairs and out into the garden and headed for the outdoor café on the other side of the lawn. This time, she had brought the diary with her, so she had something to do while she ate. She was keen to read about how Lena's application to the Wasbies had been received. She wandered across the manicured lawns on a path lined with pot plants ablaze with different coloured flowers – geraniums, marigolds, chrysanthemums, begonias, all in full bloom.

At the café, the smiling waiter showed her to a table under the shade of a fig tree and she sat down and ordered coffee and a club sandwich. She felt she needed building up after the privations of the journey the day before, having fallen asleep without supper as soon as she arrived and having missed breakfast.

When the waiter had gone off with her order, Chloe opened up the diary again, turned to the next entry, which was dated January 10th 1944, and read on.

It has taken a few days, but this morning at breakfast time, I got a letter back from the Wasbie headquarters in Shillong! I was so apprehensive when I opened it that my hands were shaking, and it was difficult to tear the envelope.

LAKSHMI AND SUNIL, whom she had told about her plans, were on tenterhooks too and watched Lena anxiously as she ripped the envelope open and pulled the letter out. On the top of the page was the emblem of the Wasbies – a chinthe, which Vicky had told her was a mythical Burmese creature, a sort of lion, that guarded temples and pagodas and was said to bring good luck.

The letter was from Major Ninian Taylor, the commanding officer of the Wasbies. She thanked Lena for her application and said she was very pleased to be able to offer her a place to train with them at their HQ in Shillong. Time was of the essence, she wrote, and there was a pressing need for more women to serve at the front so she hoped that Lena would be able to join them without delay. To that end, she asked her to respond by letter, but if she was able to telephone too, it would speed things up immeasurably.

Lena read the letter out loud to Lakshmi and Sunil, translating it into Hindi for them, and they both burst into happy applause. Lakshmi hugged her as Lena knew Sita would have done. They all became a bit tearful then, because it meant the end of her stay with them. They had grown very close since Sita had died. Lena knew that Lakshmi and Sunil thought of her as a sort of substitute daughter and to her they were substitute parents, although no one could ever replace Sita, of course.

When it was time for her to go to work, Lena set off on foot towards the rickshaw stand in Cart Road. As she neared it, she caught sight of someone running towards her and once the person got closer, Lena saw that it was Mary coming up the road from the direction of St Catherine's. She was smiling fit to burst and waving a letter in her hand. She didn't need to tell Lena her news, and when she reached Lena, breathing heavily, Lena quickly told her that she had received an offer too. They hugged and laughed and congratulated each other. The rickshaw-wallahs just stood there watching, scratching their heads in bemusement.

Mary returned to St Catherine's and Lena set off in the rickshaw towards Jalapahar with very mixed feelings. She was buzzing with excitement about the prospect of going to Shillong and eventually to Burma with the Wasbies, but this was tinged with dread and guilt at the thought of the conversation she needed to have with Lieutenant Harper. She would be sad to leave him. She was deeply grateful for the kindness he'd shown her and was still touched at how he'd gone to her mother's funeral. They had grown close over the past few months, so, parting from him would be a wrench, especially as she knew that the lieutenant was at such a low ebb.

When she arrived at the office, he was over in the main building. She felt a little nervous waiting for him to return, anticipating their discussion. She went into the little kitchen in the corner of the Nissen hut and brewed them both a coffee as she normally did. Just as she'd finished, the lieutenant came through the door. She was relieved to see that he was smiling and that he looked better than he had for a while.

'Good morning, Miss Chatterjee,' he greeted her and went into his office. Lena followed him in with the coffee.

'Could we have a word please, sir,' she asked.

He looked up from his papers, surprise in his eyes. 'Of course. Do sit down,' he said and gave her his full attention.

Lena sat down in the chair opposite his desk and just came straight out with it. She told him that a friend of hers had joined the Wasbies in Burma, that she wanted to do her bit for the war effort and that she'd applied to them herself. At first, Lieutenant Harper's mouth dropped open, but when she'd finished, he smiled and said that it was very brave and honourable to volunteer.

'I wish you the very best of luck, Miss Chatterjee. We shall be very sorry indeed to lose you, of course, but you have a very good reason.'

Lena hesitated before saying, 'I'm very sorry to be leaving you at this time... I know you are still grieving for your terrible loss.'

She wanted to be completely honest with him too, so she went on to admit that part of the reason she wanted to go to Burma was that in the back of her mind she was hoping that she might be able to find out where Billy was and find a way of contacting him.

The lieutenant smiled. 'I half-guessed that that might have something to do with it. But I don't blame you at all.' Then he leaned forward and looked into her eyes. 'Love is such a precious thing. You need to seize whatever opportunities you can.'

Lena smiled back, unable to reply, tears filling her eyes.

'I fear that it won't be an easy task, though. Burma is such a huge country, there are hundreds of thousands of troops there and the situation is often chaotic. But I wish you all the luck in the world.'

So, I only have a few days left in Darjeeling. I phoned Major Taylor from the office and left a message with her secretary accepting the offer, and said that I could come at the end of the week. Then I wrote a letter saying the same thing, which I sent with the daily post from the base. I am now in a frenzy of excitement and apprehension, wondering if this is the right thing to do, or if it is the craziest thing I've ever done in my life!

Chloe mused over her grandfather's reaction to Lena's announcement, tucking into her lunch. He and Lena had clearly grown close on their trips into the mountains in Nepal, more so since the death of Alisha. How like him it was, though, to put all thoughts of his own comfort aside and back her plans for joining the Wasbies. He had put Lena's happiness before his own and had encouraged her to seize the moment, even though it would leave him without her company and support. And, again unselfishly, he had told her to pursue her dreams of finding Billy, even though he had lost his own love. Chloe was curious as to how and when their relationship had developed into something more.

She turned to the next diary entry, dated 16th January 1944.

So here we are, Mary and I, on board the Guwahati Express. It is the sleeper train from Siliguri bound for Guwahati, which is the nearest railway station to Shillong. From there it is still another sixty miles or so, but we will go by bus.

MAJOR TAYLOR HAD SENT postal orders for their travel expenses, so they had bought their tickets at Darjeeling station, packed their bags, and set off early that morning on the Darjeeling Himalaya Railway. Lena felt a real mixture of emotions when they boarded the train with their suitcases. It was incredibly exciting to be embarking on the trip, but she was also sad to be leaving Darjeeling and so many people she knew and loved. There was no knowing when she would be back.

Joan came to the station to see them off, as did Lakshmi and Sunil, and, to Lena's surprise, Lieutenant Harper, who arrived in his staff car just moments before the train left. Lena had thought that they had said goodbye the previous day at the office, when he'd presented her with a beautiful pen as a leaving present and gave a little speech in the canteen to the assembled office staff and a few officers. He'd been very kind and said what a huge contribution Lena had made to the recent Gurkha recruitment campaigns, and how she would be sure to make a big impression wherever she went. She'd been so overcome with emotion that she couldn't say anything in reply, but everyone had clapped and cheered and wished her well.

She was sad to say goodbye to Lakshmi and Sunil too. They'd helped her to the station with her luggage, fussed around finding the right carriage and settled her on board. When it came to saying goodbye, Lakshmi burst into tears and clung to Lena, and

Sunil looked as though he was about to cry too. She hugged them both and thanked them for their incredible kindness and hospitality.

'I will write,' she said, fighting back the tears. 'And I'll be back before too long.'

Joan was tearful too. She kissed Lena on the cheek and held Mary extra tight. Lena knew it would be hard for poor Joan at St Catherine's. All her friends were away with the Wasbies and although there were other young teachers at the school still, she didn't know them as well.

They were already settled on the train when Lieutenant Harper arrived. He came up to the carriage door and Lena pulled the window down to speak to him. He looked as choked as everyone else. Tears were standing in his eyes.

'I just wanted to say goodbye, Miss Chatterjee. I will miss you terribly.'

Not knowing what to say, Lena replied, 'Oh please call me Lena. And thank you. I will miss you too.'

'You must write and let me know how you're getting on,' he said.

The train gave a blast of its horn and the stationmaster blew his whistle. Then, to Lena's astonishment, Lieutenant Harper leaned forward and gave her a peck on the cheek.

'Thank you for everything, Lena,' he said, just as the train pulled out of the station.

Lena found herself blushing furiously but doubted that he saw it in the confusion of the departure, with all the smoke and steam from the train and all the noise and hubbub that accompanied the train leaving Darjeeling station.

She always loved the trip down the mountains from Darjeeling to Siliguri; out through the town, past those beautiful temples nestled on the hillside, the tea plantations and forests, with the backdrop of Kanchenjunga in the distance. But this time the journey was tinged with sadness. She wouldn't see those

views that were so dear to her for a very long time. She was
taking a step into the unknown. She realised that Mary must feel
that way too because she looked as sad as Lena felt as the little
train made its way down the mountainside, navigating the
various loops and inclines, tooting valiantly at cattle and goats
grazing on the track as it went. They hardly spoke during that
part of the journey, both preferring to be alone with their
thoughts, but Lena did feel comforted by Mary's presence. How
much more difficult this would have been if she was setting out
alone!

When they reached Siliguri Junction, a group of porters
surrounded the carriage door, all clamouring for their custom.
They bartered a little for the best price. The man they chose was
old and skinny with very few teeth, but he put both their suitcases on his head and set off merrily at a cracking pace to the
main train station with the two of them trailing in his wake. Luckily, Major Taylor had told them to pack as little as possible
because it was going to be difficult to take much into Burma with
them, and they would be issued with uniforms when they got to
Shillong.

They didn't have to wait long on the platform at Siliguri for
the Guwahati Express. It was pulled by a huge black steam
engine belting out smoke and steam. It arrived with a fanfare of
tooting, and stopped with a great blast of the horn and hissing of
breaks, then porters and hawkers all converged on the train at
once. Their porter found his way to the first-class sleeping car
and stowed the suitcases aboard. They gave him a generous tip.
He'd done a good job and they both felt a little sorry for him. He
rewarded them by putting his hands together in a gesture of
thanks and giving them a wide, gap-toothed smile.

They had a whole compartment to themselves and it felt like
the height of luxury. Neither Mary nor Lena had ever travelled
first-class before. When Sita used to take Lena to Calcutta sometimes, they always travelled in the third-class car, with its wooden

seats and open sleeping compartments, where the fans were often broken, the bunks were three or four high, and people were wedged so tight some would sit on the floor and some outside on the roof. So, they felt slightly out of place in that rather grand compartment which had its own little bathroom with an old-fashioned sink and flushing lavatory.

The guard came and took their order for supper, which later arrived on trays when they stopped at a station farther down the line. They ate lamb curry with rice and chapattis and delicious it was too, although a little cold by the time it reached them. Before that they'd spent quite a bit of time watching the countryside slide by through the window, observing the flat plain roll by, taking them farther and farther away from home and from any sight of the Himalayas. They pulled down the window and stuck their heads out and looked behind them as they drew away from the mountains and gradually faded into the grey-blue of the misty horizon.

Sometimes the countryside they passed through was wild and jungled, with ragged coconut palms and teak trees soaring above the track. Sometimes they crossed wide rivers, sometimes sped through farmland, where rice paddies and tapioca grew in abundance, where buffalo waded in pools and cattle stood beside the tracks nibbling the undergrowth. They roared through country stations where people waited for the slow train, sitting on their baggage surrounded by their worldly goods, where children stopped playing and stood and stared at the express train passing through.

After they'd eaten their meal, the light started to fade and they were just passing through some hillier country when the guard came in and pulled the blinds down and asked them to wait in the corridor while he made the beds. They looked at each other in surprise, not used to this sort of service on the railways.

Lena volunteered to take the top bunk. She loved the feeling of snuggling down, watching shafts of light playing on the ceiling as they were carried at speed through unknown countryside. In the morning they would reach Guwahati and find the bus to Shillong. Lena couldn't wait to arrive now and to see the place where they were to spend the next few weeks. The excitement had superseded the sadness at leaving home and this had begun to feel like a real adventure.

THE JOURNEY from the train station at Guwahati to Shillong was up a winding road through wooded mountains. The views were not dissimilar from the mountains around Darjeeling, although not quite as wild and impressive as the Himalayas. Like Darjeeling, Shillong was a hill station, so it did feel a little bit like coming home for Lena and Mary. The Wasbie headquarters were in a beautiful old mansion, set in lovely, well-tended gardens, full of flowering plants and trees.

When they arrived, it was supper time and they were introduced to Major Taylor, a statuesque lady who radiated energy and bonhomie, then to all the other new recruits, of whom there were eight. Lena tried her best to remember their names; Betty, Edna, Vera, Ivy, Jessie, Patricia, Barbara and Grace.

They all sat down to a hearty meal of beef stew, dumplings and potatoes which Lena found very filling but welcome after the long journey. All the girls seemed friendly and pleasant and, just like Lena, keen to learn as much as they could and get on with their postings to Burma as soon as possible. Lena noticed that she and Mary were the only Eurasians in the group, but the other girls couldn't have been more welcoming. There was no snobbishness or frosty looks, which was so refreshing after the way they had sometimes been treated in the past, and just proved that Miss Woodcock and her attitudes were out of date.

After supper, Lena and Mary were given their own room on the first floor overlooking the beautiful gardens. Lena was glad that they were put together. Lying awake and chatting about their days after lights-out reminded her of their old dormitory days at St Catherine's.

On their first full day in Shillong, they were measured for their uniforms by the local tailor and were given an outline of what the job entailed. They would be required to make sandwiches, cakes and buns and serve them and tea to the troops wherever they were sent. They would also sell other basic supplies, such as razors, shoe polish, cigarettes, writing paper and envelopes, toothpaste and soap. They would be responsible for keeping abreast of the stock on board the mobile vans and for restocking them at local depots. In addition, they would all be taught to drive the lorries, which sounded thrilling to Lena. She'd had no idea that that might be on the cards!

They were shown round a typical truck which was kept on the grounds at Shillong for demonstration purposes. It was a big old Chevrolet with shelves and cupboards inside, cooking equipment and kettles. A hatch had been cut in the side from which food could be served. To Lena it looked quite enormous, so the thought of driving one was a little daunting.

Over the next few days, they were taught how to make cakes and buns and professional-looking sandwiches. They also learned basic bookkeeping, because they would be taking money from customers and needed to be able to balance the books. Lena found some of that tricky, arithmetic never having been her strong point, but with an effort, she managed to grasp it.

A few days later, she had her first driving lesson, which proved rather nerve-racking. She had never been in the driver's seat of a vehicle before and to learn on such a huge one felt like quite a tall order. When she climbed up the three metal steps into the cab of the truck and sat at the wheel, she wondered how she would ever manage it. It felt so high up, the steering wheel so far from the windscreen and everything designed on a scale which seemed far bigger than herself.

The lesson took place on some waste ground behind a block of barracks and the instructor was a burly Scottish sergeant from one of the regiments stationed in Shillong. He kept calling Lena 'Missy', which made her smile, but she had to suppress it because she didn't want him to think she was making fun of him. After he'd given her a bit of a lecture about how things worked, he turned to her and said, 'Now you can turn on the engine, Missy.'

Lena turned the key, but there was just a fizzing noise. She tried again. It took several attempts before the engine chugged into life and she realised that there was a bit of technique to it. When the engine was rumbling away, though, vibrating the whole cab, the sound was deafening. It was quite hard for Lena to hear the sergeant at all, so he had to yell all his instructions. That, and the sun beating down on top of the cab made him go red in the face and sweat profusely.

'Put your left foot hard down on the clutch and put the gear-stick into first,' he ordered.

The gearstick was huge and spindly and seemed to wave around when you tried to move it, but eventually she managed to do what he'd asked.

'Now, gradually lift your left foot off the clutch and press the accelerator.'

Needless to say, the truck leapt forward and the engine stalled immediately. This happened two or three times before Lena got the hang of it. When she was moving along steadily, the sergeant explained how to change into second gear.

'It's called double declutching,' he announced, but as Lena had never done anything else, it seemed quite natural to her.

By the end of the lesson, she was able to go up and down through all the gears and bring the truck to a halt without stalling.

'You've done very well for a beginner,' the sergeant said, and rewarded her with a rare smile. 'You'll have another lesson tomorrow and every day after that, until you've reached the requisite standard for a licence, but you've made a great start.'

Lena got down from the truck cock-a-hoop that the lesson had been a success and that she was well on her way to becoming a fully-fledged Wasbie.

21

SHILLONG, 1944

It is 20ᵀᴴ January already. Mary and I have been at the Wasbie HQ in Shillong for several days and are beginning to settle down and get to know the other girls. I've been so busy and have gone to bed exhausted each night, so haven't had time to write in this diary before now. I have managed to write letters to Lakshmi and Sunil and Lieutenant Harper to let them know that we've arrived safely, and Mary wrote to Joan.

Tomorrow we will have our first attempt at putting all our training into practice (apart from the driving, of course). We will be sent out to canteens that are set up around Shillong for the soldiers stationed here. It won't be quite like working on the front line, but it will be a start and both Mary and I are looking forward to it.

Chloe reluctantly shut the diary and looked round the open-air café. She'd been so absorbed in Lena's experience at Shillong that she'd hardly noticed the passing of time. But it appeared that most of the lunch time guests had gone, and the waiters were busy clearing the tables, batting away the pigeons, mynahs and other assorted bird life that had come to peck the crumbs from the tablecloths.

Thanking the waiters, she returned to her room and locked the diary in the safe inside the wardrobe. She picked up her water bottle and guidebook. She was going to take a walk around the Thamel area and see how much it had changed since Lena's day. On an impulse she opened her grandmother's photograph album and took out one of the photographs of Lena as a young woman and slipped it into her bag.

She strolled out through the front gates and checked the map in her guidebook for directions to Durbar Square. It looked to be about twenty minutes' walk from the hotel, through a lot of little streets and passageways with many twists and turns. She set off down the narrow road and soon found herself in a pedestrianised area lined with tall, brightly coloured buildings, the bottom floor of which were shops catering for tourists. There were clothes shops, handicraft shops, luggage shops, but there were also tea traders, and shops selling groceries and fruit and vegetables for the locals. Every so often, she would pass a small temple wedged between two taller buildings, and the occasional stupa too, strung with multicoloured flags. The streets were busy, crowded with tourists, backpackers and locals. Cycle rickshaws nosed their way through the thronging shoppers, ringing their bells, the riders shouting for people to move out of their way.

Progress was very slow because of the crowds and because Chloe had to keep consulting her map. She also couldn't resist browsing at the many stalls and wandering into each temple and pausing at each stupa she came across. At last, she turned a corner and in front of her was a huge square, filled with magnificent red-brick temples with tiered slate roofs. On one side was an imposing white building with a pillared portico and, beyond that, the magnificent façade of a large building with stone lions guarding its wide entrance steps. It looked like a palace.

Staring up at the majestic building, Chloe's heart missed a beat. Could that be the palace of the Kumari Devi? With its four floors and shuttered windows and a wooden balcony jutting out over the square, it looked very much as Lena had described it. Chloe's guidebook told her that the Kumari Devi was still worshipped in Nepal, so perhaps she would get a glimpse of the young goddess today, if she was patient.

She sat on some stone steps opposite and waited patiently, but to no avail. The shutters to the upper floors remained steadfastly closed, the balcony still and empty. After about half an hour, she gave up. Perhaps she would come back another time to see if she could get a glimpse of the Kumari Devi.

There were a few market stalls dotted around the square, so she wandered around them, looking at the trinkets on offer. One stall was selling many-stranded, beaded necklaces in all different colours. They were very pretty, and Chloe bought two – one for herself and one for Sophie. She enjoyed bartering with the stall-holder but had a sneaking feeling that the price they agreed upon was still far too high and that she should have driven a harder bargain.

She wandered to the edge of the square, behind the jewellery stall and noticed a side street leading away from the square that was lined with jewellers' shops. She tried to remember what Lena had written about her first visit to the fortune teller. Hadn't she walked down a street full of jewellers to reach the fortune-teller's place?

Curious, Chloe went down the steps and into the side alley, noticing that the light was fading now, amazed that the day was almost over. Was this the alley that Lena had ventured down? Would she find a fortune teller down here? She'd put off investigating because she was worried that she would be disappointed, but once she started exploring, she became more and more determined to find one. Hadn't Kiran said that there were still fortune tellers around Durbar Square?

She carried on down the narrow street. Halfway along, another, narrower alley led off to the right. She turned down it, noting that it was even darker here, that it smelled dank. She carried on cautiously. Something scuttled past her and disappeared into a drain. She shuddered. It was definitely a rat. She was about to give up and retrace her steps when she noticed a pair of wooden doors set into a stone doorframe. The doors were blackened with age and pollution, but beneath the grime she could see that they were intricately carved.

Her heart pounding, Chloe turned the brass handle and pushed the doors open. Behind them was a gloomy, vaulted room. It looked like a cave, and was lit by candles. On the far side of the room hung some heavy, red curtains. Chinks of light spilled from round the edges of them. Chloe walked forward and, her heart in her mouth, pulled one of the curtains aside.

A woman with long, black hair and extravagant make-up sat behind a small round table, surrounded by candles. She was dressed in a bright red silk robe and wore a great deal of jewellery – bangles, long, dangly earrings, many gold chains around her neck, and her fingers were covered with rings. She looked up from filing her nails and fixed Chloe with a dark-eyed gaze. Chloe hesitated.

'Don't be afraid,' the woman said. 'Please, come in. Sit down. Give me your hand.'

She motioned Chloe to sit down in the rickety old chair opposite her.

Chloe stepped into the room and sat down. Was this the same chair that her grandmother had sat in, over seventy years ago? It could well be. In fact, Chloe was experiencing the strangest feelings of déjà vu, having read all about this place in Lena's diary. It was still exactly as Lena had described. She told herself it couldn't possibly be the same fortune teller, but this woman looked just like the one Lena had depicted.

'Let me take your hand,' the woman repeated, holding her own hand out. Chloe let the woman take her hand and study it. The woman leaned forward, her head dropped, she was studying Chloe's palm intently. She seemed mesmerised. Chills went down Chloe's spine and she drew her hand away.

'I'm sorry, I should have explained. I'm not here for a palm reading, I came to see you because I was curious. My grandmother came here during the second world war and what she was told seemed to have a profound impact on her. I was wondering... I know this is silly, but I was wondering if the woman who spoke to her was still here... still alive, maybe?'

The fortune teller narrowed her eyes.

'I will pay, of course,' Chloe said quickly, sensing her hesitation, and the woman's face immediately brightened.

'It is a very long time ago,' the woman said hesitantly. 'I can ask my grandmother. She is in her eighties now, but she learned her trade from her own mother. She used to sit in on all her prophesies from a very early age.'

'I'm sure she won't remember her. I was just curious to come here and see the place... to understand why my grandmother took those prophesies so seriously,' Chloe said, getting an unsettling sense of the mystery surrounding this room.

'Do you have a photograph I can show her?' the woman asked.

Chloe looked in her bag and took out the photograph of Lena, young and fresh, standing against the backdrop of mountains. She felt reluctant to hand it to the fortune-teller, but it was the only way to get answers.

'If you come back, perhaps in a week or ten days, my grandmother will be here again. She normally listens in and helps me. She is very wise, but she is unwell at the moment.'

'Oh dear. I'm so sorry to hear that,' Chloe said. 'But I will come back again.'

'Thank you.' Chloe put several rupee notes on the table and got up to go.

'When you come again, I will tell your fortune. Free of charge,' the woman said smiling for the first time. 'You have a fascinating palm yourself. May good luck be your companion until that day.'

Chloe went back out into the alleyway and stood there blinking, adjusting her eyes to the light. Then she turned back towards Durbar square, mulling over what she'd just experienced. How incredible that the building Lena had described had remained unchanged down the decades, and that the same family still plied their trade from the strange cave-like room at the back.

Chloe retraced her steps and was soon back in the bustle of Durbar Square. Despite the darkness, it was still thronging with people. She walked across it, heading back to the hotel, when she noticed a small group of people gathered in one corner. They were looking upwards and she realised that they were staring up at the Kumari Devi's palace. She walked towards them and when she drew close, she saw that a young girl stood on the wooden balcony on the top floor that was lit up with lights. She was dressed from head to toe in red silk with an elaborate feathered headdress. She stood there motionless, staring down at the square and at the crowd of people. Chloe looked up at her, entranced. What an incredible sight it was and what a privilege to see the living goddess. Young girls had stood on that balcony like that for hundreds of years and being there in that ancient square looking up at her gave Chloe a powerful connection to the past.

She stood there for what seemed like an age and it was only when the girl stirred and moved to go inside that Chloe came out of her reverie with a shudder. People were starting to drift away, so she turned and started to walk back in the direction of the hotel. As she reached the edge of the square, she noticed a young couple coming towards her. With a start, she realised that the man was Kiran, his arm was tucked through the arm of a pretty young woman who looked as stylishly dressed as he did. They seemed very happy and were laughing at a private joke, so Chloe quickly looked the other way, hoping he wouldn't notice her.

She walked on, her thoughts in turmoil, and she tried to examine how she was feeling. One part of her wasn't surprised that Kiran had a girlfriend, or wife even, but, she had to admit to herself, part of her was disappointed too. She had to face the fact that despite their difficult first encounter, she'd got to know and like Kiran during the journey to Kathmandu and she'd been looking forward to spending more time with him on the trek to Ghorepani. She even forced herself to admit that she was actually attracted to him and that she'd been hoping he felt the same way. Now all her hopes in that direction were dashed and she suddenly felt weary and dispirited.

She made her way back to the hotel, thinking just how inept the fortune teller's words about good fortune had been a few moments before. It made her wonder why Lena had set so much store by such words seventy years ago.

22

IT IS March now and at last my training is complete and I'm on my way to the front! I'm travelling by train to Chittagong, from where I will be airlifted to wherever it is that they are sending me in Burma. They haven't told me that yet, it is all very top-secret and they are paranoid about leaks, and the Japanese finding out where the next offensive will be. That feels exciting but a bit terrifying too.

IT WAS ONLY as the train was lumbering across the vast Indian plain towards the south coast, that Lena had finally got time to stop and breathe and catch up with her diary. The past few weeks had been so intense and busy, but also, in a curious way, so mundane and repetitive, that she hadn't either had the time or the inclination to chart her daily activities.

She had written a couple of letters to Lieutenant Harper, though, and told him how she was getting on in Shillong. He always replied by return, despite how busy he must have been, and his letters were warm and witty, and full of amusing anecdotes about Lena's former colleagues and life at the base. They reminded her yet again that there were many different sides to that man, and that he wasn't just that stiff-upper-lip staff officer that he presented on the surface.

During the last few weeks at Shillong, the trainee Wasbies were sent out to work the canteens that were set up in and around the town. Lena had got used to serving tea, sandwiches and cakes, dealing with a long line of impatient customers, handling money, and making sure the accounts were kept up to date. They also did a fair amount of baking and food preparation back at the kitchens at HQ. Lena felt as though she was now ready to transfer those skills to the field. She'd been itching to get to her posting for a while, as were all the others in her group. She had also got her driving licence, much to her astonishment, so was now qualified to drive one of those enormous army trucks. The gruff Scottish sergeant had even smiled and given Lena a hug when he'd presented her with the licence.

Before she took the train, Lena had to say goodbye to Mary and to all the other girls she'd got to know and become fond of at Shillong. It was a very sad moment and there were tears shed all round. The others were being posted to other units all over Burma, so they were all travelling separately. Lena was going to join an established unit who were already operating a canteen at the front. She would be replacing someone who had developed malaria and had been transferred to hospital back in India. Lena had been issued with a supply of Mepacrine – a malaria medication. She'd started to take it religiously, although it was already turning her skin a strange shade of yellow. It was probably worth it, she reasoned, although they were told that no medication was ever one hundred per cent effective against the deadly disease, especially in the jungles of Burma which were thick with mosquitoes by all accounts.

Lena was travelling in a ladies-only compartment in a first-class carriage to Chittagong. She had it all to herself. The first part of the journey from Shillong to Gauhati was by bus, just as on the way up. She was glad in a way that she was travelling alone. It was good to have the journey to reflect and to prepare for what was to come. Was she crazy to have gone to these lengths to get near the front line partly in an attempt to see Billy? The more she'd learned about Burma, the less she thought it likely that she would get anywhere near him. It was probable that she would never even discover where he was.

She knew that the 14th Army was made up of dozens of different regiments and was fighting on many different fronts all over Burma. There were some in the Arakan on the coast, some in the Naga Hills on the border with India where there was concern that the Japanese might mount an attack against Imphal. There were more in central Burma, and yet others helping United States and Chinese forces on the Ledo Road on the border with China. The list went on.

The more Lena had learned about the campaign and about the Wasbies' role, the more she had realised what she was doing was worthwhile in itself. If she never actually found Billy, at least she would know that she had done something positive to help the cause rather than completing forms, typing letters and filing papers in Lieutenant Harper's office.

THE NEXT MORNING, she found herself in Chittagong, in a miserable room in a dormitory barracks, not unlike the room she'd stayed in on the base in Kathmandu. Only in Chittagong she knew nobody, and it seemed even more forlorn and lonely. Chittagong had the feel of a transit town. It was the place where troops assembled before they were sent into Burma either by sea or overland. There were dozens of barracks full of soldiers and parade grounds where there were constant exercises. All the time, there was movement – mule trains, army vehicles and tanks on manoeuvres and on the way in or out. It was a restless place, full of restless, nervous people.

When Lena had arrived on the night train, she had reported to the transport section and they told her that she would have to wait a day or two for a flight into Burma. She still hadn't been told where she was going. Not that it would make much difference to her. She was sure that wherever there was fighting, it would be uncomfortable and dangerous, not to mention extremely hot and humid, just as it was in Chittagong.

There wasn't much to do there except wait. At lunchtime, Lena went into the barracks' canteen, where there were many soldiers from the 14th Army on their way to the Burma front. Because she was alone, she couldn't help but overhear their conversations. A lot of it focused on rumours about Indian soldiers serving in the British Indian Army who were defecting to the Indian National Army which was fighting on the side of the Japanese. Apparently, those soldiers often betrayed their former mates by giving any intelligence they had gained to the Japs. According to the soldiers' conversations, the defectors thought that by doing so they were helping the cause of Indian independence as preached by their leader Subhas Chandra Bose. But the soldiers she overheard were sceptical. It seemed that the defection of so many had bred distrust amongst the ranks in the British Indian Army amongst those who remained.

Lena remembered Lieutenant Harper speaking to her about this. He'd said that it was happening a lot in the ranks of the British Indian Army which was partly why they were so keen on recruiting as many Gurkhas as they could. Gurkhas were trustworthy and had no real interest in Indian independence, and so were far less likely to betray their fellow soldiers and go over to fight with the Japs.

Listening to the conversations, she wondered whether these rumours were true or whether they were exaggerated. Either way, her mind went back to Billy and she wondered whether this was affecting his regiment. She remembered how he'd told her that he'd fought alongside Indian soldiers, how trustworthy they were and what great brothers in arms they made. It would really destroy his faith in that brotherhood to see some of them transfer their allegiance to the enemy.

Two days later, Lena finally found herself at the front, but not yet in Burma. She was in the heart of the jungle, somewhere in Assam, at a place called Hailakandi. The airstrip she was stationed at was, according to the pilot on the flight over, to be the HQ of a big push by the Chindit regiment, called Operation THURSDAY. It was all very hush-hush and Lena was not to tell a soul – though who there might be to tell apart from soldiers out there in the middle of nowhere she had no idea.

She had flown in on a Douglas transport plane alongside boxes and crates of supplies for the troops. They had landed on a huge grass airstrip that had been hacked out of the jungle. The landing was extremely bumpy. It was an incredible flight, out from Chittagong over the Bay of Bengal at first, which was very turbulent with all the different currents and pockets of air over the sea, but it didn't faze Lena after her flights into Nepal. She was glad that she'd already had that experience, and that Lieutenant Harper had reassured her about flying. Without that she would have been terrified when the little plane started bucketing around. She had hung onto her seat, closed her eyes and thought of his calm, soothing voice reassuring her that it was quite normal for the plane to rock around furiously and that she wasn't to worry.

When they landed, Lena noticed that parked around the landing strip were dozens of flimsy-looking gliders alongside several military airplanes.

'Those are Dakotas,' the pilot told her. 'They are here to pull the gliders.

He'd already told her on the flight that Chindit troops would be flown from the airstrip by glider over the border, into inacces-

sible parts of the jungle in Burma to establish various strongholds around the Kaukwe valley.

Just after they landed, she saw two small aircraft take off from
the strip, and while they were walking to the makeshift base, the
pilot told her that they were likely to be spotter planes, going to
do a recce in the jungle to check that it would be safe to land
gliders on the airstrips.

Most of the troops were stationed in tents around the airfield,
so many that it felt like a tented town. Lena was taken in between
the rows of tents by a private from one of the regiments stationed
there, to meet her fellow Wasbies. He took her little suitcase and
beckoned her to follow him.

There were five Wasbies already at the camp, and when Lena
arrived, they were hard at work serving men with tea and cake
from a hatch in the side of their Chevrolet lorry. The whole scene
was a sea of movement and the Wasbies were extremely busy,
handing out cups of tea, taking money, making tea or cutting cake
and sandwiches in the back of the van. The girls looked hot and
bothered, and far too occupied to stop and talk to Lena, but their
leader, June Evans, an ample Welsh lady in her fifties, came out
of the back of the van wiping her hands on her apron and greeted
Lena warmly. She looked genuinely pleased and relieved to see
her and quickly introduced her to the other four.

'This is Pamela, Kathleen, Mildred and Barbara, or Babs as
she likes to be known.'

None of them had time to do anything other than say a quick
hello and then they were straight back to their work; a long queue
of troops was waiting impatiently and rather rowdily at the front
of the van to be served. Lena was excited to see a real live canteen
in operation and although she'd got used to serving soldiers in
Shillong, this was her first glimpse of one operating at the front.

June asked the soldier who'd brought her there to take Lena
to her billet.

'Make yourself at home there, Lena. I will catch up with you after the shift.'

Lena followed the man back through the lines to a large canvas tent on the edge of the field, a little away from the troops' tents. This one belonged to the Wasbies. The soldier pointed to the flap and indicated for Lena to go in. She thanked him, took her suitcase and ducked inside.

She was pleasantly surprised by how spacious and light it was. It was a huge, old-fashioned army tent, made of camouflaged canvas. There were six little camp beds set out with mosquito nets hanging from the ceiling poles. The girls had spread colourful sarongs on the beds to make it more homely. Their clothes were hanging on a rail on the other side of the tent, and they all appeared to use their suitcases as bedside tables with an oil lamp set up on each.

Lena quickly realised that her bed must be the one at the end – the only one without a sarong spread over it, just army-issue sheets, but at least it had only got one neighbour, so as private as possible in the circumstances. She pushed the mosquito net aside, sat down on her bed, and took off her shoes which were pinching her in the heat.

Lena decided to investigate the immediate surroundings. Beside the tent was another one – slightly smaller with an awning and a trestle table and chairs set up. Inside was a Calor Gas stove and a little kitchen. This must be the Wasbies' mess tent. She quickly made herself a cup of tea. It was very welcome in the heat and she hadn't had anything since 6 a.m. in Chittagong. How long ago that seemed!

When she'd finished drinking, she investigated further. Behind the sleeping tent was another tent which served as a makeshift bathroom with a portable canvas bath, jug and bowl set out. Next door to that was another small tent which she discovered was a camp lavatory. One of the Indian workers told her that there was fresh water in the bathroom if she wanted a wash.

She thanked him in his language.

'You speak Hindi!' He rewarded her with a friendly smile. 'If you need anything, I am here to help, miss. There is also cook, a sweeper and a dhobi-whallah too just for the Wasbie ladies. I will send dhobi-wallah round for any dirty washing.'

Lena thanked him, went back to fetch her towel, and washed off the grime and sweat of the long journey from Chittagong.

When the others came back it was late afternoon – time for an early supper. The cook brought food from the kitchen tent and after the girls had washed and changed, they all sat down to eat. The others all looked equally exhausted, but they still took the trouble to be friendly and welcoming to Lena, and to ask her about herself and what had brought here there.

Several of them told her that they had husbands serving at the front, and two, Kathleen and Barbara, had grown up in India so it had seemed natural for them to join up with the Wasbies to help to defend British interests in the country. When the meal of chicken and fried rice was finished, Lena helped Pamela and Elsie to clear the table. An orderly came to collect the plates. After that, they all sat around the tent watching the sunset over the jungle and sipping beers which June had produced from somewhere. Lena had rarely sampled alcohol and even after a couple of sips found herself growing sleepy. But she soon woke up when June started talking about their duties the following morning. She repeated what the pilot had told Lena earlier.

'The boys here are going to be flown into Burma to establish strongholds behind Japanese lines. They will be heading for several airstrips, all with code names – Chowringhee, Broadway, Piccadilly, White City. Another lot will set off to go by road to the north of a town called Indaw. They will be establishing a strong-hold to be codenamed Aberdeen. It goes without saying that this information stays within the camp.'

All the Wasbies nodded their understanding.

'This all means that we will have to get up extremely early and be ready to serve the men before dawn. They might want tea before they go, or things from the shop to take with them into the jungle. So, we'll all need to get to bed early and get some sleep.'

They didn't stay up for long, all the others were dog-tired, but when they turned in, Lena took the opportunity to write her diary by the light·of the Tilley lamp.

Now there is definitely something to write about, I need to make sure I do so as soon as I can before I forget all the details. What a day to be starting my duties with the Wasbies – at the very start of a big operation. So even though I'm not yet in Burma, I am very much at the centre of things and about to start doing my bit in earnest. I need to turn in now though and get some sleep before our early start.

As PLANNED, Lena was up before sunrise with the other Wasbies. They donned their uniforms and made their way between the tents over to the Chevrolet canteen. The others had stocked it the day before, so the shelves were full of supplies, such as soap, cigarettes, shoe polish, razors and hair oil. There was also plenty of bread and sandwich ingredients and several cakes ready and waiting to be cut. Someone got the tea urn going – this one was run on bottled gas.

'Could you serve at the hatch alongside Pam?' June asked Lena.

'Of course,' Lena replied, feeling a little nervous. The nerves soon dissipated as she got the hang of the work and Pamela – who liked to be called Pam – was extremely patient with her. Lena discovered that it was very much like serving soldiers in Shillong, only this time there were many, many more of them and they were all impatient to be served and to get on, so it was important to work very quickly and efficiently.

The men she served all seemed keyed up and nervous. Their eyes darted about restlessly, and none of them could stand still for more than a second. Lena tried to serve them without a fuss, sensing that there could easily be a scene if things didn't go smoothly. She understood that they were all acutely aware that the day ahead would put them in grave danger. The airstrips they were flying to could well have already been discovered by the Japanese, so the men could be ambushed as soon as they landed, not to mention the fact that flying over these mountains and landing in the middle of the jungle in a flimsy glider was hazardous enough in itself.

Everyone wanted a last cup of tea before setting off, usually sweetened by several spoons of sugar. Most men wanted a packet of cigarettes too, and often something extra like soap or hair oil. Lena wondered what use that might be in the jungle, but guessed that they might just want a little bit of luxury to take with them. Nobody asked for cake or sandwiches, probably because they'd all just had their breakfast. Lena and Pam saved them for the afternoon shift and just concentrated on brewing and serving the tea as quickly as they could.

After they'd been serving for about an hour, the first aircraft took off with a deafening roar, a flimsy glider following on behind. From where Lena was stationed, she had a good view of the runway through the gaps in the forest of tents. She watched as men were loaded into gliders, dozens at a time, along with all their equipment, boxes of supplies, and even mules that were led up the ramps braying in protest. Once they were all on board, the gliders were hitched up to the Dakotas which then lumbered down the airstrip and eventually took off, the gliders dragging behind. Some of the Dakotas were even towing two gliders, one behind the other. That looked perilous to Lena, particularly given how overloaded the gliders must have been.

Once in the sky, the aircraft had to climb steeply to clear the great mountains which stood between Assam and Burma and for hours the air was filled with the sound of their engines straining to gain height. Some of them seemed to barely skim the tops of the hills.

When the girls had finally served the last of the men, June thanked them all and said, 'Why don't you go and sit closer to the runway and watch the rest of the aircraft take off?'

Pam ran back to the tent and grabbed a couple of sarongs and everyone took their own cups of tea and sat down beside the airstrip. It was incredible to see these tiny aircraft, loaded to the hilt, struggle into the sky and head over the hills towards Burma to land behind enemy lines. It gave Lena an incredible sense of optimism to watch them embark on this daring endeavour and brought tears to her eyes to see them disappear over the horizon. As each aircraft faded into the mist above the mountains, she prayed for the safety of each of the men.

She thought of Billy as she watched them embark on that perilous mission. She'd already ascertained that he certainly wouldn't be amongst the men in this camp. These men were all Chindits of the 77th and IIIth Brigades. She had listened to snatches of conversation as the men lined up and waited to be served, including rumours that Billy's division had been sent up to Kohima in the hills between Burma and Assam. She knew that was where the Japanese were expected to launch an offensive to take the ridge and push down towards Imphal in India, so when she heard that, she became afraid for Billy. The Japanese were expected to battle fiercely for the chance of moving into India and were known to fight to the death.

Flights continued to take off right into the late afternoon. Once the Dakotas had released the gliders in central Burma, they returned to the airfield to hook up another glider to tow out there. During the afternoon shift, a few of the pilots came for tea in between flights. Their eyes were red-rimmed with fatigue and their faces filmed with sweat and grime. Yet, they were anxious to down their tea and get back to their duties.

During the evening, while Lena was helping to cut sand-wiches and baking cakes for the next day, news of the landings began to filter back to the base and the air was thick with it. Of the sixty-one gliders that had taken off from the airfield, the rumour was that twenty-six had crashed. Some of them had gone down over the nearby hills, the nylon ropes unable to take the strain of the steep climb. Others had crash-landed when they'd arrived at the jungle airstrip in Burma and there had been a pile-up with those coming in behind them. There were many casual-ties with the injured being ferried back by plane to field hospitals in India. Tragically, twenty-three men lost their lives that day, but over four hundred landed safely and were now behind Japanese lines.

Lena felt incredibly saddened by this terrible loss of life. She wondered how many of those men they had served this morning. The mood was quite subdued, but, overall, the operation was deemed to be a success by the superior officers, and it was set to continue the following day. So Lena had to put the shock and sadness aside.

After that first day, all the days seemed to merge into one. Lena was so utterly exhausted each night that as soon as she climbed inside the mosquito net and her head had hit the thin pillow she fell straight to sleep. She was on her feet from dawn and worked until the evening stocking up the van and making preparations for the next day. But she never failed to pray for Billy's survival every day and she thought about him every hour, hoping that one day they would be reunited.

There were an average of fifty-five flights each day. The Wasbies had their work cut out serving tea and supplies to the endless stream of Chindits bound for Burma on board those flimsy gliders. One day Lena overheard that the operation was all but complete and that nine thousand men had been flown into those remote strips in the Burmese jungle, and over a thousand mules too. They had managed to establish the strongholds in the jungle behind the enemy lines as they'd set out to do, at Chowringhee and at Broadway, and from there they would be able to carry out covert guerrilla operations against the enemy. To Lena, it was both exciting and humbling to have been part of that extraordinary operation, serving tea and trying to boost morale.

As soon as Operation THURSDAY was complete, work began to pack up and remove the camp. The Wasbies were due to have one day of rest, and then were to be flown somewhere else to operate another canteen nearer to the front line. June wasn't too sure where it would be, but she thought it was near a place called Tamu, which was close to the front at Imphal and Kohima.

'According to the officers, there's fierce fighting for a ridge there, the mood amongst the troops is low and they have very little in the way of supplies. So, a mobile canteen serving tea and snacks will be a great boost to morale.'

Lena felt a shiver, a mixture of fear and excitement when she heard where they were bound. At last she would be near the front and doing what she'd signed up for. She'd heard that Billy's regiment was in that vicinity, so perhaps someone might at least have news of him or where he was.

It felt strange the next morning not heading straight off to the canteen to make an early start, but Lena and two other Wasbies had arranged to borrow a jeep and were going to pack a picnic and travel out to the countryside and have a look around. June, Babs and Kathleen were staying behind to work the canteen – they'd had the previous day off. It was the first time for weeks that Lena hadn't put her uniform on when she'd got out of bed. Not that she minded wearing it, it was very smart – a grey shirt and trousers (compulsory because of the mosquitoes) and she was very proud of it. But she had to admit that sometimes it was a little hot and stiff. It was lovely to pull on a soft cotton dress and sandals instead that morning.

One of the officers dropped the jeep off near the Wasbies' billet just after dawn. The girls loaded sandwiches and cakes, a Calor Gas stove, blankets, and tea-making equipment into the back. Then they all slid onto the front seat and set off down the dusty road that led out of the camp. Mildred insisted on driving and they sped away into the countryside. Soon, they found themselves speeding through the little town of Hailakandi. Although it was the capital of the district, it was just a strip of makeshift buildings strung out along the highway. People sitting on their porches shaded their eyes and stared at the girls as they went past. Lena realised that it must have been highly unusual to see western women travelling in an army jeep – in fact, she didn't suppose the locals had seen many western women around those parts in their lives, other than perhaps the wife of the local district officer on one of their rare visits.

They drove on along a straight highway through parched scrub and flooded paddy fields. The sun was beating down mercilessly. The jeep was open-topped and Lena was glad of the hat she'd brought, although she had to hold it down constantly to stop it flying off.

Mildred and Pam had been out that way once before Lena had arrived, and they knew the road. A few miles out of town, Mildred turned off the highway onto a tiny track that wound its way between the paddy fields, past tiny villages which consisted of groups of mud huts where buffalo wallowed in muddy pools, chickens and pigs rooted around the houses, and the village children and dogs ran out to surround the jeep as they drove through.

Eventually, they ended up beside a wide brown river that seemed to stretch for miles ahead. The far bank was only just visible.

'This is the Karkahal River,' Mildred announced. She parked the jeep under a tree and they all got out, shook the dust from their clothes and spread their picnic blankets on a little pebbly beach that jutted out into the river. They brewed up a cup of tea and laid down on the blankets to enjoy the sunshine, the lapping of the river and the sound of the pelicans and bulbul birds on the water.

They chatted easily for a while, about the operation, about some of the men they'd encountered, about the Wasbies. Then they got round to talking about their lives before they'd joined up. Mildred said that she came from Wiltshire in England.

'I joined up with the Wasbies as a cipher clerk to work in Burma at the beginning of the war. When the Japs were threatening to invade though, we were all going to be evacuated and sent home. But Major Taylor managed to persuade the powers-that-be to let her establish a unit to operate canteens at the front. I gladly stayed on to join her. I almost regretted it when Rangoon was bombed and overrun by the Japs. Everyone was trying to leave and there were hardly any trains. You should have seen the people trying to scramble on board! It was heartbreaking. Families with tiny children and babies, desperate to leave. I managed to squeeze on board one of the last trains. We could see the city burning as the train pulled out through the suburbs,' she finished with a note of sadness.

Pam told them that she'd travelled out to Burma when her husband, who was in the army, had been posted there in 1939. 'I came so I could be near him, but I've not seen him once since war broke out.'

'How very sad for you,' Lena said with feeling, 'Are you able to write?'

'We try, but he's moving around all the time. Joining the Wasbies has given my life out here some purpose, otherwise I'd have been sent home. There are hardly any ships back to England and it's so dangerous. I didn't want to do that. What about you, Lena? What led you to sign up?'

Lena hesitated for a moment, then took a deep breath and told them all about Billy, how she'd met him in the hospital in Darjeeling, how they'd got to know and like each other, how she'd helped him escape the earthquake, and how he'd had to leave while she was away in Nepal.

'I suppose, part of the reason I volunteered for the Wasbies was to try to find him,' she admitted.

Pam pulled a sympathetic face and shook her head. 'Best of luck, Lena, but judging by what's happened to me, please don't hold out too much hope.'

'I've got to try, though,' Lena said.

'You'll see him again one day, but it might not be here,' Mildred said, patting her hand.

'I need to warn him, though,' Lena blurted. 'He could be in danger and I need to let him know.'

'In danger? They're all in danger,' Pam remarked.

'But this is different. You see, when I was in Kathmandu, I went to see a fortune teller,' Lena explained. 'She told me that he was in danger from someone he trusted... I know it sounds silly and far-fetched, but I need to find him and let him know.'

Lena watched their expressions anxiously, thinking they might laugh at her, but they didn't.

'It doesn't sound silly at all,' Mildred said, and Pam murmured her agreement.

It was a huge relief to Lena to be able to unburden herself to Mildred and Pam. They were so sympathetic, and after they'd confided in each other, Lena felt that they were already firm friends.

Before they ate their picnic, they stripped down to their underwear and went for a swim in the river. It was deliciously refreshing to take a dip in the cool water after so many days sweating in the heat of the camp. They were lucky, though, that they'd already got out of the water, had dried and dressed when a local farmer came past driving a herd of goats.

23

WHEN WE GOT BACK to camp, it was after dark and we had to muck in and pack up the truck which will be taken by one of the army drivers back to Shillong. Then we packed our bags because tomorrow we have another early start – this time into the heart of the war zone, to that little place called Tamu, not too far from Kohima in the Naga Hills.

Chloe was intrigued to read Lena's first few entries about her time as a fully-fledged Wasbie, the accounts of the Chindits taking off on their daring operation into the Burmese jungle and to encounter Mildred Lightfoot for the first time between those pages. It surely *was* Mildred Lightfoot whom Lena had referred to. Mildred and Lena must have remained firm friends for life. Did the same apply to Pam? Chloe sighed. There was so much that she'd never spoken about.

She was now back at the Kathmandu Guest House after her trip to Durbar Square. She had no appetite or energy for further sightseeing that day. Perhaps it was that gruelling bus journey the day before that had sapped her energy? Perhaps it was the excitement of finding the fortune-teller's place that morning, or the less welcome surprise of seeing Kiran arm in arm with an attractive young woman. Whatever it was, she was quite content to spend the evening resting at the hotel, catching up with Lena's diary, rather than doing more exploring. She was keen to read on, so she asked a passing waiter to bring her a fruit juice and turned back to the diary and began the next entry dated 14th March 1944.

We have now arrived on the Tamu-Palel Road close to the front, and I'm writing this in my tiny tent by the light of a Tilley lamp. The tent is meant for two people, but it turns out that, sadly, tonight I'm alone due to tragic circumstances. I'm still reeling with shock at what happened just after we arrived here. It is difficult to put into words, but I must try to because I need to make sure I remember every detail of this dreadful day. I will start at the beginning.

THE FLIGHT into Burma was in one of the sturdy old Dakota aircraft that had been used to tow the gliders into Burma for Operation THURSDAY. The Wasbies all piled on board with their luggage. They had been told that there was a mobile canteen already set up on the Tamu road, so they didn't need to take any equipment with them. The mood on the flight was exuberant. The girls were glad to have completed a successful stint at Hailakandi and to be heading for pastures new. To be going even closer to the front was incredibly exciting too, if rather nerve-racking.

Lena overheard the pilot telling June some unsettling news while they were flying up towards the mountains. She was sitting behind June so couldn't help listening in.

'Apparently, the Chindits who landed at Chowringhee had heard a rumour that the Japanese had rumbled their co-ordinates. They had to disperse into the jungle. They got out in the nick of time. Just as well really, because the camp was bombed to oblivion by the Japanese afterwards.'

'Good Lord!' June exclaimed. What happened to them?'

'None of them were harmed apparently. They're now well behind enemy lines carrying out guerrilla activities.'

'That's good to know,' June replied.

'The boys at Broadway weren't so lucky. After they'd set up camp, some of them went on up the mountain to try to establish another one up there. But on the way, they were surrounded by Japs and there was a hell of a battle. Heavy casualties on both sides I heard.'

Lena thought about those men to whom she'd served a humble cup of tea before they'd been flown off to face danger. She wondered if she'd served any who'd died in that battle. It reminded her how precarious every life was, and she got to thinking about Billy again, wondering if he was still alive, or-God forbid-whether he was buried in some shallow grave in the middle of the jungle.

She was still thinking about him as the Dakota headed over the dusty plain and into the hills. She was sitting beside the window on the right of the aircraft, and she looked out over layer upon layer of forested hilltops, stretching into the distance, fading into the misty horizon. They passed over tiny hill villages where they could actually see the villagers standing there staring up at them, sometimes waving madly.

They began their descent to the airstrip at Tamu, then the pilot turned round,

'If you look out on the left, you can see Imphal and the army base there.'

All the Wasbies crowded over to that side of the plane and there it was. A whole valley full of tents, sheds, army vehicles, aircraft and supply depots stretching far into the distance. It was truly impressive, far bigger than the encampment they had just come from. It was Imphal and the surrounding area, though, which was under threat from the Japanese and which the troops they were on their way to serve were trying desperately to defend from attack.

The airstrip at Tamu was new – having been carved out of the jungle by Indian troops only the previous month – and it was very bumpy indeed, provoking surprised shrieks from some of the Wasbies as they bounced to a halt. An officer from the Indian Army 20th Division came to meet the girls and show them to their tents.

'The front line is a little way down the hill over there,' he said pointing to the horizon. 'Don't be alarmed if you hear gunfire. The battle goes on all day and all night.'

Just as the group reached the Tamu-Palel Road at the top of the hill above the airstrip, they met a convoy of army vehicles snaking along the pass. They must have been bringing supplies to the camp. The girls stopped beside the road to let them by. Pam was dragging behind because the handle on her suitcase had broken and she kept stopping to try to fix it. Suddenly came the droning of aircraft approaching from the west. Instinctively, Lena looked up. It sounded different to the noise of the Dakotas she was used to.

The officer yelled, 'Japanese aircraft. Take cover immediately.'

They all dived under a paused lorry, just as the planes were upon them. The aircraft swooped down and strafed the convoy, firing continuously on the vehicles. Lena put her hands over her ears, but she could still hear the sickening ack-ack-ack of machine-gun fire and the terrifying ping of bullets on metal, the screams of men in the convoy being hit. It seemed to go on for ever, but it could only have been a few seconds.

She was huddled under the lorry next to Mildred and when she turned round, she saw with a bolt of shock that Pam had been hit. She was lying prone on the grass, bleeding from a wound to her head. Her suitcase had burst open and all her clothes were blowing around in the eddies and currents left by the Japanese aircraft.

'Pam!' Lena started to scramble out from under the lorry to run to her friend.

'Stay put!' yelled the officer. 'That's an order.'

The planes were coming back, screaming low overhead. Lena counted three of them, firing on the convoy again. There were shouts and screams from the men. Some had been hit. Then there was a horrible, deathly silence during which Lena became aware of the drip-drip-drip of petrol draining from the tank of the lorry into the dusty road.

Once it was clear that the aircraft weren't coming back, Lena and Mildred crawled out from under the truck and ran over to Pam. She'd been hit on her forehead, her skull shattered in a great, gaping, bloody wound. Suppressing nausea and remembering the first-aid they had been taught at Shillong, Lena grabbed a shirt from the pile of Pam's clothes and tried to stem the blood. Pam's eyes were still open but flickering shut constantly, her pupils disappearing up into her eyelids.

'Stay awake!' Lena urged and she could hear Mildred saying the same thing. Mildred's cheeks were wet with tears.

Lena had no idea how long they stayed there like that, trying to keep Pam awake, but they were eventually interrupted by some medical orderlies who came running over with a bamboo stretcher. She watched as the men loaded Pam gently onto it and took her off to the field hospital in the camp the other side of the hill. Lena and Mildred ran alongside the stretcher, Lena was still trying to hold the shirt to Pam's forehead, but it was soaked with blood.

When they reached the field hospital, which was a large square tent set up in the middle of the camp, the orderlies paused outside.

'I'm sorry, but I'm afraid you can't come in,' the man in the lead said. Then they lifted the flap and disappeared inside. But in that moment, Lena got a glimpse of the horrors in the tent. Dozens of bloodied, bandaged men with all manner of wounds and disfigurements, writhing and groaning in pain on camp beds or on the floor. She exchanged appalled glances with Mildred.

When they turned to leave, four or five more stretchers turned up carrying men who'd been hit when the convoy was strafed.

They walked slowly and wordlessly away, back towards the road. The other four Wasbies were coming towards them carrying their belongings, and Pam's too. The others were all in tears, asking about Pam, desperate for news, but all Lena and Mildred could do was shake their heads and tell them that she was in the hospital. They wandered back to the convoy, where soldiers were trying to start the vehicles and move them off the road. The officer who'd been accompanying the girls was visibly shaken.

'Follow me,' he said, squaring his shoulders, and he took them to the other side of the camp and showed them to their tents, which were a lot smaller than the ones at Hailakandi. There were three two-man tents set up for them and as it had already been agreed that Pam and Lena would share, Lena agreed to sleep alone.

They got settled in, then, dazed with shock, went to the officers' mess – another big tent on the edge of the camp – where they were given some sort of unappetising stew for lunch. Lena just toyed with her food, feeling wretched. They spoke about nothing but Pam and how wonderful she was, how much fun, how much energy and enthusiasm she had, always optimistic and encouraging others. They didn't know what would happen to her, but if she lived, she would surely never be the same again.

After that dismal lunch, the Wasbies were taken to look at their mobile canteen, which was an older, more battered version of the Chevrolet trucks that they were used to operating.

'There has been a recent delivery of supplies,' the officer said, 'so the cupboards are well stocked.'

They had to set to work then, baking cakes, making sandwiches for the next day when they would start serving the frontline troops. But none of their hearts were in the task and they simply went through the motions, barely speaking. Every so often, someone would break down or let out a loud sob. When would this terrible war stop taking good people? Lena wondered.

She found it hard to sleep that night with the continuous sound of gunfire coming from the battlefield which was just behind the camp and thinking constantly about poor Pam. She'd heard that she would get used to the tragedy wrought by war in time, but Lena wasn't so sure. It was hard not to think about all the men who were dying out there, so close to where they were lying.

In the morning, she dressed quickly. Then she and Mildred went over to the medical tent and asked after Pam. The orderly furrowed his brow and ducked back inside the tent to fetch a doctor. The doctor appeared, his white coat stained with blood, lines of exhaustion ringing his eyes.

'I'm afraid to say she passed away in the night,' he told them.

Lena and Mildred clung to each other in their mutual grief and stumbled back through the camp to break the dreadful news to the others.

That afternoon, they went to the edge of the camp where there was a hastily dug graveyard with dozens of recent graves. The regiment padre conducted the service and they buried Pam, wrapped only in a sheet, tears streaming down their faces. Lena struggled to comprehend how their beautiful Pam, full of fun and laughter, who only two short days ago was swimming in the river beside her without a care in the world, had gone for ever.

June told everyone they were welcome to take the rest of the day off.

'Remember, though, these men are putting their lives on the line every day. They deserve some comfort. I think Pam would have wanted us to carry on with our work, don't you?'

The girls all murmured their agreement. It was better to be pulling together, working hard, rather than sitting in the miserable darkness of the tent wallowing in sadness.

Even so, it was hard to go back to work pouring tea, cutting

cake and taking money. They passed another long, tiring day,
serving whatever troops came for tea, cakes or supplies – Indians,
Gurkhas, British men from every part of the country. They all
looked equally muddy, exhausted and filthy. It was hardly
surprising, they had been there for days and during that time the
battle had not let up.

LENA HAD BEEN SERVING troops on the Tamu-Palel Road for five
days, and at the end of each day, she had just crawled into bed
under the mosquito net, exhausted and drained. Each night she
went to sleep with images of poor, dear Pam in her mind.

All the time the Wasbies had been stationed there, the battle
had raged around them. Guns and shells fired round the clock. It
was strange, Lena thought, but you somehow got used to it after a
time and stopped registering every bang or explosion. Sometimes
they spotted Japanese tanks moving along the ridge of the hill,
trying to get behind the British position. It was chilling to see the
enemy at such close quarters.

When the girls went for meals in the mess tent, the officers
would talk about the operation.

'When we first arrived here,' one officer, a major, told them,
'these hills were covered in jungle. All the shelling and tank
movements have destroyed all the vegetation.'

Lena looked around her thinking about what he'd said. Now
the hills were just quagmires carved up with mud-filled trenches.
It was hard to imagine it had once been jungle, rich and lush,
alive with the sound of wildlife.

'It's absolutely vital for the British to defend the ridge,' the
major went on. 'If it were to fall, the Japanese would have an easy
route along the Shenam Saddle, to take Imphal.'

'And you know what that would mean,' the man beside him, a

captain, chipped in. 'That the Japs would then have a foothold in India.'

The two officers went on to tell them that there were members of the Indian National Army fighting alongside the Japanese.

'These are men who defected from the British Indian Army,' the captain told them, his jaw clenched in anger. 'I can tell you, it causes a lot of resentment and anger amongst the men fighting here – the British and the Indian troops who have stayed loyal.'

'Yes,' the major agreed. 'Their defection is seen as the worst kind of treachery.'

Lena remembered overhearing the troops in the canteen at Chittagong talking about the same thing and how Lieutenant Harper had often mentioned how the Gurkhas were loyal and trustworthy and wouldn't even consider going over to the INA.

She felt a pang of nostalgia, thinking of Lieutenant Harper. She hadn't been able to write to him since she'd left Hailakandi and she hadn't received a letter from him since leaving Shillong. There was no post to or from the Tamu-Palel Road, and she realised that she missed his letters. They used to cheer her up and remind her of home. She wondered how he was coping with his grief, whether he was lonely, and thought again of his kindness towards her. He'd given her a job and even trusted her with his secrets.

Later that day, June told the girls that she'd received a message from Major Taylor that they were to proceed straight to Imphal. From the reports Major Taylor had received from High Command, the fighting on the Tamu-Palel Road had become too intense and dangerous for the Wasbies to be there anymore. So, that evening, after they'd finished their shift, they stowed everything away in the truck, in preparation for the next morning, when they would drive to Imphal. It was further away from the fighting and perceived to be safer.

Lena felt excited to be on the move, though leaving was

tinged with sadness too. That evening, the girls went to the grave-yard to say goodbye to Pam for the last time. They had no flowers to put on her grave, but Lena tied a little red ribbon to the crude cross that marked Pam's resting place as a gesture of remembrance.

When I lie down at night I can't get the image of her dreadful wound out of my head, her flickering eyes as the life drained from her body. Such a tragic loss. None of us will ever forget her and how she died. It is so sad that her grave is up here on a remote mountain in the midst of the jungle, and not in some country graveyard near her home in England where her family would be able to visit.

Chloe found it hard to get to sleep herself that night, thinking of poor Pam, buried out there in a remote spot in the mountains, thousands of miles from her home. Lena's descriptions went round and round in her mind. What tragic events her grand-mother had been part of as a young woman.

The next morning, Chloe felt drained. When she went down to breakfast, the receptionist called her over and handed her a note. She looked at the envelope with her name neatly written with capitals on the front and knew it must be from Kiran. It had to be. After all, she didn't know anyone else here in Kathmandu. She ripped it open.

Dear Chloe,

I hope you are enjoying Kathmandu and the Guest House. I dropped round very early and guessed you were still asleep. I have to take a tour party up to Bhaktapur today and won't be back until late. But I wanted to let you know that tomorrow I plan to go to Pokhara by bus. My mother is unwell and I'd like to see her, but it would be good if you would come to Pokhara with me. I'd be happy to guide you up into the hills. There wouldn't be a charge, I enjoyed your company on our journey from Kakarbhitta, and I'd like to spend more time with you, so it would be a gift from a friend.

I will come back after my tour is finished – around 6 p.m. to see what you have decided. I hope you do decide to come along. It would be fun to spend more time together.

Best wishes,

Kiran Rai

Chloe wandered out to the café in the garden, mulling over Kiran's words. She was flattered by them and tempted to take him up on his offer. She would love to spend more time in his company too. But she couldn't help remembering the sight of him in Durbar Square arm in arm with the pretty Nepalese girl, laughing and chatting, obviously relaxed in each other's company. She had slight qualms about leaving for Pokhara so soon, too. She'd barely scratched the surface of the sights in Kathmandu. On the other hand, she reasoned, the offer was almost too good to be true. Although she could have paid for a guide to take her up to Ghorepani, it would surely be better to go into the hills with someone she already knew. She could always come back to Kathmandu after the trip and spend more time seeing the sights. After all, she needed to return anyway to see the fortune teller again.

24

IMPHAL, 1944

So, here we are in Imphal after an eventful day on the road. We are a little farther from the fighting, but it is well-known that the Japanese are pushing forward and have Imphal in their sights.

Getting to Imphal had been a traumatic experience. At times, Lena had thought they wouldn't make it and that they would all die, trapped in their mobile canteen up there in the hills.

June had driven the truck. Lena was glad it wasn't her at the wheel. She knew she would have been terrified. She found driving difficult enough in the best of conditions, let alone navigating through a war zone where they could have been hit by shells or aircraft fire at any time.

Although they were driving away from the front and the fighting, there was constant aircraft activity above the road, with Japanese fighter planes screaming overhead. Every time the planes came over, the girls all crouched down under the counter of the truck, where at least there was some cover. But poor June, exposed up there on the driving seat, just had to soldier on.

As well as aircraft to contend with, there was shellfire too, from long-range missiles, whistling overhead, sometimes landing quite close. The explosions caused the earth to spurt up in fountains, making it even more difficult to pass.

So, for most of the journey, Lena's pulse had been racing, and she couldn't slow her heartbeat down. She tried to remind herself that they weren't totally alone. They had an army escort from the 20th Indian Division. There was an armoured car driving ahead and one bringing up the rear too.

Even so, she couldn't help wondering what the soldiers would do against an attack from the air, or if the Japanese tanks managed to burst through the British and Indian lines and begin their final advance along the road to Imphal.

The road itself was littered with burned-out and abandoned army vehicles and in places the surface had been blown away by shells leaving deep craters. Although some of these holes had been filled in with earth by the troops, it had quickly turned to mud. The journey, which was less than twenty miles, took several hours.

When they finally arrived in the huge army camp in the Imphal valley, the place was on high alert, with troops constantly coming and going to their positions in the surrounding hills. It wasn't known from which direction the Japanese would attack. They were advancing on four different fronts.

The girls were shown to a tent on the edge of the encampment, a lot larger and roomier than the ones they'd been staying in up until then. These tents were showing signs of wear, though, as if they'd been used by dozens of troops passing through. They were shabby and none too clean. The mosquito nets above the camp beds were dirty and full of holes. Lena could hear creatures scrabbling around outside, which she assumed were rats. Later, when they went along to the mess tent for a meal of bully beef and boiled potatoes, an officer told them that it would be a few days before they could be evacuated into central Burma.

'Everyone, except essential combat staff are being moved on

from Imphal. Even nurses working in the field hospital are being flown back to the hospital at Comilla tomorrow. Except a select and very brave few who will be going up near the front at Kohima to man a field hospital up there. We'll get you out as soon as we can. In the meantime,' he finished, 'you'll be able to set up your canteen in the middle of the camp and serve the soldiers who are based here. It will be a great boost to morale.'

Lena was relieved to hear that they would be fully occupied for the next few days, and not getting bored and miserable, dwelling on the loss of Pam and the horrors of the battles that were raging all around them. It would be easy to slip into despair. Just walking through the camp, she'd already seen several wounded men being loaded off aircraft or bullock carts straight from the battlefield. They were then run by orderlies on stretchers to the hospital tent.

It was truly terrible to see the extent of their wounds – limbs blown off, shocking stomach and head injuries, oozing blood. The men themselves, those that were conscious, were often screaming out in pain. Lena could only reflect once more on what a terrible toll the war was taking on their young men.

It reminded Lena sharply of Billy and all the poor wounded boys who'd surrounded him in the hospital in Darjeeling. She wondered yet again if she would ever see him again. She knew that some of his division were out there in the hills on the Shenam Ridge, but in the days she'd been up there on the Tamu-Palel Road, she hadn't met anyone who knew Billy. She had to assume he was with one of the groups dotted around elsewhere in Burma. Unless the worst had happened, and she couldn't start to think about that. She had to cling onto whatever hope there was that he was still alive and that one day they would be together again.

They were only in Imphal for a few days, but each day they rose before dawn and went over to their truck which was parked on the other side of the camp to open up.

There was always a constant stream of soldiers queuing to buy tea and sandwiches, cake and buns or supplies of shoe polish, toothpaste or hair oil. Although everyone looked jittery, they were all ready with a joke or a bit of banter. It annoyed Lena, though, to see that the officers always pushed in and tried to get served before the other men. June would step in and sort out the jostling queue. 'Everyone has to wait their turn to be served,' she would yell. 'There's no pulling rank here, gentlemen!'

While the men were queuing up, the girls would hear them exchange news about the battle. There was still fierce fighting up on the Shenam ridge, and the Japanese were making a violent and concerted attempt to take Kohima, which occupied a strategic position on the road to Imphal. They were advancing on Imphal from three other directions, but the British and Indian forces were putting up strong resistance on every front.

The Wasbies were the last non-combatants left on the Imphal plain and things around them were getting extremely tense. The fighting had been going on day and night in the hills. From outside the tent, Lena could see the machine-gun emplacements set up in strategic positions on the surrounding mountains, and hear the rattle of gunfire constantly. Her nerves were frayed. She worried constantly that the Japs would burst through the British and Indian lines and take them all prisoner. She shuddered to think what could happen. She had read chilling stories of mass rape in Nanking in China and other places when the Japanese had invaded.

But to her relief, on the fourth day, the Wasbies were told that they were going to be flown out. They were to be taken to somewhere in the Irrawaddy valley where troops were massing to attempt to take Indaw again after the failure of the Chindit expedition the previous month. It would be easier for the Wasbies to stay well back behind the lines there, whereas in Imphal the fighting went on all around them and there was a danger that the valley would be overrun by the Japanese at any time.

Lena was glad that they were finally going. The relief on each of her fellow Wasbies' faces was plain to see when they were told they would be moving out. Lena felt her heart lifting, but that feeling was mixed with sorrow for all the men who had to stay there to fight. There was no respite or relief for them.

25

BURMA, 1944

On 3 April we arrived in a tiny village called Se-U, in the Katha district in north-central Burma, on the banks of a river. It is south of the town of Indaw, and not too far from the Irrawaddy valley.

They had been flown there from Imphal in one of the trusty old Dakotas. It had taken off steeply in order to fly out of the valley. As it headed east over the Manipur Hills, the girls had a good view of the battlefields, where the lines of trenches were plain to see, the bursts of gunfire lighting up the bare brown earth. Once over the jungled hills, they flew over the Chindwin River, weaving its way through the dark green landscape like a lithe, brown snake. Then they crossed yet more hills before the land flattened out in another river valley and as they began to descend, temples, villages and rice paddies came into view. Then they were bumping along the grass landing strip beside another wide, brown river.

As soon as they had landed, an officer showed them to their billet, which this time consisted of two old wooden village houses. Like the tents at Imphal, they were none too clean, and the girls had to set to straight away, making the place habitable.

The officer in charge told the Wasbies that the troops there were all British, men of the 7th Leicester Regiment. They were there to take the nearby town of Indaw, and to make covert sorties to disrupt the Japanese wherever they could.

'There's a mobile canteen already here waiting for you. It's been driven here from somewhere in the Arakan by army drivers,' he announced.

After cleaning the houses, the girls set off to investigate it. There wasn't much stock in the truck, so they had to drive it over to the army store, which was on the edge of the camp and stock up with as much as they could. This time June asked Lena to drive and she was relieved that she did so without mishap, although it wasn't far and the track was fairly dry and flat. But it felt like an achievement all the same.

WE SPENT *the evening making sandwiches and baking cakes and buns in the mess kitchen and came back to our quarters exhausted after another eventful day. It doesn't feel quite so dangerous here as at Imphal. The fighting is farther away and there is less chance of being besieged by the enemy, but I do feel for all those men fighting for their lives in Imphal, Kohima and the surrounding hills. And I wonder about Billy too and whether he is still out there somewhere, still fighting for his own life.*

Chloe paused and looked out of the bus window. This part of the Kathmandu-Pokhara road was fairly straight and flat, and Kiran had nodded off to sleep beside her, so she'd taken the opportunity to catch up with some more entries in Lena's diary. They were travelling along a main road in the bottom of a valley beside a fast-flowing river where white rapids rushed through canyons and tumbled over huge rocks. She recalled reading about Lena's journey between Kathmandu and Pokhara, when the road had been impassable because of landslides, and they'd had to get out of the Land Rover to clear the earth and rocks away before they could proceed. It seemed as though the road had improved significantly since then, although on occasion the bus driver had had to slow down and edge past mudslides or skirt around huge potholes.

Chloe was glad that she'd decided to come along with Kiran, glad of his company again. She'd spent the day before walking around the old city alone with her map and guidebook, stopping to look at all the different temples, palaces and sights along the way. Unlike her first day in Kathmandu, when she'd been keen to get straight to Durbar Square, on the second occasion, she took her time and savoured the experience, taking dozens of pictures on her phone as she went.

Kiran had been waiting when she'd arrived back at the guest house. He'd seemed delighted when she told him she'd decided to go with him to Pokhara and into the mountains. He'd ordered her a taxi for the morning and said he would meet her at the bus station at eight o'clock. When she'd arrived there that morning, as arranged, his eyes had lit up again. She was puzzled and a little wary. She had decided to find a subtle way of asking him about his girlfriend, but hadn't found the right moment yet.

With a sigh, she turned back to the diary. After the last paragraphs, there were several pages of one- or two-line entries, simply marking the date, the location and giving a brief update about the work, Lena's fellow Wasbies, or sometimes about the progress of the Burma campaign. It seemed that for the next few months, Lena was kept very busy – too busy to spend much time writing her diary. And Chloe assumed that it felt as though every day was a repeat of the previous one and probably didn't warrant a long diary entry.

According to the diary, Lena and her fellow Wasbies were stationed at Se-U for several weeks, then they moved behind the 7th Leicester Battalion who were marching south to Indaw Lake. Lena wrote that for the men, the march was long and hard, battling through mud and incessant, heavy rain, but for the

Wasbies, travelling alongside in their mobile canteen, although at times the truck got stuck in the mud and had to be dug out by the accompanying troops, it was a chance to experience the beauty of the northern Burmese countryside close-up, the gentle hills, the timeless villages nestled amongst the paddy fields, the wide, lazy rivers, the crumbling temples rising from the misty plains.

The division set up camp near Indaw Lake, which Lena described as a beautiful, remote stretch of water full of wading birds and other exotic wildlife, nestled in a lush, green valley. The Wasbies set to work serving tea and cake again. Supplies for the canteen were dumped nearby by regular flights from India. It seemed to Chloe that Lena enjoyed this time of relative stability, although nothing in that war could be said to be safe. The girls were only too aware that the men they were serving were being sent out to face the enemy each day and that often men they'd chatted to that morning didn't return in the evening.

On 6 June 1944, Lena wrote that the Wasbies had been told that thousands of Canadian, American and British troops had landed on the beaches in Normandy and begun their advance down through northern France. Lena noted that it was good news, of course, but that she wasn't sure how it might affect them in the East. The Allies might be victorious in Europe, but the Japanese could carry on fighting. She couldn't see anything persuading them to loosen their grip on Burma and the rest of the region.

Later that month, she recorded that at last the siege of Imphal was over. The Wasbies had been told that two British and Indian Divisions had finally retaken the Imphal to Kohima road. The Japanese seemed to be losing ground in that area at long last, she noted. But still they were fighting on in the Irrawaddy valley and all over central Burma.

The Wasbies' stay at Indaw lake continued for several months and Chloe flicked through the following entries where Lena gave details of supply drops, of how many men they'd served that day, of minor illnesses the other girls were suffering from, and of the sorties the 7th Leicesters were carrying out against Japanese forces daily, how many casualties there were and how exhausted the men were looking.

Towards the end of August, Lena wrote that the 7th Leicesters were to be disbanded. They had performed incredible feats in north-central Burma and weakened the Japanese defences with all their operations and sorties, but their numbers were severely depleted. Those who were left were to be flown back to India for treatment and rehabilitation. The Wasbies, were to be sent to serve elsewhere in Burma. They were waiting for news as to where that would be.

∼

Wherever it is, we will be sad to say goodbye to these brave soldiers, many of whom, over these few incredible months, have become our friends.

Chloe closed the diary, wanting to save the next chapter in Lena's wartime experience for when she had more time and wasn't rocking and swaying along on a dilapidated bus. The road had started to get steeper and more winding over the past few miles.

Kiran was stirring beside her. He blinked awake and smiled into her eyes.

'I'm so pleased you agreed to come along with me, Chloe,' he said. 'It's great that you're going to meet my family.'

He'd already told her that she could stay free of charge in his parents' guest house. She felt awkward about accepting that offer but realised it would be rude to refuse. She would see if she could buy them a gift.

'I think you mentioned you had a brother.' she asked. 'Will be be there?'

'I have one brother and one sister actually. My brother now

runs a shop in Pokhara, selling trekking equipment. My sister is my twin, actually. She lives at home and helps my mother and father run the guest house. She's just been with me in Kathmandu for a couple of days. She went straight back home yesterday after we found out that my mother was ill.'

'Oh.' Chloe's mind started racing. Could it have been Kiran's sister he'd been with in Durbar Square? Thinking back, the young woman's face was as beautiful as Kiran's own, with the high cheekbones and dancing brown eyes.

'What did you do together in Kathmandu?' she asked, trying to sound nonchalant.

'We went up to Durbar Square for an early supper one evening. There's a great little place we know in the backstreets.'

Chloe sat back against the seat, smiled to herself and let out a long sigh, staring out of the window at the peaks opposite. Suddenly, everything became clear. Kiran hadn't been stringing her along at all. He *had* been really pleased to see her at the bus station, and his enthusiasm in her company was genuine. How stupid she'd been. She could relax now and enjoy the journey with him and drop all her suspicious thoughts.

26

POKHARA, 2015

THE BUS finally rolled into the outskirts of Pokhara. It was a much larger city than Chloe had imagined. It was spread out across a wide valley, built around a beautiful mountain lake and surrounded by snow-capped peaks. They got off the bus at the bus station on the edge of the town centre, and Kiran quickly found them a motor rickshaw.

'My parents' guest house is beside the lake,' he explained. 'A couple of kilometres from here. It's quiet there and its where all the tourists want to stay. It's the most beautiful part of Pokhara.'

They drove through the city, which to Chloe seemed like a smaller version of Kathmandu, where motor bikes buzzed to and fro, and music belted out from open-fronted shops. Lush green trees lined the roads here though, even palm trees in some places. The colours were incredible. Pastel-painted low-rise buildings, set amongst vibrant gardens. All of this contrasted with the back-drop of dark green hills, framed with the snowy Annapurnas and above them the deep blue sky.

After weaving through a maze of backstreets, they arrived at Phewa Lake and drove along beside it for a short distance. Chloe was enchanted by what she saw. Small boats painted in many different colours bobbed about on the mirror-like surface. In the middle of the lake was an island, on which was built a temple with tiered roofs. They passed several guest houses and backpacker hostels which overlooked the lake. Young, sun-kissed travellers sat out on the porches or wandered along the road in shorts and flip-flops, enjoying the late-afternoon sunshine.

At last, they drew up at a tall, square building, painted bright blue, with wide balconies on each level. A sign proclaimed *Sunset-View Guest House.*

'This is our place,' Kiran said proudly as the motor rickshaw drew to a halt outside. He jumped out, paid the driver, then helped Chloe out with her backpack. She could tell from the look in his eyes that he was both excited and a little nervous to introduce her to his parents.

They wandered inside the guest house, where a grey-haired man, who Chloe guessed was in his fifties, sat working behind the reception desk. When he looked up and saw Kiran, his face broke out in a smile, and he came from behind the desk to hug Kiran.

'This is Chloe, Dad,' Kiran announced. 'We met on the way back from Darjeeling. I'm going to take her up to Ghorepani if Amma is well enough.'

The older man's eyes alighted on Chloe and he smiled tentatively and bowed his head slightly. 'Namaste,' he said, 'And a warm welcome to our humble guest house.'

'Namaste,' Chloe replied, putting her hands together in the Nepalese gesture of greeting. In the man's eyes, she could see the love for his son, but also a slight hesitation. Could it be wariness about her?

'I said Chloe could stay here as our guest,' Kiran continued. 'If we have a spare room, that is?'

'Of course. No problem.'

The father scurried back behind his desk and consulted his booking chart.

At that moment, a woman's voice said, 'Kiran!' and someone emerged from the bottom of the staircase and ran over to embrace him.

'This is my sister, Rumi. Rumi, please meet Chloe.'

The young woman turned her attention to Chloe and Chloe saw immediately that she was the same woman she'd seen in Durbar Square with Kiran. And standing there, side by side with her brother, Chloe could see the striking likeness between them. Her spirits lifted still further.

'Lovely to meet you, Chloe. Kiran has told me all about you,' Rumi said, and Chloe sensed mischief in her words.

Kiran looked a little embarrassed and shuffled his feet and looked down at the floor.

'How's Amma today?' he asked, and Rumi's smile vanished.

'She's been up and down,' she said. 'A bit better today, I think, though. I'm hoping that's it for now.' She turned to Chloe to explain. 'I don't know if Kiran has told you, but our mother suffers from emphysema. She can go for months without any problems, but she's sometimes laid low quite suddenly. She will get better, but it could take a couple of weeks.'

'I'm so sorry to hear that, but it must be a relief to know that she will recover, at least,' Chloe said.

'Let's go up and see her, Rumi,' Kiran said. 'Chloe, would you like a bottle of cold beer? Why don't you go out onto the café-terrace over there? There's a bar out there. Just say you are staying with me, and you won't have to pay.'

'Oh no, I must pay my way,' she replied, noticing a tense look pass across the father's face.

After she'd watched Kiran and Rumi disappear upstairs, she smiled her thanks at their father, and wandered out onto the terrace where a few guests were sipping beers and watching the sun begin to drop in the sky over the mountains opposite. She asked the barman for a cold Ghorka beer and sat down at a table which had a good view over the lake and of the hills on the far side. She sipped the beer and stared out over the lake, drinking in the beauty all around her. The sun was dropping rapidly now, lighting up the clouds with golds and silvers. As it descended, it shone brighter and brighter, while the sky above it darkened to a deep violet, the clouds turning purply-grey. The colours of the sunset were perfectly reflected in the lake, and as the light faded, the boats lost their colour and became black silhouettes moving on the shimmering water.

Chloe felt the warmth of the evening and the calm of the lake wash through her. How lucky she was to be here, to already have made Nepalese friends and to have the prospect of spending a few days trekking up to Ghorepani with Kiran. Now that the niggle she'd had in the back of her mind had dissipated, she could relax and enjoy the experience. Only, why had his father looked so suspicious when they'd been introduced? She shrugged and tried to put it to the back of her mind.

After about half an hour or so, Kiran and Rumi joined her at the table. It was dark by now and the balcony was lit up by fairy lights. The atmosphere was magical. They ordered some bar snacks and more beer and sat there relaxing and chatting comfortably. Kiran said that their mother was already on the mend and that she really wanted to meet Chloe.

'She's off to sleep now, but wanted to see you in the morning. By the way, I think we should set off on our trek tomorrow. Now I know she's over the worst, there's nothing to keep us here.'

'If you're sure. Is it an early start?'

Kiran laughed. 'Not too bad. We can set off about nine. If you come down for breakfast about half-past seven, there should be time for you to drop in on Amma before we leave.

Around ten o'clock, Rumi yawned and said, 'I have to turn in now. It was lovely to meet you, Chloe. I will probably see you in the morning. You should get some rest too if you're trekking tomorrow.'

'You're right,' Kiran agreed, draining his beer. 'I'll show you up to your room.'

They went back inside the darkened reception area, where the desk was already closed for the night. Kiran picked up her rucksack and carried it upstairs. She followed him to a room on the second floor. He turned the key in the lock, opened the door and turned the light on. The room was simply furnished with pale furniture, batik paintings on the walls and a colourful tapestry bedspread.

'This is one of our best rooms,' Kiran said. 'It's got great views over the lake that you'll see in the morning, and even a balcony.'

'It's very kind of your parents to put me up,' Chloe remarked. 'I wanted to buy them a gift, but if we're going early tomorrow there won't be time.'

'They won't expect anything. They are happy for you to stay as our guest.'

She went into the room and he put her rucksack down at the end of the bed.

'Goodnight then,' he said with a smile, looking into her eyes. 'I will see you tomorrow.'

'Yes. I'll set my alarm. And thanks so much for this, Kiran. It's lovely here. I do appreciate it.'

He hesitated for a moment, and for a split second she thought he was going to kiss her. Excitement tinged with panic rushed through her. But he turned away and left the room, closing the door quietly behind him.

IN THE MORNING, Chloe was up bright and early and wandered downstairs to the terrace, where breakfast tables were laid out under sunshades. The sun was already high in the sky. Kiran had started eating, so she sat down opposite him.

'Sleep well?' he asked.

'Very well thanks. It's so peaceful here.' She picked up the menu. The backpackers on nearby tables were tucking into bacon and eggs, or muesli and fruit.

'Good. I'd recommend the guwa mari for breakfast. With a cup of tea. That's what we locals tend to eat,' Kiran told her.

She eyed his plate and saw that it was piled with crispy dough balls that looked a bit like doughnuts. She decided to go with his suggestion and when they arrived and she bit into one, she understood why this was such a popular breakfast.

'Shall I take you to see Amma now?' Kiran asked when she'd finished, and she nodded, wiping the grease from her mouth with a napkin.

She followed him up to the top floor, to a spacious apartment where the family lived, furnished simply but tastefully with teak furniture and colourful wall hangings. He took her into a bedroom at the front of the building.

They stood at the end of a big, carved, wooden bed. The woman propped up on the pillows looked tired, the skin under her eyes was puffy and her black hair that was streaked with grey was scraped back from her face. Despite that, she radiated a serene sort of beauty and Chloe was drawn to her. It was easy to see where Kiran and Rumi got their good looks.

'Amma, this is Chloe,' Kiran said. His mother stirred and smiled weakly.

'So pleased to meet you, Chloe. Kiran mentioned that you were staying. Welcome to our home,' then she paused and glanced at her son.

'Kiran, why don't you leave us together for a short while?'

Kiran glanced quickly at Chloe. 'I'll see you downstairs then,' he said and left discreetly.

When he'd gone, his mother held out her hand and Chloe moved forward and took it in her own. The hand was clammy and cold.

'My name is Ehani, by the way,' she said. 'My family call me Amma. But I do have a name of my own. Please... sit down.'

Ehani inclined her head towards a stool beside the bed and Chloe obeyed. Despite her weakened state, it was clear that Ehani was a woman of strength.

Ehani smiled at her and examined her face. 'You are indeed a pretty girl. Just as Kiran said.'

Chloe felt her cheeks warming up. She wondered what sort of conversation the two of them had had about her. Despite her embarrassment, she couldn't help feeling flattered that Kiran had described her that way.

'You have Indian blood. That is clear. To me that is a good sign. Kiran told me that you've come here to find out more about your grandmother's journey. That is an interesting and worthwhile thing to do.'

'Yes. She came to Nepal during the war with my grandfather who was in the army. She went up to Ghorepani a couple of times to recruit Gurkhas for the British Indian Army.'

Ehani smiled, her eyes misty. 'It is beautiful in those hills. You will see. Nothing much has changed since those days, either. I'm pleased that Kiran is going to take you. You will learn so much from him.'

Chloe nodded, wondering what to say. Ehani started to cough, holding a handkerchief up to her mouth, but it soon subsided.

'I grew up in a mud hut in the hills where the fire smoked day and night. That's why I have this bad chest. But it can't be helped.'

'I hope you're better very soon,' Chloe said.

'Thank you. There is something I wanted to talk to you about, though. That's why I wanted to see you alone.'

'Oh?'

'This is a bit delicate. But I know my son is getting very fond of you and I want to be sure you're going to be right for him. That you're not going to hurt him.'

Now Chloe's cheeks were definitely flaming. 'Hurt him?'

'I want you to know that, despite appearances, Kiran has a soft heart. He is easily hurt.'

Chloe took a deep breath. She had no idea how to respond. This seemed very premature, after all, nothing more than friendship had passed between her and Kiran. Her eyes strayed to the window and the lake, which glittered in the morning sun, the boats bobbing on the surface already.

'You might think that this is a little strange, me talking like this to you. So let me explain. Last year, Kiran was in love with a girl from America. He met her in one of the bars in Kathmandu. She was very pretty, but I could see as soon as I met her that she wasn't going to make him happy. They went off together on a tour of the country and, sure enough, he came back here devastated after a couple of weeks. She'd gone off with another trekker they'd met on the way up to Everest base camp. It took him a long time to recover, so I wouldn't want something like that to happen again.' Ehani fixed Chloe with a steely look, but Chloe met it.

'I can assure you that I'm not going to hurt Kiran,' she said, finding her voice. 'At the moment, we are just friends. We get on well and we like each other and I don't know if it will ever be any more than that. But if it does become more, or if it doesn't, I promise you that I will do my level best not to hurt him. I've been hurt myself recently, and I certainly wouldn't want to inflict that on anyone else.'

Ehani smiled and held out her hand again. She took Chloe's in hers and patted it. 'That is good to know. Very good to know. Now, don't let me delay you any further. Please... go, and enjoy the mountains.'

Chloe left the room and made her way down the stairs, reeling from the strange conversation. Despite her embarrassment, she realised that she was touched by the obvious bond between mother and son.

Kiran was waiting for her at the bottom of the stairs. He looked into her eyes anxiously. 'All good?' he asked.

'All good,' she said, giving him a reassuring smile. She wasn't going to tell him what his mother had spoken about.

'Great,' he said, relief in his voice. 'Let's head off to the mountains then.'

27

CHLOE CLAMBERED into the narrow bed upstairs in the tea house in a tiny village deep in the foothills of the Annapurna range. It was the first night of the trek and all her bones were aching from climbing all day and carrying her backpack. The trail up from the end of the metalled road at Nayapul had been a mixture of unmade track and stone-built path. Where the path climbed, which was frequently, flights of stone steps were built into the surface. She had lost track of how many she'd climbed after a couple of hundred.

She'd left most of her clothes at Kiran's guest house, but despite that, her backpack still seemed to drag mercilessly on her shoulders and sweat poured down her body, collecting on her back between her shirt and her pack. She recalled that Lena had come up on a pony, so would have been able to enjoy the spectacular scenery without all the exertion. But despite the discomforts, Chloe had enjoyed the climb. The path rose steadily through a river valley, through rice paddies, fields of vegetables and patches of wild forest. Sometimes they went through a farm or a group of traditionally built houses, but most of the time they were out in the open country, drinking in the beauty of the hills all around them.

Conversation had flowed easily between her and Kiran and she had put behind her the slight awkwardness shown by his father and the conversation she'd had with his mother that morning. Instead, they talked about their surroundings, and he'd filled her in with information about how people in the hills survived, their farming methods and way of life, and how goods were brought up into the mountains. They saw many mule trains trudging along the path carrying heavy loads, packed on saddlebags either side of their bodies, and many sherpas too, hauling unfeasibly large loads on their backs, secured by a 'tumpline,' as Kiran called it, around their foreheads. They all greeted them cheerily, despite the strain they must have been under. Chloe had noticed their bulging leg muscles and how their compact bodies were a mass of muscle.

That evening, over a beer on the veranda of the teahouse, Chloe had confided in Kiran about Fergal, how their relationship had faltered, how she'd finally had the strength to walk away, but how when she'd seen him with another woman soon after her grandmother's death it had shaken her to the core.

He'd listened intently and said, 'I could see the sadness in your eyes the very first time I saw you. I wanted to make things better for you, even then.'

Chloe laughed. 'What, when we had that terse exchange about the rickshaw-wallah?'

Kiran had laughed too. 'Well... perhaps not at that precise moment...'

She had wondered then if he would tell her about his sadness too, but he didn't, and the moment moved on.

Now, she turned over in bed, fished for Lena's diary in her rucksack and put on her head-torch. Tomorrow they would reach Ghorepani, and she was looking forward to seeing if there was anyone there who remembered Alisha and her grandfather. She was almost sure there wasn't going to be. But it would still be fascinating to see the place where her seemingly reserved grandfather had fallen in love for the first time. They had to be up early in the morning, but it was not yet late and although her bones ached, her mind was buzzing, so she turned to the point she'd left off in her grandmother's journal and carried on reading.

We stayed near Indaw Lake with the 7th Leicesters until the regiment was completely disbanded a couple of days ago. It was a beautiful place, and we got to know the surrounding countryside and villages quite well. Sometimes we would stroll out of the camp on our free afternoons, swim in the lake, or walk through the rice paddies. The villagers would welcome us with cups of tea and little snacks they'd baked. We could hardly understand a word of each other's language, but it didn't matter, we got by with smiles and nods and hand gestures.

THERE WERE STILL dribs and drabs of the Leicesters in the camp, and the Wasbies carried on opening up the canteen, baking cakes and making sandwiches for the men that remained. They stood ready to serve them right to the end.

But on 10 December, they were transported to the banks of the Chindwin, where regiments of the 33rd Division of the 14th Army were massing to cross the river and take on the Japanese on their march towards Mandalay.

It felt good to be starting afresh in a new environment, serving front-line troops once again, although Lena, like the other girls, was sad to say goodbye to the Leicesters. At least they had each other.

The five girls had grown close, having struggled on together through rough conditions, living for several months under canvas, with all the discomforts that had brought. June had reported to Wasbie HQ that they didn't need Pam to be replaced, that they could manage without a sixth team member. On the odd occasion, there had been minor squabbles and resentments, but, if anything, the experience had brought them closer than ever before. Lena now counted the other four as firm friends, especially Mildred, who was of a similar age, as well as being single too.

Mildred had remembered what Lena told her about Billy and sometimes asked about him. What could Lena say in response?

'I will never forget him, Mildred. I think about him every day, but I have to face facts. The chances that he has survived this long at the front grow more remote each day.'

She yearned to speak to Billy and to tell him what the fortune teller had said the second time she'd visited but realised that it might well be too late even for that now. She was terrified that the prophesy might have materialised in the months they'd been apart, but she did her best not to dwell on that thought and to keep her hopes and prayers alive in her heart.

The girls were flown into a jungle airstrip on the east bank of the Chindwin river, a few miles north of where it joined the Irrawaddy to form one great confluence. 33 Corps, which included the 20th Indian Division – some of whom they'd encountered up on the Tamu-Palel Road – had been crossing the Chindwin to reach that point over the previous few days and were still arriving, unit by unit.

The Wasbies were stationed in thick jungle amongst steep hills that ran all the way down to the river, with very little land for an army to camp on. There were no roads, so the girls didn't have a mobile canteen to work in, just a couple of trestle tables and some rudimentary equipment. It was impossible to bake there, but they were able to make tea and sell supplies which had been airdropped in, including biscuits.

The men were gathering there before on the river bank before pushing on south to Monywa, a riverside port which was occupied by Japanese forces. The Wasbies had been told that they would be travelling on behind the men. Once the port had been taken, the plan was to push on to the Irrawaddy, Schwebo and finally Mandalay.

It was beautiful there, beside the wide, lazy river, but incredibly hot and steamy and mosquitoes plagued the girls, especially at night. Looking round at the other Wasbies, Lena realised how much weight they'd all lost over the past few months in the camps. Their cheeks were hollow, their arms and legs like sticks and their skin had a strange yellow tinge from the malaria medication. Of course, here they needed the medication even more than ever. They often heard stories of soldiers laid low by the disease and having to be flown back to hospital in India to recover.

The girls would be staying in tiny tents again and once again Lena volunteered to sleep alone. It really didn't bother her and because she had been billeted with Pam it made sense. Lena quite liked her own company and to have some time to herself so she could write her diary.

The next day, Lena went with the other girls over to open the canteen, quite early on, when the mist was rising in clouds from the river and the chorus of jungle creatures was still rattling away as it did throughout the night. Even as they opened up, there was a steady stream of men queuing for tea, all of whom looked exhausted. They'd been on the march for weeks, some of them from as far away as Imphal and Kohima where they'd spent months fighting in the most gruelling conditions. They had crossed the river the day before, some on floating bridges, others wading across a shallow stretch with their packs, holding their weapons above their heads. When they got to the other side, they'd had to set up camp in their wet clothes and cook their own food.

The girls did their best to cheer them up, chatting away and trying to engage the men in conversation, but it was difficult to get a response, or to raise a smile on any of the faces.

Lena was just bending down to put some rubbish in the bin under the table, when she heard a voice say, 'Lena?'

That voice spoke straight to her subconscious, and chills of shock and recognition went right through her. She stood up and there he was. Thin and gaunt, black smudges of exhaustion under his bloodshot eyes, but it was unmistakeably him.

'Billy?' she said weakly, looking at the man whose safety she'd been praying for and whom she'd been dreaming of all those months.

She stood staring at him, her mouth open, and he stared back, wide-eyed with shock. It seemed as though everything else around went into a sort of blurry slow-motion.

After a few seconds, men behind him in the queue started getting restless.

'Move on there, Billy Thomas, we're all waiting back here.'

Luckily, Mildred saw what was happening. 'I'll look after these men, Lena,' she said hastily. She stepped in and started serving the men behind Billy and the queue moved on again.

Her hand shaking, Lena poured some tea into Billy's tin mug and handed it to him.

'I had no idea that you were here,' he said, his soft eyes on her face.

'I wanted to do something more to help the war effort,' she told him, swallowing the lump in her throat, wondering if he could see the truth in her eyes, that she'd done it partly to see if she could find him. It sounded so ridiculous, somehow.

'That's very... brave of you,' he replied. 'It's so good to see you, Lena.'

'It's good to see you too. I can't believe it...'

Words seemed inadequate to convey the strength of her feeling, but gradually the ice thawed and they began asking each other question after question. There were long gaps in the conversation though, during which they just stood there staring at each other, marvelling that they'd found one another again.

Billy sipped his tea while they talked, his eyes glued on Lena's face, the other men surging around him to be served by Mildred.

Too soon, he'd finished his tea and handed Lena the mug. Their fingers touched and a bolt of electricity went through her.

'What time do you finish your shift?' he asked.

'About four o'clock.'

'I'll be waiting for you under the big tree,' he said, nodding towards a giant teak tree that towered over the camp on a bend in the river. 'If you'd like to, of course,' he added, a little shyly.

'I'd *love* to. See you then.'

Lena couldn't wait until the end of the shift. Mildred was remarkably restrained in her questioning. Perhaps she sensed that Lena's emotions were in turmoil and that she didn't really want to talk about Billy at that moment. When they'd finally finished serving, done the washing up in an old oil drum and packed everything away, Mildred went back to her tent and Lena rushed along the camp to the teak tree.

There he was, waiting for her. He looked less surprised and a bit more relaxed than earlier on. He took Lena in his arms and they hugged briefly. They felt too conspicuous to kiss though, because there were army tents all around.

'Why don't we stroll along the bank?' Billy suggested, taking her arm.

Walking wasn't easy, they were tripping over tent pegs and guy ropes all the way. At the end of the camp, there was a pile of logs that must have been left by some nearby villagers. They were covered in moss and creepers, but it was at least a place to stop, with some privacy. Lena sat down beside Billy. It was wonderful to feel the warmth of him next to her after so long apart.

'I've thought about you all the time,' she said. 'Wondering where you were. Tell me everything that's happened to you since we last met.'

'I've been fighting. Ever since I left Darjeeling, I've been fighting. All over Burma, most recently at Kohima.'

Lena could see from the look in his eyes what he must have lived through. 'It must have been terrible.'

'It was,' he said simply. 'We were living in muddy ditches. There wasn't enough to eat or drink. There were bodies every-where... littering the mud. Dead and wounded too. We were under fire all the time. No time to rest.' He bowed his head, 'I've lost count of how many of my mates I've lost.'

Lena felt for his hand then and entwined her fingers between his. 'How dreadful, Billy. How terrible for you.'

'But I survived. I was lucky. To tell you the truth, I can't help feeling a bit guilty that I'm still alive.'

Lena squeezed his hand. 'I for one am very, very glad that you did survive.'

He slid his arms around her and kissed her full on the lips then, a long, lingering kiss, like those they used to exchange in the convalescent home all those months ago.

They kissed for a long time, then, when they paused, Lena took a deep breath.

'I have something to tell you, Billy,' she began. 'I went to see the fortune teller in Kathmandu again and she told me that you are still in danger. I came straight to the convalescent home to tell you about it when I got back to Darjeeling, but you'd already left. I tried to find out where you were, but it was impossible.'

Billy frowned. 'I left a note for you. With the matron. Didn't she give it to you?'

'No! I could tell she was hiding something... She was so disap-proving of me. That woman!'

'It wouldn't have made much difference, to be honest. I had no idea where we were bound, so I couldn't leave an address. You couldn't have written to me anyway.'

'But still... She should have given it to me. What did the note say?'

'Oh,' Billy stroked her cheek and looked into her eyes. 'Just that I wouldn't forget you and that I would come back to find you as soon as I could.'

A warm feeling stole through Lena and she beamed back at him, but then she remembered the fortune-teller's words.

'The fortune teller said that you were still in danger. It wasn't the earthquake she'd seen. It was something else. Or *someone* else. It involved you and another person. Someone you trust.'

Billy smiled incredulously, just as he'd done before. 'I've been in mortal danger dozens of times over the past few months, especially at Kohima. If I was going to die, it would have been then. It sounds like your fortune-teller's prophesy, whatever it meant, has been and gone.'

Lena had to admit that it was possible. But she couldn't forget the vehemence in the woman's look and the feeling of certainty she'd had then that the woman was speaking the truth. 'She really believed it, Billy. She was sure that you were in danger and that I needed to warn you.'

'Oh Lena, you're so kind to worry about me, but you don't need to worry anymore.'

'Are there people you trust around you?'

Billy shrugged. 'Of course. All the men in my charge. I've been promoted to sub-conductor since I was in Darjeeling. That's the equivalent of Warrant Officer in the British Army. The Indian men in my platoon are solid fighters and completely loyal.' Then he thought for a moment. 'Actually, there *is* a chap. Another sub-conductor. Roy Carnie. He's the same rank as I am. He's often lazy and doesn't pull his weight...'

'Well, perhaps that's who the fortune teller was talking about. You need to watch that man very closely. Be wary of him. Please, for me.'

'I'm already keeping a close eye on Roy. He could put the whole unit in danger with the shortcuts he takes and his slapdash ways.'

'Good,' said Lena. 'Make sure you do.'

After that, they kissed again, then Billy walked her back to her tent, gave her another kiss, more chaste this time, before returning to his men. Lena watched him go, hoping fervently that he would take the warnings seriously and that he would keep a close watch on the other sub-conductor.

She went back to do her shift as usual in the afternoon, her cheeks glowing and her eyes alight with passion for life for the first time in months. Billy had said he would come along to the canteen the next morning and that they could go for another walk again after her shift. She couldn't wait for that to come around.

I HOPE that he will remain here by the Chindwin for a while and not get posted downriver to Monywa before we've spent enough time together and caught up properly. As I lie down tonight, for the first time since I left Darjeeling, I won't be tormented with worry about Billy. I will sleep soundly in the knowledge that he is sleeping just a few yards away from me, that I have delivered the fortune-teller's message and that, for the time being at least, he is safe.

Chloe put the diary down, overcome with sleep herself now, her bones and muscles comfortably relaxed after the day's exertions. She was glad that Lena had finally been reunited with Billy again and felt a comfortable glow steal over her thinking about the relief that Lena must have felt and the happiness she must have experienced being in his presence again. Thinking about it, she realised that it was not dissimilar to the feeling she herself was experiencing being with Kiran, spending time with him, walking alongside him through this beautiful landscape, chatting easily or just strolling together in comfortable silence. She closed her eyes, feeling the happiness and excitement of anticipating the days ahead that would be spent the same way. Soon she felt herself drifting off into a blissful sleep.

28

THEY NEXT MORNING, after plenty of tea and breakfast of fruit and porridge, Chloe and Kiran set out from Tikedhunga towards Ghorepani.

'It normally takes about seven hours,' Kiran told her. 'But that counts stopping for lunch and as many tea stops as you need.'

'Sounds perfect,' Chloe said, shouldering her backpack and following him down the paved, narrow path and out of the little village. The trail followed a tree-lined valley for half an hour or so and then started to rise further into the hills. The stone steps seemed endless, and Chloe found herself breathing heavily, her heart hammering with exertion, while Kiran sprang ahead of her, turning back every so often to smile or give words of encouragement. 'I'm not as fit as you are,' she said, stopping at a break in the steps, wiping her forehead with the back of her hand.

'I was born in these hills,' he said, smiling down at her. 'I know them really well and I come here often. It must be hard if you're doing it for the first time.'

He came back down, took her arm, and they carried on up the steps together. She found it easier to climb with him supporting her.

At the top of that rise, there was a teahouse where they stopped for a drink and to admire the views of the surrounding peaks.

'I told you, didn't I,' she said, sipping her green tea, 'that Gran came up here by pony in 1943.'

'Yes, you did,' he smiled. 'Are you thinking you'd have liked to do that?'

'No. I'm thinking how fit I'll be at the end.'

'You must have been very close to your grandmother to make this trip into her past,' Kiran said.

'We were close. After Mum died, Dad got married again pretty quickly and took off to Australia. Gran was basically a replacement mother to me,' Chloe explained.

'That must have been very difficult for you,' Kiran said gently. 'Losing your mother. How old were you.'

'I was seventeen. And it was... it was terrible. She developed an aggressive form of breast cancer. She was perfectly fit and healthy, but she got ill and died within a matter of months. It was really hard to cope with at that age. But Gran was always there for me. She filled the void, somehow. My mother was very like her actually. Strong and funny and unconventional. Gran took up where Mum left off...' She felt her voice catching and her eyes filling with tears. She rarely spoke about her mother. She'd buried her grief and built a hard shell around it. Losing her grandmother too had softened that shell and allowed her to speak about it, but she still felt very vulnerable.

They sat in silence for a time, then he said softly. 'It must be hard to talk about it. Especially losing both parents like that. Do you keep in touch with your father?'

She shook her head. Although he'd sent Christmas and birthday cards and they'd spoken on the phone occasionally, she'd only seen him on three occasions since he'd left, when he'd come back to England on business. Conversation had always been stilted.

'I've never forgiven him, I suppose, for leaving me like that. And now he has another family. Two more daughters. It's too late.'

Kiran smiled gently. 'It's never too late to try to heal wounds,' he said. 'Especially with family.' Chloe remained silent, thinking about his words.

After another pause, he said, 'I worry about my own mother. She's not strong... physically, that is. I dread losing here. She's like a rock to all of us.'

'She seems quite a personality,' Chloe remarked.

Kiran drew in a deep breath. 'Did she tell you about... well, about what happened to me last year?'

'She told me some of it.'

Kiran sighed. 'I wish she wouldn't interfere. I was stupid. I lost my head, and I got hurt. But I'm completely over it now.'

'I'm sure she was only doing what she thought was best,' Chloe replied, diplomatically.

'Well, I hope it didn't... how can I put this? I hope it didn't put you off wanting to spend time with me?'

She glanced up into his eyes and he was looking at her with an intensity that was palpable. She reached out and took his hand in hers and squeezed it.

'Of course it didn't,' she said. 'Why on earth would it? I'm having a fabulous time and nothing your mother could have said would change that.'

He relaxed and squeezed her hand in return. She felt the warmth and softness of his skin and a sense of well-being spread through her body.

'That's so good to know,' he said, relaxing visibly.

She returned his smile, and they sat there like that for a while, staring into each other's eyes, the beauty of their surroundings all but forgotten.

'Let's push on, shall we?' Kiran said at last, breaking the silence. 'There's still several hours trekking until we reach Ghorepani.'

They left the teahouse and carried on, walking quickly now, deeper and deeper into the mountains, getting closer to the towering peaks of the Annapurnas, and Kiran told her their names.

'That's Dhaulgiri, that's Annapurna South, then the other Annapurna mountains, 1, 2 and 3' he said as they climbed.

The sight of those sparkling, snow-covered peaks, stark against the bright blue sky, kept Chloe going, step after gruelling step until, towards the end of the long afternoon, a largeish village came into view halfway up a valley ahead of them, with painted, wooden houses built into the hillside, surrounded by farmed terraces planted out with fruit and vegetables.

'We will go to the guest house first,' Kiran told her. 'I know quite a few villagers here. Some of them are very old, and they might remember something about your grandparents.'

They checked into a two-storey lodge where the rooms opened off balconies on the upper floors. Once again, as on the previous night, Chloe's room was just bare boards and a hard wooden bed, but the lodge owners were friendly, the place was clean, and there were plenty of blankets on the bed, which Chloe was grateful for. There was a definite nip in the air now, a chill breeze funnelling down the valley from the high mountains.

She put on an extra fleece and went downstairs to the large open room which served as both kitchen and eating area. It was already growing dark, and the woman who owned the lodge was preparing the meal on a wood-burning stove in the corner of the room. Delicious smells wafted over to Chloe: frying spices and garlic, the evocative smell of rice boiling. Chloe's mouth watered.

She sat down at one of the simple wooden tables and ordered a Gorhka beer from the woman's husband and sipped it slowly, wondering where Kiran had got to. Just when she was beginning to get worried, he arrived, just in time for the meal to be dished up.

'I've been asking around to see if anyone is still alive who remembers the 1940s,' he said. 'There are a couple of old men who were around at that time. I've arranged for us to go and speak to them in the morning. So, let's hope they have good memories.'

After the delicious meal of dal baht and curry, washed down with a couple of beers, they went upstairs to bed. Kiran stopped outside Chloe's room and, in the starlight, looked into her eyes for a moment, then kissed her full on the lips. She responded, kissing him back, drinking in the taste of him, putting her arms around his neck, pulling him close. When it was over, he drew back.

'Goodnight, Chloe,' he said, tucking a lock of her hair behind her ear. 'Sleep well. See you in the morning. I'm going to wake you bright and early. I want to take you up to see the sunrise on Poon Hill. It is a bit of a walk from here, but I think you'll agree that it's well worth it.'

'Sounds good, see you in the morning,' she whispered, still reeling from what had just happened.

She went inside the room, closed the door and stood with her back against it, breathing deeply, recovering from the kiss, coming down from the high that it had given her. She'd been on the point of asking him in, but she was glad that she hadn't, and that he hadn't asked. It was right to take this slowly. They both needed to be sure of their feelings before taking things further, and she knew he was aware of that.

She got changed, slipped into bed and took out her grand-mother's diary, keen to find out what happened between Billy and Lena in that camp beside the Chindwin River. She turned to the next entry, dated 13 December 1944.

Billy has been told that his unit will move on down the Chindwin to Monywa tomorrow morning at first light. He broke the news to me this morning, when we met after my morning shift to take our usual walk to the pile of logs at the end of the camp. I knew it would happen at some point, of course, but I was devastated when he told me. For some reason, I'd got lulled into a false sense of security here in this transit camp, thinking that this little interlude could go on indefinitely, when deep inside I always knew that it must come to an end sometime.

THEY HAD DONE the same walk at the same time every day since Billy had arrived. Each time, they'd wandered hand in hand along the path behind the camp, sat down on the pile of logs and talked. They'd told each other a bit more about what had happened to them during the months that they'd been apart, then, when the talking was over, they'd kissed and hugged and held each other tight, until it had been time to go back.

It had been incredible catching up with Billy and spending time with him. Lena had had to keep pinching herself to make sure she wasn't dreaming. It all seemed just too good to be true, but it was really happening. She hoped and prayed that he would remain safe for the rest of the campaign, and that when the war was finally over, as it surely would be, they would be together again. Surely, it could not go on for much longer, just one or two more battles, to drive the Japanese back from central Burma, and for the Allies to go on to take Mandalay.

That afternoon, when he'd delivered the news that he would soon be leaving, he'd lingered for a moment, then he'd said, 'Can I come again tonight? To say goodbye properly? We have to leave before dawn and there won't be a chance in the morning.'

Lena dropped her gaze to the dry, bare soil in front of her tent. She knew what this meant.

'Of course,' she whispered. She agreed because she loved him so dearly and it was what she wanted, too. She would be a fool not to take this opportunity to show him the depth of that love.

As she waited in her tent for him, her nerves were taut with anticipation. This was what she'd longed for since she'd first fallen in love with Billy, but still, she felt nervous. She knew what she was about to do would be regarded as a sin by many – by her mother and by the teachers at St Catherine's and by the Church. But their world wasn't a world torn apart by war and uncertainty. Lena needed to do this, to prove her love to Billy once and for all, and to send him into battle with the knowledge that she would always be true.

Billy left the next morning before dawn without ceremony. Just a kiss on the lips and a promise that they would be together again just as soon as was humanly possible in that mad, mad war. He left her a photograph of himself in uniform.

'They took it in the camp when I was promoted to sub-conductor,' he said and she took it gratefully and held it to her lips. After he'd gone, she lay in her camp bed, picturing him marching down to Monywa. She knew that the next day, he and the rest of his battalion would be in combat against the Japanese. She hoped and prayed that the fighting would be short-lived, and that he would soon be back with her again. Until that time, she vowed to carry on as best she could. Serving tea and cake alongside her friends and colleagues, stocking up the canteen, baking cakes and buns for another day.

≈

So, now I'm lying here, in my tent, writing this by the light of a Tilley lamp, basking in the memory of what passed between us. I had no idea that the human body was capable of such physical joy, and I'm glad that it happened, that I got to experience it with the man I truly love. Nothing can take that away from me now. Billy and I are truly joined as one and I know we'll be together until the end.

Chloe closed the diary and put out the light and pulled the blankets tightly around her. She was happy for Lena that she and

Billy had been reunited and had had the opportunity to show each other the extent of their love. The warmth that stole over her, thinking about it, mingled with the delicious feelings she was still experiencing from Kiran's kiss. Things had shifted between them now, and there was no going back.

29

GHOREPANI, 2015

CHLOE AWOKE before dawn to a gentle knock on her bedroom door. It was Kiran.

'I've made you tea downstairs,' he said.

'Thanks, I'll get up now.'

She slipped out of bed and, shivering, pulled on her underwear, trousers and plenty of layers. Then she went down to the kitchen where a steaming cup of tea awaited her. Once she'd downed it, she followed Kiran, by the light of torches, out of the sleeping village and onto a nearby trail that rose steeply up the mountainside on stone steps. They climbed for twenty minutes or so and when they emerged at the top of the hill, their feet were crunching over snow-covered ground and the grey dawn was beginning to light up the sky.

There was quite a crowd of trekkers and guides gathering to see the sunrise. Kiran put his arm around Chloe's shoulders and took her to a quiet spot away from the growing crowd.

'Look,' he said, pointing east to where there was a glint of red-gold light emerging from behind one of the distant mountains. This first chink of light winked on the horizon for a few seconds, then spread its glow wider as, very slowly, the sun began to appear behind the mountain. As it rose higher in the sky, the peaks of the Annapurnas emerged, one by one, from the rosy pink light of the dawning sun.

Chloe watched, spellbound as the colours gradually deepened and the sky behind the mountains changed from grey to deep blue to the startling bright blue that she'd seen the day before. All too soon it was over, and the crowds began to head down the mountainside to their breakfasts. It was a moment she would never forget, and she turned to Kiran smiling.

'Thank you for bringing me here,' she said.

'Well, thank *you* for coming. I wanted to be with you to see the sunrise. But it's quite a climb before breakfast! Let's go back to the lodge and eat, shall we? After that, we can go and see the village elders.'

When they got back to the lodge, Chloe warmed her fingers and toes by the kitchen fire while the lodge owner prepared porridge and tea for them. When it was ready, although she was hungry, she found it hard to eat much because her stomach was churning with excitement. Would the men remember Lena and her grandfather? She couldn't wait to speak to them.

Kiran gave her a sympathetic smile as they set off after breakfast. 'Don't hold out too much hope, Chloe. These village elders are very old. Their memories might not be what they once were.'

'All right,' she said, 'I'll try not to.'

Lena knew Kiran was right, but it was impossible not to feel hopeful.

Kiran took her to an old, stone-built house on the edge of the village. Two old men sat at a table outside, under the veranda. Both wore long cotton tunics and trousers covered by overcoats, and the ubiquitous Nepalese fez on their heads. They were smoking bidis and enjoying the morning sunshine. They greeted Kiran warmly and he introduced them to Chloe. The older man gestured to them to sit down opposite him at the table.

'This is the Headman, Rajesh and this is Sorash, who is going to tell you what he remembers,' Kiran explained.

While they were settling in their seats, an old woman emerged from the house with a teapot and cups and proceeded to pour out four cups of green tea and put one in front of each of them. She smiled broadly when they thanked her, but quickly went back inside.

The old man, Sorash, began to speak then, and Kiran translated his words for Chloe.

'Sorash says he grew up in the village,' Kiran began. 'He is eighty years old now. When I was asking around yesterday, I mentioned the name Alisha, your grandfather's fiancé. Sorash remembers her well. He attended the school where she was a teacher, and he was also a distant cousin of Alisha's. He was about eight years old when she died. He says her parents were devastated and never really recovered from her death.

'He also remembers your grandfather coming up to recruit for the Gurkhas and how he used to stay at Alisha's house. Sorash remembers him well because he would have liked to become a Gurkha soldier himself, but he was far too young during the war and, afterwards, recruitment tailed off. In any case, his parents would have stopped him. He was their only son and was needed at home to look after their land and animals. He used to hang around when your grandfather was here and watch young men from the village and from the surrounding countryside queuing to sign up, wishing it was him.'

Chloe listened, amazed that this old man in front of her had actually met her grandfather during the war when he was still a young man. 'Does he remember the times that my grandmother came up with him?'

'Do you have the photograph of her when she was young to show him?'

'Of course.'

She dipped in her bag and drew out the photograph of Lena in her Wasbie uniform.

Kiran translated her question and held out the photograph for the old man to look at. The old man took the photo and stared at it. He went silent for a while, screwing up his eyes in deep thought, but finally shook his head, passed the photograph to the Headman and they had a brief conversation. The Headman too shook his head and handed the photo back to Chloe.

'He doesn't remember her, I'm afraid,' Kiran said. 'He only remembers your grandfather because he was so interested in the Gurkhas and because of Alisha. He says your grandfather still came up here sometimes even after Alisha died, but he looked very troubled when he did, and barely spoke to anyone. When the war ended, he stopped coming.'

Sorash continued to speak and then got up slowly from the table.

'He wants us to go inside his house. He has something to show you.'

Chloe followed the old man and Kiran over the threshold. It was gloomy inside the house and the smoke from a wood-fired stove lingered on the air. It took her eyes a few seconds to adjust. The old man was beckoning her over to the far wall where some pictures of the Buddha hung and beside them some framed charcoal sketches of Nepalese people. Some were individual portraits, others were family groups. In many of them, the people were wearing traditional dress, so Chloe guessed they were quite old.

The man urged her to look at a particular picture. It was a framed sketch of two people. A man and a woman. Sorash beckoned her to come closer. Chloe peered at it, trying to make out what she was looking at, and then it struck her. This was a sketch of her grandfather, when he was a young man, with a full head of hair, looking very handsome and very proud. He was wearing military uniform and had his arm around the shoulders of a young Nepalese woman, with big, beautiful eyes. Their love and happiness shone out from this picture all these years later.

She turned to Kiran, her eyes suddenly blurring. 'It's him. It's my Grandpa,' she said, feeling him slip his arm around her and hold her to him.

'Sorash says that Alisha's father sketched it and all the other pictures on the wall. He was a good artist and was in demand in the village to sketch likenesses for people because they didn't have cameras. When he died, Sorash inherited them and brought them to his house.'

'Do you think he would mind if I took a photo of it on my phone?' she asked, and Kiran spoke to the man.

Sorash took the picture down from the wall and handed it to Chloe.

'He wants you to keep it.'

'Keep it?' She began to push it away, but Kiran shook his head. 'He will be offended if you won't accept it. It is very generous of him, so best not to refuse the gift.'

'Thank you,' she said to Sorash, putting her hands together. 'That's so kind of you. Thank you very much.'

He smiled and bowed his head, his wrinkled face lighting up in a smile.

LATER THAT MORNING, they set off back down the mountainside towards Pokhara. In her backpack, Chloe carried the framed sketch of George and Alisha, having wrapped it in several layers of clothing to make sure the glass didn't break. They retraced the steps they'd taken the previous day and arrived back at Tirked-hunga in the late afternoon. After an early supper, they went upstairs to bed early. Once again, Kiran held her to him and kissed her full on the lips as they said goodnight, but she went to her room alone.

Chloe was glad once again that things were progressing slowly and comfortably between them. She was also glad of an opportunity to read more of the diary, anxious to find out what happened to Lena and Billy. The next entry was dated early January 1945.

It is many days since Billy left the camp with his unit, and I've been on tenterhooks to hear any news of him. I've also been waiting anxiously to be told we can move downriver behind the troops. But my hopes were dashed this morning, when we were told by one of the officers that there has been a change of plan.

Now, the Wasbies would not be following the troops of the 20th Division down the Chindwin River to Monywa. They were to be taken somewhere nearer the Irrawaddy, where British troops had broken through Japanese lines and things were more stable.

'The fighting at Monywa has been fierce. It's taken days of heavy action to push the Japanese back from the town. It's a river port and of crucial strategic importance to them. We've had reports that the Japs were supported by units of the Indian National Army. Casualties have been heavy, I'm afraid.'

Shock washed through Lena like an electric pulse and she found her hands shaking, unable to concentrate on what the officer was saying. She felt Mildred's eyes on her. She must have known what Lena was thinking. What if Billy had been one of those casualties? What if he was injured, killed even? She tried to stop her fears running away with her, but it was difficult. When she managed to tune back into what was being said, it was to hear further shocking news.

'The Japs admitted defeat at Monywa in the end. Dozens of their soldiers walked into the Chindwin River to drown themselves. They couldn't take the humiliation.'

What a dreadful, chilling sight that must have been to

witness, Lena thought. What a terrible war it was continuing to be.

Later on, when the girls had finished their morning shift, they packed up everything yet again, said goodbye to those officers and troops they'd got to know and who were still in the camp, then they carried their little suitcases over to the tiny airstrip that had been hewn out of the forest. They boarded one of the Dakotas and were flown out over the jungle again, skimming the tops of the paddle-leafed teak trees as they went. The flight was very short, but it was the only way out of the camp. If they had followed the troops downriver, they would have come upon the aftermath of the battle and all the danger and chaos that would have entailed.

They flew over jungle and the flat plain, with its square patches of rice paddies, then over the wide Irrawaddy River, then, spread out below them was the most extraordinary sight.

'That's the Pagan valley,' the pilot shouted over his shoulder.

The plain below was filled with temples as far as the eye could see. Hundreds of them dotted the landscape, built of gold or sandstone, rising to the sky from the undergrowth. Looking down at them through the dust-haze of the shimmering morning, it seemed as though they belonged to some sort of surreal, magical land, not modern-day Burma ravaged as it was by war.

Finally, they landed at an army camp beside another lake. The pilot told them it was a place called Meiktila and that British troops were massing there to divert attention from an advance on Mandalay.

The Wasbies' camp this time consisted of three small tents. To Lena's relief, June volunteered to sleep alone so that Lena and Mildred could share. Lena didn't think she could bear to be alone in the state of mind she was in. At least Mildred understood what she was going through.

We've had a couple of hours' rest, but in a few minutes we are due to resume duties again at a mobile canteen that has somehow made its way here ahead of us. I feel exhausted after all these months with barely a break, but when I think of what the troops are going through, it is easy to put my own discomfort aside and get on with the task in hand.

30

Two days later, Chloe sat beside Kiran on the narrow bus seat, bouncing around on the uneven surface of the Pokhara to Kathmandu highway. She'd tried to get him to take the window seat for the eight- or nine-hour journey back to Kathmandu, but he'd insisted.

'No. I've done this journey many, many times. It is all new for you. I want you to remember these views when you go back to your own country.'

She'd looked at him sharply then, wondering why he'd mentioned her leaving. Up until that point, it had been a sort of taboo between them. Perhaps he was testing her, seeing what her reaction might be? Perhaps he was feeling insecure because of what had happened in his previous relationship? They hadn't spoken about the future at all yet, but Chloe was clear in her own mind that she wasn't just going to up and leave as if nothing had happened between them. But she'd ignored his remark and kept quiet, sliding into the window seat while he stood aside in the aisle waiting for her, holding up a queue of impatient passengers. The bus journey might not be the best time and place to discuss their feelings. Also, she was aware that Kiran had decided to return to Kathmandu, not just because he had work commitments, but also because he clearly found it difficult to be in the same house as his mother for any length of time. But she wasn't going to mention that to him either, sensing that it was a highly sensitive subject.

Ehani had been up and about by the time they returned from their trek to Ghorepani. Chloe could see immediately that she was used to giving orders in her home and business, and to everyone in her family falling into line, including her husband. She fussed around Kiran as if he was a small child and was clearly still suspicious of Chloe, despite the conversation they'd had before the trek. She made a few barbed remarks at mealtimes and if Chloe came into a room, she would lapse into Nepalese so Chloe couldn't understand what was being said. After a couple of days, although she'd enjoyed some time in Pokhara, the atmosphere in the house was so strained, it had been a relief when Kiran had said he needed to get back to Kathmandu.

On their last day in Pokhara, Kiran had rowed her to a little beach on the other side of the lake, and they'd trekked up many flights of stone steps to the Japanese Peace Pagoda on a hill opposite the town. It was a huge, startling white stupa, with four enormous golden insets, one on each surface, each depicting a different cycle in the life of the Buddha. At the entrance, a sign explained that a Japanese Buddhist had built the pagoda along with dozens of others throughout the world in order to spread peace, having seen the effects of the atomic bomb at Hiroshima.

Chloe had wandered around the outside, gazing at the views of the lake and the mountains in the morning mist, thinking about the war and what her grandmother and countless others had experienced. She hoped fervently that the message of peace the pagoda was built to convey had been heard and noted. As she'd walked, she'd realised that Kiran was no longer with her.

She had found him, sitting quietly on one of the benches, his eyes faraway. She had sat down beside him and he took her hand.

'Everything all right?' she had asked gently.

He'd shrugged. 'I'm looking forward to getting back to Kathmandu, to be honest, even though I love it here.'

'I understand,' she had replied, not wanting to say anything derogatory about his mother.

He had turned to look at her. 'You will come and stay with me, won't you? In Kathmandu?' he'd asked, his eyes on her face.

She'd been wondering if he'd ask that, and she already had her answer. She had looked down at her lap. 'I think it would be better for me to go back to the Kathmandu Guest House, for a few days at least.'

His face had fallen and she could sense his disappointment.

'I just think... well, I really think we should take things slowly,' she had explained. 'After all, we have all the time in the world, don't we?'

'Of course. I suppose so. You're quite right.'

He had soon recovered his composure and on the way down the hillside from the Peace Pagoda, he had put his arm around her, and they had walked together in comfortable silence. She knew it was the right thing to do, and that it was far too soon in their relationship for her to take up his invitation. He'd already told her in passing how small the apartment was, that it was in fact just a studio, sharing a bathroom with the other apartments on the floor, and that when his sister stayed, he'd slept on the couch, but they'd felt cramped and on top of each other and started bickering after a day or so.

Now, Chloe watched the scenery roll by as the bus sped through the straggly outskirts of Pokhara and started labouring uphill on the first of its many mountain passes. Kiran's eyes were already closed, he seemed programmed to fall asleep on bus journeys, so she took out Lena's diary and started to read from where she'd left off. The next entry was dated February 1945.

We are still here on the edge of the 33rd Division's HQ at Meiktila, still serving the troops tea, cakes and provisions virtually round the clock. It seems that things are building up to a big battle as every day new troops arrive with all their machinery and equipment and proceed to set up camp on the flat ground around the town.

WHEN NEW TROOPS FIRST ARRIVED, June always made a point of opening up the canteen, whatever time of day or night it might be, to serve the men a welcoming cup of tea. The camp grew in size every day and just as at her first camp in Hailakandi, Lena could sense tension in the men in the build-up to battle. They clearly knew that they were on the brink of a big push that could be make or break for the British in Burma and that, one way or another, they would shortly be experiencing front-line action.

To her dismay and frustration, there had still been no news of Billy, although she'd asked every possible soldier and officer if they had any news of the 20th Indian Division. All she ever heard in response was how the division had had great success at Monywa and how they drove the Japanese out of there after a long, fierce battle.

At the time Billy left, they had both thought that Lena would be following him downriver and that they would be together again shortly. So they hadn't made any arrangements for contacting each other. She comforted herself with the thought that Billy knew that Lakshmi and Sunil's house had become her home in Darjeeling, and also that he could always write to her c/o Wasbie HQ if all else failed.

She tried to hold onto the fact that he would get in touch with her as soon as he was able, and that, in a sense, no news was good news. The memory of the night they'd been together stayed with her. The way they'd held each other, the feel of his lips on her skin, his body loving hers. Thinking about it, she would go into a sort of dreamy reverie and Mildred would give her a sympathetic but knowing look. Lena hadn't told Mildred what had happened that last night, but she suspected that Mildred had guessed.

Since arriving at the new camp, Lena had been suffering from extreme exhaustion. She put it partly down to the strain of not knowing about Billy, but also to the fact that she'd been working in the field for almost a year with only the odd day's break. She had also been feeling vaguely nauseous at times and was worried that perhaps she had contracted malaria. Time would tell, but she decided that if she wasn't feeling any better in a few days she would go to the MO in the hospital tent and ask his advice.

BUT THE FOLLOWING WEEK, Lena was packing her bags ready to ship out of the camp the next morning. She had to keep pinching herself, and she was still struggling to work out how she felt about her news. Partly joyful, but partly apprehensive and a touch guilty too that she would be leaving June and the girls when they'd looked out for each other for almost a year, but she had no choice, not after the news she had received earlier when she'd been to see the Medical Officer.

She'd had to wait outside the hospital tent for a long time to see him. She could hear the groans and cries of severely wounded men inside, and each time one of the orderlies went in or out, she'd caught a glimpse of the horrors in there. Just as before on the Tamu Road, this tent was filled with men with shocking injuries – amputations, head and stomach wounds, broken limbs – all of them lying in cramped conditions on mats or camp beds on the floor, waiting to be evacuated to a proper hospital. As before, it shook Lena to the core. She had to sit down and take deep breaths. It was all she could do to keep her breakfast down.

The MO was abrupt with her when she finally saw him, and

she was a little put off by his manner, but she understood that he had far more pressing matters to attend to than a mildly sick Wasbie. He listened grudgingly while she told him her symptoms.

'Lie down on the table,' he told her and once she had clambered up there, he examined her expertly with deft hands. He listened to her heart and lungs, looked down her throat and into her eyes and ears, and generally prodded her about. 'Sit down please,' he'd said to her when he'd finished.

Lena had climbed off the table and sat down on a wooden chair beside his desk.

'You need to be evacuated back to India without delay.'

Lena had stared at him. 'Really? Is it that serious? What's wrong with me, doctor?'

The doctor looked straight at her, unblinking, and delivered the news. 'I believe you're expecting a baby. And the front line is no place for a pregnant woman, Miss Chatterjee.'

Shock went through her like a thunderbolt. Speechless, she had watched the doctor write a chit for her to take to the transport officer.

'You must leave as soon as possible for either Comilla or Chittagong – whichever there is transport too first. You must go straight to one of the doctors there. They will be able to confirm your condition.'

Lena had left the tent reeling with the impact of the news. It was incredible, although she realised, not impossible. Her cycles had been very erratic over the past year, and when Billy and she were together, it might have been a more risky time than she'd thought.

She had felt her stomach as she walked back to the mobile canteen, wondering at the fact that she could be carrying Billy's child. She didn't feel ready to be a mother, and she had no idea what to tell June and the others.

In the end, she didn't tell June anything. She simply said that the doctor had ordered her back to India for a check-up because of her exhaustion and nausea. June had looked at her with narrowed, sceptical eyes for a few seconds, then said, 'I'm so sorry, Lena. I had no idea you were so ill. You must go straight to the transport officer. I'll go along to the admin tent to cable Wasbie HQ. We won't be able to do without a replacement for you, my dear.'

Lena had felt a stab of guilt. It had been hard enough to cope without Pam, but to lose another pair of hands would make it impossible for the others. Abandoning them when they'd all been together through thick and thin for so long tore at her conscience.

That evening, the others put on a little party for her, with tea and cakes leftover from the afternoon shift. They were all tearful as they hugged goodbye.

I said my final, sad farewells to June, Babs and Kathleen and came back to the tent to pack. Only Mildred will get up in the morning at 4 a.m. to see me off. Now, I must turn out the Tilley lamp and try to get some sleep before my journey. If the doctor's prediction is correct, my days as a Wasbie are at an end. It is bittersweet – a sad day for me as well as a joyful one.

Chloe put the diary down and stared out of the window of the bus at the wide Trisuli river that ran through foamy rapids over rocks at the bottom of the valley. She wasn't surprised to learn Lena's news. She'd wondered about it after having read that Lena had spent the night with Billy, but had Lena actually been pregnant? There was a possibility that the camp doctor was incorrect and that the second doctor at either Chittagong or Comilla had found some other explanation for her symptoms. Perhaps she'd had malaria after all. After all, if she had been pregnant, what had happened to the baby?

Chloe wanted to read on, but Kiran was beginning to stir, and the bus was slowing down and pulling into a pit stop so the weary passengers could stretch their legs, buy a drink or queue for the washroom.

When the bus pulled out of the refreshment stop and back onto the road, Kiran said, 'Have you discovered anything interesting in the diary?'

'Yes – I think my grandmother might have become pregnant by the soldier I told you about.'

'You think? You're not sure?'

'Not yet. I'll need to carry on reading to find out.'

'Go ahead.'

She shook her head, 'No, I want to see the scenery and I want to talk to you. This can wait until I'm in Kathmandu.'

Chloe closed the diary firmly and turned her attention to Kiran. He took her hand and held it in her lap and said, 'When we're back in Kathmandu, maybe you'd like to come up to Nagarakot with me. It's about thirty kilometres out of town and you get the most stunning views of the Himalayas from there. You can even see Mount Everest on a clear day. I have a couple of days work up there – a group to guide around the area – but there's plenty to do while I'm out during the daytime or you could even join in with the group.'

'I'd love to, Kiran. As long as there's enough time in Kathmandu for me to go back to the fortune teller I told you about. She said she was going to ask her mother if there was any chance that she remembered my grandmother. So, if I have time to do that before we have to leave, I could come along with you.'

'Do you think the fortune teller would remember her?' asked Kiran. 'After all, its many decades ago.'

'Maybe not, but I want to explore every angle I can while I'm here.'

'While you're here?' She felt his hand tense inside hers.

'Yes... while I'm here. You mentioned that I should be making the most of my time while I'm here and it got me thinking.'

'Oh, I didn't mean anything by that,' he said, looking inquiringly at her. 'I just assumed—'

'Well, it made me think that I should really be making some plans. I have an open plane ticket. I could go back anytime. I can't stay here forever. You're quite right.'

'I wish you could stay forever,' he muttered, so softly that she had to strain to hear his words. 'Perhaps you could find work here? Extend your visa?'

Chloe paused for a moment, looking away from him – out at the opposite mountain, its outline fuzzy as the bus bumped along, the rice terraces, the traditional houses dotted over the hillside.

'Perhaps I could,' she agreed at last. 'It's just that, well... there's so much for me to sort out at home. I need to work out what to do with Gran's property, sort out her estate with the lawyers. My friend, Sophie, is looking after Gran's dog Kip, and I can't leave him there forever. I came away on a bit of an impulse, you see.'

'I understand, but I want to be with you, Chloe. There's something special between us, don't you agree?'

She turned back to look at him, into his deep, brown eyes that were gazing at her with such intense emotion. His words had brought home to her just how much he meant to her, how serious things had got between them just in the space of a couple of short weeks. She knew it was time for honesty. 'I do. I agree with you. I love being with you. You make me feel... whole somehow. And whenever we're not together, I think about you all the time.'

'I'm glad you feel that way. And I'm sorry that my mother made you uncomfortable over the past couple of days.'

'It's fine,' Chloe said. 'She's only trying to protect you.'

'Still – she shouldn't have behaved that way.'

'Please don't worry. It doesn't make any difference to the way I feel about you.'

He kissed her gently on the cheek and they fell silent for a time. Then they passed the rest of the journey chatting amicably, making plans for Kathmandu and Nagarkot and reminiscing about their trek up to Ghorepani.

When the bus arrived at the bus station in Kathmandu, Kiran helped her off with her rucksack and quickly found Chloe a taxi. Despite her resolutions about not staying with him, she'd half-hoped that he would ask if he could come back to the Kathmandu guest house with her, but he kissed her tenderly as she got into the taxi and said he would call round for her in the morning.

The staff at the guest house greeted her like a long-lost friend. Ensconced in her room once again, Chloe was glad of the solitude after all, so she could turn back to Lena's diary.

31

CHITTAGONG, 1945

I AM REELING with the news that the doctor in Chittagong gave me this morning and I don't really know how I feel about it. He confirmed that I'm definitely expecting a baby and that all is progressing well with the pregnancy. My symptoms are perfectly normal, apparently, and he ruled out malaria or any other tropical disease.

Lena came away from the military hospital experiencing a jumble of emotions: surprise, joy, trepidation and even fear. It was now even more pressing for her to get in touch with Billy. She needed to let him know the news and, in her heart of hearts, she was hoping that he would ask her to marry him.

If he were to ask her, it would make Lena's dreams come true. She would be with the man she loved for the rest of her life, and they would raise their child together in happiness. But if she couldn't get in touch with him, or he didn't ask her, Lena had no idea what she would do.

She knew that her time with the Wasbies was over, however. As the doctor had said, there was no place for an expectant mother at the front, and God, willing, the war would be over soon in any case. She would have to return to Darjeeling because there was nowhere else for her to go. The army accommodation in

Chittagong was dismal and uncomfortable, and she couldn't stay there forever, nor did she want to. Especially as she would soon no longer be a member of the armed forces.

Although she'd decided that she must go back to Darjeeling, she knew it would only be temporary. Lakshmi and Sunil were strict Hindus and she was worried that there would be no room in their home for a baby born out of wedlock. For the time being, she reasoned, nobody would know about her condition, and by the time she was no longer able to hide it, she hoped and prayed that she would have worked out what to do.

She contemplated throwing herself on the charity of one of the many convents in Darjeeling, although she would surely be made to pay the price for her sinful ways. That would be soul-destroying – like returning to St Catherine's. But going back to Darjeeling was the only immediate solution she could think of. So, she went straight to the railway station to book a train. The next one, the overnight one via Guwahati, was due to leave the following evening.

On her way back to the barracks, she passed a little shop selling stationery, and bought some cheap writing paper and envelopes. When she got back to her room, she sat down to write to Major Taylor at Shillong with her resignation. She couldn't bring herself to admit her circumstances, so cited ill health as the reason. She cried as she wrote, and had to make sure her tears didn't fall on the paper and smudge the ink.

Being a Wasbie had been such an incredible and humbling experience. She'd met so many formidable women. She knew that working alongside them had made her stronger and more confident in so many ways. She still felt as though she was letting them all down. She would miss the friendships they had all forged in adversity, although she was hoping to keep in touch with some of the girls. Certainly, Mildred had asked for her address in Darjeeling, and they'd promised each other that they would write as soon as they could.

When she'd sealed and addressed Major Taylor's letter, Lena wrote to Billy. She propped his photograph in front of her on the desk and sat staring at the blank sheet of paper for a long time, wondering what to say. Her initial plan was to let him know that she had something important to tell him, and tell him that she needed to see him face to face to do so. However, after some thought, she decided that it would be better to let him know the truth sooner rather than later. So, in the end, she broke the news to him in the letter that he was to become a father. She asked him to try to get some emergency leave to visit her in Darjeeling. She told him that she loved him and that she thought about him every moment of every day.

'Please write to me at Sunil and Lakshmi's house as soon as you possibly can,' she wrote. 'I hope and pray to hold you safely in my arms once again very soon. All my love, Lena.'

Then she went out onto those busy, chaotic streets, walked to Army HQ and handed the letter into the office. She'd addressed it to Sub-Conductor Billy Thomas, 20th Indian Division, 14th Army, Monywa, Burma. That was the last place she knew for certain that Billy had been headed.

The officer at the desk shook his head. 'You know it's virtually impossible to get post to troops on the front line, don't you, miss?'

Lena couldn't stop the tears falling. She knew what he said was true, but had hoped against hope anyway.

'Don't worry,' the officer said quickly, seeing her despair. 'We can sometimes get letters through alongside reports and orders. I will do my level best to ensure that the letter gets to the 20th Indian Division.'

She left the office with at least a little hope in her heart that the letter would reach Billy. She headed back to her room, on what was to be her last full day as a Wasbie and on the day that she learned for definite that she was to become a mother. It was strange to think that a new human being was growing inside her. A special human being, made from love. She felt exhausted and drained too but still uncertain about the future. There was so much to think about!

LAKSHMI AND SUNIL were amazed and delighted when Lena turned up on their doorstep. She had walked up from the station carrying her small bag of belongings and was hot and sweaty when she knocked on their door. She had written to them from Chittagong to tell them she was coming, but the letter hadn't yet arrived.

Luckily, they were so pleased to see Lena that they didn't ask her too many questions about why she'd left the Wasbies – they seemed satisfied with her explanation that she had been suffering from general ill health and exhaustion. After all, just one look at her was enough to confirm the truth of that statement. It had been impossible for Lena to keep in touch with them from the front line, so they had no idea whether she was dead or alive until the moment she'd walked through the door. Lakshmi took Lena in her arms and hugged her tight, tears streaming down her face.

Lena's old room was ready and waiting for her. When she stepped inside, it looked as if she'd never left. All the things she'd managed to salvage from her mother's house were still there, just as she'd left them over a year ago. Alone in the room, she went over to the mirror. The face she saw staring back shocked her to the core. In most of the camps, the Wasbies hadn't had any access to mirrors, and it was the first time for many months that Lena had had a full view of herself. She touched her hollow cheek. Her skin was tinged with yellow from the malaria medication, and her eyes had a strained, anxious look that hadn't there before she went away. No wonder Lakshmi and Sunil looked worried.

Lakshmi went off to the market and came back laden with fresh meat and vegetables. Then she set about cooking a great feast. Sunil went to speak to the neighbours – all those who had known and loved Sita – and when the feast was finally ready, ten people were assembled downstairs to sit and eat with Lena and celebrate her return. She was glad to be back amongst the Indian community, talking Hindi again after such a long time. She felt the warm glow of acceptance, looking round at those welcoming, friendly faces. But she also wondered how they would all react if they knew the truth about her homecoming. She shuddered, hoping that she would be able to keep her secret at least until Billy had returned to her.

The following day, Lena walked round to St Catherine's looking for Joan. She wanted to catch up with her old friend. Also, Joan might be the one person she could confide in. She was craving a sympathetic shoulder to lean on. As she walked down the road towards the school, her nerves began to jangle. She was dreading meeting Miss Woodcock, even now, and even after everything she'd been through. But she didn't get as far as the building itself.

Abdul, the guard at the gate greeted her warmly. 'Miss Lena! So good to see you after all this time. How are you?'

'I'm fine, thank you. Good to see you too!'

He peered at her with anxious eyes. 'Are you sure?' Too polite to say she looked pale and thin.

'Of course. Thank you. I've come to look for my old friend, Joan.'

The old man's face fell. 'Miss Joan has left St Catherine's, I'm afraid. Around three months ago.'

'Oh!' Disappointment washed through Lena. 'Do you know where she's gone?'

'I believe she went to teach at a school in Calcutta, miss. Her younger sister went too.'

'Do you know the name of the school?' she asked, but the old man shook his head again.

Lena stayed and chatted to him for a while, then thanked him for his help and walked away, reflecting how nice it was to see the kindly old man and catch up on his news. It had cheered her up, despite the trepidation she'd felt at being near that place again. She was a little surprised that Joan had left Darjeeling without even leaving a note with Lakshmi for her. Perhaps she'd written to Mary or Vicky and expected them to pass on the message, though.

She'd done little since then except wait anxiously for the post to arrive. Each morning, she watched the postman from her bedroom window, pedalling up the hill on his bicycle towards the bazaar. Each time she saw him approaching through the stalls with his postbag over his shoulder, her heart had beat a little faster, but each time she'd been disappointed. He'd never once stopped at the house.

How long would she have to wait before a letter came from Billy? She ran through the possible scenarios constantly. Perhaps her letter hadn't got to him yet? Perhaps he hadn't read her news? She would take out his photograph and look at it tenderly, willing him to write. The wait was agony, but she had to try to be patient and positive.

THREE DAYS LATER, Lena bumped into Lieutenant Harper in Chowrasta. She had wandered up to the stalls there on an errand for Lakshmi, who had wanted some mangoes and limes which were difficult to get down in the bazaar. Lena was glad to get out of the house and to have something to do for once to take her mind off her anxieties. Now that she was home and eating properly, her nausea had eased a little. When she was bargaining with a stallholder, she saw an army car nosing its way through the market, and instantly recognised it as belonging to the lieutenant.

Over the past months, she'd often thought about him and his kindness towards her, and wondered how he was faring, whether he was still grieving heavily for Alisha. Their correspondence had dwindled to nothing after she was sent to the front line – it became virtually impossible to send and receive letters, but she'd kept his letters and sometimes used to re-read them to cheer her up and remind her of Darjeeling. Since returning, she'd felt so alone, she'd even been contemplating visiting him at the base to say 'hello' but felt that might not be appropriate and she didn't want to answer any awkward questions about her early homecoming.

All those thoughts were running through her mind when she spotted his car in Chowrasta.. When it drew alongside her, she saw that Lieutenant Harper himself was in the back seat, and while she stood there wondering whether to wave to him, he must have noticed her. He signalled to his driver to stop, then got out of the car and came towards her, a smile spreading all over his face, and when she caught sight of his friendly smile, she realised that she was genuinely pleased to see him too.

'Lena! What a wonderful surprise.'

Before she knew it, his arms were around her and he was kissing her on the cheek. 'Are you home on leave?' he asked.

'No. I'm afraid I'm home for good. I've been... quite unwell,' she replied, feeling a little guilty, as she always did, at not telling the whole truth.

Lieutenant Harper looked concerned. 'Nothing serious I hope?'

He was a genuine gentleman so didn't ask for any details when she shook her head and dropped her gaze.

'Well, do you have time to come for a cup of tea? We could go to that teahouse over there.'

'I'd like that, thank you,' Lena said, picking up her bag of fruit.

'I'll take that,' the lieutenant said. She thanked him, and followed him to a little teahouse on the square where traders who'd come over the mountains from Nepal and Tibet rested while their ponies and mules were fed and watered in the stables next door.

The half-hour they spent together took Lena out of herself and made her feel less desperate than she'd been feeling since her return. There was something so safe and reassuring about Lieutenant Harper. She was glad to see that he seemed a lot more cheerful now than when she'd left. He told her that he still thought about Alisha a lot, but that he was no longer grieving like he had at the beginning.

'I'm so thankful now for having known and loved her and for the time we had together,' he said, reflectively, looking into his tea. 'But what about you, Lena? Did you manage to find Billy?'

Lena looked into his earnest, caring eyes and everything came out in a rush.

'We did meet up for a short time, yes. On the banks of the Chindwin, just before the battle of Monywa. He went on to Monywa and we were supposed to follow, but our orders changed. I'm so, so worried. I've tried to get in touch with him through the regiment, but I haven't heard anything from him and I'm... well, I'm getting sick with worry.'

She stopped short of telling him the full story. She couldn't bring herself to, even though she knew that the lieutenant wouldn't judge her. After all, he had been in a similar position not too long ago. In fact, part of the reason she didn't say anything about it to him was because she didn't want to remind him of the loss of his own baby, which must still feel very raw.

'I'm wondering if there's anything I could do to help,' he said. 'I do have some channels of communication into the 14th Army. I could tap up some of my contacts.'

'Oh, would you?' Lena asked.

'Of course. I'll do whatever I can. You know though, don't you, that both Meiktila and Mandalay have been recaptured by the Allies? It's quite likely that in the confusion of battle and all the troop movements, your letter never actually reached him.'

'I suppose you're right,' she agreed, brightening a little.

When they'd finished their tea, they walked together across the square towards his car. As they parted, he said, 'Look, I'll send telegrams to senior officers in the 20th Indian Division today. If you come down to the base tomorrow afternoon, I will let you know if there is any news.'

Then, to her surprise, he took her hand in his and looked into her eyes. 'I'm very pleased to see you back, Lena. I've missed you. If you want your old job back when you're better, then all you have to do is ask.'

She watched him get into his car and drive away, then walked home with a bit of a spring in her step for the first time in days. At last, it felt as if there was a glimmer of hope that she would soon find out where Billy was and perhaps be able to contact him. She could barely wait until the next afternoon.

THE NEXT DAY, Lena arrived at Lieutenant Harper's office around 2 p.m. and was ushered in by the clerk who'd replaced her. It was strange going back to the place where she'd taken her first tentative steps into the real world having broken away from St Catherine's. It made her feel vulnerable again somehow.

When she entered Lieutenant Harper's office and he stood up to greet her, she knew immediately from his expression that he'd had some bad news, but she didn't realise at first quite how devastating that news would be.

'Do sit down, Lena,' he said, then, instead of taking a seat himself behind his desk, he pulled up another chair to sit beside her. He leaned forward and looked into her eyes.

'I'm afraid I have some terrible news for you. I've heard back from Sub-Conductor Billy Thomas' commanding officer. I'm sorry to have to tell you that Billy perished in the battle of Monywa.'

Lena stared at him for a second, then let out a howl of pain, as if she'd been physically hurt. Everything around went into a panicked blur, and she thought for a moment that she was going to faint.

She felt the lieutenant take her hand and put his arm around her shoulder. He kept repeating, 'I'm so, so sorry, Lena, I know how you must feel.'

He handed her a shot of brandy which she gulped down. It coursed like fire through her veins, relaxing her a little. It was a long time before she could even speak.

'Do you know how it happened?' she finally asked.

Lieutenant Harper shook his head. 'I'm afraid I don't have any more details. I can tell you that Billy was buried in one of the many makeshift cemeteries along the Chindwin River. His grave is marked by a simple wooden cross.'

'What about his family?' Lena asked weakly.

'I know that his mother has been told, as his next of kin.'

Lena's heart went out to that poor, poor woman, whom Billy had told her suffered from ill-health. Two of her sons had now been lost to the Burma Campaign. How truly terrible.

All she could think of was the tragic loss. Of Billy with his beautiful eyes and his gentle ways, his innate kindness and his wry sense of humour. The way he would look at her with pure love in his gaze; the way he would make her feel as if she was floating on a cloud of happiness when he took her hand or put his arms around her. The tenderness of that one precious night they'd had together which would never be repeated.

The one glimmer of daylight was that he had left Lena a precious gift that would remind her of him forever. She would do her utmost to protect and care for that living reminder of their love.

Lena's mind kept going back, too, to the fortune teller and her face as she'd uttered her ominous prophesy. Had her words come true? Had Billy been betrayed? Had that led to him losing his life?

She had tried to warn him, to persuade him to take notice, to not necessarily trust everyone around him. But perhaps her words hadn't hit home? Perhaps she could have done more?

She asked Lieutenant Harper if he would try to find out what had happened and he promised he would.

'I'll come into town tomorrow and tell you if I find anything more about the circumstances of his death.'

He took Lena home in his car, sitting beside her on the back seat, holding her hand. When the car pulled up outside Lakshmi and Sunil's place, all the stallholders stopped what they were doing to stare; it was so rare that a motor vehicle came to that part of town.

Lieutenant Harper led Lena to the door and explained to Lakshmi in Hindi that Lena had lost a dear friend in battle. Lakshmi went very pale. Lena had mentioned to her that she was concerned about Billy and Lakshmi knew a little about Lena's close friendship with him. She took Lena in her arms and ushered her inside the house, where she brewed some herbal tea.

'Drink this down. It will help with the shock,' she said, handing the drink to Lena. She also made Lena eat some garlic soup and nan bread, which she forced down. Then Lakshmi helped Lena upstairs and laid her down on the bed, drew the curtains and left her to rest.

32

When I awoke half an hour ago, the pain of loss hit me afresh. I dragged myself up to write this diary, to record the events of this terrible day. Perhaps tomorrow Lieutenant Harper will have some news for me, but whatever it is, it is unlikely to bring me any comfort. Nothing really could.

Sleep eluded Chloe for hours when she finally closed Lena's diary and put out the light. She'd read the latest four entries straight through without pausing, and when she'd finished, it was well after midnight. She was exhausted from the long bus journey and from the emotional turmoil of reading her grandmother's diary. It was as if she was experiencing the loss and grief Lena herself had, seventy years before.

It brought to mind the pain of losing her own mother when she was seventeen and then her grandfather a couple of years after that. Lena had grieved then too, but stoically, with dignity. Chloe had remarked at the time on her grandmother's courage and composure. Now she reflected that perhaps Lena had learned a lot about grief in her youth – the loss of her own mother, the loss of her first love. She must have understood grief intimately and known how to deal with it, like an unwelcome visitor, one that had to be tolerated and humoured for as long as they wanted to stay.

At last, these thoughts all began to jumble and become confused. Eventually, Chloe dropped off to sleep but kept on waking, revisiting the diary, thinking about poor Billy cut down in his prime, poor Lena and the terrible blow she'd suffered.

In the morning, she felt as though she hadn't slept a wink. She showered quickly and went down to the courtyard. She was taking breakfast in the fresh morning air, when Kiran appeared, striding across the garden towards her, waving. Her heart lifted as she watched him approach. He exuded energy and warmth and life. Just looking at him filled her with a warm glow. He bent down to kiss her on the cheek and sat down opposite her.

'Did you sleep OK?' he asked, peering into her eyes. 'You look a bit tired.'

'I'm OK,' she said. 'I was awake reading quite late. I just need some more strong coffee.'

The waiter hovered and Kiran ordered a lassi and Chloe another coffee.

'I came to let you know that I need to go to Bhaktapur later on this morning to meet the tour group. They went straight there from the airport. Have you decided whether to come with me or not?'

'I'd love to, but I was going to try to see the fortune teller this morning.'

'The bus leaves at quarter to twelve,' he said. 'Why don't you text me? You could always come later, or join us tomorrow.'

He took her hand on the table and she smiled into his eyes. She knew that he was sceptical about the fortune teller, but she was glad that he didn't try to discourage her from going there.

'I was going to go along to see her as soon as I've finished breakfast. Do you want to come with me?'

'No, it's OK. I've got a few errands to run here in Thamel, then

I need to go back to the flat and get my things. That's why I came to see you early.'

He sat there in the garden with her, while she finished her breakfast, told her a bit about Bhaktapur – that it was an ancient, medieval capital, with narrow, paved streets, full of historic buildings, even more beautiful and impressive than Durbar Square in Kathmandu. He described it with such passion that by the time he'd finished, Chloe's mind was made up.

'I can't wait to see it.'

'And I can't wait to show it to you,' he said, beaming.

She walked him to the gate, and they kissed goodbye.

'Good luck with your fortune teller,' he said with a wry smile. 'Call me later. Either way, we'll see each other today or tomorrow. There are plenty of rooms at the guest house in Bhaktapur, so there's bound to be one for you. They're not often booked up.'

'I'll call you,' she called, blowing him a kiss, then fondly watching him walk away down the road between the street stalls, rickshaws and motor bikes, under the many rows of flapping prayer flags. Then she turned back towards the garden, full of fresh enthusiasm for the day ahead.

IT TOOK her twenty minutes or so to walk through the busy streets of Thamel to Durbar Square, past the many open-fronted shops selling everything from masks of Hindu gods to yak wool scarfs and hats, to Tibetan Thanka paintings to trekking expeditions. The streets were thronging with people, tourists and backpackers mingling with the locals. Chloe realised that she felt at home here now, far more so than when she'd first walked through these streets only a few weeks back.

Leaving Durbar Square and making her way down the narrow, gloomy side-street, she felt herself stiffen. She'd retraced her steps to the fortune-teller's place without much difficulty. But the place suddenly felt alien and frightening. She approached the huge oak door to the fortune-teller's premises with trepidation and gave it a gentle push. It opened, just as it had the first time, and her heart began to pound with anticipation. She walked slowly towards the back room and, taking a deep breath, drew the curtain aside and gasped. There were two women there, mother and daughter, sitting side by side, both dressed in bright red sarees and shawls and a lot of jewellery. It was as if they were waiting for her.

The younger woman looked up and beckoned to Chloe. 'Come in, my child. We hoped you would come. My mother has been waiting here for three days to speak to you.'

Chloe couldn't take her eyes off the old woman. If she'd been a child when Lena had visited in the early 1940s, she must be in her eighties at least by now. She looked bent and frail, her skin was heavily lined and wrinkled, but she still wore a line of heavy black kohl round her eyes and many ropes of red and black beads around her neck. Chloe could see immediately that the old woman was still sharp and perceptive.

Chloe sat down opposite the two women, facing them.

'I have kept the picture of your grandmother. It is here.' The younger woman pushed the photograph of Lena that Chloe had left with her across the table. Chloe picked it up, relieved to have it back. 'My mother does remember her,' the woman added.

'Really?' A bolt of excitement went through Chloe. She turned towards the old lady and looked her in the eye. 'Would you be able to tell me what you remember about my grandmother?'

The old woman fumbled in the folds of her saree and produced something from a pocket. She put it on the table. Chloe peered at it, frowning. It was a small piece of black leather, and looking closer, she could see that it had been fashioned in the shape of a bow.

'This belonged to your grandmother,' the old woman said,

her voice hoarse and croaky. 'It dropped off her shoe while she was here. I remember her. She was very graceful. Very beautiful.'

Chloe examined the leather bow, incredulous. Had this scrap of leather really belonged to Lena? Then she recalled Lena having mentioned about losing a bow from one of her shoes in the diary and her scalp tingled.

'My mother kept the bow until the day she died,' the old woman went on. 'She was confused by your grandmother, you see. She had an aura of tragedy and sadness around her, but my mother couldn't quite work out what it all meant at first, although she knew it involved trust. Having one of her belongings gave my mother greater insight into her prophesy.'

Chloe turned the leather bow over and over in her hand, amazed that this relic from another age connected her to her grandmother as a young woman. 'And *did* it give your mother greater insight?' she asked.

'Yes,' the old woman nodded. 'She realised that a breach of trust was definitely at the heart of what she saw, and that the danger she could foresee for your grandmother's friend lay in some sort of betrayal. But that was all she said. Fortune telling isn't science... sometimes we cannot predict exactly.'

Chloe fell silent. It struck her that whatever Lena had said to Billy, however much she'd tried to persuade him, his fate might already have been predetermined, it might have been impossible for him to avoid.

'Let me look at *your* palm, my child,' the younger woman said suddenly.

Chloe tore her eyes away from the old woman and moved her gaze to look at her daughter. She met the woman's dark, all-seeing eyes. Their intensity shook her. 'Oh no, I didn't come here for me,' she said hastily.

'But it is always helpful to know a little about what the future holds,' the woman said, cajoling. 'And today would be a propitious day to have your palm read. There is something in the air today, some shift in the balance of things...'

Chloe felt a little reluctant, thinking of the prophesies her grandmother had heard in this very room and how they had affected her life. What if the woman told her something she didn't want to hear? What if she told her that she and Kiran had no future together? She wasn't sure she wanted to know that. But the woman was persistent, beckoning to Chloe to hold out her hand.

'Go on, my child,' the old woman chipped in. 'It is always useful to know about the future. That way, you can plan ahead...'

Reluctantly, Chloe offered her hand to the younger woman, who held it between her own warm palms and lowered her face to get a better look in the flickering candlelight. She remained motionless, studying Chloe's palm for several minutes. Eventually she looked up, her expression deadly serious.

'You will be in grave danger if you make a journey today. I foresee something momentous about to happen. It is shrouded in clouds and dust. It is some sort of accident. Were you planning to go somewhere today?'

Shock rolled through Chloe. She nodded. 'Bhaktapur. With a friend...'

'You should *not* go. Please heed my warning,' the fortune-teller's voice was urgent, her eyes intense, looking deeply into Chloe's own. 'My advice is this. Go back to your hotel room and wait there until it's safe. Do not leave until the danger has passed.'

'But how will I know if the danger has passed?' Chloe was puzzled, her mind in turmoil now. She wanted to brush this aside and carry on as normal, but a superstitious streak, perhaps inherited from Lena, urged her to take this seriously.

It was then that it dawned on her that she needed to warn Kiran. He shouldn't go to Bhaktapur either, not if there was going to be an accident. She stood up and glanced at her watch. It was half-past ten. There was still time to warn him. She would tell him to come to the guest house and they could catch another bus together, tomorrow.

'I have to go now. Thank you. Thank you so much for everything.'

Chloe stood up, took a thousand-rupee note out of her purse and put it down on the table.

The old woman handed her the leather bow. 'Take this. It will bring you luck.'

'Remember, stay in your room until the danger has passed,' the daughter shouted after her as Chloe ducked out through the curtains and headed across the outer room.

Once in the street, she dialled Kiran's number and waited breathlessly for him to answer.

When he did, she said, 'Kiran, the fortune teller warned me not to go to Bhaktapur. There's going to be an accident or something. You shouldn't go either.'

There was a short pause, then he said, 'You're not serious, surely?'

She swallowed, her heartbeat speeding up. 'Yes, I am! Deadly serious. You should have seen her face, Kiran. She told me to go back to my hotel room and not go anywhere. *Please* don't go to Bhaktapur. Come back to the guest house with me.'

She heard him laugh. 'Oh, come on, Chloe. These people are just after your money.'

The amusement in his voice exasperated and worried her in equal measure. 'It's not true. They were absolutely right about Billy being in danger. He died in action. It was in the diary. *Please,* Kiran. You need to take this seriously.'

Kiran sighed. 'Are you sure this isn't just... well... it sounds as though you aren't quite sure you want to come along with me.'

She fell silent then, his words felt like a slap in the face.

'Chloe? Are you still there?'

'Kiran, I really want to come with you. It's just the fortune teller...' She realised how strange and implausible that probably sounded and paused, wondering how to explain it better to him, but he cut into the silence.

'Look, I'm going to head off to the bus station now. If you're really worried, you can come along this afternoon or this evening. I need to get over there and meet the tour group as soon as I can. I can't really delay. I'm sure it will be fine. Don't worry.'

'Kiran, please,' she urged.

'Chloe, it will be fine,' he repeated. 'I need to go now. I'll call you when I've arrived. Please come this afternoon or this evening. I really want you there. I love you.'

This was the first time he'd said those words to her and her heart did a somersault hearing them.

'I love you too,' she said. 'But please don't go, Kiran.'

'Look, I'll see you later. I really need to set off now. Goodbye, Chloe.'

'Kiran. Kiran?'

But he'd already hung up.

Chloe began to hurry back towards Durbar Square, her mind in turmoil. The rush of pleasure she'd experienced when Kiran had said he loved her was quickly displaced when she recalled that he had doubted her commitment. How could she convince him that she wanted to be with him? Part of her wanted to rush to the bus station to prove her commitment to him, but the fortune-teller's words echoed in her mind. Perhaps Kiran was right, perhaps it was all mumbo-jumbo. But something deep inside told her otherwise.

She gripped the leather bow that was still in the palm of her hand, thinking of Lena, and walked as quickly as she could back to the guest house.

33

KATHMANDU, 2015

REACHING THE GUEST HOUSE, Chloe hurried across the garden, into the building, then ran up the stairs to her room. Once inside, she paced about, letting her heartbeat slow down. She glanced at her watch. It was eleven o'clock now. Kiran would be on his way to the bus station.

She sat down beside the window and looked down into the garden, where guests were eating and drinking, relaxing in the sunshine on recliners. She felt a little foolish. Perhaps she should have gone to Bhaktapur after all?

But the more she thought about it, the less comfortable she felt about letting Kiran go alone. The fortune-teller's words kept coming back to her. She made a decision. She needed to go to him and persuade him not to get on that bus.

She ran down the stairs, out of the hotel, and onto the street. It was hot and noisy, and difficult to make progress through the throng of morning shoppers and she was breathless and damp with sweat by the time she emerged from the narrow streets of the old quarter and onto a main road. She started walking in the direction of the bus station and before long was able to flag down a taxi.

The driver huffed when she asked him to take her to the bus station as quickly as he could.

'Traffic bad today,' he said frowning.

'I'll pay extra,' she told him. He said no more and pulled out into the heavy traffic. Progress was slow. Chloe kept glancing at her watch impatiently. The time was going maddeningly quickly. She tried to text Kiran, but her phone had too little charge for the texts to go through. Even before she arrived at the station, she knew she'd be too late. When they pulled up outside, she handed the taxi driver a wad of notes and ran across the busy bus concourse, searching desperately for the right stand.

Sure enough, when she finally reached the stand for the Bhaktapur bus, it was empty and the bus had already gone. Feeling deflated and even more anxious than before, she headed back to where the taxi was still parked and asked the driver to take her back to Thamel. She would go back to the guesthouse, pack her things and wait until the afternoon bus.

Back in her room, she plugged her phone into charge and reached for Lena's diary. Reading it seemed an ideal way to pass the time and to distract herself from her anxiety. She was keen to find out whether Lena had discovered how Billy had died and whether the fortune teller was right that it had to do with a breach of trust. She turned to the next entry.

Lieutenant Harper called again this morning. He has just left the house, and I feel as wretched and helpless as I did yesterday when I first heard about Billy's death.

~

LENA WAS UPSTAIRS when the lieutenant came that day. She saw his car parked below her window and heard Lakshmi letting him in, then some muttered words between them and Lakshmi's voice calling up the stairs.

'Lena, my dear. Please come down. Lieutenant Harper is here.'

Lena was trembling all over as she went down the stairs. Lakshmi made some tea and then went straight out to the market. Lena was grateful to her for understanding how distressing all this was for her and for giving them privacy.

They sat down in the living room, either side of the little, low table. It was odd to see the lieutenant in that environment, in his pristine uniform, sitting cross-legged on the floor cushions and sipping the green tea that Lakshmi had made. It flashed through Lena's mind how at home he'd been amongst the villagers up in the mountains in Nepal. But now his face was grave and it made her stomach churn with nerves.

'I have managed to glean some details from Sub-Conductor Thomas' Commanding Officer,' he began, his eyes steady on her face. 'I'm afraid he made it clear to me that the circumstances of Billy's death mustn't be disclosed to anyone other than you. If the truth of what happened gets out, it will severely affect morale amongst the troops. I know I can trust you, Lena.'

'Of course,' she whispered, hardly able to bear it.

'I'm afraid, Sub-Conductor Thomas was betrayed in the worst possible way. He had put complete trust in one of his subordinates, an Indian soldier, whom he'd treated as his right-hand man in the lead-up to the battle at Monywa.'

Lena listened anxiously, afraid at what was to follow.

'But it turned out that this soldier didn't deserve that trust. During the battle, the unit was advancing down river. Sub-Conductor Thomas had sent this man ahead to recce a spinney on the riverbank. He returned and told Thomas that it was safe to advance with the rest of his men. When Thomas and his unit entered the trees, they were immediately surrounded by Japanese and Indian National Army troops and mown to the ground with machine guns.'

Lena gasped and felt the tears fill her eyes.

'The Indian soldier hung back, along with two or three of his comrades, who were then seen to run over to the enemy lines. He was a turncoat and a traitor. A defector to the Indian National Army.' Lieutenant Harper was clenching his fists as he said this, his eyes were full of rage. 'He'd been working on Thomas, gaining his trust for weeks, waiting for an opportunity to betray him.'

Waves of shock went through Lena. It was exactly what the fortune teller had predicted – that he would be betrayed by someone close to him. She'd tried to warn him, but he'd misunderstood the message, assuming that the person he needed to be wary of was the other sub-conductor, the slapdash one whom he said was putting lives in danger. But it turned out not to be that man at all.

She was racked with anxiety and remorse about her own role in Billy's death. Had she done more harm than good by trying to warn him? He'd clearly mistrusted the wrong man. She wondered if perhaps he felt, having identified someone untrustworthy, that it was safe to trust all the others around him when he should have been more wary? She would never know.

She thought about how poor Billy had died, what might have gone through his mind, the terrible fear he must have felt. She realised too that it must have happened before she'd even written her letter to him, so he would never have even known that he was to be a father. That's what upset her most of all and when she realised that, she couldn't stop the tears falling.

Lieutenant Harper put his arm around her shoulders and tried to comfort her and because she felt safe with him and was desperate to talk to someone about her terrible situation, she decided to tell him everything, there and then. She took a deep breath.

'I'm expecting Billy's child,' she began.

Although she felt Lieutenant Harper stiffen beside her

momentarily, his voice was steady when he said, 'I'm so very sorry, Lena. I'm listening if you want to talk about it.

So, she told him that she'd been waiting for Billy to come to her, that she had a little money and must make immediate plans to leave Darjeeling. 'I know it won't be possible for me to stay here once my secret is known,' she finished, dabbing her wet cheeks.

'Please don't worry. I will do everything I can to help you. I'm sure there's a way to figure this out.'

He stayed for a long time, until Lena had stopped crying and had calmed down a little. It felt reassuring to have him by her side.

When finally he got up to leave, he said, 'I will go away and do some thinking. And I'll come back tomorrow to see you if you like. Check you're all right.'

'I'd like that very much. Thank you,' she replied.

Now I'm in my room resting. When Lakshmi came home, she gave me some more herbal tea and helped me upstairs. I lie here listening to the sounds of the market outside, the shouts of vendors, the hubbub of conversation, the occasional vehicle rumbling past. It's strange that life goes on here just as normal despite Billy's death and my grief. I wish the world would stop and acknowledge its loss, not carry on as if nothing had happened.

Chills went through Chloe when she read the description of how Billy had died. It meant the fortune teller had been right about the breach of trust. It reinforced Chloe's belief in the fortune teller. She was doubly sure now that she was right not to have gone to Bhaktapur. But what did that mean for Kiran? She felt helpless. There had been nothing she could do to stop him going.

Suddenly, there was a long, low rumble. Chloe looked up

from the diary. The sound seemed to come from deep, deep below her, somewhere underground. The floor beneath her began to vibrate, then it lifted and rolled, like a great wave on the sea. Her chair tipped forward and she jumped up, alarmed, gripping the windowsill. The building was buckling and swaying. Down in the garden, terrified people were running about, shouting, waving their hands, clutching each other. Then, even as she watched through the window, the building opposite, which was part of the guest house, formed a series of cracks in the front wall, like rips in material, then the wall crumbled in front of her eyes, collapsing in a cloud of powdery dust, coming to rest in the garden beneath.

Shaking, panic rising in her throat, Chloe instinctively grabbed her phone, left her room and ran downstairs, taking the stairs two at a time. Other guests were doing the same, emerging from rooms and making for the staircase. When she reached the ground floor, she looked around wildly. The reception area was deserted, the plate-glass doors had smashed, piles of glass lay in shards all around. Rubble and dust billowed in from outside, filling her mouth and nostrils. Coughing, she followed other guests running out of the building.

Outside, through the clouds of dust, she could just about make out people staggering about. She could hear their confused, panicked cries. A group of hotel staff and guests had gathered in the courtyard. Some had been struck by flying glass, blood oozing from their wounds, but none of them looked seriously injured. One of the security guards was already taking water around to the assembled guests.

'Sit down, sit down, miss,' he said, handing Chloe a paper cup.

She sat down on the ground, gulping the water gratefully. She felt the tremors of aftershocks through the grass. Everyone fell silent and stared up at the damaged building, fearful that it would collapse completely, but although it tottered slightly, it stood firm.

In all the panic and confusion, the fortune-teller's words came back to Chloe with full force. This must be the accident the woman had been predicting, the momentous event which she could somehow sense in the air. Chloe's mind flew to Kiran. He would have been on the bus when the earthquake struck. What had happened to it?

Her phone was in her pocket. She snatched it out and punched in his number again, but the line was dead. She stood up, feeling unsteady, and looked around for an exit. She needed to get out of there straightaway. The lion statues that guarded the entrance to the guest house had fallen over, one of them lay smashed and headless on the tarmac drive. She ran past them and out onto the narrow street. It was thronging with dazed and injured people. Bikes, rickshaws and motorbikes had fallen over and were lying on their side in the road. People were sitting on the steps of shops with their heads in their hands.

Chloe pushed through the crowds to the end of the road, and turned into the next street, heading for the main road that she knew led out of the city. But that street was blocked by a collapsed building, a film of dust hung in the air. She turned away and headed in the other direction. This street was strewn with bricks and plaster from the damaged buildings, and debris that had been thrown out of shops in the few seconds that had devastated the city. She picked her way along the street and eventually emerged onto the main road.

This road was the scene of chaos too. Overturned motorbikes, abandoned vehicles, collapsed buildings. People wandered about the carriageway, dazed and bewildered. Chloe began to walk along the road, weaving between the stationery vehicles, the people sitting on the road, the upturned bicycles and motorbikes. She remembered Kiran saying that it was around twenty kilometres to Bhaktapur. If necessary, if she just kept going, she could walk all the way there.

She walked on for a couple of kilometres, making slow progress, passing many devastated buildings where people were digging through the rubble. A man pedalling a rickshaw slowed down as he pulled alongside her.

'Where are you going, madam?' he asked. 'You want help?'

'I'm going to Bhaktapur.'

'It's a long way. But I will take you. You look very tired.'

She looked at the man. He looked tired too, his hair was full of dust, his eyes bloodshot.

'It's all right, thank you,' she replied. 'I'm OK walking.'

'Please, madam. I will take you. I need customers,' he said.

'All right, if I can pay you to take me, I will come.'

He motioned her to get in.

She felt a little guilty, allowing this man to pedal her, but it would be far quicker than walking and she needed to get to Kiran, to know that he was safe.

The rickshaw was able to weave between the obstructions and debris on the road quickly and deftly. Occasionally, Chloe felt the ground tremble beneath the seat and braced herself, but the aftershocks were short-lived now and less violent than the earthquake itself.

She saw the overturned bus up ahead when they'd been going for fifteen minutes or so. Shock washed through her. It was lying on its side, half submerged in rubble. When the rickshaw drew closer, she saw that a building must have collapsed right onto it, pushing it over, smashing the windows and buckling the side panels. Rescuers were hauling people out of the windows, some were already lying, injured, by the roadside, the faces of three others had been covered with clothes.

'Stop, please!'

The rickshaw ground to a halt. She thrust some notes into the man's hand, scrambled out and ran to the bus.

'Hey, lady!' the rickshaw man shouted.

But Chloe didn't stop running and the rickshaw man shrugged and pedalled slowly away.

'Which bus is this?' she asked frantically.

People stared, many not speaking English. In the end, someone said, 'Bhaktapur bus,' and her heart stood still.

She looked around wildly, searching for Kiran. People were being dragged out of the crumpled bus, bloodied and white-faced. Chloe moved forward, and soon found herself helping passengers out, holding their hands as they climbed up and safely reached the ground. Some were bleeding, others clearly had broken limbs and all looked dazed and shaken. As each passenger emerged from the stricken bus, she studied their faces, searching desperately for Kiran, but he was nowhere to be seen.

When she'd been helping for about half an hour, she noticed an ambulance making its way towards them between the wrecked vehicles. It pulled up beside the bus. She watched as some of the worst injured passengers were loaded into the vehicle. Then it drew away and sped back towards Kathmandu, its light flashing, sirens blaring.

'Where's it going?' she asked the man beside her.

'Bir Hospital,' he said. 'In the centre of the city. They've taken three lots of people already from this bus. People who were very badly injured.'

Chloe watched the ambulance as it began to weave its way back towards the city centre between the abandoned vehicles on the road. Perhaps Kiran had already been taken to the hospital, or, God forbid, he was one of those motionless forms lying on the ground beside the wrecked vehicle. She couldn't bear to contemplate that.

She pulled out her phone and flicked through to a photograph of Kiran. She'd taken it on the boat trip in Pokhara; he was smiling at her from the bow, an oar in one hand. 'Did you see this man?' she asked the man.

He peered, then nodded. 'They took him to the hospital,' he said.

'Was he OK?' Her voice was shaking.

The man looked away. 'I'm not sure. You should go there,' he muttered.

'Thanks.'

She turned away from the bus and began to run then, following the flashing lights of the ambulance. It could only proceed at a crawl, weaving between the abandoned and crashed vehicles, the motorbikes strewn across the road, the people wandering about and sitting in groups on the road. The sun was high in the sky and her T-shirt was soon soaked in sweat and clinging to her body. She was thirsty and breathless, but she went as quickly as she could, her eyes pinned on those flashing lights, thinking about the prophesy. The accident the fortune teller was talking about. She would have been on that bus if she'd not believed the old woman's words. If only she'd been able to persuade Kiran! If only he'd taken her seriously. She couldn't stop reminding herself that Billy hadn't listened to Lena, with tragic consequences.

It took about forty minutes to get back to the centre of the city, by which time Chloe had lost sight of the ambulance. She asked directions to the hospital and eventually arrived in front of a long, modern, concrete building. It was on Kanti Path, one of the main thoroughfares, which was choked with slow-moving vehicles and thronging with crowds of agitated people. Ambulances were drawn up on the pavement outside the hospital entrance. She eased her way through the crowds to the reception hall. It was full of wounded people waiting for medical attention. They filled every available seat, some were sitting on the floor, others standing.

The woman at the desk was harassed, scribbling down details of patient after patient and waving them aside to wait. She looked up when Chloe neared the front of the queue.

'I'm looking for Kiran Rai,' she said and held up the photograph on her phone.

The woman peered at it, consulted her list, then nodded. 'Upstairs,' she said, her voice showing the strain and exhaustion of the past couple of hours. 'He was sent straight up to surgery.'

Chloe's mouth dropped open, and she felt tears well in her eyes for the first time since the earthquake. Her legs were suddenly weak. She leaned on the reception desk and took a breath.

'You're a relative?' the woman asked, frowning.

Chloe shook her head. 'Close friend.'

'You can go on up. First-floor ward.'

Like a sleepwalker, Chloe found the staircase. Injured people were sitting on the stairs. She picked her way up between them. As she climbed, she felt another aftershock shiver the building. A spontaneous gasp went up and then a couple of seconds of silence.

The first floor was as crowded as the reception area. People were sitting in plastic chairs in a waiting area. On the far wall were some double doors marked, 'Emergency Room, Private'. A nurse stood beside the doors. Chloe approached her and explained that she'd come to see Kiran Rai.

'He's in theatre at the moment. He may be a few hours, I'm afraid. Come back this evening.'

'What's wrong with him?'

'Bleed on the brain. He suffered head injuries when a building collapsed on his bus. Come back later on. We will know more then.'

Blinded by tears, hardly able to see where she was going, Chloe groped her way down the stairs, through the thronging, agitated crowds and out onto the street. Looking around, she realised that she wasn't actually very far from Thamel and the guest house. Her feet were sore and she was physically and emotionally exhausted, but she took a deep breath and began to walk.

Once she was back at the guest house, she made her way past the collapsed building. A security guard waved her through into the main building that remained untouched and she went up to her room. She tried to dial the number for the Sunset View Guest House in Pokhara. She needed to let Kiran's family know he was in hospital, but although she tried to dial it several times, she had no signal and her phone kept cutting out. She decided to try again once she had some firm news about Kiran's condition.

Lena's diary was on the floor beside her upturned chair. How incredible, that just a few hours previously, she'd been sitting there, looking out at the garden, reading the diary. How much had happened since then. She picked it up. There weren't many pages left to read. It might distract her from her overwhelming anxiety while she waited. She turned back to the point she'd left off, and read on.

34

DARJEELING, 1945

Lieutenant Harper (I mean George – I must remember to call him that now) has been to see me every day for the past week and I've found myself looking forward to his visits more and more each time.

Lena was aware that by visiting her, he was trying to take her out of herself, trying to help her not exactly put aside her grief, but rather to accept it and yet realise too that she still had a life to live. That day, for the first time, she had felt a slight shift in her emotions and realised that she was no longer feeling quite the weight of grief that she had been up until then. Afterwards, she was consumed with guilt, thinking that in letting go of those feelings, she was somehow betraying Billy's memory.

That was the day that George persuaded her to go out for the first time since she'd heard the news of Billy's death. His driver took them up to Tiger Point. It had been a long time since she'd ventured up the narrow road that wound through the forest and emerged on top of the hill with its fabulous views of the Indian Himalayas. It was wonderful to be out in the fresh air in that magnificent place.

Lena stood there, breathing in the fresh, mountain air and

drinking in the sight of the majestic hills. It made her realise how much she'd missed it over the months she'd been in Burma and how dear to her heart those mountains had always been.

She turned to George and smiled, and he took her hand.

'All right?' he asked solicitously and she nodded.

'Thank you for getting me to come out.'

But walking back down the hill, she felt a little faint and stumbled on the uneven surface. She felt George's arm as he slipped it through hers. They walked slowly back to the car, and he helped her into the back seat. It was so nice to be cared for, to know that someone was there to look after her and to look out for her.

When they arrived back in Darjeeling, he walked her from the car to the house and because Lakshmi was out, he went inside with her and made sure she was comfortable.

'Are you sure you're going to be all right?' he asked before he left.

'I'm fine, thank you.'

'I'll come again tomorrow.'

'I'd like that... but only if you're sure.'

'Of course. I have an idea as to how I can help you. I've been thinking it over for a while. When I come tomorrow, I will tell you.'

Lena wondered what it might be and how it would help her. Perhaps he had found her a place in some sort of institution either in Darjeeling or elsewhere in India? She would know for sure the next day, but at least she could go to bed with a little hope in her heart.

THE FOLLOWING MORNING, George turned up at the front door and asked if Lena would like to walk up to Observatory Hill with him.

He had a mysterious look in his eyes and she was intrigued. They walked together through the market on Chowrasta and up the many steps and winding paths up to the little temple on the hill, from which there was that stunning view of the mountains.

There, they sat down on a wooden bench, and he told Lena what was on his mind.

'I'm very fond of you, Lena. You must know that, and I've been thinking about this for a long time, but it has taken me a while to pluck up the courage to ask. So, I'll come straight to the point. Will you marry me?'

A wave of surprise went through her, although it wasn't completely unexpected. She felt the colour rise in her cheeks.

'I wanted to wait until you were grieving a little less,' he said. 'And I would have asked you anyway, but I'm asking now because in practical terms, we have very little time.'

He paused for a few seconds and when she said nothing, he carried on.

'You and I understand each other very well. We have both suffered the sad loss of our first loves, but we can comfort each other. We are already very good companions.'

'I'm amazed and flattered,' she said when she finally found her voice. 'But... but... what about...?' She looked down at her little bump, trying to articulate what was on her mind.

'I'd be honoured to take on the role of the father of your child, Lena. I have thought this all through very carefully and it makes perfect sense. If we marry in the next few weeks, no one will ever know that the baby isn't mine. We could arrange a short trip away to another hill station when the time comes if there is any doubt about that.'

She stared at him. He really had thought it all through.

'And as soon as the war is over, if you are happy, I'd like to return to a posting back in England. I'd love it if you'd come with me. It could be the start of a new life for both of us.'

'I... I'm not sure...' This was all too fast. Lena was grateful for his offer. It could be an answer to all her problems, but it was a lot to take in.

'You don't have to decide now,' he said gently. 'Please take your time. Think about it carefully. But the sooner we make a decision, the easier everything will be.'

Lena's mind was reeling as they walked back to the house together, she was going over and over what he'd said, thinking of all the possibilities and implications of it all. If only there was someone to help her decide, but there was no one. Not even Joan or any of her St Catherine's friends. She would have to make this decision alone.

A WEEK PASSED without Lena seeing George or even having contacted him. She had needed time to think it over and he had said that she must take as long as she needed. But he was right, there wasn't actually much time. Already Lena could feel her belly swelling and the first tiny movements of the growing baby inside.

That morning she'd heard on the BBC World Service on Sunil's radio that Rangoon had finally been retaken by Allied forces. Listening to the report, Lena imagined all the soldiers marching, triumphant through the devastated city. A wave of sadness went through her at the thought that Billy, and so many other young men, didn't get to see the victory, despite playing such an important part in the campaign. She thought about the Wasbies too. How she'd loved to have been there with them. She imagined the girls celebrating in style, wherever they were, when the news came through. She hadn't heard from Mildred at all and assumed the team had been following the front line throughout and were thus unable to write.

This news of victory had made her realise how swiftly time

was moving on. Soon the war would be over, and George would go home to England. She knew she had to decide whether to accept his offer and go with him. She'd always wanted to see England, especially having been taught at St Catherine's that everything in England was magical and everyone fortunate to live there. She knew from speaking to Billy that that wasn't quite true, but she still had that burning desire to experience it for herself. Of course, it would mean leaving Darjeeling, Sunil and Lakshmi, and all the friends and neighbours there. The prospect made Lena sad, but when she thought of how they might react if they knew about her baby, she realised that staying in this community wasn't an option.

On 5 May 1945, Lena made her decision, for better or worse.

She took a rickshaw along to the army base, just as she used to when she was working there. When George looked up and saw her standing there, she saw his eyes light up with pleasure. It did her heart good to see it. He really was a very good-looking man, she thought, in a solid, well-bred, English sort of way, although so very different to Billy.

'I've come to tell you that I will marry you,' she said, her voice trembling.

He looked as though he would burst with pleasure. He came out from behind the desk and they hugged briefly, then he kissed her on the lips.

'Thank you. Thank you, Lena. You've made me a very happy man. Why don't we go somewhere and talk about it? It's not easy to talk here.'

So, they went out to his car. George drove her along the hilltop road and stopped the car in a remote place. They got out and walked along the ridge with the backdrop of Kanchenjunga on one side, and they talked.

Putting his arm around her shoulders, he pulled her close. 'I've always admired you, Lena. Ever since you came into my office on that first day, so full of energy and bursting with enthusiasm for life. My heart belonged to Alisha then, but you've always been my rock and, without realising it almost, I was growing fonder and fonder of you every day.'

Lena looked up at him and smiled.

'You know, as I said the other day,' he went on, 'I often thought about asking you, and even if you hadn't been in... well, in such a difficult situation, I would still have asked you to marry me. I don't want you to think I only asked because of that.'

As he talked, Lena realised that she felt the same way about him, that although her heart belonged and would always belong to Billy, she'd had very warm feelings for George too.

When they got back to the car, he took her in his arms and kissed her, properly this time. It wasn't a passionate kiss, but it wasn't a platonic one either. It felt a little odd at first, but given time, Lena knew she would be able to return his affection.

SO THAT IS IT. *The decision is made. Tomorrow George will announce our engagement and start making arrangements for our wedding which will take place in Darjeeling within the next couple of weeks. I know Lakshmi and Sunil will be very pleased. They have become very fond of George and can see that he is a kind man who will be very good for me.*

When the war is finally over, we will sail for England and our new lives, and I will put all of this behind me and embrace life in my new home. Perhaps one day I might visit Darjeeling, but once I've made the break, I know it will be hard to come back to the place where Billy and I fell in love and where I lost my dear old Ma.

On our walk this afternoon, George and I decided that we will be the only ones who ever know about my pregnancy. Billy's child will be George's child and he or she will never know otherwise. It is better that way. If the world weren't the way it is, I would tell my child about its father, how much we loved each other and what a good, brave man

Billy was. However, the world is full of prejudice and ignorance and snobbery. I don't want my child to grow up feeling any sort of stigma, and I am confident that George will be an excellent father to my child, so we have taken this decision for the best.

I am lying down to sleep now, with this book under my pillow, looking forward to what tomorrow will bring, and at last with some hope in my heart for the future.

Chloe closed the battered blue book with tears in her eyes, mulling over Lena's final revelation. She now knew for sure what she'd suspected from the start. It meant that her Uncle Andrew, her cousin Daniel's father, must be Billy's child. It was hard to take on board. In all the shock and turmoil of the day, her anxiety about Kiran, her mind wasn't functioning very well, but she could just about remember that Uncle Andrew's birthday was in September and that he would be seventy this year. That meant that he would have been conceived in December 1944.

Thinking about it further, that similarity she'd seen in Billy's eyes when she'd first seen the photograph of him in the drawer of Lena's bureau, the line of his brow, the shape of his eyes. Those were Uncle Andrew's eyes too, but she'd not realised it at the time.

How ironic it all was. She thought about her uncle and about her cousin Daniel, how important status and tradition were to them, how they identified with her grandfather and his military career, and seemed not to hold Lena in such high esteem. If only they knew the truth about how courageous Lena had been during the war, and that Andrew was the son of a humble dock worker from the East End of London, not someone from the officer class! Lena had obviously kept the secret from him and from everyone, and taken it to her grave, as had George.

Chloe put the diary aside. This was all too much to process at the moment. She would think about it later. Now, she needed to focus on Kiran. She glanced at her watch. It was almost time to set off back to the hospital. She took a quick shower and changed into some clean clothes and then it was time to go.

The roads were still in chaos and there was no chance of getting a rickshaw or a taxi, but she went as quickly as she could, half running, half walking, skirting around collapsed buildings, abandoned vehicles. She was anxious to be there for Kiran when he came out of theatre.

The hospital was as busy, if not busier than it had been earlier in the day. A tarpaulin awning had been constructed outside the front entrance, to shelter people waiting for medical attention. Chloe made her way through the reception hall and up the stairs. Her nerves were taut, her stomach churning, she was dreading what she might discover. She crossed the first floor to the door of the Emergency Room and told the nurse that she'd come to see Kiran Rai. She tried to read the woman's expression when she said his name, but the woman just nodded.

'He is out of surgery now, but unconscious,' the nurse said without smiling.

'Can I see him?'

'I'll ask the doctor.' The nurse disappeared for a few seconds and when she returned, she beckoned Chloe to follow her.

Through the double doors was a long corridor lined on either side with stretchers, on which people lay, either unconscious or barely so. Chloe averted her eyes and followed the nurse to a ward at the end of the corridor. Families were gathered around the beds of loved ones and there was a hubbub of subdued conversation.

The nurse headed for a bed in the corner that was curtained off. She pulled the curtain aside and nodded Chloe through. 'He's here. You can see him, but he isn't awake yet.'

Chloe went straight to the bed and stared down at Kiran, shock rolling through her. He was lying against the pillows, his head swathed in bandages, his eyes closed. Dried blood crusted around his mouth. She knelt down beside him and felt for his hand. 'Oh, Kiran,' she breathed.

She stayed there for a long time, just holding his hand, whispering words of love, her eyes fixed on his for any sign of life, but they remained firmly closed.

After a time, the curtain was pulled aside, and a male doctor in a grubby white coat put his head round.

'Is he going to be all right?' she asked, her voice trembling.

'I wish I could say yes, but you never know with head injuries. It was touch-and-go in theatre for a while.'

'But he will wake up, won't he?' Tears caught in her throat.

'I sincerely hope so... Look, it's probably a bit too soon for you to be here. Why don't you come back again tomorrow morning?'

'I'd prefer to stay with him,' she said weakly, beginning to panic. Now she'd finally found him, how could she tear herself away?

'It would be better if he was left to rest,' the doctor said gently. 'Come again tomorrow, as early as you like... we should have more of a prognosis by then.'

He held the curtain aside for her. She wanted to protest, but the doctor looked exhausted and stressed.

Blindly, she retraced her steps across the ward, back down the corridor, through the double doors, down the stairs and out into the street. The skies were darkening. There were no street lights on anywhere, just pinpricks of light from gas lamps and torches. She wandered back towards Thamel, distraught, the image of Kiran's inert face fresh in her mind. She entered the backstreets, not really knowing where she was, hardly paying attention to where she was going. She must have taken a wrong turn somewhere along the route because suddenly she realised that Durbar Square was ahead of her.

Chloe stopped, staring at the scenes of devastation. Hurricane lamps had been set up all around the square and she could see that where the ancient temples had been only the day before, there were now just piles of rubble, red bricks, roofs roof timbers, all collapsed into heaps. There were few people in the square as a police cordon was stopping people entering.

She wandered on for a few minutes and realised she was in the fortune-teller's street. It was quiet there and the solid buildings were unchanged. It was as if nothing had happened. Something, some instinct, guided her to the fortune-teller's door. She pushed it open and went through the inner room.

The younger woman was sitting alone and she looked up at Chloe with fear in her eyes. 'Come in,' she said. 'Sit down. Today is a terrible day. I predicted something of it, but I couldn't foresee it all.'

Chloe sat down and, without being asked, held out her palm. 'I did what you said, I didn't travel today. But my friend did. He went on the bus to Bhaktapur... he was badly hurt.'

The woman shook her head in dismay. 'I'm so sorry to hear that.'

Then she took Chloe's hand and studied it for a long time.

'Will he recover?' Chloe asked, her voice tremulous.

The woman looked up and into Chloe's eyes, pain and confusion in her own, and shook her head. 'I'm sorry, but I cannot see. I cannot see what will happen to him. I am truly sorry... but I believe that if you love him there is hope... but I cannot say for sure.'

Chloe swallowed hard, drew her hand away and got up to go. She was wasting her time here.

'Please... wait!' the woman cried.

Chloe paused.

'I *can* see, though, that you have discovered a secret today,' the fortune teller said. 'A family secret. You will wonder whether to tell what you know, but my advice to you is this. You must wait – wait until the time is right. It could be days or weeks; it could be years. You will know when the time has come.'

Chloe and stared back into the fortune-teller's eyes, amazed.

In amongst the pain and trauma of the day, she'd been wondering vaguely what she should do with the information she'd discovered from Lena's diary. Should she tell Uncle Andrew and Daniel the truth? They surely had the right to know? On the other hand, what good would it do? It would be breaching Lena's vow for him never to know. Besides, Uncle Andrew was getting old and frail, why introduce such a complication into his twilight years, why not let him just enjoy them without the disruption that this new knowledge would bring?

'Thank you,' she murmured. Then she went back through the darkened outer room and, as quickly as she could, made her way back through the stricken streets to the Kathmandu Guest House.

CHLOE HAD A RESTLESS NIGHT. The shock of the earthquake and of everything that had happened that day kept sleep at bay for hours. When she finally did drift off, her alarm woke her around five thirty. She got out of bed and pulled on her clothes, gulped down some mineral water and went straight out onto the street, which was already a hive of activity. People were up and about clearing up the debris from the earthquake, shovelling piles of bricks, sweeping up rubbish.

As she walked, she tried to call Kiran's family. To her surprise, the line was working and after a couple of rings, his mother answered.

'Kiran? Chloe? Is that you?'

'It's me, Chloe.'

'Are you all right? How is Kiran? I've been trying to get hold of him since I heard about the earthquake. He's not answering.'

'He's in hospital, I'm afraid, Ehani. I'm going to see him now...' her voice broke, her hands were shaking.

'Hospital? What happened?'

'He was on a bus to Bhaktapur. A building collapsed onto it. He was injured, I'm afraid. Head injuries.'

'Oh, Chloe! How terrible...' Ehani's voice broke. 'My poor boy! We will come. We will come to Kathmandu straightaway. Which hospital is he in?'

'The Bir Hospital. I'm going there now.'

'Please give him our love.'

'Of course.'

'And Chloe... I'm sorry, I'm so sorry that I was... well, *off* with you. I just wanted to protect my son from more hurt. But I know now that you're a good person. That you're good for *him*. I see that now. I want to say that you have my love and my blessing, Chloe.'

Chloe swallowed, unable to respond.

'Let me know when you have more news. We will be there as soon as we can.'

'Goodbye, Ehani,' Chloe said. 'And thank you.'

The hospital was as busy as it had been the day before and Chloe made her now familiar way upstairs and along to the emergency ward. A nurse let her in through the double doors and she went straight to Kiran's bed. She half expected him to look up and smile at her when she drew the curtain aside, but her hopes were dashed. His face looked exactly as it had when she'd left the previous evening. His eyes were closed, his skin sallow and waxy.

Someone had put a stool beside the bed, so she sat down beside him and took his hands in hers. The fortune-teller's words were fresh in her mind. *If you love him, there is hope.* She did love him, but she needed to let him know that. Even if he couldn't hear her, she knew she had to talk to him, to tell him what he meant to her, how much she cared.

At first, it felt a little awkward talking to someone who wasn't conscious, and she didn't know where to begin. So, she went back to the first moment they had set eyes on each other, in the restaurant on the Indian border, the first terse exchange about the cheating rickshaw-wallah, and how from an unpromising start their conversation on the journey to Kathmandu had thawed the ice between them and changed her mind completely about him.

'By the end of that journey, I was falling for you, Kiran, and when you suggested taking me up to Ghorepani, I was so happy. But the next day I saw you in Durbar Square with your sister. I jumped to the wrong conclusion and thought it was your girl-friend, but my reaction to seeing you with her made me realise that you already meant a lot to me.'

She carried on talking, describing their trip to Pokhara and their trek into the mountains, going over everything they'd done together, all the conversations they'd had. She spoke about how full of joy she was in his company, how good being with him made her feel.

She hardly noticed the passing of time. The doctor came in a couple of times and checked on Kiran, and at one point a nurse brought her a cup of black tea. But Chloe just carried on into the afternoon, oblivious to the comings and goings on the ward, talking and talking until her voice was hoarse, but still she forced the words to come.

As the sun went down on the day, just as she was beginning to give up hope, Kiran's eyelids fluttered. Chloe held her breath and leaned in closer and, gradually, his eyes blinked open. She thought her heart would burst with joy and relief.

Kiran frowned, shook his head gently, then gradually fixed his gaze on Chloe. She didn't know whether to call for the doctor, but she didn't want to leave him, not just at that moment.

'Chloe?' he said, his voice rough and groggy. 'Where am I?'

'You were in an accident. You're in hospital in Kathmandu. You've been asleep for a long time.'

She felt him grip her hand. 'I dreamed we were walking together through the mountains...' he said, then broke off and frowned again. 'And that you were worried that I had someone else. That's not true, is it?'

She shook her head. 'No, not now.'

'You will stay with me, Chloe, won't you?' he asked, looking into her eyes. 'I've got a feeling we might have talked about you going home to England. I couldn't bear that. I love you so much.'

'Of course I'll stay,' she whispered through the tears. 'I love you too.'

EPILOGUE

April 2016

CHLOE WAITED on the steps of the monastery while Ehani fussed around her, adjusting Chloe's headdress, tweaking an imaginary hair from her cream brocade jacket.

Rumi's eyes twinkled mischievously as she handed Chloe a bunch of lotus flowers. 'Good luck,' she whispered. 'Come on, Amma. Let's go inside.'

Ehani and Rumi bustled away ahead of her into the shrine room and Chloe was left on the steps alone, waiting for everyone to settle before she made her entrance. Her hands were shaking so much that the lotus flowers and the hem of her long robe trembled too. Her stomach was churning, with a mixture of nerves and excitement. She could already see Kiran from where she waited, standing there at the front of the shrine room, elegant in his traditional silk robes. Her heart swelled with pride and love for him.

They were all there waiting for her now – Kiran's parents, his brother and her wife, his sister Rumi, and many assorted friends and extended family members too. There were colleagues from the Earthquake Relief charity where Chloe had been working for almost a year now, and friends and family from England too. Sophie stood beside Dan and his wife and his two teenage children and, most amazing of all, Chloe's own father was there, a tall, distinguished figure, standing right at the front beside Kiran.

So much had happened in the past year. It had been a tough few months while Kiran recovered from his head injuries, but Chloe had moved into his studio flat to help him through it. Once he was over the worst, she'd found a job helping those made homeless by the earthquake. She loved the work; although harrowing sometimes, it was so rewarding. She often thought back to her former life finding homes for the wealthy in Surrey, without regret. There was no comparison.

Once Kiran was well enough to cope on his own, she'd gone home briefly to clear Lena's house, find a tenant for it and to sort out Lena's estate. To her relief, Sophie had agreed to keep Kip. Sadly, she'd had to return six months later for Uncle Andrew's funeral. He'd died quite suddenly and unexpectedly of a heart attack in his sleep.

Chloe had felt in her bones that the time was right then to let Daniel know about Billy. It wouldn't be breaching any of Lena's promises, but just to make sure, she'd driven down to Wiltshire to visit Mildred Lightfoot, to thank her for giving her Lena's diary and to ask her advice. Mildred had agreed with her that the time was right. Chloe decided that the best way to let Daniel know was to let him find out from Lena herself, so she'd simply handed him the diary and the photograph of Billy that Lena had kept in her bureau.

He'd called her two weeks later when she was back in Kathmandu to thank her and to say he'd read the diary straight through and was stunned. He'd already been to the East End of London to try to find where Billy had lived and worked, and had done some online research to see if he could find out anything else about his grandfather. He was planning to write to the Ministry of Defence too to get copies of Billy's military records. He'd told Chloe that his children were very interested and involved in his research and that they were planning a family trip to Myanmar to see where Billy had fought and died, and to Darjeeling at some point too.

'Perhaps you'll come to Nepal too, if you have time? It would be great to see you.'

She could hardly believe she was saying that, but Lena's diary and Billy's story had brought them together. It was strange how she felt closer to Dan than she ever had before, now that they were separated by continents.

There was someone else she felt closer too as well. Lena's story had emphasised the importance of family to her as had her love for Kiran. After Kiran had proposed to her, Chloe had taken the plunge and called her father in Australia. He was surprised but delighted to hear from her and even more delighted to hear her news. After that, they'd spoken weekly, and he'd promised to bring his new family to the wedding in Pokhara. There they all were, standing beside him, his wife Rosie and their two girls, Chloe's Australian half-sisters, she was looking forward to getting to know.

A hush fell over the prayer hall and the chanting of the monks began. It was time.

Nervously, Chloe fingered Lena's pearl necklace she'd brought all the way from England especially for today. It matched the dew-drop pearl earrings that had belonged to her own mother. 'I know you're both with me, Mum and Gran,' she whispered. 'Thank you, and I love you.'

Then, lifting the folds of her long dress so she didn't trip, she went slowly up the marble steps and entered the shrine room. She walked forward, into the cacophony of sound and the heady cloud of incense, to stand beside the man she loved, and to take her vows.

Thank you for reading *The Fortune Teller of Kathmandu*. I hope you enjoyed reading it as much as I loved writing it! Please sign up to my newsletter on annbennettauthor.com for information about my upcoming releases. If you do, you will receive a free download of one of my books. You can also follow my Facebook page for updates about my writing.

If you've enjoyed the book I would really appreciate it if you could leave a review on Amazon. It will help inform potential readers about the book and raise its profile. It will also help me to reach more readers.

ACKNOWLEDGMENTS

I was inspired to write a book set in Nepal when I first visited as a backpacker 1987 and it has taken a very long time and a more recent trip for me to do so! I'd like to thank Bhimsen and Rajesh from Outfitter Himalaya for guiding us up to Ghorepani and back earlier this year. Thanks also to Arjun Rijal and team for showing us around fabulous Kathmandu, as well as Nagarkot and Bhak-tapur in the Kathmandu Valley. I'm really grateful to Subash Tamang from Ashmita Trek and Tours for organising our trip to Darjeeling and the Indian Himalaya in 2019.

I stumbled across the story of the Wasbies while researching *The Lake Palace* - another book about the Burma Campaign during WWII. I was inspired to do more research about those brave women who were unsung heroes of the Burma Campaign. I've also been fascinated by the Gurkhas since my first visit to Nepal and because nowadays I live quite close to their HQ in the UK. In Pokhara we visited the fascinating Gurkha museum, which features many stories of incredible bravery from the war years and beyond.

I'd like to thank my sister, Mary, for reading and commenting on an early draft, Mandy Lyon-Brown for her brilliant proof-reading and all those who kindly read and commented on an advance copy. Thanks also to everyone who has supported me down the years by reading my books.

ABOUT THE AUTHOR

Ann Bennett has written several historical fiction novels, many set in India or South East Asia. This is her fifteenth book. Her first novel, *Bamboo Heart: A Daughter's Quest*, was inspired by her father's experience as a prisoner of war on the Thai-Burma Railway. *Bamboo Island: The Planter's Wife*, *A Daughter's Promise*, *Bamboo Road: The Homecoming*, *The Tea Planter's Club* and *The Amulet* are also about WWII in South East Asia. With *The Fortune Teller of Kathmandu,* they form the Echoes of Empire collection.

Ann is also author of *The Lake Pavilion* and *The Lake Palace*, set in British India during the Burma Campaign in WWII, *The Lake Pagoda* and *The Lake Villa*, both set in French Indochina during WWII. Ann's other books, *The Runaway Sisters, The Forgotten Children, The Child Without a Home* and bestselling *The Orphan House*, are published by Bookouture.

Ann is married with three grown up sons and a grand-daughter and works as a lawyer.

For more details please visit www.annbennettauthor.com

ALSO BY ANN BENNETT

Printed in Great Britain
by Amazon

32273483R00209